ISLAND

OTHER BOOKS BY ALISTAIR MacLEOD

The Lost Salt Gift of Blood
As Birds Bring Forth the Sun
No Great Mischief

ISLAND

Collected Stories

Alistair MacLeod

With a Foreword by John McGahern

JONATHAN CAPE
LONDON

Published by Jonathan Cape 2001

2 4 6 8 10 9 7 5 3 1

First published in Great Britain in 2001 by
Jonathan Cape
Random House, 20 Vauxhall Bridge Road,
London SW1V 2SA

Random House Australia (Pty) Limited
20 Alfred Street, Milsons Point, Sydney,
New South Wales 2061, Australia

Random House New Zealand Limited
18 Poland Road, Glenfield,
Auckland 10, New Zealand

Random House (Pty) Limited
Endulini, 5A Jubilee Road, Parktown 2193, South Africa

The Random House Group Limited Reg. No. 954009
www.randomhouse.co.uk

A CIP catalogue record for this book
ia available from the British Library

ISBN 0-224-06194-1

Papers used by Random House are natural, recyclable products made
from wood grown in sustainable forests; the manufacturing processes
conform to the environmental regulations of the country of origin

Printed and bound in Great Britain by Mackays of Chatham PLC

CONTENTS

FOREWORD

Alistair MacLeod's stories have a uniqueness that is rare in the writing of any time. This quality is easily recognisable but is almost impossible to describe.

A different kind of genius marks every magical page of *The Great Gatsby* and 'The Rich Boy' and stories like 'May Day', yet in much of Scott Fitzgerald's other work, where this rare quality is missing, the writing never rises above the level of a compe tent journeyman, in spite of its unfailing good manners and charm. In true work we see a talent dramatising a particular area of human experience within a recognisable social setting. Once the talent moves outside these limitations we see it begin to fail, or to work at a less exciting level.

MacLeod's careful work never appears to stray outside what quickens it, and his uniqueness is present in every weighted sentence and the smallest of gestures. He writes about people and a way of life on Cape Breton, Nova Scotia, that has continued relatively unchanged for several generations, since the first settlers went there from Scotland at the time of the Clearances. They work as fishermen, miners, smallholders, loggers, lighthouse keepers, migrant workers. They live in a dramatically beautiful setting provided mostly by nature and hostile to much human endeavour. Animals too have their own place within this proud and fragile interdependence and are part of a fierce and unsentimental tribal affection. The poetic, the religious, and the superstitious instincts are always close. As we come to know this world, it is poised on the edge of extinction, like the bald eagles MacLeod writes about so well:

> He looked up to the sound of the whooshing eagles' wings. They were flying up the mountain, almost wavering in their flight. Like weary commuters trying to make it home. He had watched them through the long winter as they were forced to fly farther and farther in search of food and open water. He had noticed the dullness of their feathers and the dimming luster in their intense angle of vision, the female's wing tips seemed almost to graze the bare branches of the trees as if she might falter and fall.

The eagles had known other seasons and circumstances when their universe was unthreatened:

> He had seen the male seize a branch in his powerful talons and soar towards the sky in the sheer exuberance of his power

and strength; had seen him snap the branch in two (in a way a strong man might snap a kindling across his knee) letting the sections fall towards the earth before plummeting after one or the other and snatching it from the air, wheeling and somersaulting and flipping the branch in front of him and swooping under it again and again until, tired of the game, he let it fall to earth. And had seen them in the aerial courtship of their mating; had seen them feinting and swerving high above the mountain, outlined against the sky. Had seen them come together and with talons locked, fall cartwheeling over and over for what seemed like hundreds of feet down towards the land. Separating and braking, like lucky parachutists, at the last minute and gliding individually and parallel to the earth before starting their ascent once more.

MacLeod's world is masculine, in its strengths and its vulnerabilities. The men and women of the stories inhabit separate worlds. They are drawn together for love or procreation, and then part, withdrawing further and further into their own separate worlds:

Now my wife seems to have gone permanently into a world of avocado appliances and household cleanliness and the vicarious experiences provided by the interminable soap operas that fill her television afternoons. She has perhaps gone as deeply into that life as I have into the life of the shafts. . . . Yet we are not surprised or critical of each other for she too is from a mining family and grew up largely on funds sent home by an absentee father. Perhaps we are but becoming our previous generation.

Sometimes they drift apart naturally through absence, as in the case of the migrant workers – through silence, or the inability to communicate, or through sudden death. This is stated with gentleness and sympathy and palpable regret, but it is also seen to be as unavoidable as fate. In the moving and beautiful 'In the Fall', it is the actual violence that their conflict engenders in the child that draws the man and the women together:

> My father puts his arms around my mother's waist and she does not remove them as I have always seen her do. Instead she reaches up and removes the comb or coral from the heaviness of her hair. I have never seen her hair in all its length before and it stretches out now almost parallel to the earth, its shining blackness whipped by the wind and glistening like the snow that settles and melts upon it. It surrounds and engulfs my father's head and he buries his face within its heavy darkness, and draws my mother closer toward him.

It is no accident that the man and the woman work together, against all the conventions, in the building of their house, and sing together as they work in the one pure love the stories detail:

> On clear still days all of the people living down along the mountain's side and even below in the valley could hear the banging of their hammers and the youthful power of their voices . . . They were married for five years in an intensity which it seemed could never last, going more and more into each other and excluding most others for the company of themselves.

Such is the purity and perfection that it can only endure finally in song:

> Every note was perfect, as perfect and clear as the waiting water droplet hanging on the fragile leaf or the high suspended eagle outlined against the sky at the apex of its arc. She sang to him until four in the morning when the first rays of light began to touch the mountain top. And then she was gone.

Often the men need dangerous work for their own physical self-expression. Sometimes they are like gladiators, where women have no place:

> For we are always expanding the perimeters of our seeming incarceration. We are always moving downward or inward or forward or in the driving of our raises even upward. We are big men engaged in perhaps the most violent of occupations and we have chosen as our adversary walls and faces of massive stone. It is as if the stone of the spherical earth had challenged us to move its weight and find its treasure and we have accepted the challenge and responded with drill and steel and powder and strength and all our ingenuity. In the chill and damp we have given ourselves to the breaking down of walls and barriers. We have sentenced ourselves to enclosures so that we might taste the giddy joy of breaking through. Always hopeful of breaking through though we know we will never break free.

The miners can be seen in their enclosures as a metaphor for MacLeod's sophisticated yet simple, his sensuous and very supple art:

> I have always wished that my children could see me at my work. That they might journey down with me in the dripping cage to the shaft's bottom or walk the eerie tunnels of the drifts that end in walls of staring stone. And that they might see how articulate we are in the accomplishment of what we do . . .
>
> I would like to show them how professional we are and how, in spite of the chill and the water and the dark and the danger there is perhaps a certain eloquent beauty to be found in what we do. Not the beauty of stillness to be found in gleaming crystal or in the polished hardwood floors to which my wife devotes such care but rather the beauty of motion on the edge of violence, which by its very nature can never long endure.

Running through the work is the deep irony that it is human ingenuity that is bringing to an end this ancient, traditional world just as MacLeod is bringing it to such vivid life. Often this is faced with grim humour, as when Archibald sells his young mare from a breed he has worked with all his life:

> 'This guy says, I don't know if it's true, that there's this farm outside of Montreal that's connected to a lab or something. Anyway, they've got all these mares there and they keep them

bred all the time and they use their water for birth control pills.'

It seemed so preposterous that Archibald was not sure how to react. He scrutinized Carver's scarred yet open face, looking for a hint, some kind of touch, but he could find nothing.

'Yeah,' said Carver. 'They keep the mares pregnant all the time so the women won't be.'

'What do they do with the colts?' said Archibald, thinking that he might try a question for a change.

In the largeness of the vision, even differences are viewed with the same deep sympathy and understanding as likenesses:

She was out of the door immediately, turning her truck in a spray of gravel that flicked against his house, the small stones pinging against his windowpane. A muddied bumper sticker read: 'If you're horny, honk your horn.'

He was reminded, as he often was, of Cora, who had been dead now for some fifteen years and who had married another man within a year of her visit to him with her open proposal. And he was touched that his granddaughter should seem so much like his brother's wife instead of like his own.

I think of the novel as the most social of all the art forms, the most closely linked to an idea of society, a shared leisure, and a system of manners. The short story does not generally flourish in such a society but comes into its own like song or prayer or superstition in poorer more fragmented communities where individualism and tradition and family and localities and chance or luck are dominant. This appears to be particularly true of Alistair MacLeod's imagined world. The form is inseparable from his material, and his sure talent is happy and at one with them both: it is as if he was sentenced to these small enclosures and made of them his plough. He has turned them into a strength and a glory: the effect is the very opposite of confinement.

The work has a largeness, of feeling, of intellect, of vision, a great openness and generosity, even an old-fashioned courtliness. The stories stand securely outside of fashion while reflecting deep change. In imagination they can move with naturalness across several generations as if they all shared the same eternal day. The small world on Cape Breton opens out to the vast spaces and distances of Canada and the oceans that surround its granite coasts and their people, returning in the summer, or at Christmas, for weddings or bereavements, bringing these vast distances home. In their surefootedness and the slow, sensuous unfolding, the stories gradually acquire the richness and unity of an epic poem or an important novel. Unwittingly, or through that high art that conceals itself, we have been introduced into a complete representation of existence, and the stories take on the truth of the Gaelic songs their people sing. In the mystery of their art they take joy from that very oblivion of which they so movingly sing.

John McGahern

THE BOAT

(1 9 6 8)

There are times even now, when I awake at four
o'clock in the morning with the terrible fear that
I have overslept; when I imagine that my father is
waiting for me in the room below the darkened stairs or that the
shorebound men are tossing pebbles against my window while
blowing their hands and stomping their feet impatiently on the
frozen steadfast earth. There are times when I am half out of bed
and fumbling for socks and mumbling for words before I realize
that I am foolishly alone, that no one waits at the base of the
stairs and no boat rides restlessly in the waters by the pier.

At such times only the grey corpses on the overflowing
ashtray beside my bed bear witness to the extinction of the latest
spark and silently await the crushing out of the most recent of
their fellows. And then because I am afraid to be alone with
death, I dress rapidly, make a great to-do about clearing my
throat, turn on both faucets in the sink and proceed to make

loud splashing ineffectual noises. Later I go out and walk the mile to the all-night restaurant.

In the winter it is a very cold walk, and there are often tears in my eyes when I arrive. The waitress usually gives a sympathetic little shiver and says, "Boy, it must be really cold out there; you got tears in your eyes."

"Yes," I say, "it sure is; it really is."

And then the three or four of us who are always in such places at such times make uninteresting little protective chit-chat until the dawn reluctantly arrives. Then I swallow the coffee, which is always bitter, and leave with a great busy rush because by that time I have to worry about being late and whether I have a clean shirt and whether my car will start and about all the other countless things one must worry about when one teaches at a great Midwestern university. And I know then that that day will go by as have all the days of the past ten years, for the call and the voices and the shapes and the boat were not really there in the early morning's darkness and I have all kinds of comforting reality to prove it. They are only shadows and echoes, the animals a child's hands make on the wall by lamplight, and the voices from the rain barrel; the cuttings from an old movie made in the black and white of long ago.

I first became conscious of the boat in the same way and at almost the same time that I became aware of the people it supported. My earliest recollection of my father is a view from the floor of gigantic rubber boots and then of being suddenly elevated and having my face pressed against the stubble of his cheek, and of how it tasted of salt and of how he smelled of salt from his red-soled rubber boots to the shaggy whiteness of his hair.

When I was very small, he took me for my first ride in the boat. I rode the half-mile from our house to the wharf on his shoulders and I remember the sound of his rubber boots galumphing along the gravel beach, the tune of the indecent little song he used to sing, and the odour of the salt.

The floor of the boat was permeated with the same odour and in its constancy I was not aware of change. In the harbour we made our little circle and returned. He tied the boat by its painter, fastened the stern to its permanent anchor and lifted me high over his head to the solidity of the wharf. Then he climbed up the little iron ladder that led to the wharf's cap, placed me once more upon his shoulders and galumphed off again.

When we returned to the house everyone made a great fuss over my precocious excursion and asked, "How did you like the boat?" "Were you afraid in the boat?" "Did you cry in the boat?" They repeated "the boat" at the end of all their questions and I knew it must be very important to everyone.

My earliest recollection of my mother is of being alone with her in the mornings while my father was away in the boat. She seemed to be always repairing clothes that were "torn in the boat," preparing food "to be eaten in the boat" or looking for "the boat" through our kitchen window which faced upon the sea. When my father returned about noon, she would ask, "Well, how did things go in the boat today?" It was the first question I remember asking: "Well, how did things go in the boat today?" "Well, how did things go in the boat today?"

The boat in our lives was registered at Port Hawkesbury. She was what Nova Scotians called a Cape Island boat and was designed for the small inshore fishermen who sought the lobsters

3

of the spring and the mackerel of summer and later the cod and haddock and hake. She was thirty-two feet long and nine wide, and was powered by an engine from a Chevrolet truck. She had a marine clutch and a high-speed reverse gear and was painted light green with the name *Jenny Lynn* stencilled in black letters on her bow and painted on an oblong plate across her stern. Jenny Lynn had been my mother's maiden name and the boat was called after her as another link in the chain of tradition. Most of the boats that berthed at the wharf bore the names of some female member of their owner's household.

I say this now as if I knew it all then. All at once, all about boat dimensions and engines, and as if on the day of my first childish voyage I noticed the difference between a stencilled name and a painted name. But of course it was not that way at all, for I learned it all very slowly and there was not time enough.

I learned first about our house, which was one of about fifty that marched around the horseshoe of our harbour and the wharf that was its heart. Some of them were so close to the water that during a storm the sea spray splashed against their windows while others were built farther along the beach, as was the case with ours. The houses and their people, like those of the neighbouring towns and villages, were the result of Ireland's discontent and Scotland's Highland Clearances and America's War of Independence. Impulsive, emotional Catholic Celts who could not bear to live with England and shrewd, determined Protestant Puritans who, in the years after 1776, could not bear to live without.

The most important room in our house was one of those oblong old-fashioned kitchens heated by a wood- and

4

coal-burning stove. Behind the stove was a box of kindlings and beside it a coal scuttle. A heavy wooden table with leaves that expanded or reduced its dimensions stood in the middle of the floor. There were five wooden homemade chairs which had been chipped and hacked by a variety of knives. Against the east wall, opposite the stove, there was a couch which sagged in the middle and had a cushion for a pillow, and above it a shelf which contained matches, tobacco, pencils, odd fish-hooks, bits of twine, and a tin can filled with bills and receipts. The south wall was dominated by a window which faced the sea and on the north there was a five-foot board which bore a variety of clothes hooks and the burdens of each. Beneath the board there was a jumble of odd footwear, mostly of rubber. There was also, on this wall, a barometer, a map of the marine area and a shelf which held a tiny radio. The kitchen was shared by all of us and was a buffer zone between the immaculate order of ten other rooms and the disruptive chaos of the single room that was my father's.

My mother ran her house as her brothers ran their boats. Everything was clean and spotless and in order. She was tall and dark and powerfully energetic. In later years she reminded me of the women of Thomas Hardy, particularly Eustacia Vye, in a physical way. She fed and clothed a family of seven children, making all of the meals and most of the clothes. She grew miraculous gardens and magnificent flowers and raised broods of hens and ducks. She would walk miles on berry-picking expeditions and hoist her skirts to dig for clams when the tide was low. She was fourteen years younger than my father, whom she had married when she was twenty-six and had been a local beauty for a period of ten years. My mother was of the sea, as were all of her people, and her horizons were the very literal ones she scanned with her dark and fearless eyes.

Between the kitchen clothes rack and barometer, a door opened into my father's bedroom. It was a room of disorder and disarray. It was as if the wind which so often clamoured about the house succeeded in entering this single room and after whipping it into turmoil stole quietly away to renew its knowing laughter from without.

My father's bed was against the south wall. It always looked rumpled and unmade because he lay on top of it more than he slept within any folds it might have had. Beside it, there was a little brown table. An archaic goose-necked reading light, a battered table radio, a mound of wooden matches, one or two packages of tobacco, a deck of cigarette papers and an overflowing ashtray cluttered its surface. The brown larvae of tobacco shreds and the grey flecks of ash covered both the table and the floor beneath it. The once-varnished surface of the table was disfigured by numerous black scars and gashes inflicted by the neglected burning cigarettes of many years. They had tumbled from the ashtray unnoticed and branded their statements permanently and quietly into the wood until the odour of their burning caused the snuffing out of their lives. At the bed's foot there was a single window which looked upon the sea.

Against the adjacent wall there was a battered bureau and beside it there was a closet which held his single ill-fitting serge suit, the two or three white shirts that strangled him and the square black shoes that pinched. When he took off his more friendly clothes, the heavy woollen sweaters, mitts and socks which my mother knitted for him and the woollen and doeskin shirts, he dumped them unceremoniously on a single chair. If a visitor entered the room while he was lying on the bed, he would be told to throw the clothes on the floor and take their place upon the chair.

Magazines and books covered the bureau and competed with the clothes for domination of the chair. They further overburdened the heroic little table and lay on top of the radio. They filled a baffling and unknowable cave beneath the bed, and in the corner by the bureau they spilled from the walls and grew up from the floor.

The magazines were the most conventional: *Time, Newsweek, Life, Maclean's, The Family Herald, The Reader's Digest.* They were the result of various cut-rate subscriptions or of the gift subscriptions associated with Christmas, "the two whole years for only $3.50."

The books were more varied. There were a few hardcover magnificents and bygone Book-of-the-Month wonders and some were Christmas or birthday gifts. The majority of them, however, were used paperbacks which came from those second-hand bookstores that advertise in the backs of magazines: "Miscellaneous Used Paperbacks 10¢ Each." At first he sent for them himself, although my mother resented the expense, but in later years they came more and more often from my sisters who had moved to the cities. Especially at first they were very weird and varied. Mickey Spillane and Ernest Haycox vied with Dostoyevsky and Faulkner, and the Penguin Poets edition of Gerard Manley Hopkins arrived in the same box as a little book on sex technique called *Getting the Most Out of Love.* The former had been assiduously annotated by a very fine hand using a very blue-inked fountain pen while the latter had been studied by someone with very large thumbs, the prints of which were still visible in the margins. At the slightest provocation it would open almost automatically to particularly graphic and well-smudged pages.

When he was not in the boat, my father spent most of his time lying on the bed in his socks, the top two buttons of his trousers undone, his discarded shirt on the ever-ready chair and the sleeves of the woollen Stanfield underwear, which he wore both summer and winter, drawn half way up to his elbows. The pillows propped up the whiteness of his head and the goose-necked lamp illuminated the pages in his hands. The cigarettes smoked and smouldered on the ashtray and on the table and the radio played constantly, sometimes low and sometimes loud. At midnight and at one, two, three and four, one could sometimes hear the radio, his occasional cough, the rustling thud of a completed book being tossed to the corner heap, or the movement necessitated by his sitting on the edge of the bed to roll the thousandth cigarette. He seemed never to sleep, only to doze, and the light shone constantly from his window to the sea.

My mother despised the room and all it stood for and she had stopped sleeping in it after I was born. She despised disorder in rooms and in houses and in hours and in lives, and she had not read a book since high school. There she had read *Ivanhoe* and considered it a colossal waste of time. Still the room remained, like a rock of opposition in the sparkling waters of a clear deep harbour, opening off the kitchen where we really lived our lives, with its door always open and its contents visible to all.

The daughters of the room and of the house were very beautiful. They were tall and willowy like my mother and had her fine facial features set off by the reddish copper-coloured hair that had apparently once been my father's before it turned to white. All of them were very clever in school and helped my mother a great deal about the house. When they were young they sang and were very happy and very nice to me because I was the youngest, and the family's only boy.

My father never approved of their playing about the wharf like the other children, and they went there only when my mother sent them on an errand. At such times they almost always overstayed, playing screaming games of tag or hide-and-seek in and about the fishing shanties, the piled traps and tubs of trawl, shouting down to the perch that swam languidly about the wharf's algae-covered piles, or jumping in and out of the boats that tugged gently at their lines. My mother was never uneasy about them at such times, and when her husband criticized her she would say, "Nothing will happen to them there," or "They could be doing worse things in worse places."

By about the ninth or tenth grade my sisters one by one discovered my father's bedroom, and then the change would begin. Each would go into the room one morning when he was out. She would go with the ideal hope of imposing order or with the more practical objective of emptying the ashtray, and later she would be found spellbound by the volume in her hand. My mother's reaction was always abrupt, bordering on the angry. "Take your nose out of that trash and come and do your work," she would say, and once I saw her slap my youngest sister so hard that the print of her hand was scarletly emblazoned upon her daughter's cheek while the broken-spined paperback fluttered uselessly to the floor.

Thereafter my mother would launch a campaign against what she had discovered but could not understand. At times, although she was not overly religious, she would bring in God to bolster her arguments, saying, "In the next world God will see to those who waste their lives reading useless books when they should be about their work." Or without theological aid, "I would like to know how books help anyone to live a life." If my father were in, she would repeat the remarks louder than necessary, and her voice would carry into his room where he lay upon his bed. His usual reaction was to turn up the volume of the radio, although that action in itself betrayed the success of the initial thrust.

Shortly after my sisters began to read the books, they grew restless and lost interest in darning socks and baking bread, and all of them eventually went to work as summer waitresses in the Sea Food Restaurant. The restaurant was run by a big American concern from Boston and catered to the tourists that flooded the area during July and August. My mother despised the whole operation. She said the restaurant was not run by "our people," and "our people" did not eat there, and that it was run by outsiders for outsiders.

"Who are these people anyway?" she would ask, tossing back her dark hair, "and what do they, though they go about with their cameras for a hundred years, know about the way it is here, and what do they care about me and mine, and why should I care about them?"

She was angry that my sisters should even conceive of working in such a place, and more angry when my father made no move to prevent it, and she was worried about herself and about her family and about her life. Sometimes she would say softly to her sisters, "I don't know what's the matter with my girls. It seems none of them are interested in any of the right things." And sometimes there would be bitter savage arguments. One afternoon I was coming in with three mackerel I'd been given at the wharf when I heard her say, "Well, I hope you'll be satisfied when they come home knocked up and you'll have had your way."

It was the most savage thing I'd ever heard my mother say. Not just the words but the way she said them, and I stood there in the porch afraid to breathe for what seemed like the years from ten to fifteen, feeling the damp, moist mackerel with their silver glassy eyes growing clammy against my leg.

Through the angle in the screen door I saw my father, who had been walking into his room, wheel around on one of his rubber-booted heels and look at her with his blue eyes flashing like clearest ice beneath the snow that was his hair. His usually ruddy face was drawn and grey, reflecting the exhaustion of a man of sixty-five who had been working in those rubber boots for eleven hours on an August day, and for a fleeting moment I wondered what I would do if he killed my mother while I stood there in the porch with those three foolish mackerel in my hand. Then he turned and went into his room and the radio blared forth the next day's weather forecast and I retreated under the noise and returned again, stamping my feet and slamming the door too loudly to signal my approach. My mother was busy at the stove when I came in, and did not raise her head when I threw the mackerel in a pan. As I looked into my father's room, I said, "Well, how did things go in the boat today?" and he replied, "Oh, not too badly, all things considered." He was lying on his back and lighting the first cigarette and the radio was talking about the Virginia coast.

All of my sisters made good money on tips. They bought my father an electric razor, which he tried to use for a while, and they took out even more magazine subscriptions. They bought my mother a great many clothes of the type she was very fond of, the wide-brimmed hats and the brocaded dresses, but she locked them all in trunks and refused to wear any of them.

On one August day my sisters prevailed upon my father to take some of their restaurant customers for an afternoon ride in the boat. The tourists with their expensive clothes and cameras and sun glasses awkwardly backed down the iron ladder at the wharf's side to where my father waited below, holding the rocking *Jenny Lynn* in snug against the wharf with one hand on the iron ladder and steadying his descending passengers with the other. They tried to look both prim and wind-blown like the girls in the Pepsi-Cola ads and did the best they could, sitting on the thwarts where the newspapers were spread to cover the splattered blood and fish entrails, crowding to one side so that they were in danger of capsizing the boat, taking the inevitable pictures or merely trailing their fingers through the water of their dreams.

All of them liked my father very much and, after he'd brought them back from their circles in the harbour, they invited him to their rented cabins which were located high on a hill overlooking the village to which they were so alien. He proceeded to get very drunk up there with the beautiful view and the strange company and the abundant liquor, and late in the afternoon he began to sing.

I was just approaching the wharf to deliver my mother's summons when he began, and the familiar yet unfamiliar voice that rolled down from the cabins made me feel as I had never felt before in my young life, or perhaps as I had always felt without really knowing it, and I was ashamed yet proud, young yet old and saved yet forever lost, and there was nothing I could do to control my legs which trembled nor my eyes which wept, for what they could not tell.

The tourists were equipped with tape recorders and my father sang for more than three hours. His voice boomed down the hill and bounced off the surface of the harbour, which was an unearthly blue on that hot August day, and was then reflected to the wharf and the fishing shanties, where it was absorbed amidst the men who were baiting lines for the next day's haul.

He sang all the old sea chanteys that had come across from the old world and by which men like him had pulled ropes for generations, and he sang the East Coast sea songs that celebrated the scaling vessels of Northumberland Strait and the long liners of the Grand Banks, and of Anticosti, Sable Island, Grand Manan, Boston Harbor, Nantucket and Block Island. Gradually he shifted to the seemingly unending Gaelic drinking songs with their twenty or more verses and inevitable refrains, and the men in the shanties smiled at the coarseness of some of the verses and at the thought that the singer's immediate audience did not know what they were applauding nor recording to take back to staid old Boston. Later as the sun was setting he switched to the laments and the wild and haunting Gaelic war songs of those spattered Highland ancestors he had never seen, and when his voice ceased, the savage melancholy of three hundred years seemed to hang over the peaceful harbour and the quiet boats and the men leaning in the doorways of their shanties with their cigarettes glowing in the dusk and the women looking to the sea from their open windows with their children in their arms.

When he came home he threw the money he had earned on the kitchen table as he did with all his earnings but my mother refused to touch it, and the next day he went with the rest of the men to bait his trawl in the shanties. The tourists came to the door that evening and my mother met them there and told them that her husband was not in, although he was lying on the bed only a few feet away, with the radio playing and the cigarette upon his lips. She stood in the doorway until they reluctantly went away.

In the winter they sent him a picture which had been taken on the day of the singing. On the back it said, "To Our Ernest Hemingway" and the "Our" was underlined. There was also an accompanying letter telling how much they had enjoyed themselves, how popular the tape was proving and explaining who Ernest Hemingway was. In a way it almost did look like one of those unshaven, taken-in-Cuba pictures of Hemingway. My father looked both massive and incongruous in the setting. His bulky fisherman's clothes were too big for the green and white lawn chair in which he sat, and his rubber boots seemed to take up all of the well-clipped grass square. The beach umbrella jarred with his sunburned face and because he had already been singing for some time, his lips, which chapped in the winds of spring and burned in the water glare of summer, had already cracked in several places, producing tiny flecks of blood at their corners and on the whiteness of his teeth. The bracelets of brass chain which he wore to protect his wrists from chafing seemed abnormally large and his broad leather belt had been slackened and his heavy shirt and underwear were open at the throat, revealing an uncultivated wilderness of white chest hair bordering on the semi-controlled stubble of his neck and chin. His blue eyes had looked directly into the camera and his hair was whiter than the two tiny clouds that hung over his left shoulder. The sea was behind him and its immense blue flatness stretched out to touch the arching blueness of the sky. It seemed very far away from him or else he was so much in the foreground that he seemed too big for it.

Each year another of my sisters would read the books and work in the restaurant. Sometimes they would stay out quite late on the hot summer nights and when they came up the stairs my mother would ask them many long and involved questions which they resented and tried to avoid. Before ascending the stairs they would go into my father's room, and those of us who waited above could hear them throwing his clothes off the chair before sitting on it, or the squeak of the bed as they sat on its edge. Sometimes they would talk to him a long time, the murmur of their voices blending with the music of the radio into a mysterious vapour-like sound which floated softly up the stairs.

I say this again as if it all happened at once and as if all of my sisters were of identical ages and like so many lemmings going into another sea and, again, it was of course not that way at all. Yet go they did, to Boston, to Montreal, to New York with the young men they met during the summers and later married in those far-away cities. The young men were very articulate and handsome and wore fine clothes and drove expensive cars and my sisters, as I said, were very tall and beautiful with their copper-coloured hair, and were tired of darning socks and baking bread.

One by one they went. My mother had each of her daughters for fifteen years, then lost them for two and finally forever. None married a fisherman. My mother never accepted any of the young men, for in her eyes they seemed always a combination of the lazy, the effeminate, the dishonest and the unknown. They never seemed to do any physical work and she could not comprehend their luxurious vacations and she did not know whence they came nor who they were. And in the end she did not really care, for they were not of her people and they were not of her sea.

I say this now with a sense of wonder at my own stupidity in thinking I was somehow free and would go on doing well in school and playing and helping in the boat and passing into my early teens while streaks of grey began to appear in my mother's dark hair and my father's rubber boots dragged sometimes on the pebbles of the beach as he trudged home from the wharf. And there were but three of us in the house that had at one time been so loud.

Then during the winter that I was fifteen he seemed to grow old and ill all at once. Most of January he lay upon the bed, smoking and reading and listening to the radio while the wind howled about the house and the needle-like snow blistered off the ice-covered harbour and the doors flew out of people's hands if they did not cling to them like death.

In February, when the men began overhauling their lobster traps, he still did not move, and my mother and I began to knit lobster trap headings in the evenings. The twine was as always very sharp and harsh, and blisters formed upon our thumbs and little paths of blood snaked quietly down between our fingers while the seals that had drifted down from distant Labrador wept and moaned like human children on the ice-floes of the Gulf.

In the daytime my mother's brother, who had been my father's partner as long as I could remember, also came to work upon the gear. He was a year older than my mother and was tall and dark and the father of twelve children.

By March we were very far behind and although I began to work very hard in the evenings I knew it was not hard enough and that there were but eight weeks left before the opening of the season on May first. And I knew that my mother worried and my uncle was uneasy and that all of our very lives depended on the boat being ready with her gear and two men, by the date of May the first. And I knew then that *David Copperfield* and *The Tempest* and all of those friends I had dearly come to love must really go forever. So I bade them all good-bye.

The night after my first full day at home and after my mother had gone upstairs he called me into his room, where I sat upon the chair beside his bed. "You will go back tomorrow," he said simply.

I refused then, saying I had made my decision and was satisfied.

"That is no way to make a decision," he said, "and if you are satisfied I am not. It is best that you go back." I was almost angry then and told him as all children do that I wished he would leave me alone and stop telling me what to do.

He looked at me a long time then, lying there on the same bed on which he had fathered me those sixteen years before, fathered me his only son, out of who knew what emotions when he was already fifty-six and his hair had turned to snow. Then he swung his legs over the edge of the squeaking bed and sat facing me and looked into my own dark eyes with his of crystal blue and placed his hand upon my knee. "I am not telling you to do anything," he said softly, "only asking you."

The next morning I returned to school. As I left, my mother followed me to the porch and said, "I never thought a son of mine would choose useless books over the parents that gave him life."

In the weeks that followed he got up rather miraculously, and the gear was ready and the *Jenny Lynn* was freshly painted by the last two weeks of April when the ice began to break up and the lonely screaming gulls returned to haunt the silver herring as they flashed within the sea.

On the first day of May the boats raced out as they had always done, laden down almost to the gunwales with their heavy cargoes of traps. They were almost like living things as they plunged through the waters of the spring and manoeuvred between the still floating icebergs of crystal-white and emerald green on their way to the traditional grounds that they sought out every May. And those of us who sat that day in the high school on the hill, discussing the water imagery of Tennyson, watched them as they passed back and forth beneath us until by afternoon the piles of traps which had been stacked upon the wharf were no longer visible but were spread about the bottoms of the sea. And the *Jenny Lynn* went too, all day, with my uncle tall and dark, like a latter-day Tashtego standing at the tiller with his legs wide apart and guiding her deftly between the floating pans of ice and my father in the stern standing in the same way with his hands upon the ropes that lashed the cargo to the deck. And at night my mother asked, "Well, how did things go in the boat today?"

And the spring wore on and the summer came and school ended in the third week of June and the lobster season on July first and I wished that the two things I loved so dearly did not exclude each other in a manner that was so blunt and too clear.

At the conclusion of the lobster season my uncle said he had been offered a berth on a deep-sea dragger and had decided to accept. We all knew that he was leaving the *Jenny Lynn* forever and that before the next lobster season he would buy a boat of his own. He was expecting another child and would be supporting fifteen people by the next spring and could not chance my father against the family that he loved.

I joined my father then for the trawling season, and he made no protest and my mother was quite happy. Through the summer

19

we baited the tubs of trawl in the afternoon and set them at sunset and revisited them in the darkness of the early morning. The men would come tramping by our house at four A.M. and we would join them and walk with them to the wharf and be on our way before the sun rose out of the ocean where it seemed to spend the night. If I was not up they would toss pebbles to my window and I would be very embarrassed and tumble downstairs to where my father lay fully clothed atop his bed, reading his book and listening to his radio and smoking his cigarette. When I appeared he would swing off his bed and put on his boots and be instantly ready and then we would take the lunches my mother had prepared the night before and walk off toward the sea. He would make no attempt to wake me himself.

It was in many ways a good summer. There were few storms and we were out almost every day and we lost a minimum of gear and seemed to land a maximum of fish and I tanned dark and brown after the manner of my uncles.

My father did not tan – he never tanned – because of his reddish complexion, and the salt water irritated his skin as it had for sixty years. He burned and reburned over and over again and his lips still cracked so that they bled when he smiled, and his arms, especially the left, still broke out into the oozing salt-water boils as they had ever since as a child I had first watched him soaking and bathing them in a variety of ineffectual solutions. The chafe-preventing bracelets of brass linked chain that all the men wore about their wrists in early spring were his the full season and he shaved but painfully and only once a week.

And I saw then, that summer, many things that I had seen all my life as if for the first time and I thought that perhaps my father had never been intended for a fisherman either physically or mentally. At least not in the manner of my uncles; he had never really loved it. And I remembered that, one evening in his room when we were talking about *David Copperfield*, he had said that he had always wanted to go to the university and I had dismissed it then in the way one dismisses one's father's saying he would like to be a tight-rope walker, and we had gone on to talk about the Peggottys and how they loved the sea.

And I thought then to myself that there were many things wrong with all of us and all our lives and I wondered why my father, who was himself an only son, had not married before he was forty and then I wondered why he had. I even thought that perhaps he had had to marry my mother and checked the dates on the flyleaf of the Bible where I learned that my oldest sister had been born a prosaic eleven months after the marriage, and I felt myself then very dirty and debased for my lack of faith and for what I had thought and done.

And then there came into my heart a very great love for my father and I thought it was very much braver to spend a life doing what you really do not want rather than selfishly following forever your own dreams and inclinations. And I knew then that I could never leave him alone to suffer the iron-tipped harpoons which my mother would forever hurl into his soul because he was a failure as a husband and a father who had retained none of his own. And I felt that I had been very small in a little secret place within me and that even the completion of high school was for me a silly shallow selfish dream.

So I told him one night very resolutely and very powerfully that I would remain with him as long as he lived and we would fish the sea together. And he made no protest but only smiled through the cigarette smoke that wreathed his bed and replied, "I hope you will remember what you've said."

The room was now so filled with books as to be almost Dickensian, but he would not allow my mother to move or change them and he continued to read them, sometimes two or three a night. They came with great regularity now, and there were more hardcovers, sent by my sisters who had gone so long ago and now seemed so distant and so prosperous, and sent also pictures of small red-haired grandchildren with baseball bats and dolls, which he placed upon his bureau and which my mother gazed at wistfully when she thought no one would see. Red-haired grandchildren with baseball bats and dolls who would never know the sea in hatred or in love.

And so we fished through the heat of August and into the cooler days of September when the water was so clear we could almost see the bottom and the white mists rose like delicate ghosts in the early morning dawn. And one day my mother said to me, "You have given added years to his life."

And we fished on into October when it began to roughen and we could no longer risk night sets but took our gear out each morning and returned at the first sign of the squalls; and on into November when we lost three tubs of trawl and the clear blue water turned to a sullen grey and the trochoidal waves rolled rough and high and washed across our bows and decks as we ran within their troughs. We wore heavy sweaters now and the awkward rubber slickers and the heavy woollen mitts which soaked and froze into masses of ice that hung from our wrists like the limbs of gigantic monsters until we thawed them against the exhaust pipe's heat. And almost every day we would leave for home before noon, driven by the blasts of the northwest wind coating our eyebrows with ice and freezing our eyelids closed as we leaned into a visibility that was hardly there, charting our course from the compass and the sea, running with the waves and between them but never confronting their towering might.

And I stood at the tiller now, on these homeward lunges, stood in the place and in the manner of my uncle, turning to look at my father and to shout over the roar of the engine and the slop of the sea to where he stood in the stern, drenched and dripping with the snow and the salt and the spray and his bushy eyebrows caked in ice. But on November twenty-first, when it seemed we might be making the final run of the season, I turned and he was not there and I knew even in that instant that he would never be again.

On November twenty-first the waves of the grey Atlantic are very high and the waters are very cold and there are no sign-posts on the surface of the sea. You cannot tell where you have been five minutes before and in the squalls of snow you cannot see. And it takes longer than you would believe to check a boat that has been running before a gale and turn her ever so carefully in a wide and stupid circle, with timbers creaking and straining, back into the face of storm. And you know that it is useless and that your voice does not carry the length of the boat and that even if you knew the original spot, the relentless waves would carry such a burden perhaps a mile or so by the time you could return. And you know also, the final irony, that your father, like your uncles and all the men that form your past, cannot swim a stroke.

The lobster beds off the Cape Breton coast are still very rich and now, from May to July, their offerings are packed in crates of ice, and thundered by the gigantic transport trucks, day and night, through New Glasgow, Amherst, Saint John and Bangor and Portland and into Boston where they are tossed still living into boiling pots of water, their final home.

And though the prices are higher and the competition tighter, the grounds to which the *Jenny Lynn* once went remain untouched and unfished as they have for the last ten years. For if there are no signposts on the sea in storm, there are certain ones in calm, and the lobster bottoms were distributed in calm before any of us can remember, and the grounds my father fished were those his father fished before him and there were others before and before and before. Twice the big boats have come from forty and fifty miles, lured by the promise of the grounds, and strewn the bottom with their traps, and twice they have returned to find their buoys cut adrift and their gear lost and destroyed. Twice the Fisheries Officer and the Mounted Police have come and asked many long and involved questions, and twice they have received no answers from the men leaning in the doors of their shanties and the women standing at their windows with their children in their arms. Twice they have gone away saying: "There are no legal boundaries in the Marine area"; "No one can own the sea"; "Those grounds don't wait for anyone."

But the men and the women, with my mother dark among them, do not care for what they say, for to them the grounds are sacred and they think they wait for me.

It is not an easy thing to know that your mother lives alone on an inadequate insurance policy and that she is too proud to accept any other aid. And that she looks through her lonely window onto the ice of winter and the hot flat calm of summer and the rolling waves of fall. And that she lies awake in the early morning's darkness when the rubber boots of the men scrunch upon the gravel as they pass beside her house on their way down to the wharf. And she knows that the footsteps never stop, because no man goes from her house, and she alone of all the Lynns has neither son nor son-in-law who walks toward the boat that will take him to the sea. And it is not an easy thing to know that your mother looks upon the sea with love and on you with bitterness because the one has been so constant and the other so untrue.

But neither is it easy to know that your father was found on November twenty-eighth, ten miles to the north and wedged between two boulders at the base of the rock-strewn cliffs where he had been hurled and slammed so many many times. His hands were shredded ribbons, as were his feet which had lost their boots to the suction of the sea, and his shoulders came apart in our hands when we tried to move him from the rocks. And the fish had eaten his testicles and the gulls had pecked out his eyes and the white-green stubble of his whiskers had continued to grow in death, like the grass on graves, upon the purple, bloated mass that was his face. There was not much left of my father, physically, as he lay there with the brass chains on his wrists and the seaweed in his hair.

THE VASTNESS OF THE DARK

(1 9 7 1)

On the twenty-eighth day of June, 1960, which is the planned day of my deliverance, I awake at exactly six A.M. to find myself on my eighteenth birthday, listening to the ringing of the bells from the Catholic church which I now attend only reluctantly on Sundays. "Well," I say to the bells and to myself, "at least tomorrow I will be free of you." And yet I do not move but lie quietly for a while looking up and through the window at the green poplar leaves rustling softly and easily in the Nova Scotian dawn.

The reason that I do not arise immediately on such a momentous day is partially due, at least, to a second sound that is very unlike the regular, majestic booming of the bells. It is the irregular and moistly rattling-rasping sound of my father's snoring which comes from the adjoining room. And although I can only hear him I can see very vividly in my mind how he must be: lying there on his back with his thinning iron-grey hair

26

tousled upon the pillow and with his hollow cheeks and even his jet-black eyebrows rising and falling slightly with the erratic pattern of his breathing. His mouth is slightly open and there are little bubbles of saliva forming and breaking at its corners, and his left arm and perhaps even his left leg are hanging over the bed's edge and resting upon the floor. It seems, with his arm and leg like that, as if he were prepared within his sleeping consciousness for any kind of unexpected emergency that might arise; so that if and when it does he will only have to roll slightly to his left and straighten and be immediately standing. Half of his body already touches the floor in readiness.

In our home no one gets up before he does; but in a little while, I think, that too will happen. He will sort of gasp in a strangled way and the snoring will cease. Then there will be a few stealthy movements and the ill-fitting door will open and close and he will come walking through my room carrying his shoes in his left hand while at the same time trying to support his trousers and also to button and buckle them with his right. As long as I can remember he has finished dressing while walking, but he does not handle buttons nor buckles so well since the dynamite stick at the little mine where he used to work ripped the first two fingers from his scarred right hand. Now the remaining fingers try to do what is expected of them: to hold, to button, to buckle, to adjust, but they do so with what seems a sort of groping uncertainty bordering on despair. As if they realized that there is now just too much for them to do, even though they try as best they can.

When he comes through this room he will be walking softly so as not to awaken me and I will close my eyes and do my imitation of sleep so that he will think himself successful. After he has gone downstairs to start the fire there will be a pause and perhaps a few exploratory coughs exchanged between my mother and me in an unworded attempt to decide who is going to make the next move. If I cough it will indicate that I am awake and usually that means I will get up next and follow the route of my father downstairs. If, on the other hand, I make no sound, in a few minutes my mother also will come walking through my room. As she passes I will close my eyes a second time but I have always the feeling that it does not work for her; that unlike my father she can tell the difference between sleep which is real and that which is feigned. And I feel always dishonest about my deception. But today, I think, it will be the last time, and I want both of them down the stairs before I myself descend. For today I have private things to do which can only be done in the brief interval between the descent of my parents and the rising of my seven younger brothers and sisters.

Those brothers and sisters are now sleeping in a very different world across the hallway in two large rooms called generally "the girls' room" and "the boys' room." In the former there are my sisters and their names and ages are: Mary, 15, Judy, 14, Catherine, 12, and Bernadette, 3. In the other there are Daniel, 9, Harvey, 7, and David, 5. They live there, across the hall, in an alien but sociable world of half-suppressed giggles, impromptu pantomimes and muffled-silent pillow fights, and fall to sleep in beds filled with oft-exchanged comic books and the crumbs of smuggled cookies. On "our" side of the hall it is very different. There is only one door for the two rooms and my parents, as I have said, have always to walk through my room to get to theirs.

It is not a very good arrangement and at one time my father intended to cut another door from the hallway into their room and to close off the inadequate connecting door between their room and mine. But at one time he also probably planned to seal and cover the wooden beams and ribs that support the roof in all our rooms and he has not done that either. On the very coldest winter mornings you can look up and see the frost on the icy heads of the silver nails and see your breath in the coldly crystal air.

Sleeping over here on this side of the hall I have always felt very adult and separated from my younger brothers and sisters and their muffled worlds of laughter. I suppose it has something to do with the fact that I am the oldest by three years and circumstances have made me more alone. At one time each of us has slept in a crib in my parents' room and as I was the first I was not moved very far – only into the next room. Perhaps they kept me close because they were more nervous about me, and for a longer time, as they had not had much experience at that time with babies or younger children. So I have been here in this bed all by myself for as long as I can remember. The next three in our family are girls and I am separated from Daniel, the nearest boy, by an unbridgeable abyss of nine years. And by that time it seems my parents felt there was no point in either moving him in with me or me across the hall with him, as if they had somehow gotten used to hearing me breathing in the room so close to theirs and knew that I knew a great deal about them and about their habits and had been kind of backed into trusting me as if I were, perhaps, a younger brother or perhaps more intimately a friend. It is a strange and lonely thing to lie awake at night and listen to your parents making love in the next room and to be able even to count the strokes. And to know that they really do not know how much you know, but to know that they do know that you know; and not to know when the knowledge of your knowing came to them any more than they know when it came to you. And during these last four or five years lying here while the waves of embarrassed horniness roll over me, I have developed, apart from the problems of my own tumescent flesh, a sort of sympathy for the problem that must be theirs and for the awful violation of privacy that all of us represent. For it must be a very difficult thing for two people to try to have a sex life together when they know that the first product of that life is lying listening to them only a few feet away. Also, I know something else that I do not think they know I know.

I was told it by my paternal grandfather seven years ago when I was ten and he was eighty, on a spring day when, warmed by the sun, he had gone downtown and sat in a tavern most of the afternoon, drinking beer and spitting on the floor and slapping the table and his knee with the palm of his hand, his head wreathed in the pipe smoke of the mine-mutilated old men who were his friends. And as I passed the tavern's open door with my bag of papers he had hailed me as if I were some minia-ture taxi-cab and had said that he wished to go home. And so we had wended our way through the side streets and the back alleys, a small slightly embarrassed boy and a staggering but sur-prisingly erect old man who wanted me beside him but not to physically support him as that would hurt his pride.

"I am perfectly capable of walking home by myself, James," he said, looking down at me off the tip of his nose and over his walrus moustache. "No one is taking me home. I only want company. So you stay over on your side and I will stay on mine and we will just be friends going for a walk as indeed we are."

But then we had turned into an alley where he had placed his left arm against a building's brick wall and leaned, half-resting, his forehead against it while his right hand fumbled at his fly. And standing there with his head against the wall and with his shoes two feet from its base he had seemed like some strange, speaking hypotenuse from the geometry books at school and standing in the stream of his urine he had mumbled into the wall that he loved me, although he didn't often say so, and that he had loved me even before I was born.

"You know," he said, "when I learned that your mother was knocked up I was so happy I was just ashamed. And my wife was in a rage and your mother's parents were weeping and wringing their silly hands and whenever I was near them I would walk around looking at my shoes. But I think that, God forgive me, I may have even prayed for something like that and when I heard it I said, 'Well, he will have to stay now and marry her because that's the kind of man he is, and he will work in my place now just as I've always wanted.'"

Then his forehead seemed to slide off his resting arm and he lurched unsteadily, almost bumping into me and seeming to see me for the first time. "Oh God," he said, with a startled, frightened expression, "what a selfish old fool! What have I done now? Forget everything I said!" And he had squeezed my shoulder too tightly at first but then relaxed his grip and let his gigantic hand lie there limply all the way to his home. As soon as he entered his door, he flopped into the nearest chair and said almost on the verge of tears, "I think I told him. I think I told him." And my grandmother who was ten years younger turned on him in alarm but only asked, "What?" and he, raising both hands off his lap and letting them fall back in a sort of helpless gesture of despair, said, "Oh you know, you know," as if he were very much afraid.

"Go on home, James," she said to me evenly and kindly although I knew she was very angry, "and pay no attention to this old fool. He has never in all his life known when to open and close his pants or his mouth." As I turned to leave, I noticed for the first time that he had not redone his trousers after urinating in the alley and that his underwear was awry.

No one has ever mentioned it since but because one of my grandparents was so frightened and the other so angry I know that it is true because they do not react that strongly to anything that is not real. And knowing so I have never checked it further. And it is strange too with this added knowledge to lie in bed at night and to hear the actual beginnings of your brothers and sisters, to almost share in it in an odd way and to know that you did not begin really in that same way or at least not in that bed. And I have imagined the back seats of the old cars I've seen in pictures, or the grassy hills behind the now torn-down dance halls or the beaches of sand beside the sea. I like to think somehow that it had been different for them at my conception and that there had been joy instead of grim release. But I suppose we, all of us, like to think of ourselves as children of love rather than of necessity. That we have come about because there was a feeling of peace and well-being before the erection rather than its being the other way around. But of course I may be as wrong about that as I am about many things and perhaps I do not know what they feel now any more than what they might have felt then.

But after today, I will probably not have to think about it any more. For today I leave behind this grimy Cape Breton coal-mining town whose prisoner I have been all of my life. And I have decided that almost any place must be better than this one with its worn-out mines and smoke-black houses; and the feeling has been building within me for the last few years. It seems to have come almost with the first waves of sexual desire and with it to have grown stronger and stronger with the passing months and years. For I must not become as my father whom I now hear banging the stove-lids below me as if there were some desperate rush about it all and some place that he must be in a very short time. Only to go nowhere. And I must not be as my grandfather who is now an almost senile old man, nearing ninety, who sits by the window all day saying his prayers and who in his moments of clarity remembers mostly his conquests over coal, and recounts tales of how straight were the timbers he and my father erected in the now caved in underground drifts of twenty-five years ago when he was sixty-two and my father twenty-five and I not yet conceived.

It is a long, long time since my grandfather has worked and all the big mines he worked in and which he so romanticizes now are closed. And my father has not worked since early March, and his presence in a house where he does not want to be breeds a tension in us all that is heightened now since school is closed and we are all home and forced in upon ourselves. And as he moves about on this morning, banging stove-lids, pretending it is important that he does so, that he is wanted somewhere soon and therefore must make this noisy rush, I feel myself separated from him by a wide and variegated gulf and very far away from the man, who, shortly after he became my father, would take me for rides upon his shoulders to buy ice-cream at the drugstore, to see the baseball games I did not understand, or into the open fields to pat the pit-horses and be placed upon their broad and gentle backs. As we would approach the horses he would speak softly to them so that they might know where we were and be unafraid when he finally placed his hand upon them, for all of them were blind. They had been so long in the darkness of the mine that their eyes did not know the light, and the darkness of their labour had become that of their lives.

But now my father does not do such things with his younger children even as he no longer works. And he is older and greyer and apart from the missing fingers on his right hand, there is a scar from a broken bit that begins at his hairline and runs like violent lightning down the right side of his face and at night I can hear him coughing and wheezing from the rock dust on his lungs. And perhaps that coughing means that because he has worked in bad mines with bad air these last few years he will not live so very much longer. And perhaps my brothers and sisters across the hall will never hear him, when they are eighteen, rattling the stove-lids as I do now.

And as I lie here now on my back for the last time, I think of when I lay on my stomach in the underground for the first time with him there beside me in the small bootleg mine which ran beneath the sea and in which he had been working since the previous January. I had joined him at the end of the school year for a few short weeks before the little mine finally closed and I had been rather surprisingly proud to work there, and my grandfather in one of his clearer moments said, "Once you start, it takes a hold of you, once you drink underground water, you will always come back to drink some more. The water gets in your blood. It is in all of our blood. We have been working in the mines here since 1873."

The little mine paid very low wages and was poorly equipped and ventilated and since it was itself illegal there were no safety regulations. And I had thought, that first day, that I might die as we lay on our stomachs on the broken shale and on the lumps of coal while the water seeped around us and into us and chilled us with unflagging constancy whenever we ceased our mole-like movements. It was a very narrow little seam that we attacked, first with our drilling steels and bits, and then with our dynamite, and finally with our picks and shovels. And there was scarcely thirty-six inches of headroom where we sprawled, my father shovelling over his shoulders like the machine he had almost become while I tried to do what I was told and to be unafraid of the roof coming in or of the rats that brushed my face, or of the water that numbed my legs, my stomach and my testicles or of the fact that at times I could not breathe because the powder-heavy air was so foul and had been breathed before.

And I was aware once of the whistling wind of movement beside me and over me and saw by the light of my lamp the gigantic pipe-wrench of my father describing an arc over me and landing with a squealing crunch an arm's length before me; and then I saw the rat, lying on its back and inches from my eyes. Its head was splattered on the coal and on the wrench and it was still squeaking while a dying stream of yellow urine trickled down between its convulsively jerking legs. And then my father released the wrench and seizing the not-quite-dead rat by the tail hurled it savagely back over his shoulder so that the thud of its body could be heard behind us as it bounced off the wall and then splashed into the water. "You dirty son of a bitch," he said between clenched teeth and wiped the back of the wrench against the rocky wall. And we lay there then for a while without moving, chilled together in the dampness and the dark.

And now, strangely enough, I do not know if that is what I hate and so must leave, or if it is the fact that now there is not even that mine, awful as it was, to go to, and perhaps it is better to have a place to go to that you hate than to have no place at all. And it is the latter which makes my father now increasingly tense and nervous because he has always used his body as if it were a car with its accelerator always to the floor, and now as it becomes more scarred and wasted, he can use it only for sex or taut too-rapid walks along the seashore or back into the hills; and when everything else fails he will try to numb himself with rum, and his friends will bring him home in the evenings and dump him with his legs buckling beneath him, inside his kitchen door. And my mother and I will half carry and half drag him through the dining room to the base of the stairs and up the fourteen steps, counting them to ourselves, one by one. We do not always get that far; once he drove his left fist through the glass of the dining room window and I wrestled with him back and forth across the floor while the wildly swinging and still-clenched fist flashed and flecked its scarlet blood upon the floor and the wallpaper and the curtains and the dishes and the foolish sad dolls and colouring books and *Great Expectations* which lay upon the table. And when he was subdued and the fist became a hand we had to ask him politely to clench it again so that the wounds would reopen while the screaming iodine was poured over and into them and the tweezers probed for the flashing slivers of glass. And we had prayed then, he included, that no tendons were damaged and that no infection would set in because it was the only good hand that he had and all of us rode upon it as perilous passengers on an unpredictably violent sea.

Sometimes when he drinks so heavily my mother and I cannot always get him to his bed and leave him instead on mine, trying to undress him as best we can, amidst his flailing arms and legs and shouted obscenities, hoping at least to get his shoes off, and loosen his collar and belt and trousers. And during the nights that follow such days I lie rigid beside him, trying to overcome the nausea caused by the sticky, sweet stench of the rum and listening to the sleep-talker's mumbled, incoherent words, his uneven snoring, and the frightening catches in his breathing caused by the phlegm within his throat. Sometimes he will swing out unexpectedly with either hand and once his forearm landed across my nose with such force that the blood and tears welled to the surface simultaneously and I had to stuff the bed-clothes into my mouth to stifle the cry that rose upon my lips.

But yet it seems that all storms subside first into gusts and then into calm and perhaps without storms and gusts we might never have any calm, or perhaps having it we would not recognize it for what it is; and so when he awakens at one or two A.M. and lies there quietly in the dark it is the most peaceful of all times, like the quiet of the sea, and it is only then that I catch glimpses of the man who took me for the rides upon his shoulders. And I arise and go down the stairs as silently as I can, through the sleeping house, and fetch the milk which soothes the thickness of his tongue and the parched and fevered dryness of his throat and he says, "Thank you," and that he is sorry, and I say that it is all right and that there is really nothing to be sorry for. And he says that he is sorry that he has acted the way he has and that he is sorry he has been able to give me so little but if he cannot give he will try very hard not to take. And that I am free and owe my parents nothing. That in itself is perhaps quite a lot to give, for many people like myself go to work very young here or did when there was work to go to, and not everyone gets into high school or out of it. And perhaps even the completion of high school is the gift that he has given me along with that of life.

But that is also now ended, I think, the life here and the high school, and the thought jolts me into the realization that I have somehow been half-dozing, for although I think I clearly remember everything, my mother has obviously already passed through this room, for now I hear her moving about downstairs preparing breakfast. I am rather grateful that at least I have not had to pretend to be asleep on this the last of all these days.

Moving now as quickly as I can, I remove from beneath the mattress the battered old packsack that was my father's in earlier, younger days. "Would it be all right if I use that old packsack sometime?" I had asked as casually as possible some months before, trying to make my plans for it sound like some weary camping expedition. "Sure," he had said in an even, non-committal fashion.

Now I pack it quietly, checking with my ballpoint pen the items that I have listed on the back of the envelope kept beneath my pillow. Four pairs of underwear, five pairs of socks, two pairs of pants, four shirts, one towel, some handkerchiefs, a gabardine jacket, a plastic raincoat and a shaving set. The latter is the only item that is new and unused and is the cheapest that Gillette manufactures. Up until this time I have always used my father's razor, which is battered and verdigris green from years of use. I have used it for some years now — more often, at times, than my questionable beard demanded.

As I move down the stairs there is still no movement from the two larger rooms across the hall and for this I am most grateful. I do not really know how to say good-bye as I have never before said it to anyone and, because I am uncertain, I wish to say it now to as few as possible. Who knows, though, perhaps I may even be rather good at it. I lay the packsack down on the second stair from the bottom where it is not awfully visible and walk into the kitchen. My mother is busy at her stove and my father is standing with his back to the room looking through the window over a view of slate-grey slag heaps and ruined skeletal mine tipples and out toward the rolling sea. They are not greatly surprised to see me as it is often like this, just the three of us in the quiet early morning. But today I cannot afford to be casual and I must say what must be said in the short space of time occupied by only the three of us. "I think I'll go away today," I say, trying to sound as offhand as possible. Only a slight change in the rhythm of my mother's poking at the stove indicates that she has heard me, and my father still stands looking through the window out to sea. "I think I'll go right now," I add, my voice sort of trailing off, "before the others get up. It will be easier that way."

My mother moves the kettle, which has started to boil, toward the back of the stove, as if stalling for time, then she turns and says, "Where will you go? To Blind River?"

Her response is so little like that which I anticipated that I feel strangely numb. For I had somehow expected her to be greatly surprised, astounded, astonished, and she is none of these. And her mention of Blind River, the centre of Northern Ontario's uranium mines, is something and someplace that I had never even thought of. It is as if my mother had not only known that I was to leave but had even planned my route and final destination. I am reminded of my reading in school of the way Charles Dickens felt about the blacking factory and his mother's being so fully in favour of it. In favour of a life for him which he considered so terrible and so far beneath his imagined destiny.

My father turns from the window and says, "You are only eighteen today, perhaps you could wait awhile. Something might turn up." But within his eyes I see no strong commitment to his words and I know he feels that waiting is at best weary and at worst hopeless. This also makes me somehow rather disappointed and angry as I had thought somehow my parents would cling to me in a kind of desperate fashion and I would have to be very firm and strong.

"What is there to wait for?" I say, asking a question that is useless and to which I know the all-too-obvious answer. "Why do you want me to stay here?"

"You misunderstand," says my father, "you are free to go if you want to. We are not forcing you or asking you to do anything. I am only saying that you do not *have* to go now."

But suddenly it becomes very important that I *do* go now, because it seems things cannot help but get worse. So I say, "Good-bye. I will write, but it will not be from Blind River." I add the last as an almost unconscious little gibe at my mother.

I go and retrieve my packsack and then pass back through the house, out the door and even through the little gate. My parents follow me to the gate. My mother says, "I was planning a cake for today . . ." and then stops uncertainly, her sentence left hanging in the early morning air. She is trying to make amends for her earlier statement and rather desperately gropes her way back to the fact of my birthday. My father says, "Perhaps you should go over home. They may not be there if and when you come again."

It is but a half block to "over home," the house of my father's parents, who have always been there as long as I can remember and who have always provided a sort of haven for all of us through all our little storms, and my father's statement that they will not be there forever is an intimation of something that I have never really considered before. So now I move with a sort of apprehension over the ashes and cinder-filled potholes of the tired street toward the old house blackened with the coal dust of generations. It is as yet hardly seven A.M. and it is as if I am some early morning milkman moving from one house to another to leave good-byes instead of bottles beside such quiet doors.

Inside my grandparents' house, my grandfather sits puffing his pipe by the window, while passing the beads of his rosary through fingers which are gnarled and have been broken more times than he can remember. He has been going deaf for some time and he does not turn his head when the door closes behind me. I decide that I will not start with him because it will mean shouting and repetition and I am not sure I will be able to handle that. My grandmother, like my mother, is busy at her stove. She is tall and white-haired and although approaching eighty she is still physically imposing. She has powerful, almost masculine hands and has always been a big-boned person without ever having been heavy or ever having any difficulty with her legs. She still moves swiftly and easily and her eyesight and hearing are perfect.

"I am going away today," I say as simply as I can.

She pokes with renewed energy at her stove and then answers: "It is just as well. There is nothing for one to do here anyway. There was never anything for one to do here."

She has always spoken with the Gaelic inflection of her youth and in that detached third-person form which I had long ago suggested that she modernize.

"Come here, James," she says and takes me into her pantry, where with surprising agility she climbs up on a chair and takes from the cupboard's top shelf a huge cracked and ancient sugar bowl. Within it there are dusty picture postcards, some faded yellow payslips which seem ready to disintegrate at the touch, and two yellowed letters tied together with a shoelace. The locations on the payslips and on the postcards leap at me across a gulf of dust and years: Springhill, Scranton, Wilkes-Barre, Yellowknife, Britannia Beach, Butte, Virginia City, Escanaba, Sudbury, Whitehorse, Drumheller, Harlan, Ky., Elkins, W. Va., Fernie, B.C., Trinidad, Colo. – coal and gold, copper and lead, gold and iron, nickel and gold and coal. East and West and North and South. Mementoes and messages from places that I so young and my grandmother so old have never seen.

"Your father was under the ground in all those places," she says half-angrily, "the same way he was under the ground here before he left and under it after he came back. It seems we will be underground long enough when we are dead without seeking it out while we are still alive."

"But still," she says after a quiet pause and in a sober tone, "it was what he was good at and wanted to do. It was just not what I wanted him to do, or at least I did not want him to do it here."

She unties the shoelace and shows me the two letters. The first is dated March 12, 1938, and addressed General Delivery, Kellogg, Idaho: "I am getting old now and I would like very much if you would come back and take my working place at the mine. The seam is good for years yet. No one has been killed for some time now. It is getting better. The weather is mild and we are all fine. Don't bother writing. Just come. We will be waiting for you. Your fond father."

The second bears the same date and is also addressed General Delivery, Kellogg, Idaho: "Don't listen to him. If you return here you will never get out and this is no place to lead one's life. They say the seam will be finished in another few years. Love, Mother."

I have never seen my grandfather's handwriting before and for some reason, although I knew he read, I had always thought him unable to write. Perhaps, I think now, it is because his hands have been so broken and misshapen; and, with increasing age, hard to control for such a fine task as writing.

The letters are written with the same broad-nibbed pen in an ink which is of a blackness that I have never seen and somehow these letters now seem like a strangely old and incompatible married couple, each cancelling out the other's desires while bound together by a single worn and dusty lace.

I go out of the pantry and to the window where my grandfather sits. "I am going away today," I shout, leaning over him.

"Oh yes," he says in a neutral tone of voice, while continuing to look out the window and finger his rosary. He does not move and the pipe smoke curls upward from his pipe which is clenched between his worn and strongly stained teeth. Lately he has taken to saying, "Oh yes," to almost everything as a means of concealing his deafness and now I do not know if he has really heard me or is merely giving what seems a standard and safe response to all of the things he hears but partially if at all. I do not feel that I can say it again without my voice breaking and so I turn away. At the door I find that he has shuffled behind me.

"Don't forget to come back, James," he says, "it's the only way you'll be content. Once you drink underground water it becomes a part of you like the blood a man puts into a woman. It changes her forever and never goes away. There's always a part of him running there deep inside her. It's what will wake you up at night and never ever leave you alone."

Because he knows how much my grandmother is opposed to what he says he has tried to whisper to me. But he is so deaf that he can hardly hear his own voice and he has almost shouted in the way deaf people do; his voice seems to echo and bounce off the walls of his house and to escape out into the sunshot morning air. I offer him my hand to shake and find it almost crushed in the crooked broken force of his. I can feel the awful power of his oddly misshapen fingers, his splayed and flattened too-broad thumb, the ridges of the toughened, blackened scars and the abnormally large knobs that are his twisted misplaced knuckles. And I have a feeling for a terrible moment that I may never ever get away or be again released. But he finally relaxes and I feel that I am free.

Even potholed streets are lonely ones when you think you may not see them again for a very long time or perhaps forever. And I travel now mostly the back streets because I am conspicuous with my packsack and I do not want any more conversations or attempted and failed and futile explanations. At the outskirts of the town a coal truck stops for me and we travel for twenty-five miles along the shoreline of the sea. The truck makes so much noise and rides so roughly that conversation with the driver is impossible and I am very grateful for the noisy silence in which we are encased.

By noon, after a succession of short rides in a series of oddly assorted vehicles, I am finally across the Strait of Canso, off Cape Breton Island and at last upon my way. It is only when I have left the Island that I can feel free to assume my new identity, which I don like carefully preserved new clothes taken from within their pristine wrappings. It assumes that I am from Vancouver, which is as far away as I can imagine.

I have been somehow apprehensive about even getting off Cape Breton Island, as if at the last moment it might extend gigantic tentacles, or huge monstrous hands like my grandfather's to seize and hold me back. Now as I finally set foot on the mainland I look across at the heightened mount that is Cape

Breton now, rising mistily out of the greenness and the white-capped blueness of the sea.

My first ride on the mainland is offered by three Negroes in a battered blue Dodge pickup truck that bears the information "Rayfield Clyke, Lincolnville, N.S., Light Trucking" on its side. They say they are going the approximately eighty miles to New Glasgow and will take me if I wish. They will not go very fast, they say, because their truck is old and I might get a better ride if I choose to wait. On the other hand, the driver says, I will at least be moving and I will get there sooner or later. Any time I am sick of it and want to stop I can bang on the roof of the cab. They would take me in the cab but it is illegal to have four men in the cab of a commercial vehicle and they do not want any trouble with the police. I climb into the back and sit on the worn spare tire and the truck moves on. By now the sun is fairly high and when I remove the packsack from my shoulders I can feel, although I cannot see, the two broad bands of perspiration traced and crossing upon my back. I realize now that I am very hungry and have eaten nothing since last evening's supper.

In New Glasgow I am let off at a small gas station and my Negro benefactors point out the shortest route to the western outskirts of the town. It leads through cluttered back streets where the scent of the greasy hamburgers reeks out of the doors of the little lunch-counters with their overloud juke-boxes; simultaneously pushing Elvis Presley and the rancid odours of the badly cooked food through the half open doors. I would like to stop but somehow there is a desperate sense of urgency now as if each of the cars on the one-way street is bound for a magical destination and I feel that should I stop for even a moment's hamburger I might miss the one ride that is worthwhile. The sweat is running down my forehead now and stings my eyes, and I know the two dark patches of perspiration upon my back and beneath the straps are very wide.

The sun seems at its highest when the heavy red car pulls over to the highway's gravelled shoulder and its driver leans over to unlock the door on the passenger side. He is a very heavy man of about fifty with a red perspiring face and a brown cowlick of hair plastered down upon his damply glistening forehead. His coat is thrown across the back of the seat and his shirt pocket contains one of those plastic shields bristling with pens and pencils. The collar of the shirt is open and his tie is loosened and awry; his belt is also undone, as is the button at the waistband of his trousers. His pants are grey and although stretched tautly over his enormous thighs they still appear as damply wrinkled. Through his white shirt the sweat is showing darkly under his armpits and also in large blotches on his back which are visible when he leans forward. His hands seem very white and dispro-portionately small.

As we move off down the shimmering highway with its mesmerizing white line, he takes a soiled handkerchief that has been lying on the seat beside him and wipes the wet palms of his hands and also the glistening wet blackness of the steer-ing wheel.

"Boy, it sure is hot," he says, "hotter'n a whore in hell."

"Yes," I say, "it sure is. It really is."

"Dirty little town back there," he says, "you can spend a week there just driving through."

"Yes, it isn't much."

"Just travelling through?"

"Yes, I'm going back to Vancouver."

"You got a whole lot of road ahead of you boy, a whole lot of road. I never been to Vancouver, never west of Toronto. Been trying to get my company to send me west for a long while now but they always send me down here. Three or four times a year. Weather's always miserable. Hotter'n hell like this here or in the winter cold enough to freeze the balls off a brass monkey." He beats out a salvo of hornblasts at a teenage girl who is standing uncertainly by the roadside.

Although the windows of the car are open, it is very hot and the redness of the car seems to intensify the feeling and sense of heat. All afternoon the road curves and winds ahead of us like a bucking, shimmering snake with a dirty white streak running down its back. We seem to ride its dips and bends like captive passengers on a roller coaster, leaning our bodies into the curves, and bracing our feet against the tension of the floorboards. My stomach vanishes as we hurtle into the sudden unexpected troughs and returns as quickly as we emerge to continue our twists and turns. Insects ping and splatter against the windshield and are transformed into yellow splotches. The tires hiss on the superheated asphalt and seem almost to leave tracks. I can feel my clothes sticking to me, to my legs and thighs and back. On my companion's shirt the blotches of sweat are larger and more plentiful. Leaning his neck and shoulders back against the seat he lifts his heavy body from the sweat-stained upholstery and thrusts his right hand through his opened trousers and deep into his crotch. "Let a little air in there," he says, as he manoeuvres his genitals, "must be an Indian made this underwear, it keeps creeping up on me."

All afternoon as we travel we talk, or rather he talks and I listen, which I really do not mind. I have never met anyone like him before. The talk is of his business (so much salary, so much commission plus other "deals" on the side), of his boss (a dumb bastard who is lucky he has good men on the road), of his family (a wife, one son and one daughter, one of each is enough), of sex (he can't get enough of it and will be after it until he dies), of Toronto (it is getting bigger every day and it is not like it used to be), of taxes (they keep getting higher and it doesn't pay a man to keep up his property, also too many Federal giveaways). He goes on and on. I have never listened to anyone like him before. He seems so confident and sure of everything. It is as if he knows that he knows everything and is on top of everything and he seems never to have to hesitate nor stop nor run down nor even to think; as if he were a jukebox fed from some mysterious source by an inexhaustible supply of nickels, dimes and quarters.

The towns and villages and train stations speed by. Fast and hot; Truro, Glenholme and Wentworth and Oxford. We are almost out of Nova Scotia with scarcely thirty miles of it ahead according to my companion. We are almost at the New Brunswick border. I am again in a stage of something like exhausted relief as I approach yet another boundary over which I can escape and leave so much behind. It is the feeling I originally had on leaving Cape Breton, only now it has been heavied and dulled by the journey of the day. For it has been long and hot and exhausting.

Suddenly the road veers to the left and no longer hooks and curves but extends up and away from us into a long, long hill, the top of which we can see almost a half mile away. Houses appear on either side as we begin the climb and then there are more and more of them strung out loosely along the road.

My companion blasts out a rhythm of hornblasts at a young girl and her mother who are stretching up on their tiptoes to hang some washing on a clothesline. There is a basket of newly washed clothes on the ground between them and their hands are busy on the line. They have some clothespins in their teeth so they will not have to bend to reach them and lose their hand-hold on the line.

"If I had my way, they'd have something better'n that in their mouths," he says, "wouldn't mind resting my balls on the young one's chin for the second round."

He has been looking at them quite closely and the car's tires rattle in the roadside gravel before he pulls it back to the quiet of the pavement.

The houses are closer together now and more blackened, and the yards are filled with children and bicycles and dogs. As we move toward what seems to be the main intersection I am aware of the hurrying women in their kerchiefs, and the boys with their bags of papers and baseball gloves and the men sitting or squatting on their heels in tight little compact knots. There are other men who neither sit nor squat but lean against the buildings or rest upon canes or crutches or stand awkwardly on artificial limbs. They are the old and the crippled. The faces of all of them are gaunt and sallow as if they had been allowed to see the sun only recently, when it was already too late for it to do them any good.

"Springhill is a hell of a place," says the man beside me, "unless you want to get laid. It's one of the best there is for that. Lots of mine accidents here and the men killed off. Women used to getting it all the time. Mining towns are always like this. Look at all the kids. This here little province of Nova Scotia leads the country in illegitimacy. They don't give a damn."

The mention of the name Springhill and the realization that this is where I have come is more of a shock than I would ever have imagined. As if in spite of signposts and geography and knowing it was "there," I have never thought of it as ever being "here."

And I remember November 1956: the old cars, mud-splattered by the land and rusted by the moisture of the sea, parked outside our house with their motors running. Waiting for the all-night journey to Springhill which seemed to me then, in my fourteenth year, so very far away and more a name than even a place. Waiting for the lunches my mother packed in wax paper and in newspaper and the thermos bottles of coffee and tea, and waiting for my father and the same packsack which now on this sweating day accompanies me. Only then it was filled with the miners' clothes he would need for the rescue that they hoped they might perform. The permanently blackened underwear, the heavy woollen socks, the boots with the steel-reinforced toes, the blackened, sweat-stained miner's belt which sagged on the side that carried his lamp, the crescent wrench, the dried and dustied water-bag, trousers and gloves and the hard hat chipped and dented and broken by the years of falling rock.

And all of that night my grandfather with his best ear held to the tiny radio for news of the buried men and of their rescuers. And at school the teachers taking up collections in all of the classrooms and writing in large letters on the blackboard, "Springhill Miners' Relief Fund, Springhill, N.S." which was where we were sending the money, and I remember also my sisters' reluctance at giving up their hoarded nickels, dimes and quarters because noble causes and death do not mean very much when you are eleven, ten and eight and it is difficult to comprehend how children you have never known may never see their fathers any more, not walking through the door nor perhaps even being carried through the door in the heavy coffins for the last and final look. Other people's buried fathers are very strange and far away but licorice and movie matinees are very close and real.

"Yeah," says the voice beside me, "I was in here six months ago and got this little, round woman. Really giving it to her, pumping away and all of a sudden she starts kind of crying and calling me by this guy's name I never heard of. Must have been her dead husband or something. Kind of scared the hell out of me. Felt like a goddamn ghost or something. Almost lost my rod. Might have too but I was almost ready to shoot it into her."

We are downtown now and it is late afternoon in the period before the coming of the evening. The sun is no longer as fierce as it was earlier and it slants off the blackened buildings, many of which are shells, bleak and fire-gutted and austere. A Negro woman with two light-skinned little boys crosses the street before us. She is carrying a bag of groceries and the little boys have each an opened sixteen-ounce bottle of Pepsi-Cola. They put their hands over the bottles' mouths and shake them vigorously to make the contents fizz.

"Lots of people around here marry niggers," says the voice. "Guess they're so black underground they can't tell the difference in the light. All the same in the dark as the fellow says. Had an explosion here a few years ago and some guys trapped down there, I dunno how long. Eaten the lunches of the dead guys and the bark off the timbers and drinking one another's piss. Some guy in Georgia offered the ones they got out a trip down there but there was a nigger in the bunch so he said he couldn't take him. Then the rest wouldn't go. Damned if I'd lose a trip to Georgia because of a single nigger that worked for the same company. Like I say, I'm old enough to be your father or even your grandfather and I haven't even been to Vancouver."

It is 1958 that he is talking about now, and it is much clearer in my mind than 1956, which is perhaps the difference between being fourteen and sixteen when something happens in your life. A series of facts or near-facts that I did not even realize I possessed flash now in succession upon my mind: the explosion in 1958 occurred on a Thursday, as did the one in 1956; Cumberland No. 2 at the time of the explosion was the deepest coal mine in North America; in 1891, 125 men were killed in that same mine; that 174 men went down to work that 1958 evening; that most were feared lost; that 18 were found alive after being buried beneath 1,000 tons of rock for more than a week; that Cumberland No. 2 once employed 900 men and now employs none.

And I remember again the cars before our house with their motors running, and the lunches and the equipment and the waiting of the week: the school collections, my grandfather with his radio, this time the added reality of a TV at a neighbour's house; and the quietness of our muted lives, our footsteps without sound. And then the return of my father and the haunted greyness of his face and after the younger children were in bed the quiet and hushed conversations of seeping gas and lack of oxygen and the wild and belching smoke and flames of the subterranean fires nourished there by the everlasting seams of the dark and diamond coal. And also of the finding of the remains of men flattened and crushed if they had died beneath the downrushing roofs of rock or if they had been blown apart by the explosion itself, transformed into forever lost and irredeemable pieces of themselves; hands and feet and blown-away faces and reproductive organs and severed ropes of intestines festooning the twisted pipes and spikes like grotesque Christmas-tree loops and chunks of hair-clinging flesh. Men transformed into grisly jigsaw puzzles that could never more be solved.

"I don't know what the people do around here now," says the voice at my side. "They should get out and work like the rest of us. The Government tries to resettle them but they won't stay in a place like Toronto. They always come back to their graveyards like dogs around a bitch in heat. They have no guts."

The red car has stopped now before what I am sure is this small town's only drugstore. "Maybe we'll stop here for a while," he says. "I've just about had it and need something else. All work and no play, you know. I'm going in here for a minute first to try my luck. As the fellow says, an ounce of prevention beats a pound of cure."

As he closes the door he says, "Maybe later you'd like to come along. There's always some left over."

The reality of where I am and of what I think he is going to do seems now to press down upon me as if it were the pressure of the caving-in roof which was so recently within my thoughts. Although it is still hot I roll up the windows of the car. The people on the street regard me casually in this car of too-bright red which bears Ontario licence plates. And I recognize now upon their faces a look that I have seen upon my grandfather's face and on the faces of hundreds of the people from my past and even on my own when seeing it reflected from the mirrors and windows of such a car as this. For it is as if I am not part of their lives at all but am here only in a sort of movable red and glass showcase that has come for a while to their private anguish-ridden streets and will soon roll on and leave them the same as before my coming; part of a movement that passes through their lives but does not really touch them. Like flotsam on yet another uninteresting river that flows through their permanent banks and is bound for some invisible destination around a bend where they have never been and cannot go. Their glances have summed me up and dismissed me as casually as that. "What can he know of our near-deaths and pain and who lies buried in our graves?"

And I am overwhelmed now by the awfulness of oversimplification. For I realize that not only have I been guilty of it through this long and burning day but also through most of my yet-young life and it is only now that I am doubly its victim that I begin vaguely to understand. For I had somehow thought that "going away" was but a physical thing. And that it had only to

55

do with movement and with labels like the silly "Vancouver" that I had glibly rolled off my tongue; or with the crossing of bodies of water or with the boundaries of borders. And because my father had told me I was "free" I had foolishly felt that it was really so. Just like that. And I realize now that the older people of my past are more complicated than perhaps I had ever thought. And that there are distinctions between my sentimental, romantic grandfather and his love for coal, and my stern and practical grandmother and her hatred of it; and my quietly strong but passive mother and the soaring extremes of my father's passionate violence and the quiet power of his love. They are all so different. But yet they have somehow endured and given me the only life I know for all these eighteen years. Their lives flowing into mine and mine from out of theirs. Different but in some ways more similar than I had ever thought. Perhaps it is possible I think now to be both and yet to see only the one. For the man in whose glassed-in car I now sit sees only similarity. For him the people of this multi-scarred little town are reduced to but a few phrases and the act of sexual intercourse. They are only so many identical goldfish leading identical, incomprehensible lives within the glass prison of their bowl. And the people on the street view me behind my own glass in much the same way, and it is the way that I have looked at others in their "foreign licence" cars, and it is the kind of judgement that I myself have made. And yet it seems that neither these people nor this man are in any way unkind and not to understand does not necessarily mean that one is cruel. But one should at least be honest. And perhaps I have tried too hard to be someone else without realizing at first what I presently am. I do not know. I am not sure. But I do know that I cannot follow this man into a house that is so much like the one I have left this morning and go down into the sexual embrace of a woman who might well be my mother. And I do not know what she, my mother, may be like in the years to come when she is deprived of the lightning movement of my father's body and the hammered pounding of his heart. For I do not know when he may die. And I do not know in what darkness she may then cry out his name nor to whom. I do not know very much of anything, it seems, except that I have been wrong and dishonest with others and myself. And perhaps this man has left footprints on a soul I did not even know that I possessed.

It is dark now on the outskirts of Springhill when the car's headlights pick me up in their advancing beams. It pulls over to the side and I get into its back seat. I have trouble closing the door behind me because there is no handle so I pull on the crank that is used for the window. I am afraid that even it may come off in my hand. There are two men in the front seat and I can see only the outlines of the backs of their heads and I cannot tell very much about them. The man in the back seat beside me is not awfully visible either. He is tall and lean but from what I see of his face it is difficult to tell whether he is thirty or fifty. There are two sacks of miner's gear on the floor at his feet and I put my sack there too because there isn't any other place.

"Where are you from?" he asks as the car moves forward. "From Cape Breton," I say and tell him the name of my home.

"We are too," he says, "but we're from the Island's other side. I guess the mines are pretty well finished where you're from. They're the old ones. They're playing out where we're from too. Where are you going now?"

"I don't know," I say, "I don't know."

"We're going to Blind River," he says. "If it doesn't work there we hear they've found uranium in Colorado and are getting ready to start sinking shafts. We might try that, but this is an old car and we don't think it'll make it to Colorado. You're welcome to come along with us, though, if you want. We'll carry you for a while."

"I don't know," I say, "I don't know. I'll have to think about it. I'll have to make up my mind."

The car moves forward into the night. Its headlights seek out and follow the beckoning white line which seems to lift and draw us forward, upward and inward, forever into the vastness of the dark.

"I guess your people have been on the coal over there for a long time?" asks the voice beside me.

"Yes," I say, "since 1873."

"Son of a bitch," he says, after a pause, "it seems to bust your balls and it's bound to break your heart."

THE GOLDEN GIFT OF GREY

(1 9 7 1)

At midnight he looked up at the neon Coca-Cola clock and realized with a taut emptiness that he had already stayed too late and perhaps was even now forever lost. He lowered his eyes and then quickly raised them again with the rather desperate hope that he might on a second try somehow catch the clock by surprise and find the hands somewhere else, at nine or ten perhaps, but it was no use. There they were, perfectly vertical, like a rigid arrow of accusation seeming to condemn by their very rigidity and righteousness everything in the world that was not so straight and stern as they themselves

He felt sick at first and almost numb along his arms and down through his wrists and into his fingers, the way he had felt the time he had been knocked out in the high school football game. He moved his shoulders beneath his shirt in an attempt to shake off the chill and ran his tongue nervously over his lips and travelled his eyes then around the pool table to the men with the cue-sticks in their hands and to the stained brown-black wood that framed the table's squareness. There were three quarters on the wood indicating that three challengers still remained. And he looked then at the soft, velvet green of the table itself, that held him, he thought, like a lotus land, and finally to the blackness of the eight-ball and the whiteness of the cue, good and evil he thought, paradoxically flowering here on the greenness of this plain. He was in his first real game, and it had somehow become a series of games, a marathon that had begun at eight when he had paused, books in hand at the doorway, and it had gone on and on, the night's hours fleeing with the swiftness and unreality of a dream. The type of dream that holds you in a delicate tensile web, even while a certain part of you knows that you will not remember in the morning, and you do not quite know if the feeling is one of ecstasy or pain, or if the awakening is victory or defeat, or if you are forever saved or yet forever doomed.

And now a voice said, "Boy, you goen to wait all night? I ain't got time." And he moved with a jolt, out of the dream but in it, and said, "Side pocket," indicating the direction with his head, and taking the cue he leaned over and across the table, raising his right leg and feeling his belt buckle press into his stomach, and the brown-black wood strong against his testicles and then the sensation of the smoothly polished wood running slickly through his fingers as he shot and then watched the gently nudged eight-ball roll softly and silently across the field of green until it vanished quietly before his eyes, and he could hear it then, clanging and rolling noisily now somewhere beneath and within the table on its clattering way to join its predecessors in an underworld of dark. And then he saw the green dollar bill flutter down to the table before his eyes and even as he reached for it, someone else was pushing one of the quarters into the slot and redeeming the balls from their cavern and preparing to arrange them within the rack. And it was now after midnight and he knew he had stayed too long.

He had not been home since before eight that morning when he had walked out into the early October sunshine with his books beneath his arm. He could see the books now lying just inside the door on the end of the narrow bench that ran along the wall. They were covered defensively by his jacket and from beneath the sleeve he could see the algebra, and the red-covered geometry into which he had pencilled his marks, 90's mostly, and the English text whose poems he had almost totally committed to memory. They looked incongruous in this setting and he vaguely wished that somehow he could cover them more adequately; to protect them and perhaps to protect himself from the questions that they asked and the questions that the men might ask about them. He flicked his eyes nervously down the canyon-like room. It was long and narrow and he could hardly discern the far end with its hazy EXIT sign because of the tobacco smoke that seemed to hang in wavering layers in the stale and sour air. A long uneven bar ran almost the total length of the room, beginning near the pool table and stretching like a trackless narrow-gauge railway toward a distant bandstand where two guitarist-singers and a drummer perspired beneath the ever-changing coloured lights and blasted the heavy air with the twanging heartbreak sound of Nashville. On the bar itself three bloated no-longer-young go-go girls moved with heavy unimaginative movements, their net-stockinged feet not always avoiding the sad little puddles of spilled beer. Beneath them and along the bar the men they were supposed to entertain looked up at them dutifully and wearily, although one with hair of snow moved his heavy, calloused hand rhythmically up and down the neck of his beer bottle with a slow and thoughtful masturbating motion.

Over everything and all of them the odour hung and covered and pressed like the roof of a gigantic invisible tent from which there could be no escape. It smelled of work clothes, soaked and dried in sweat and seldom washed, and of spilled beer and of the sour rags used to mop it up, and of the damp and decaying wood that lay beneath the floor, and of the reek that issued forth from the constantly swinging doors of the men's washroom: the exhausted urine and the powerful disinfectant and the shreds of tobacco and soggy cigarette papers which appeared in the trough beneath the crudely lettered signs: This is *not* an ashtray; Please don't throw cigarette butts in our toilet, we don't urinate in your ashtray; DON'T THROW CIGARETTE BUTTS HERE.

And as it all assailed his senses he felt that everything was wrong with his life and that all of it was ruined, though he was yet but in his eighteenth year. And he wished that he were home.

He could see the situation at home now. The five younger children would be in bed and his sister Mary, who was sixteen, would be helping his mother prepare the lunch that his father would carry in his pail to the meat-packing plant. His younger brother, Donny, who was thirteen, would be desperately hoping, though he knew his hopes were doomed, that the television might remain on longer. And his father who had been propped in front of the television in his undershirt, and in his sock feet and with the waistband of his trousers undone, and with his greying reddish head flopping occasionally from side to side as he dozed and slept more than he dared admit, would have risen and gone to lock the door for the night. And then he would stop and ask gruffly, "Where's Jesse?" And then there would be the awful, awkward silence, and, "Well, don't he live here no more?" And they would all squirm and his mother would dry glasses that were already dry, and Mary and Donny would glance furtively at one another, while the heavy-set man, now fully awake and puffing on his pipe, would walk from one window to the next, shielding his eyes against the glass while trying to catch a glimpse of his eldest son approaching beneath the street lights. He would walk ceaselessly back and forth with the long, loping outdoor stride which he had brought to the northern Indiana city from eastern Kentucky and which he could not or would not change and he would mutter: "Where is that fella?" or more strongly, "Where'n hell's that boy at and it goen on past twelve midnight?" And his wife would watch too, as intently but secretly, so that her husband would not see and become more agitated because of her awareness. And sometimes to make it better she would lie or tell one of the young children to say, "Jesse is studyen over at Caudell's tonight with Earl. He said he wouldn't be in till late."

Then she alone bore the burden of the watching and the waiting and it was much easier then, for unlike her husband she bore her burdens silently and you did not realize that she worried at all unless you happened to catch her at an unguarded moment and saw the trace of strain about her high cheekbones and the tautness of her jaw or the tight compression of her lips. So she would say or cause others to say, "studyen at Caudell's," because if it was not the best answer it was better than any other that she knew. And she realized that her husband, even like herself, looked upon "studyen" and whatever it might entail with a deep respect not far removed from fear. For they were both of them barely literate and found even the signing of the magnificent report cards that their children triumphantly and relentlessly presented to them something of a task. Yet while they were sometimes angry and tried to be contemptuous of "book learnen" and people who were just "book smart" they encouraged both as much as they could, seeing in them a light that had never visited their darkness, but realizing that even as they fanned the flame they were losing a grip on almost all they had of life. And feeling themselves as if washed by a flood down the side of a shale-covered Kentucky mountain, clutching and grasping at twigs and roots with their hopeful fingers bloodied raw.

They had been at the base of a very real Kentucky mountain ten years ago when Everett Caudell had finally convinced them to come North. He had been a friend of the boy's father in the isolation of that squirrel-hunting, pie-social youth and their girls had become the wives they had taken with them to the anguish of the coal camps where jobs and life were at best uncertain amidst an awful certainty of poverty and pain. Caudell had come North and secured the job in the meat-packing plant and then returned with the battered half-ton truck for his family and their belongings and then again for the friend of his youth. The friend who had recently been almost killed when the roof of the illegal little mine that burrowed into the hillside had come crashing down. He had escaped only because he saw the rats racing by him toward the light and had dropped his tools and followed, sprinting after them and almost stepping on their scaly tails as the beginning roar of the crashing rock and the shotgun pops of the snapping timbers sounded in his ears.

Ever since, both he and his wife had been more strongly religious than before, because they felt somehow that God had either sent the fleeing rats as a sign or had physically propelled the man upon his way, and perhaps had even planned it so that they might come North to a new life. A life that found them ten years later waiting after midnight for the sound of footsteps at their door.

Always before, he had been home by eleven-thirty. Always. Always. But now he was here with the music and the odour in his ears and in his nose, with the cue-stick in his hand and with the green table beneath the tarnished yellow light flat before him. He could see the quarters of the challengers and hear the voices of the men quietly placing side bets behind him and he knew somehow that no matter what the cost, and almost against his soul, he would not, could not go. For it had taken him a long time to reach this night and it could never be again.

It was two years since he had first stopped outside the open door and gazed in at the life that moved beyond it. It had been a hot night in midsummer with the heat moving in little waves off the sidewalk and he had been returning from his job at the Grocery. He had been first attracted by the music, the sound of Eddy Arnold and Jim Reeves, that his father played constantly and of which both he and his sister were ashamed. They did not know the aching loneliness of which it spoke and when it floated from the windows of their house on warm summer nights it branded their parents indelibly as hillbillies and they themselves as well, as extensions of those parents. And it was a label that they hated and did not wish to bear.

He had watched, that night, fascinated, from the sidewalk and when people began to jostle him he had stood in the doorway and then with one foot inside the door, mindful of the signs that read: We do not serve minors; If you are under 21, do not enter; but entering nevertheless, although with one eye always careful of the door, while wearing that expression that he had often noticed on the faces of nervous gentle Negroes on the fringes of all-white crowds.

He had stopped then almost every evening for a week on his way home, standing outside or just inside the door, captured by the music and the odour, but most of all by the heavy men moving around the pool table. And then one night he had looked up at the man who was then holding the cue-stick and his eyes had looked into the eyes of Everett Caudell and their glances had met and held, somewhere there in the emptiness of the space above the table like the probing, seeking beams of two lonely mountain freight trains which round a bend at midnight and find themselves even in that instant forever committed to each other. And he had sensed even then the way that it would be; that Everett Caudell would never tell his father "I seen Jesse the other night," nor would he tell Earl Caudell, who was in the same grade and played football in the same backfield, "I saw your father playing pool in a bar the other night." Because some things transcend all differences in age, and chronology in the end is but an empty word.

And so he had begun. At night on the way home from the Grocery he would stop for ten or twenty minutes to watch, standing just within the door and against the wall. Always mindful of the sign which reminded him that he was a "minor" and as such should "not enter"; but realizing with the passage of time that no one really cared, no more than they cared for the other sign which read, NO GAMBLING. And he moved farther away from the door and deeper and deeper into the room, becoming slowly aware that the strange, violent, profane men seemed to like him, and winked at him when they sank the good shots and complained to him when they missed. And he discovered still later that the door was open even at four when he went to work as well as at seven when he returned. Often in the time when there was no football practice he would almost run from school to get there for a few precious moments, hoping with a desperate hope that the table would be empty and waiting so that he might deposit the quarter which was always sweaty because he held it so tightly while almost running. And then he would watch and listen to the balls as they rolled to their release and practise by himself the shots he had seen the night before; practise intently and relentlessly until four o'clock when the heavy men began to appear from the completion of their shifts. He had done all of this somehow without even daring to think that he would ever play in a real game himself, and now, seeing and feeling his body leaning over the table, he felt a strange sensation and kinship with those boys in the F. Scott Fitzgerald stories who practise and practise but never play until a certain moment comes along in their lives and changes them forever.

There had been four men playing when he had entered and taken his stand beside the wall and beneath the signs that forbade his presence. Two sets of middle-aged men who circled the table, first swiftly with their eyes and then slowly with their bodies, speaking to the balls with pleading profanity and wiping away the tiny beads of perspiration that formed upon their brows. They played for only the token dollar, which too was forbidden by a sign, and when the losers had paid, one of them said that he must go home and had gone almost instantly. And then his partner had turned and said to the figure that he had so often seen there beside the wall, "Me and you," and offered him the cue-stick. So he had taken it, almost instinctively and if feeling like the boys of Fitzgerald, feeling also, and perhaps more, like the many youths of Conrad who never thought they would do what is now already done. And the commitment had been made and the night had so begun.

At first he was so preoccupied with the thought that he would lose, and have to pay a dollar he was not sure he had, that he played very badly, and they won only because of the shots his partner made, but in the second and third games he became stronger, playing cautiously and deliberately, and while he was not spectacular at least he did not lose, and he was surprised at how much he had learned from the solitary practice sessions and from the hours of standing and watching beneath the signs. And when the men they had played went out into the darkness he and his partner played against each other and after what seemed like a very long time he won and pocketed the dollar and stayed and stayed, seeing from the corner of his eye the challenging quarters being laid on the brown-black wood by the broken-nailed fingers of the faceless unknown men, until he had recognized one set of fingers and looked into the face of Everett Caudell but said nothing, as nothing had been said on that first meeting here in a time that seemed so long ago. So they played quietly, both of them, very carefully and very slowly until only the eight-ball remained and the older man took his shot and scratched and then laid his dollar upon the table and went out into the night and was replaced by a set of nameless hands and another nameless face.

He had thought while playing against Caudell many different things. First he had been embarrassed and afraid that the man would attempt to make conversation, and then he had thought, that if he were to lose, it would be very fitting that his loss should be to the only man of all those present that he really knew. And then he had, right until the end, been very much afraid that Everett Caudell would purposely lose the game, the way a fond father loses at checkers to his seven-year-old child, and he had hoped and almost prayed that they would both not have to go through such an emasculating loss of dignity on this his night of realization. And when he finally was certain that Caudell was playing his very best he felt deeply grateful for the unspoken acknowledgement and when the defeated man departed he was overcome by a mingled feeling of loneliness and sorrow, regret and anger and fierce exultant pride that made him almost ashamed. The way one feels when standing at the grave-side of a loved one who has died.

And the night flashed on and he played as if still in the dream, unaddled by the beer that began to affect his opponents with the hours passing and unaddled by the music or the activities that became more frenzied as the night wore on. Once he had raised his head, to the twanging bass chords of a Duane Eddy composition, and looked along the bar's surface where one of the perspiring middle-aged dancers spread her heavy net-stockinged limbs and lowered herself gradually and gradually until she was almost sitting on the bald head of the man who had leaned forward across the bar, holding him there with a hot, heavy inner thigh against each of his ears and grinding herself backwards and forwards across the baldness of his pate. And he had felt almost sick then and had quickly averted his eyes and taken his shot too quickly and missed.

At one-thirty a man tapped him on the shoulder and told him someone wanted to speak to him and he had turned to see his younger brother, Donny, beckoning him from the street through the door that was still open. He excused himself and went out quickly, pulling the solid door behind him so powerfully that it slammed, as if by doing so he protected his brother from the woman on the bar and perhaps himself from the men within.

Donny's brown eyes were wide in their sockets and he began to speak in fast little uneven sentences: "Gee, you better come home. They're walking around looking out the windows. It's awful, especially Dad. He's smoking like mad. He's got that funny look on his face. They don't know where you're at."

At first he was afraid but he tried to act amused. "Look, what's the difference? I'm too late now. I might as well stay out all night, eh?"

"But Jesse, you know what it'll be like when you come home."

"So? Will it be any worse in the morning?" The look on Donny's face plainly indicated that it would.

"Jesse, what will I tell them?"

"Tell them I'm playing pool."

"They don't know what pool is, and what if they ask where?"

"Tell them."

"Jesse, you're nuts. The old man will be down here in five minutes if he knows. You know what he's like. There's no telling what he'll do."

He thought then of the awful violence that was within his father; a something that rumbled deep below like some subterranean mountain stream of roaring white water, splashing and pounding dark rocks within deep unseen caves. He remembered seeing it only once as a child, in Hazard or Harlan and he could not now remember which, the man his father had hit, literally flying like a grotesque rag doll across the space of the behind-the-store parking lot and how he had lain there so crumpled and still for so long with the blood trickling past his broken teeth in slender, threadlike, crimson streams. And his mother had prayed, "O Lord, may this man not die, I'm asken you." And his father had buried his head within his arms and leaned against the wall of the store, perhaps praying too while his fists remained so tightly clenched that the knuckles showed white, as if he were trying to hang on to something very desperately but was uncertain what it was. And after a while they, as children, cried too, because they knew there was something wrong but did not know what else to do.

Behind him now, the door opened and as he turned he saw the dancers again along the bar, and the man framed in the doorway saying, "you goen to finish this game? I ain't got time," and he started nervously and said to Donny, "Look, I gotta go.

Make up your own story. Tell them I'm okay. I'll be home later."
As he turned to the building he averted his eyes from his
brother's face in order to avoid the tears that he sensed but did
not wish to see.

So he went back in and thought of how Donny was the
greatest little brother in the world. Of how he had never broken
any of his brother's confidences, of how he would spend hours
shining that brother's shoes or running faithfully after the base-
balls he lofted into the skies and of how when the brother had
first started smoking he would go all over town like a tireless
little robot gathering bottles until he had acquired enough for
the precious package of cigarettes. Sometimes he had the feeling
that if he told Donny to walk off the edge of a towering building he would do so without a moment's hesitation, and the
thought of the awful power seemed to tighten around his heart.

At three he left the bar that had officially closed at two and
felt that he had no place to go. It was both too late and too early
to go home. He went into the street and then entered an alley
and stood in the darkness, listening to the scuffle of the rats and
waiting for the dawn; he shivered in the cold and tried to think
of what he would say if anyone should come along and see him
standing there, shivering in an alley with his books beneath his
arm. Almost fearfully he backed into the shadow of a building
and shoved his hands into the pockets of his trousers. It was then
that he felt the money and jumped as if he had been shocked.
He had been so intent on playing that he had forgotten about
the dollar bills he had been pocketing. But now he felt them
in two tangled, crumpled lumps. Lumps that were now a chilly
damp, but had once been warm and almost soggy from the

perspiration of his thighs. He tried to count them without light and without taking them from his pockets, fingering what he thought was a new corner, and then another, and counting the corners of one pocket and then the other, and finally in despair, because he never got the same number twice, giving it up altogether and starting suddenly back into the street.

When he entered the all-night coffee shop he sat on the second last stool and laid his books on the very last, hoping that he would not be noticed there and that he might have at least some privacy. The cloth of his trousers pulled tight against his thighs when he sat and he could feel and sense the protruding of the pockets' bulges, knowing what they looked like without even looking down, and afraid to look down lest his worst fears be confirmed, or that by so doing he should draw attention to something he had no wish to publicize. Thinking it was like the mysterious coming of the ill-timed adolescent erection, when one knows that it is there, unbidden and unwanted and unbecomingly wrong.

He ordered the coffee and then slowly drew the crumpled bills from the right pocket. Probably, he thought, because he was right-handed. One by one he uncrumpled and flattened them. They were still damp and smelled faintly of salt. There were nineteen. Then he did the same with the contents of the left. There were twelve. Thirty-one dollars.

He left the coffee shop with the bills neatly folded in the breast-pocket of his shirt and with his mood completely changed. He would go home and he would give it to them, he thought. It would be the first worthwhile gift that he would give to those from whom he had always taken. And he was filled with a great love for the strange people that were his parents. Parents whom he found so difficult to understand, who still made treks to Kentucky and who were not above being openly emotional when their battered old car crossed the mighty bridge from Cincinnati to Covington, and who would not wash the red hill mud from that car on their return, waiting for the rains to do so as it stood out in the yard, and who listened always to their hill-billy music.

And he was ashamed now of the times he had been ashamed of them. He remembered the awful experience of the "Parents' Night" when he had been in fourth grade, the year after the move, and of how he had wildly begged them to accompany him to view the wonders of his school, and of how they them-selves had become even mildly excited and had washed and scrubbed themselves to redness in anticipation of the big event. Once inside the great building, however, what natural dignity they possessed had seemed to drain from them immediately, as if some magic stoppers had been pulled beneath their shoes. And they had become blank and dumb and very nearly overcome by panic in that strange foreign world of animated numerals and foot-high ABC's and posters that told one how to do everything it seemed, from brushing one's teeth to crossing at street corners to feeding birds in winter. His mother had said, "Mighty fine," "This sure is mighty fine," "It sure is mighty fine," over and over again as if her mind were locked in a groove, and his father's line, while crushing his hat in his massive hands, had been, "Ah sure do appreciate all this here," and he had said it indiscriminately, to teachers, to other parents and to janitors alike. And in the eyes of Miss Downs, the fourth-grade teacher, he had seen the unspoken question: "How can such a bright little boy as Jesse have parents such as these?" He remembered now that he had rather wondered how, himself.

At five-forty-five he went home after stopping at an all-night service station to convert thirty-one dollar bills into a twenty and a ten. Everybody was up; his mother was getting breakfast although it was too early; the table was set and his father's lunch pail lay open on its side. No one said a word, and he had a strange feeling that he had gone deaf. He had never thought the house could be so quiet. He looked at his mother, but she kept her eyes on the stove, and then he looked at Donny who seemed about to burst into tears.

And then it was like the beginning of a play in which his father had the first lines, "And where the hell have you been?" Lines that came out clear and well rehearsed, as if he had been practising and practising, and they were not loud nor hard as he had expected. And he – he had not rehearsed, he had not studied his lines well enough, but he stumbled out into the middle of the stage and began to take his part, and a voice within him said, "Tell him the truth," and the peculiar unrehearsed voice said, "I was playing pool."

"We have been waiting for you all night," said his mother evenly, sounding the endings to all her words, "we thought something had happened to you, that you'd been beaten or that you'd been robbed."

He was very happy suddenly and filled with love because of their concern. His voice said excitedly: "No, no, nothing happened. I didn't lose anything. I won. Look!" And he began to withdraw the thirty-one dollars from his pocket. Someone said,

"How much?" and he almost laughed and said, "Thirty-one dollars," drawing the gift completely from his pocket and laying it on the table.

His mother said, "Before you have a bite of breakfast in this house, go and give it back."

He was stopped then in full tilt and almost crushed, as if he were bolting for the hole in the football line and suddenly found that the daylight had vanished and the hole had closed and the opposition's weight was squeezing out his life.

And then he was angry and shouted, "Give it back? Who to?"

And his mother said, still evenly, "To the people you took it from. The Lord has been good to us and it seems He wouldn't want none of this."

He burst into tears of anger and sorrow and hopelessness, and tried to explain: "But you don't understand. The Lord has nothing to do with it. I didn't steal it. It's mine. I won it. I can't give it back. I don't even know their names."

His father said, "You heard your mother," so he stormed out of the house and stood at the gate, crying, until Donny came out and he was forced to stop. In his pocket his hand clutched the little ball that was now the thirty-one dollars, three bills that were soaked from the sweat of his perspiring palms. He looked at the sleeping soon-to-be-awakened city and did not know what to do.

He started to walk then but soon he was running. Down several streets and across several others in the almost-light of early morning. He slowed down just as he entered the Caudells' yard, trying to walk slowly as if just out for a stroll, though breathing heavily.

He found Everett Caudell in the kitchen, sitting by himself with a cup of coffee and listening to his little radio as it valiantly tried to pull in the fast-fading signal from Wheeling, West Virginia. The others were still in bed and he himself was not completely dressed, being still in his stockinged feet, and with his heavy shirt yet unbuttoned and his trousers not yet firmly fastened by the broadness of his heavy belt.

"How do, Jesse?" he said as casually as if he had been whittling a stick on his doorstep in the middle of a Sunday afternoon. "How ya bin? Coffee?"

He was surprised first because he hadn't been asked why he was about at such an hour but the surprise was short-lived and soon buried beneath the avalanche of his reason for coming. "Here," he said, pulling the three criminal, sweat-stained bills from his pocket and thrusting them at the man, "here, take them. They're for you – you lost last night."

The big man said kindly: "Take it easy, lad. Sit down now. What's all this? What's all this?" and he began to fill his pipe as if there were all the time in the world and the world were never to end. And the words tumbled out then, one after the other, on top of one another, passed and thundered and banged one against the other, like the coal when it comes bounding down the chutes, which was one of the few images he remembered from Kentucky, crashing and rolling and pounding, in big lumps and little ones, and the big being broken into the small, and he ended saying: "I've got to give it to someone, and it's for you because you lost and I won – and I shouldn't have."

The man took them then, the three dirty bills, the twenty, the ten and the one, and put them in the pocket of his still unbuttoned shirt. "Aye lad," he said, "your father is a good man and your mother a good woman; now go on back and tell them what you've done, and if they come to me, why I'll tell them, 'Sure, he give it to me, a twenty, a ten, and a one,' just like you did."

When he was at the door he heard his name immediately behind him and turned to find that Caudell had followed him on silent stockinged feet and was now standing directly in front of him. And then before he could move he saw the older man quickly and quietly tuck the three bills into the shirt pocket of his guest. "Now there," he said, "there ain't nothen wrong. There's no lie. You give it to me and I took it. We'll leave it be like that. Now go on home as I hear the army starten to move upstairs."

And he went out then into the new day and after a while he even whistled a bit, and he thought of how he'd knock the geometry exam dead next week and of how the football pads would settle with familiar friendliness upon his waiting shoulders that very afternoon. Already he could sense the shouts and hand-claps from the sun-drenched field and as he began to jog, he could hear the golden leaves as they turned beneath his feet.

THE RETURN

(1 9 7 1)

It is an evening during the summer that I am ten years old and I am on a train with my parents as it rushes toward the end of eastern Nova Scotia. "You'll be able to see it any minute now, Alex," says my father excitedly, "look out the window, any minute now."

He is standing in the aisle by this time with his left hand against the overhead baggage rack while leaning over me and over my mother who is in the seat by the window. He has grasped my right hand in his right and when I look up it is first into the whiteness of his shirt front arching over me and then into the fine features of his face, the blueness of his eyes and his wavy reddish hair. He is very tall and athletic-looking. He is forty-five.

"Oh, Angus, sit down," says my mother with mingled patience and exasperation, "he'll see it soon enough. We're almost there. Please sit down; people are looking at you."

My left hand lies beside my mother's right on the green upholstered cushion. My mother has brown eyes and brown hair and is three years younger than my father. She is very beautiful and her picture is often in the society pages of the papers in Montreal, which is where we live.

"There it is," shouts my father triumphantly. "Look, Alex, there's Cape Breton!" He takes his left hand down from the baggage rack and points across us to the blueness that is the Strait of Canso, with the gulls hanging almost stationary above the tiny fishing boats and the dark green of the spruce and fir mountains rising out of the water and trailing white wisps of mist about them like discarded ribbons hanging about a newly opened package.

The train lurches and he almost loses his balance and quickly has to replace his hand on the baggage rack. He is squeezing my right hand so hard he is hurting me and I can feel my fingers going numb within his grip. I would like to mention it but I do not know how to do so politely and I know he does not mean to cause me pain.

"Yes, there it is," says my mother without much enthusiasm. "Now you can sit down like everybody else."

He does so but continues to hold my hand very fiercely. "Here," says my mother not unkindly, and passes him a Kleenex over my head. He takes it quietly and I am reminded of the violin records which he has at home in Montreal. My mother does not like them and says they all sound the same so he only plays them when she is out and we are alone. Then it is a time like church, very solemn and serious and sad and I am not supposed to talk but I do not know what else I am supposed to do; especially when my father cries.

Now the train is getting ready to go across the water on a boat. My father releases my hand and starts gathering our luggage because we are to change trains on the other side. After this is done we all go out on the deck of the ferry and watch the Strait as we groan over its placid surface and churn its tranquillity into the roiling turmoil of our own white-watered wake.

My father goes back into the train and reappears with the cheese sandwich which I did not eat and then we go to the stern of the ferry where the other people are tossing food to the convoy of screaming gulls which follows us on our way. The gulls are the whitest things that I have ever seen; whiter than the sheets on my bed at home, or the pink-eyed rabbit that died, or the winter's first snow. I think that since they are so beautiful they should somehow have more manners and in some way be more refined. There is one mottled brown, who feels very ill at ease and flies low and to the left of the noisy main flock. When he ventures into the thick of the fray his fellows scream and peck at him and drive him away. All three of us try to toss our pieces of cheese sandwich to him or into the water directly before him. He is so lonesome and all alone.

When we get to the other side we change trains. A blond young man is hanging from a slowly chugging train with one hand and drinking from a bottle which he holds in the other. I think it is a very fine idea and ask my father to buy me some pop. He says he will later but is strangely embarrassed. As we cross the tracks to our train, the blond young man begins to sing: "There once was an Indian maid." It is not the nice version but the dirty one which I and my friends have learned from the bigger boys in the sixth grade. I have somehow never before thought of grown-ups singing it. My parents are now walking very fast, practically dragging me by the hand over the troublesome tracks. They are both very red-faced and we all pretend we do not hear the voice that is receding in the distance.

When we are seated on the new train I see that my mother is very angry. "Ten years," she snaps at my father, "ten years I've raised this child in the city of Montreal and he has never seen an adult drink liquor out of a bottle, nor heard that kind of language. We have not been here five minutes and that is the first thing he sees and hears." She is on the verge of tears.

"Take it easy, Mary," says my father soothingly. "He doesn't understand. It's all right."

"It's not all right," says my mother passionately. "It's not all right at all. It's dirty and filthy and I must have been out of my mind to agree to this trip. I wish we were going back tomorrow."

The train starts to move and before long we are rattling along the shore. There are fishermen in little boats who wave good-naturedly at the train and I wave back. Later there are the black gashes of coal mines which look like scabs upon the greenness of the hills and the blueness of the ocean and I wonder if these are the mines in which my relatives work.

This train goes much slower than the last one and seems to stop every five minutes. Some of the people around us are talking in a language that I know is Gaelic although I do not understand it, others are sprawled out in their seats, some of them drowsing with their feet stuck out in the aisle. At the far end of the aisle two empty bottles roll endlessly back and forth, clinking against themselves and the steel-bottomed seats. The coach creaks and sways.

The station is small and brown. There is a wooden platform in front of it illuminated by lights which shine down from two tall poles and are bombarded by squads of suicidal moths and June bugs. Beneath the lights there are little clusters of darkly clad men who talk and chew tobacco, and some ragged boys about my own age who lean against battered bicycles waiting for the bundles of newspapers that thud on the platform before their feet.

Two tall men detach themselves from one of the groups and approach us. I know they are both my uncles although I have seen only the younger one before. He lived at our house during part of the year that was the first grade, and used to wrestle with me on the floor and play the violin records when no one was in. Then one day he was gone forever, to survive only in my mother's neutral "It was the year your brother was here," or the more pointed "It was the year your drunken brother was here."

Now both men are very polite. They shake hands with my father and say "Hello, Angie" and then, taking off their caps, "How do you do" to my mother. Then each of them lifts me up in the air. The younger one asks me if I remember him and I say "Yes" and he laughs and puts me down. They carry our suitcases to a taxi and then we all bounce along a very rough street and up a hill, bump, bump, and stop before a large dark house which we enter.

In the kitchen of the house there are a great many people sitting around a big coal-burning stove even though it is summer. They all get up when we come in and shake hands and the women put their arms around my mother. Then I am introduced to the grandparents I have never seen. My grandmother is very tall with hair almost as white as the afternoon's gulls and eyes like the sea over which they flew. She wears a long black dress with a blue checkered apron over it and lifts me off my feet in powerful hands so that I can kiss her and look into her eyes. She smells of soap and water and hot rolls and asks me how I like living in Montreal. I have never lived anywhere else so I say I guess it is all right.

My grandfather is short and stocky with heavy arms and very big hands. He has brown eyes and his once-red hair is almost all white now except for his eyebrows and the hair of his nostrils. He has a white moustache which reminds me of the walrus picture at school and the bottom of it is stained brown by the tobacco that he is chewing even now and spitting the juice into a coal scuttle which he keeps beside his chair. He is wearing a blue plaid shirt and brown trousers supported by heavy suspenders. He too lifts me up although he does not kiss me, and he smells of soap and water and tobacco and leather. He asks me if I saw any girls that I liked on the train. I say "No," and he laughs and lowers me to the floor.

And now it is later and the conversation has died down and the people have gradually filtered out into the night until there are just the three of us, and my grandparents, and after a while my grandmother and my mother go upstairs to finalize the sleeping arrangements. My grandfather puts rum and hot water and sugar into two glasses and gives one to my father and then allows me to sit on his lap even though I am ten, and gives me sips from his glass. He is very different from Grandpa Gilbert in Montreal who wears white shirts and dark suits with a vest and a gold watch–chain across the front.

"You have been a long time coming home," he says to my father. "If you had come through that door as often as I've thought of you, I'd've replaced the hinges a good many times."

"I know, I've tried, I've wanted to, but it's different in Montreal, you know."

"Yes, I guess so. I just never figured it would be like this. It seems so far away and we get old so quickly and a man always feels a certain way about his oldest son. I guess in some ways it is a good thing that we do not all go to school. I could never see myself being owned by my woman's family."

"Please don't start that already," says my father a little angrily. "I am not owned by anybody and you know it. I am a lawyer and I am in partnership with another lawyer who just happens to be my father–in–law. That's all."

"Yes, that's all," says my grandfather and gives me another sip from his glass. "Well, to change the subject, is this the only one you have after being married eleven years?"

My father is now red–faced like he was when we heard the young man singing. He says heatedly, "You know you're not changing the subject at all. I know what you're getting at. I know what you mean."

"Do you?" asks my grandfather quietly. "I thought perhaps that was different in Montreal too."

The two women come downstairs just as I am having another sip from the glass. "Oh, Angus, what can you be thinking of?" screams my mother rushing protectively toward me.

"Mary, please!" says my father almost desperately, "there's nothing wrong."

My grandfather gets up very rapidly, sets me on the chair he has just vacated, drains the controversial glass, rinses it in the sink and says, "Well, time for the working class to be in bed. Good night all." He goes up the stairs walking very heavily and we can hear his boots as he thumps them on the floor.

"I'll put him to bed, Mary," says my father nodding toward me. "I know where he sleeps. Why don't you go to bed now? You're tired."

"Yes, all right," says my mother very gently. "I'm sorry. I didn't mean to hurt his feelings. Good night." She kisses me and also my grandmother and her footsteps fade quietly up the stairs.

"I'm sorry, Ma, she didn't mean it the way it sounded," says my father.

"I know. She finds it very different from what she's used to. And we are older and don't bounce back the way we once did. He is seventy-six now and the mine is hard on him and he feels he must work harder than ever to do his share. He works with different ones of the boys and he tells me that sometimes he thinks they are carrying him just because he is their father. He never felt that way with you or Alex but of course you were all much younger then. Still, he always somehow felt that because those years between high school and college were so good that you would both come back to him some day."

"But Ma, it can't be that way. I was twenty then and Alex nineteen and he was only in his early fifties and we both wanted to go to college so we could be something else. And we paid him back the money he loaned us and he seemed to want us to go to school then."

"He did not know what it was then. Nor I. And when you gave him back the money it was as if that was not what he'd had in mind at all. And what is the something you two became? A lawyer whom we never see and a doctor who committed suicide when he was twenty-seven. Lost to us the both of you. More lost than Andrew who is buried under tons of rock two miles beneath the sea and who never saw a college door."

"Well, he should have," says my father bitterly, "so should they all instead of being exploited and burrowing beneath the sea or becoming alcoholics that cannot even do that."

"I have my alcoholic," says my grandmother now standing very tall, "who was turned out of my Montreal lawyer's home."

"But I couldn't do anything with him, Ma, and it's different there. You just can't be that way, and – and – oh hell, I don't know. If I were by myself he could have stayed forever."

"I know," says my grandmother now very softly, putting her hand upon his shoulder, "it's not you. But it seems that we can only stay forever if we stay right here. As we have stayed to the seventh generation. Because in the end that is all there is – just staying. I have lost three children at birth but I've raised eight sons. I have one a lawyer and one a doctor who committed suicide, one who died in coal beneath the sea and one who is a drunkard and four who still work the coal like their father and those four are all that I have that stand by me. It is these four that carry their father now that he needs it, and it is these four that carry the drunkard, that dug two days for Andrew's body and that have given me thirty grandchildren in my old age."

"I know, Ma," says my father, "I know that and I appreciate it all, everything. It is just that, well somehow we just can't live in a clan system any more. We have to see beyond ourselves and our own families. We have to live in the twentieth century."

"Twentieth century?" says my grandmother spreading her big hands across her checkered apron. "What is the twentieth century to me if I cannot have my own?"

It is morning now and I awake to the argument of the English sparrows outside my window and the fingers of the sun upon the floor. My parents are in my room discussing my clothes. "He really doesn't need them," says my father patiently. "But, Angus, I don't want him to look like a little savage," replies my mother as she lays out my newly pressed pants and shirt at the foot of the bed.

Downstairs I learn that my grandfather has already gone to work, and as I solemnly eat my breakfast like a little old man beyond my years, I listen to the violin music on the radio and watch my grandmother as she spreads butter on the top of the baking loaves and pokes the coals of her fire with a fierce enthusiasm that sends clouds of smoke billowing up to spread themselves against the yellowed paint upon her ceiling.

Then the little boys come in and stand shyly against the wall. There are seven of them and they are all between six and ten. "These are your cousins," says my grandmother to me and to them she says, "this is Alex from Montreal. He is come to visit with us and you are to be nice to him because he is one of our own."

Then I and my cousins go outside because it is what we are supposed to do and we ask one another what grades we are in and I say I dislike my teacher and they mostly say they like theirs which is a possibility I have never considered before. And then we talk about hockey and I try to remember the times I have been to the Forum in Montreal and what I think about Richard.

And then we go down through the town, which is black and smoky and has no nice streets nor flashing lights like Montreal, and when I dawdle behind I suddenly find myself confronted by two older boys who say: "Hey, where'd y'get them sissy clothes?" I do not know what I am supposed to do until my cousins come back and surround me like the covered wagons around the women and children of the cowboy shows, when the Indians attack.

"This is our cousin," say the oldest two simultaneously and I think they are very fine and brave for they too are probably a little bit ashamed of me, and I wonder if I would do the same for them. I have never before thought that perhaps I have been lonely all of my short life and I wish that I had brothers of my own – even sisters perhaps.

My almost-attackers wait awhile, scuffing their shoes on the ashy sidewalk, and then they separate and allow us to pass like a little band of cavalry going through the mountains.

We continue down through the town and farther beyond to the seashore where the fishermen are mending their gear and pumping the little boats in which they allow us to play. Then we skip rocks on the surface of the sea and I skip one six times and then stop because I know I have made an impression and doubt if I am capable of an encore.

And then we climb up a high, high hill that tumbles into the sea and a cousin says we will go to see the bull who apparently lives about a mile away. We are really out in the country now and it is getting hot and when I go to loosen my tie the collar button comes off and is forever lost in the grass through which we pass.

The bull lives in a big barn and my cousins ask an old man who looks like my grandfather if he expects any cows today. He says that he does not know, that you cannot tell about those things. We can look at the bull if we wish but we must not tease him nor go too close. He is very big and brown and white with a ring in his nose and he paws the floor of his stall and makes low noises while lowering his head and swinging it from side to side. Just as we are ready to leave, the old man comes in carrying a long wooden staff which he snaps onto the bull's nose ring. "Well, it looks like you laddies are in luck," he says, "now be careful and get out of the way." I follow my cousins, who run out into a yard where a man who has just arrived is standing, holding a nervous cow by a halter and we sit appreciatively on the top rail of the wooden fence and watch the old man as he leads out the bull who is now moaning and dripping and frothing at the mouth. I have never seen anything like this before and watch with awe this something that is both beautiful and terrible, and I know that I will somehow not be able to tell my mother, to whom I have told almost everything important that has happened in my young life.

And later as we leave, the old man's wife gives us some apples and says, "John, you should be ashamed of yourself; in front of

these children. There are some things that have to be but are not
for children's eyes." The chastised old man nods and looks down
upon his shoes but then looks up at us very gravely from beneath
his bushy eyebrows, looks at us in a very special way and I know
that it is only because we are all boys that he does this and that
the look as it excludes the woman simultaneously includes us in
something that I know and feel but cannot understand.

We go back then to the town and it is late afternoon and we
have eaten nothing but the apples and as we climb the hill
toward my grandparents' house I see my father striding down
upon us with his newspaper under his arm.

He is not disturbed that I have stayed away so long and seems
almost to envy us our unity and our dirt as he stands so straight
and lonely in the prison of his suit and inquires of our day. And
so we reply, as children do, that we have been "playing," which
is the old inadequate message sent forth across the chasm of our
intervening years to fall undelivered and unreceived into the
nothingness between.

He is going down to the mine, he says, to meet the men
when they come off their shift at four and he will take me if I
wish. So I separate from my comrade-cousins and go back down
the hill holding on to his hand, which is something I do not
often do. I think that I will tell him about the bull but instead I
ask, "Why do all the men chew tobacco?"

"Oh," he says, "because it is a part of them and of their way
of life. They do that instead of smoking."

"But why don't they smoke?"

"Because they are underground so much of their lives and
they cannot light a match or a lighter or carry any open flame

down there. It's because of the gas. Flame might cause an explosion and kill them all."

"But when they're not down there they could smoke cigarettes like Grandpa Gilbert in a silver cigarette holder and Mama says that chewing tobacco is a filthy habit."

"I know, but these people are not at all like Grandpa Gilbert and there are things that Mama doesn't understand. It is not that easy to change what is a part of you."

We are approaching the mine now and everything is black and grimy and the heavily laden trucks are groaning past us. "Did you used to chew tobacco?"

"Yes, a very long time ago, before you were ever thought of."

"And was it hard for you to stop?"

"Yes it was, Alex," he says quietly, "more difficult than you will ever know."

We are now at the wash-house and the trains from the underground are thundering up out of the darkness and the men are jumping off and laughing and shouting to one another in a way that reminds me of recess. They are completely black, with the exception of little white half-moons beneath their eyes and the eyes themselves. My grandfather is walking toward us between two of my uncles. He is not so tall as they nor does he take such long strides and they are pacing themselves to keep even with him the way my father sometimes does with me. Even his moustache is black or a very dirty grey except for the bottom of it where the tobacco stains it brown.

As they walk they are taking off their headlamps and unfastening the batteries from the broad belts which I feel would be very fine for carrying holsters and six-guns. They are also fishing for the little brass discs which bear their identification numbers. My father says that if they should be killed in the underground these little discs would tell who each man was. It does not seem like much consolation to me.

At a wicket that looks like the post office the men line up and pass their lamps and the little discs to an old man with glasses. He puts the lamps on a rack and the discs on a large board behind his back. Each disc goes on its special little numbered hook and this shows that its owner has returned. My grandfather is 572.

Inside the adjoining wash-house it is very hot and steamy like when you are in the bathroom a long, long time with the hot water running. There are long rows of numbered lockers with wooden benches before them. The floor is cement with little wooden slatted paths for the men to walk on as they pass bare-footed to and from the noisy showers at the building's farthest end.

"And did you have a good day today, Alex?" asks my grandfather as we stop before his locker. And then unexpectedly and before I can reply he places his two big hands on either side of my head and turns it back and forth very powerfully upon my shoulders. I can feel the pressure of his calloused fingers squeezing hard against my cheeks and pressing my ears into my head and I can feel the fine, fine, coal dust which I know is covering my face and I can taste it from his thumbs which are close against my lips. It is not gritty as I had expected but is more like smoke than sand and almost like my mother's powder. And now he presses my face into his waist and holds me there for a long, long time with my nose bent over against the blackened buckle of his belt. Unable to see or hear or feel or taste or smell anything that is not black; holding me there engulfed and drowning in blackness until I am unable to breathe.

And my father is saying from a great distance: "What are you doing? Let him go! He'll suffocate." And then the big hands come away from my ears and my father's voice is louder and he sounds like my mother.

Now I am so black that I am almost afraid to move and the two men are standing over me looking into one another's eyes. "Oh, well," says my grandfather turning reluctantly toward his locker and beginning to open his shirt.

"I guess there is only one thing to do now," says my father quietly and he bends down slowly and pulls loose the laces of my shoes. Soon I am standing naked upon the wooden slats and my grandfather is the same beside me and then he guides and follows me along the wooden path that leads us to the showers and away from where my father sits. I look back once and see him sitting all alone on the bench which he has covered with his newspaper so that his suit will not be soiled.

When I come to the door of the vast shower room I hesitate because for a moment I feel afraid but I feel my grandfather strong and hairy behind me and we venture out into the pouring water and the lathered, shouting bodies and the cakes of skidding yellow soap. We cannot find a shower at first until one of my uncles shouts to us and a soap-covered man points us in the right direction. We are already wet and the blackness of my grandfather's face is running down in two grey rivulets from the corners of his moustache.

My uncle at first steps out of the main stream but then the three of us stand and move and wash beneath the torrent that spills upon us. The soap is very yellow and strong. It smells like the men's washroom in the Montreal Forum and my grandfather tells me not to get it in my eyes. Before we leave he gradually turns off the hot water and increases the cold. He says this is so we will not catch cold when we leave. It gets colder and colder but he tells me to stay under it as long as I can and I am covered with goose pimples and my teeth are chattering when I jump out for the last time. We walk back through the washing men, who are not so numerous now. Then along the wooden path and I look at the tracks our bare feet leave behind.

My father is still sitting on the bench by himself as we had left him. He is glad to see us return, and smiles. My grandfather takes two heavy towels out of his locker and after we are dry he puts on his clean clothes and I put on the only ones I have except the bedraggled tie which my father stuffs into his pocket. So we go out into the sun and walk up the long, long hill and I am allowed to carry the lunch pail with the thermos bottle rattling inside. We walk very slowly and say very little. Every once in a while my grandfather stops and turns to look back the way we have come. It is very beautiful. The sun is moving into the sea as if it is tired and the sea is very blue and very wide – wide enough it seems for a hundred suns. It touches the sand of the beach which is a slender boundary of gold separating the blue from the greenness of the grass which comes rolling down upon it. Then there is the mine silhouetted against it all, looking like a toy from a Meccano set; yet its bells ring as the coal-laden cars fly up out of the deep, grumble as they are unloaded, and flee with thundering power down the slopes they leave behind. Then the blackened houses begin and march row and row up the hill to where we stand and beyond to where we go. Overhead the gulls are flying inland, slowly but steadily, as if they are somehow very sure of everything. My grandfather says they always fly inland in the evening. They have done so as long as he can remember.

And now we are entering the yard and my mother is rushing toward me and pressing me to her and saying to everyone and no one, "Where has this child been all day? He has not been here since morning and has eaten nothing. I have been almost out of my mind." She buries her fingers in my hair and I feel very sorry for my mother because I think she loves me very much. "Playing," I say.

At supper I am so tired that I can hardly sit up at the table and my father takes me to bed before it is yet completely dark. I wake up once when I hear my parents talking softly at my door. "I am trying very hard. I really am," says my mother. "Yes, yes, I know you are," says my father gently and they move off down the hall.

And now it is in the morning two weeks later and the train that takes us back will be leaving very soon. All our suitcases are in the taxi and the good-byes are almost all completed. I am the last to leave my grandmother as she stands beside her stove. She lifts me up as she did the first night and says, "Good-bye, Alex, you are the only grandchild I will never know," and presses into my hand the crinkled dollar that is never spent.

My grandfather is not in, although he has not gone to work, and they say he has walked on ahead of us to the station. We bump down the hill to where the train is waiting beside the small brown building, and he is on the platform talking with some other men and spitting tobacco over the side.

He walks over to us and everyone says good-bye at once. I am again the last and he shakes hands very formally this time. "Good-bye, Alex," he says, "it was ten years before you saw me. In another ten I will not be here to see." And then I get on the train and none too soon for already it is beginning to move. Everyone waves but the train goes on because it must and it does not care for waving. From very far away I see my grandfather turn and begin walking back up his hill. And then there is nothing but the creak and sway of the coach and the blue sea with its gulls and the green hills with the gashes of their coal embedded deeply in their sides. And we do not say anything but sit silent and alone. We have come from a great distance and have a long way now to go.

IN THE FALL

(1 9 7 3)

 "We'll just have to sell him," I remember my mother saying with finality. "It will be a long winter and I will be alone here with only these children to help me. Besides, he eats too much and we will not have enough feed for the cattle as it is."

It is the second Saturday of November and already the sun seems to have vanished for the year. Each day dawns duller and more glowering and the waves of the grey Atlantic are sullen and almost yellow at their peaks as they pound relentlessly against the round smooth boulders that lie scattered as if by a careless giant at the base of the ever-resisting cliffs. At night, when we lie in our beds, we can hear the waves rolling in and smashing, rolling in and smashing, so relentless and regular that it is possible to count rhythmically between the thunder of each: one, two, three, four; one, two, three, four.

It is hard to realize that this is the same ocean that is the crystal blue of summer when only the thin oil-slicks left by the fishing boats or the startling whiteness of the riding seagulls mar its azure sameness. Now it is roiled and angry, and almost anguished; hurling up the brown dirty balls of scudding foam, the sticks of pulpwood from some lonely freighter, the caps of unknown men, buoys from mangled fishing nets and the inevitable bottles that contain no messages. And always also the shreds of blackened and stringy seaweed that it has ripped and torn from its own lower regions, as if this is the season for self-mutilation – the pulling out of the secret, private, unseen hair.

We are in the kitchen of our house and my mother is speaking as she energetically pokes at the wood and coal within her stove. The smoke escapes, billows upward and flattens itself out against the ceiling. Whenever she speaks she does something with her hands. It is as if the private voice within her can only be liberated by some kind of physical action. She is tall and dark with high cheekbones and brown eyes. Her hair, which is very long and very black, is pulled back severely and coiled in a bun at the base of her neck, where it is kept in place by combs of coral.

My father is standing with his back toward us and is looking out the window to where the ocean pounds against the cliffs. His hands are clasped behind his back. He must be squeezing them together very tightly because they are almost white – especially the left. My father's left hand is larger than his right and his left arm is about three inches longer than normal. That is because he holds his stevedore's hook in his left hand when he works upon the waterfront in Halifax. His complexion is lighter than my mother's and his eyes are grey, which is also the predominant colour of his thinning hair.

We have always lived on the small farm between the ocean and the coal mining town. My father has always worked on his land in the summer and at one time he would spend his winters working within the caverns of the coal mine. Later when he could bear the underground no longer he had spent the time from November to April as an independent coal-hauler, or working in his woodlot where he cut timbers for the mine roof's support. But it must have been a long time ago, for I can scarcely remember a time when the mine worked steadily or a winter when he has been with us, and I am almost fourteen. Now each winter he goes to Halifax but he is often a long time in going. He will stand as he does now, before the window, for perhaps a week or more and then he will be gone and we will see him only at Christmas and on the odd weekend; for he will be over two hundred miles away and the winter storms will make travelling difficult and uncertain. Once, two years ago, he came home for a weekend and the blizzard came so savagely and with such intensity that he could not return until Thursday. My mother told him he was a fool to make such a journey and that he had lost a week's wages for nothing – a week's wages that she and six children could certainly use. After that he did not come again until it was almost spring.

"It wouldn't hurt to keep him another winter," he says now, still looking out the window. "We've kept him through all of them before. He doesn't eat much now since his teeth have gone bad."

"He was of some use before," says my mother shortly and rattling the lids of her stove. "When you were home you used him in the woods or to haul coal — not that it ever got us much. These last years he's been worthless. It would be cheaper to rent a horse for the summer or perhaps even hire a tractor. We don't need a horse any more, not even a young one, let alone one that will probably die in March after we've fed him all that time." She replaces the stove-lids — all in their proper places.

They are talking about our old horse Scott, who has been with us all of my life. My father had been his driver for two winters in the underground and they had become fond of one another and in the time of the second spring, when he left the mine forever, the man had purchased the horse from the Company so that they might both come out together to see the sun and walk upon the grass. And that the horse might be saved from the blindness that would inevitably come if he remained within the deeps; the darkness that would make him like itself.

At one time he had even looked like coal, when his coat was black and shiny strong, relieved by only a single white star in the centre of his forehead; but that too was a long time ago and now he is very grey about the eyes, and his legs are stiff when he first begins to walk.

"Oh, he won't die in March," says my father, "he'll be okay. You said the same thing last fall and he came through okay. Once he was on the grass again he was like a two-year-old."

For the past three or four years Scott has had heaves. I guess heaves come to horses from living too near the ocean and its dampness; like asthma comes to people, making them cough and sweat and struggle for breath. Or perhaps from eating dry and

dusty hay for too many winters in the prison of a narrow stall.
Perhaps from old age too. Perhaps from all of them. I don't
know. Someone told my little brother David who is ten that
dampening the hay would help, and last winter from early
January when Scott began to cough really bad, David would take
a dipper of water and sprinkle it on the hay after we'd put it in
the manger. Then David would say the coughing was much
better and I would say so too.

"He's not a two-year-old," says my mother shortly and begins
to put on her coat before going out to feed her chickens. "He's
old and useless and we're not running a rest home for retired
horses. I am alone here with six children and I have plenty to do."

Long ago when my father was a coal-hauler and before he
was married he would sometimes become drunk, perhaps
because of his loneliness, and during a short February day and a
long February night he had drunk and talked and slept inside the
bootlegger's, oblivious to the frozen world without, until in the
next morning's dehydrated despair he had staggered to the door
and seen both horse and sleigh where he had left them and
where there was no reason for them to be. The coal was glowing
black on the sleigh beneath the fine powdered snow that seems
to come even when it is coldest, seeming more to form like dew
than fall like rain, and the horse was standing like a grey ghostly
form in the early morning's darkness. His own black coat was
covered with the hoar frost that had formed of yesterday's sweat,
and tiny icicles hung from his nose.

My father could not believe that the horse had waited for him
throughout the night of bitter cold, untied and unnecessary,
shifting his feet on the squeaking snow, and flickering his

muscles beneath the frozen harness. Before that night he had never been waited for by any living thing and he had buried his face in the hoar-frost mane and stood there quietly for a long, long time, his face in the heavy black hair and the ice beading on his cheeks.

He has told us this story many times, even though it bores my mother. When he tells it David sits on his lap and says that he would have waited too, no matter how long and no matter how cold. My mother says she hopes David would have more sense.

"Well, I have called MacRae and he is to come for him today," my mother says as she puts on her coat and prepares to feed her chickens. "I wanted to get it over with while you were still here. The next thing I know you'll be gone and we'll be stuck with him for another winter. Grab the pail, James," she says to me, "come and help me feed the chickens. At least there's some point in feeding them."

"Just a minute," he says, "just a goddamn minute." He turns quickly from the window and I see his hands turn into fists and his knuckles white and cold. My mother points to the younger children and shakes her head. He is temporarily stymied because she has so often told him he must not swear before them and while he hesitates we take our pails and escape.

As we go to where the chickens are kept, the ocean waves are even higher, and the wind has risen so that we have to use our bodies to shield the pails that we carry. If we do not, their contents will be scooped out and scattered wildly to the skies. It is beginning to rain and the drops are so driven by the fierceness of the wind that they ping against the galvanized sides of the pails and sting and then burn upon our cheeks.

Inside the chicken-house it is warm and acrid as the chickens press around us. They are really not chickens any more but full grown capons which my mother has been raising all summer and will soon sell on the Christmas market. Each spring she gets day-old chicks and we feed them ground-up hardboiled eggs and chick-starter. Later we put them into outside pens and then in the fall into this house where they are fattened. They are Light Sussex which is the breed my mother favours because they are hardy and good weight-producers. They are very, very white now with red combs and black and gold glittering eyes and with a ring of startling black at the base of their white, shining necks. It is as if a white fluid had been poured over their heads and cascaded down their necks to where it suddenly and magically changed to black after exposure to the air. The opposite in colour but the same in lustre. Like piano keys.

My mother moves about them with ease and they are accustomed to her and jostle about her as she fills their troughs with mash and the warm water we have brought. Sometimes I like them and sometimes I do not. The worst part seems to be that it doesn't really matter. Before Christmas they will all be killed and dressed and then in the spring there will be another group and they will always look and act and end in the same way. It is hard to really like what you are planning to kill and almost as hard to feel dislike, and when there are many instead of one they begin to seem almost as the blueberries and strawberries we pick in summer. Just a whole lot of them to be alive in their way for a little while and then to be picked and eaten, except it seems the berries would be there anyway but the capons we are responsible for and encourage them to eat a great deal, and try our best to make them warm and healthy and strong so that we may kill them in the end. My father is always uncomfortable around them and avoids them as much as possible. My friend Henry Van Dyken says that my father feels that way because he is Scottish, and that Scotsmen are never any good at raising poultry or flowers because they think such tasks are for women and that they make a man ashamed. Henry's father is very good at raising both.

As we move about the closeness of the chicken-house the door bangs open and David is almost blown in upon us by the force of the wind and the rain. "There's a man with a big truck that's got an old bull on it," he says, "he just went in the house."

When we enter the kitchen MacRae is standing beside the table, just inside the door. My father is still at the window, although now with his back to it. It does not seem that they have said anything.

MacRae, the drover, is in his fifties. He is short and heavy-set with a red face and a cigar in the corner of his mouth. His eyes are small and bloodshot. He wears Wellington boots with his trousers tucked inside them, a broad western-style belt, and a brown suede jacket over a flannel shirt which is open at the neck exposing his reddish chest-hair. He carries a heavy stock whip in his hand and taps it against the side of his boot. Because of his short walk in the wind-driven rain, his clothes are wet and now in the warmth of the kitchen they give off a steamy, strong odour that mingles uncomfortably with that of his cigar. An odour that comes of his jostling and shoving the countless frightened animals that have been carried on the back of his truck, an odour of manure and sweat and fear.

"I hear you've got an old knacker," he says now around the corner of his cigar. "Might get rid of him for mink-feed if I'm lucky. The price is twenty dollars."

My father says nothing, but his eyes, which seem the grey of the ocean behind him, remind me of a time when the log which Scott was hauling seemed to ricochet wildly off some half-submerged obstacle, catching the man's legs beneath its onrushing force and dragging and grinding him beneath it until it smashed into a protruding stump, almost uprooting it and knocking Scott back upon his haunches. And his eyes then in their greyness had reflected fear and pain and almost a mute wonder at finding himself so painfully trapped by what seemed all too familiar.

And it seemed now that we had, all of us, conspired against him, his wife and six children and the cigar-smoking MacRae, and that we had almost brought him to bay with his back against the ocean-scarred window so pounded by the driving rain and with all of us ringed before him. But still he says nothing, although I think his mind is racing down all the possible avenues of argument, and rejecting them all because he knows the devastating truth that awaits him at the end of each: "There is no need of postponing it; the truck is here and there will never be a better opportunity; you will soon be gone; he will never be any younger; the price will never be any higher; he may die this winter and we will get nothing at all; we are not running a rest home for retired horses; I am alone here with six children and I have more than enough to do; the money for his feed could be spent on your children; don't your children mean more to you than a horse; it is unfair to go and leave us here with him to care for."

Then with a nod he moves from the window and starts toward the door. "You're not . . ." begins David, but he is immediately silenced by his mother. "Be quiet," she says, "go and finish feeding the chickens," and then, as if she cannot help it, "at least there is some point in feeding them." Almost before my father stops, I know she is sorry about the last part. That she fears that she has reached for too much and perhaps even now has lost all she had before. It is like when you attempt to climb one of the almost vertical sea-washed cliffs, edging upward slowly and groping with blue-tipped fingers from one tiny crevice to the next and then seeing the tantalizing twig which you cannot resist seizing, although even as you do, you know it can be grounded in nothing, for there is no vegetation there nor soil to support it and the twig is but a reject tossed up there by the sea, and even then you are tensing yourself for the painful, bruising slide that must inevitably follow. But this time for my mother, it does not. He only stops and looks at her for a moment before forcing open the door and going out into the wind. David does not move.

"I think he's going to the barn," says my mother then with surprising softness in her voice, and telling me with her eyes that I should go with him. By the time MacRae and I are outside he is already halfway to the barn; he has no hat nor coat and is walking sideways and leaning and knifing himself into the wind which blows his trousers taut against the outlines of his legs.

As MacRae and I pass the truck I cannot help but look at the bull. He is huge and old and is an Ayrshire. He is mostly white except for the almost cherry-red markings of his massive shoulders and on his neck and jowls. His heavy head is forced down almost to the truck's floor by a reinforced chain halter and by a rope that has been doubled through his nose ring and fastened to an iron bar bolted to the floor. He has tried to turn his back into the lashing wind and rain, and his bulk is pressed against the truck's slatted side at an unnatural angle to his grotesquely fastened head. The floor of the truck is greasy and slippery with a mixture of the rain and his own excrement, and each time he attempts to move, his feet slide and threaten to slip from under him. He is trembling with the strain, and the muscles in his shoulders give involuntary little twitches and his eyes roll upward in their sockets. The rain mingles with his sweat and courses down his flanks in rivulets of grey.

"How'd you like to have a pecker on you like that fella?" shouts MacRae into the wind. "Bet he's had his share and driven it into them little heifers a good many times. Boy, you get hung like that, you'll have all them horny little girls squealin' for you to take 'em behind the bushes. No time like it with them little girls, just when the juice starts runnin' in 'em and they're findin' out what it's for." He runs his tongue over his lips appreciatively and thwacks his whip against the sodden wetness of his boot.

Inside the barn it is still and sheltered from the storm. Scott is in the first stall and then there is a vacant one and then those of the cattle. My father has gone up beside Scott and is stroking his nose but saying nothing. Scott rubs his head up and down against my father's chest. Although he is old he is still strong and the force of his neck as he rubs almost lifts my father off his feet and pushes him against the wall.

"Well, no time like the present," says MacRae, as he unzips his fly and begins to urinate in the alleyway behind the stalls. The barn is warm and close and silent, and the odour from the animals and from the hay is almost sweet. Only the sound of MacRae's urine and the faint steam that rises from it disturb the silence and the scene. "Ah, sweet relief," he says, rezipping his trousers and giving his knees a little bend for adjustment as he turns toward us. "Now let's see what we've got here."

He puts his back against Scott's haunches and almost heaves him across the stall before walking up beside him to where my father stands. The inspection does not take long; I suppose because not much is expected of future mink-feed. "You've got a good halter on him there," says MacRae, "I'll throw in a dollar for it, you won't be needin' it anyway." My father looks at him for what seems a very long time and then almost imperceptibly nods his head. "Okay," says MacRae, "twenty-one dollars, a deal's a deal." My father takes the money, still without saying anything, opens the barn door and without looking backward walks through the rain toward his house. And I follow him because I do not know what else to do.

Within the house it is almost soundless. My mother goes to the stove and begins rinsing her teapot and moving her kettle about. Outside we hear MacRae starting the engine of his truck and we know he is going to back it against the little hill beside the barn. It will be easier to load his purchase from there. Then it is silent again, except for the hissing of the kettle which is now too hot and which someone should move to the back of the stove; but nobody does.

And then all of us are drawn with a strange fascination to the window, and, yes, the truck is backed against the little hill as we knew and MacRae is going into the barn with his whip still in his hand. In a moment he reappears, leading Scott behind him.

As he steps out of the barn the horse almost stumbles but regains his balance quickly. Then the two ascend the little hill, both of them turning their faces from the driving rain. Scott stands quietly while MacRae lets down the tailgate of his truck. When the tailgate is lowered it forms a little ramp from the hill to the truck and MacRae climbs it with the halter-shank in his hand, tugging it impatiently. Scott places one foot on the ramp and we can almost hear, or perhaps I just imagine it, the hollow thump of his hoof upon the wet planking; but then he hesitates, withdraws his foot and stops. MacRae tugs at the rope but it has no effect. He tugs again. He comes halfway down the little ramp, reaches out his hand, grasps the halter itself and pulls; we can see his lips moving and he is either coaxing or cursing or both; he is facing directly into the rain now and it is streaming down his face. Scott does not move. MacRae comes down from the truck and leads Scott in a wide circle through the wet grass. He goes faster and faster, building up speed and soon both man and horse are almost running. Through the greyness of the blurring, slanting rain they look almost like a black-and-white movie that is badly out of focus. Suddenly, without changing speed, MacRae hurries up the ramp of the truck and the almost-trotting horse follows him, until his hoof strikes the tailboard. Then he stops suddenly. As the rope jerks taut, MacRae, who is now in the truck and has been carried forward by his own momentum, is snapped backward; he bounces off the side of the bull, loses his footing on the slimy planking and falls into the wet filth of the truck box's floor. Almost before we can wonder if he is hurt, he is back upon his feet; his face is livid and his clothes are smeared with manure and running brown rivulets; he brings the whip, which he has somehow never relinquished even in his fall, down savagely between the eyes of Scott, who is still standing rigidly at the tailgate. Scott shakes his head as if dazed and backs off into the wet grass trailing the rope behind him.

It has all happened so rapidly that we in the window do not really know what to do, and are strangely embarrassed by finding ourselves where we are. It is almost as if we have caught ourselves and each other doing something that is shameful. Then David breaks the spell. "He is not going to go," he says, and then almost shouts, "he is just not going to go – ever. Good for him. Now that he's hit him, it's for sure. He'll never go and he'll have to stay." He rushes toward my father and throws his arms around his legs.

And then the door is jerked open and MacRae is standing there angrily with his whip still in his hand. His clothes are still soggy from his fall and the water trails from them in brown drops upon my mother's floor. His face is almost purple as he says, "Unless I get that fuckin' horse on the truck in the next five minutes, the deal's off and you'll be a goddamn long time tryin' to get anybody else to pay that kinda money for the useless old cocksucker."

It is as if all of the worst things one imagines happening suddenly have. But it is not at all as you expected. And I think I begin to understand for the first time how difficult and perhaps how fearful it is to be an adult and I am suddenly and selfishly afraid not only for myself now but for what it seems I am to be. For I had somehow always thought that if one talked like that before women or small children or perhaps even certain men, the earth would open up or lightning would strike or that at least many people would scream and clap their hands over their ears in horror or that the offender, if not turned to stone, would certainly be beaten by a noble, clean-limbed hero. But it does not happen that way at all. All that happens is the deepening of the thundercloud greyness in my father's eyes and the heightening of the colour in my mother's cheeks. And I realize also with a sort of shock that in spite of Scott's refusal to go on the truck, nothing has really changed. I mean not really; and that all of the facts remain awfully and simply the same: that Scott is old and that we are poor and that my father must soon go away and that he must leave us either with Scott or without him. And that it is somehow like my mother's shielding her children from "swearing" for so many years, only to find one day that it too is there in its awful reality, in spite of everything that she had wished and wanted. And even as I am thinking this, my father goes by MacRae, who is still standing in the ever-widening puddles of brown, seeming like some huge growth that is nourished by the foul-smelling waters that he himself has brought.

David, who had released my father's legs with the entrance of MacRae, makes a sort of flying tackle for them now, but I intercept him and find myself saying as if from a great distance my mother's phrases in something that sounds almost like her voice, "Let's go and finish feeding the chickens." I tighten my grip on his arm and we almost have to squeeze past MacRae whose bulk is blocking the doorway and who has not yet made a motion to leave.

Out of doors my father is striding directly into the slashing rain to where Scott is standing in something like puzzlement with his back to the rain and his halter-shank dangling before him. When he sees my father approach he cocks his ears and nickers in recognition. My father who looks surprisingly slight with his wet clothes plastered to his body takes the rope in his hand and moves off with the huge horse following him eagerly. Their movement seems almost that of the small tug docking the huge ocean freighter, except that they are so individually and collectively alive. As they approach the truck's ramp, it is my father who hesitates and seems to flinch, and it is his foot which seems to recoil as it touches the planking; but on the part of Scott there is no hesitation at all; his hooves echo firmly and confidently on the strong wet wood and his head is almost pressed into the small of my father's back; he is so eager to get to wherever they are going.

He follows him as I have remembered them all of my life and imagined them even before. Following wildly through the darkened caverns of the mine in its dryness as his shoes flashed sparks from the tracks and the stone; and in its wetness with both of them up to their knees in water, feeling rather than seeing the landing of their splashing feet and with the coal cars thundering behind them with such momentum that were the horse to stumble, the very cars he had set in motion would roll over him, leaving him mangled and grisly to be hauled above ground only as carrion for the wheeling gulls. And on the surface, following, in the summer's heat with the jolting haywagon and the sweat churned to froth between his legs and beneath his collar, fluttering white on the blackness of his glistening coat. And in the winter, following, over the semi-frozen swamps as the snapping, whistling logs snaked behind him, grunting as he broke through the shimmering crystal ice which slashed his fetlocks and caused a scarlet trail of bloodied perforations on the whiteness of the snow. And in the winter, too, with the ton of coal upon the sleigh, following, even over the snowless stretches, driven bare by the wind, leaning low with his underside parallel and almost touching the ground, grunting, and swinging with violent jolts to the right and then to the left, moving the sleigh forward only by moving it sideways, which he had learned was the only way it would move at all.

Even as my father is knotting the rope, MacRae is hurrying past us and slamming shut the tailgate and dropping down the iron bolts that will hold it in its place. My father climbs over the side of the box and down as MacRae steps onto the running-board and up into the cab. The motor roars and the truck lurches forward. It leaves two broad wet tracks in the grass like the trails of two slimy, giant slugs and the smell of its exhaust hangs heavy on the air. As it takes the turn at the bottom of the lane Scott tries to turn his head and look back but the rope has been tied very short and he is unable to do so. The sheets of rain come down like so many slanted, beaded curtains, making it impossible to see what we know is there, and then there is only the receding sound of the motor, the wet trails on the grass and the exhaust fumes in the air.

It is only then that I realize that David is no longer with me, but even as the question comes to the surface so also does its answer and I run toward the squawking of the chicken-house.

Within the building it is difficult to see and difficult to breathe and difficult to believe that so small a boy could wreak such havoc in so short a time. The air is thick with myriad dust particles from the disturbed floor, and bits of straw and tiny white scarlet-flecked feathers eddy and dip and swirl. The frightened capons, many of them already bloodied and mangled, attempt short and ungainly flights, often colliding with each other in midair. Their overfed bodies are too heavy for their weak and unused wings and they are barely able to get off the floor and flounder for a few feet before thumping down to dusty crippled landings. They are screaming with terror and their screams seem as unnatural as their flights, as if they had been terribly miscast in the most unsuitable of roles. Many of them are already lifeless and crumpled and dustied and bloodied on the floor, like sad, grey, wadded newspapers that have been used to wipe up blood. The sheen of their feathers forever gone.

In the midst of it all David moves like a small blood-spattered dervish, swinging his axe in all directions and almost unknowingly, as if he were blindfolded. Dust has settled on the dampness of his face and the tears make tiny trails through its greyness, like lonely little rivers that have really nothing to water. A single tiny feather is plastered to his forehead and he is coughing and sobbing, both at the same time.

When my father appears beside me in the doorway he seems to notice for the first time that he is not alone. With a final exhausted heave he throws the axe at my father. "Cocksucker," he says in some kind of small, sad parody of MacRae, and bolts past us through the door, almost colliding with my mother, who now comes from out of the rain. He has had very little strength with which to throw the axe and it clatters uselessly off the wall and comes to rest against my father's boot, wet and bloodied, with feathers and bits of flesh still clinging to its blade.

I am tremendously sorry for the capons, now so ruined and so useless, and for my mother and for all the time and work she has put into them for all of us. But I do not know what to do and I know not what to say.

As we leave the melancholy little building the wind cuts in from the ocean with renewed fury. It threatens to lift you off your feet and blow you to the skies and your crotch is numb and cold as your clothes are flattened hard against the front of your body, even as they tug and snap at your back in insistent, bil-lowing balloons. Unless you turn or lower your head it is impossible to breathe, for the air is blown back almost immedi-ately into your lungs, and your throat convulses and heaves. The rain is now a stinging sleet which is rapidly becoming the winter's first snow. It is impossible to see into it, and the ocean off which it rushes is lost in the swirling whiteness, although it thunders and roars in its invisible nearness like the heavy bass blending with the shrieking tenor of the wind. You hear so much that you can hardly hear at all. And you are almost immo-bile and breathless and blind and deaf. Almost but not quite. For by turning and leaning your body and your head, you can move and breathe and see and hear a little at a time. You do not gain much but you can hang on to what little you have and your toes curl almost instinctively within your shoes as if they are trying to grasp the earth.

I stop and turn my face from the wind and look back the way I have come. My parents are there, blown together behind me. They are not moving, either, only trying to hold their place. They have turned sideways to the wind and are facing and leaning into each other with their shoulders touching, like the end-timbers of a gabled roof. My father puts his arms around my mother's waist and she does not remove them as I have always seen her do. Instead she reaches up and removes the combs of coral from the heaviness of her hair. I have never seen her hair in all its length before and it stretches out now almost parallel to the earth, its shining blackness whipped by the wind and glistening like the snow that settles and melts upon it. It surrounds and engulfs my father's head and he buries his face within its heavy darkness, and draws my mother closer toward him. I think they will stand there for a long, long time, leaning into each other and into the wind-whipped snow and with the ice freezing to their cheeks. It seems that perhaps they should be left alone, so I turn and take one step and then another and move forward a little at a time. I think I will try to find David, that perhaps he may understand.

THE LOST SALT GIFT OF BLOOD

(1 9 7 4)

Now in the early evening the sun is flashing everything in gold. It bathes the blunt grey rocks that loom yearningly out toward Europe and it touches upon the stunted spruce and the low-lying lichens and the delicate hardy ferns and the ganglia-rooted moss and the tiny tough rock cranberries. The grey and slanting rain squalls have swept in from the sea and then departed with all the suddenness of surprise marauders. Everything before them and beneath them has been rapidly, briefly and thoroughly drenched and now the clear droplets catch and hold the sun's infusion in a myriad of rainbow colours. Far beyond the harbour's mouth more tiny squalls seem to be forming, moving rapidly across the surface of the sea out there beyond land's end where the blue ocean turns to grey in rain and distance and the strain of eyes. Even farther out, somewhere beyond Cape Spear lies Dublin and the Irish coast; far away but still the nearest land, and closer now than is Toronto or Detroit, to say nothing of North America's more western cities; seeming almost hazily visible now in imagination's mist.

Overhead the ivory white gulls wheel and cry, flashing also in the purity of the sun and the clean, freshly washed air. Sometimes they glide to the blue-green surface of the harbour, squawking and garbling; at times almost standing on their pink webbed feet as if they would walk on water, flapping their wings pompously against their breasts like overconditioned he-men who have successfully passed their body-building courses. At other times they gather in lazy groups on the rocks above the harbour's entrance, murmuring softly to themselves or looking also quietly out toward what must be Ireland and the vastness of the sea.

The harbour itself is very small and softly curving, seeming like a tiny, peaceful womb nurturing the life that now lies within it but which originated from without; came from without and through the narrow, rock-tight channel that admits the entering and withdrawing sea. That sea is entering again now, forcing itself gently but inevitably through the tightness of the opening and laving the rocky walls and rising and rolling into the harbour's inner cove. The dories rise at their moorings and the tide laps higher on the piles and advances upward toward the high-water marks upon the land; the running moon-drawn tides of spring.

Around the edges of the harbour brightly coloured houses dot the wet and glistening rocks. In some ways they seem almost like defiantly optimistic horseshoe nails: yellow and scarlet and green and pink; buoyantly yet firmly permanent in the grey unsundered rock.

At the harbour's entrance the small boys are jigging for the beautifully speckled salmon-pink sea trout. Barefootedly they stand on the tide-wet rocks, flicking their wrists and sending their glistening lines in shimmering golden arcs out into the rising tide. Their voices mount excitedly as they shout to one another encouragement, advice, consolation. The trout fleck dazzlingly on their sides as they are drawn toward the rocks, turning to seeming silver as they flash within the sea.

It is all of this that I see now, standing at the final road's end of my twenty-five-hundred-mile journey. The road ends here – quite literally ends at the door of a now-abandoned fishing shanty some six brief yards in front of where I stand. The shanty is grey and weatherbeaten with two boarded-up windows, vanishing wind-whipped shingles and a heavy rusted padlock chained fast to a twisted door. Piled before the twisted door and its equally twisted frame are some marker buoys, a small pile of rotted rope, a broken oar and an old and rust-flaked anchor.

The option of driving my small rented Volkswagen the remaining six yards and then negotiating a tight many-twists-of-the-steering-wheel turn still exists. I would be then facing toward the west and could simply retrace the manner of my coming. I could easily drive away before anything might begin.

Instead I walk beyond the road's end and the fishing shanty and begin to descend the rocky path that winds tortuously and narrowly along and down the cliff's edge to the sea. The small stones roll and turn and scrape beside and beneath my shoes and after only a few steps the leather is nicked and scratched. My toes press hard against its straining surface.

As I approach the actual water's edge four small boys are jumping excitedly upon the glistening rocks. One of them has made a strike and is attempting to reel in his silver-turning prize. The other three have laid down their rods in their enthusiasm and are shouting encouragement and giving almost physical moral support: "Don't let him get away, John," they say. "Keep the line steady." "Hold the end of the rod up." "Reel in the slack." "Good." "What a dandy!"

Across the harbour's clear water another six or seven shout the same delirious messages. The silver-turning fish is drawn toward the rock. In the shallows he flips and arcs, his flashing body breaking the water's surface as he walks upon his tail. The small fisherman has now his rod almost completely vertical. Its tip sings and vibrates high above his head while at his feet the trout spins and curves. Both of his hands are clenched around the rod and his knuckles strain white through the water-roughened redness of small-boy hands. He does not know whether he should relinquish the rod and grasp at the lurching trout or merely heave the rod backward and flip the fish behind him. Suddenly he decides upon the latter but even as he heaves, his bare feet slide out from beneath him on the smooth wetness of the rock and he slips down into the water. With a pirouetting leap the trout turns glisteningly and tears itself free. In a darting flash of darkened greenness it rights itself within the regained water and is gone. "Oh damn!" says the small fisherman, struggling upright onto his rock. He bites his lower lip to hold back the tears welling within his eyes. There is a small trickle of blood coursing down from a tiny scratch on the inside of his wrist and he is wet up to his knees. I reach down to retrieve the rod and return it to him.

Suddenly a shout rises from the opposite shore. Another line zings tautly through the water, throwing off fine showers of iridescent droplets. The shouts and contagious excitement spread anew. "Don't let him get away!" "Good for you." "Hang on!" "Hang on!"

I am caught up in it myself and wish also to shout some enthusiastic advice but I do not know what to say. The trout curves up from the water in a wriggling arch and lands behind the boys in the moss and lichen that grow down to the sea-washed rocks. They race to free it from the line and exclaim about its size.

On our side of the harbour the boys begin to talk. "Where do you live?" they ask and is it far away and is it bigger than St. John's? Awkwardly I try to tell them the nature of the North American midwest. In turn I ask them if they go to school. "Yes," they say. Some of them go to St. Bonaventure's, which is the Catholic school, and others go to Twilling Memorial. They are all in either grade four or grade five. All of them say that they like school and that they like their teachers.

The fishing is good they say and they come here almost every evening. "Yesterday I caught me a nine-pounder," says John. Eagerly they show me all of their simple equipment. The rods are of all varieties, as are the lines. At the lines' ends the leaders are thin transparencies terminating in grotesque three-clustered hooks. A foot or so from each hook there is a silver spike knotted into the leader. Some of the boys say the trout are attracted by the flashing of the spike; others say that it acts only as a weight or sinker. No line is without one.

"Here, sir," says John, "have a go. Don't get your shoes wet." Standing on the slippery rocks in my smooth-soled shoes I twice attempt awkward casts. Both times the line loops up too high and the spike splashes down far short of the running, rising life of the channel.

"Just a flick of the wrist, sir," he says, "just a flick of the wrist. You'll soon get the hang of it." His hair is red and curly and his face is splashed with freckles and his eyes are clear and blue. I attempt three or four more casts and then pass the rod back to the hands where it belongs.

And now it is time for supper. The calls float down from the women standing in the doorways of the multicoloured houses and obediently the small fishermen gather up their equipment and their catches and prepare to ascend the narrow upward-winding paths. The sun has descended deeper into the sea and the evening has become quite cool. I recognize this with surprise and a slight shiver. In spite of the advice given to me, and my own precautions, my feet are wet and chilled within my shoes. No place to be unless barefooted or in rubber boots. Perhaps for me no place at all.

As we lean into the steepness of the path my young companions continue to talk, their accents broad and Irish. One of them used to have a tame seagull at his house, had it for seven years. His older brother found it on the rocks and brought it home. His grandfather called it Joey. "Because it talked so much," explains John. It died last week and they held a funeral about a mile away from the shore where there was enough soil to dig a grave. Along the shore itself it is almost solid rock and there is no ground for a grave. It's the same with people, they say. All week they have been hopefully looking along the base of the cliffs for another seagull but have not found one. You cannot kill a seagull, they say, the government protects them because they are scavengers and keep the harbours clean.

The path is narrow and we walk in single file. By the time we reach the shanty and my rented car, I am wheezing and badly out of breath. So badly out of shape for a man of thirty-three; sauna baths do nothing for your wind. The boys walk easily, laughing and talking beside me. With polite enthusiasm they comment upon my car. Again there exists the possibility of restarting the car's engine and driving back the road that I have come. After all, I have not seen a single adult except for the women calling down the news of supper. I stand and fiddle with my keys.

The appearance of the man and the dog is sudden and unexpected. We have been so casual and unaware in front of the small automobile that we have neither seen nor heard their approach along the rock-worn road. The dog is short, stocky and black and white. White hair floats and feathers freely from his sturdy legs and paws as he trots along the rock looking expectantly out into the harbour. He takes no notice of me. The man is short and stocky as well and he also appears as black and white. His rubber boots are black and his dark heavy worsted trousers are supported by a broadly scarred and blackened belt. The buckle is shaped like a dory with a fisherman standing in the bow. Above the belt there is a dark navy woollen jersey and upon his head a toque of the same material. His hair beneath the toque is white, as is the three-or-four-day stubble on his face. His eyes are blue and his hands heavy, gnarled and misshapen. It is hard to tell from looking at him whether he is in his sixties, seventies or eighties.

"Well, it is a nice evening tonight," he says, looking first at John and then to me. "The barometer has not dropped, so perhaps fair weather will continue for a day or two. It will be good for the fishing."

He picks a piece of gnarled grey driftwood from the roadside and swings it slowly back and forth in his right hand. With desperate anticipation the dog dances back and forth before him, his intense eyes glittering at the stick. When it is thrown into the harbour he barks joyously and disappears, hurling himself down the bank in a scrambling avalanche of small stones. In seconds he reappears with only his head visible, cutting a silent but rapidly advancing V through the quiet serenity of the harbour. The boys run to the bank's edge and shout encouragement to him – much as they had been doing earlier for one another. "It's farther out," they cry, "to the right, to the right." Almost totally submerged, he cannot see the stick he swims to find. The boys toss stones in its general direction and he raises himself out of the water to see their landing splashdowns and to change his wide-waked course.

"How have you been?" asks the old man, reaching for a pipe and a pouch of tobacco and then, without waiting for an answer, "perhaps you'll stay for supper. There are just the three of us now."

We begin to walk along the road in the direction that he has come. Before long the boys rejoin us, accompanied by the dripping dog with the recovered stick. He waits for the old man to take it from him and then showers us all with a spray of water from his shaggy coat. The man pats and scratches the damp head and the dripping ears. He keeps the returned stick and thwacks it against his rubber boots as we continue to walk along the rocky road I have so recently travelled in my Volkswagen.

Within a few yards the houses begin to appear upon our left. Frame and flat-roofed, they cling to the rocks, looking down into the harbour. In storms their windows are splashed by the sea but now their bright colours are buoyantly brave in the shadows of the descending dusk. At the third gate, John, the man and the dog turn in. I follow them. The remaining boys continue on; they wave and say, "So long."

The path that leads through the narrow whitewashed gate has had its stone worn smooth by the passing of countless feet. On either side there is a row of small, smooth stones, also neatly whitewashed, and seeming like a procession of large white eggs or tiny unbaked loaves of bread. Beyond these stones and also on either side, there are some cast-off tires also whitewashed and serving as flower beds. Within each whitened circumference the colourful low-lying flowers nod; some hardy strain of pansies or perhaps marigolds. The path leads on to the square green house, with its white borders and shutters. On one side of the wooden doorstep a skate blade has been nailed, for the wiping off of feet, and beyond the swinging screen door there is a porch which smells saltily of the sea. A variety of sou'westers and rubber boots and mitts and caps hang from the driven nails or lie at the base of the wooden walls.

Beyond the porch there is the kitchen where the woman is at work. All of us enter. The dog walks across the linoleum-covered floor, his nails clacking, and flings himself with a contented sigh beneath the wooden table. Almost instantly he is asleep, his coat still wet from his swim within the sea.

The kitchen is small. It has an iron cookstove, a table against one wall and three or four handmade chairs of wood. There is also a wooden rocking-chair covered by a cushion. The rockers are so thin from years of use that it is hard to believe they still function. Close by the table there is a washstand with two pails of water upon it. A washbasin hangs from a driven nail in its side and above it is an old-fashioned mirrored medicine cabinet. There is also a large cupboard, a low-lying couch and a window facing upon the sea. On the walls a barometer hangs as well as two pictures, one of a rather jaunty young couple taken many years ago. It is yellowed and rather indistinct; the woman in a long dress with her hair done up in ringlets, the man in a serge suit that is slightly too large for him and with a tweed cap pulled rakishly over his right eye. He has an accordion strapped over his shoulders and his hands are fanned out on the buttons and keys. The other picture is of the Christ-child. Beneath it is written, "Sweet Heart of Jesus Pray for Us."

The woman at the stove is tall and fine featured. Her grey hair is combed briskly back from her forehead and neatly coiled with a large pin at the base of her neck. Her eyes are as grey as the storm scud of the sea. Her age, like her husband's, is difficult to guess. She wears a blue print dress, a plain blue apron and low-heeled brown shoes. She is turning fish within a frying pan when we enter.

Her eyes contain only mild surprise as she first regards me. Then with recognition they glow in open hostility, which in turn subsides and yields to self-control. She continues at the stove while the rest of us sit upon the chairs.

During the meal that follows we are reserved and shy in our lonely adult ways; groping for and protecting what perhaps may be the only awful dignity we possess. John, unheedingly, talks on and on. He is in the fifth grade and is doing well. They are learning percentages and the mysteries of decimals; to change a percent to a decimal fraction you move the decimal point two places to the left and drop the percent sign. You always, always do so. They are learning the different breeds of domestic animals: the four main breeds of dairy cattle are Holstein, Ayrshire, Guernsey and Jersey. He can play the mouth organ and will demonstrate after supper. He has twelve lobster traps of his own. They were originally broken ones thrown up on the rocky shore by storms. Ira, he says nodding toward the old man, helped him fix them, nailing on new lathes and knitting new headings. Now they are set along the rocks near the harbour's entrance. He is averaging a pound a trap and the "big" fishermen say that that is better than some of them are doing. He is saving his money in a little imitation keg that was also washed up on the shore. He would like to buy an outboard motor for the small reconditioned skiff he now uses to visit his traps. At present he has only oars.

"John here has the makings of a good fisherman," says the old man. "He's up at five most every morning when I am putting on the fire. He and the dog are already out along the shore and back before I've made tea."

"When I was in Toronto," says John, "no one was ever up before seven. I would make my own tea and wait. It was wonderful sad. There were gulls there though, flying over Toronto harbour. We went to see them on two Sundays."

After the supper we move the chairs back from the table. The woman clears away the dishes and the old man turns on the radio. First he listens to the weather forecast and then turns to short wave where he picks up the conversations from the offshore fishing boats. They are conversations of catches and winds and tides and of the women left behind on the rocky shores. John appears with his mouth organ, standing at a respectful distance. The old man notices him, nods and shuts off the radio. Rising, he goes upstairs, the sound of his feet echoing down to us. Returning, he carries an old and battered accordion. "My fingers have so much rheumatism," he says, "that I find it hard to play anymore."

Seated, he slips his arms through the straps and begins the squeezing accordion motions. His wife takes off her apron and stands behind him with one hand upon his shoulder. For a moment they take on the essence of the once-young people in the photograph. They begin to sing:

Come all ye fair and tender ladies
Take warning how you court your men
They're like the stars on a summer's morning
First they'll appear and then they're gone.

I wish I were a tiny sparrow
And I had wings and I could fly

I'd fly away to my own true lover
And all he'd ask I would deny.

Alas I'm not a tiny sparrow
I have not wings nor can I fly
And on this earth in grief and sorrow
I am bound until I die.

John sits on one of the homemade chairs playing his mouth organ. He seems as all mouth-organ players the world over: his right foot tapping out the measures and his small shoulders now round and hunched above the cupped hand instrument.

"Come now and sing with us, John," says the old man.

Obediently he takes the mouth organ from his mouth and shakes the moisture drops upon his sleeve. All three of them begin to sing, spanning easily the half-century that touches their extremes. The old and the young singing now their songs of loss in different comprehensions. Stranded here, alien of my middle generation, I tap my leather foot self-consciously upon the linoleum. The words sweep up and swirl about my head. Fog does not touch like snow yet it is more heavy and more dense. Oh moisture comes in many forms!

All alone as I strayed by the banks of the river
Watching the moonbeams at evening of day
All alone as I wandered I spied a young stranger
Weeping and wailing with many a sigh.

Weeping for one who is now lying lonely
Weeping for one who no mortal can save
As the foaming dark waters flow silently past him
Onward they flow over young Jenny's grave.

Oh Jenny, my darling, come tarry here with me
Don't leave me alone, love, distracted in pain
For as death is the dagger that plied us asunder
Wide is the gulf, love, between you and I.

After the singing stops we all sit rather uncomfortably for a moment, the mood seeming to hang heavily upon our shoulders. Then, with my single exception, all come suddenly to action. John gets up and takes his battered school books to the kitchen table. The dog jumps up on a chair beside him and watches solemnly in a supervisory manner. The woman takes some navy yarn the colour of her husband's jersey and begins to knit. She is making another jersey and is working on the sleeve. The old man rises and beckons me to follow him into the tiny parlour. The stuffed furniture is old and worn. There is a tiny wood-burning heater in the centre of the room. It stands on a square of galvanized metal which protects the floor from falling, burning coals. The stovepipe rises and vanishes into the wall on its way to the upstairs. There is an old-fashioned mantelpiece on the wall behind the stove. It is covered with odd shapes of driftwood from the shore and a variety of exotically shaped bottles, blue and green and red, which are from the shore as well. There are pictures here too: of the couple in the other picture; and one of them with their five daughters; and one of the five daughters by themselves. In that far-off picture time all of the daughters seem roughly between the ages of ten and eighteen. The youngest has the reddest hair of all. So red that it seems to triumph over the non-photographic colours of lonely black and white. The pictures are in standard wooden frames.

From behind the ancient chesterfield the old man pulls a collapsible card table and pulls down its warped and shaky legs. Also from behind the chesterfield he takes a faded checkerboard and a large old-fashioned matchbox of rattling wooden checkers. The spine of the board is almost cracked through and is strengthened by layers of adhesive tape. The checkers are circumferences of wood sawed from a length of broom handle. They are about three quarters of an inch thick. Half of them are painted a very bright blue and the other half an equally eye-catching red. "John made these," says the old man, "all of them are not really the same thickness but they are good enough. He gave it a good try."

We begin to play checkers. He takes the blue and I the red. The house is silent, with only the click-clack of the knitting needles sounding through the quiet rooms. From time to time the old man lights his pipe, digging out the old ashes with a flattened nail and tamping in the fresh tobacco with the same nail's head. The blue smoke winds lazily and haphazardly toward the low-beamed ceiling. The game is solemn, as is the next, and then the next. Neither of us loses all of the time.

"It is time for some of us to be in bed," says the old woman after a while. She gathers up her knitting and rises from her chair. In the kitchen John neatly stacks his school books on one corner of the table in anticipation of the morning. He goes outside for a moment and then returns. Saying good night very formally, he goes up the stairs to bed. In a short while the old woman follows, her footsteps travelling the same route.

We continue to play our checkers, wreathed in smoke and only partially aware of the muffled footfalls sounding softly above our heads.

When the old man gets up to go outside I am not really surprised, any more than I am when he returns with the brown, ostensible vinegar jug. Poking at the declining kitchen fire, he moves the kettle about, seeking the warmest spot on the cooling stove. He takes two glasses from the cupboard, a sugar bowl and two spoons. The kettle begins to boil.

Even before tasting it, I know the rum to be strong and over-proof. It comes at night and in fog from the French islands of St. Pierre and Miquelon. Coming over in the low-throttled fishing boats, riding in imitation gas cans. He mixes the rum and the sugar first, watching them marry and dissolve. Then, to prevent the breakage of the glasses, he places a teaspoon in each and adds the boiling water. The odour rises richly, its sweetness hung in steam. He brings the glasses to the table, holding them by their tops so that his fingers will not burn.

We do not say anything for some time, sitting upon the chairs, while the sweetened, heated richness moves warmly through and from our stomachs and spreads upward to our brains. Outside the wind begins to blow, moaning and faintly rattling the window's whitened shutters. He rises and brings refills. We are warm within the dark and still within the wind. A clock strikes regularly the strokes of ten.

It is difficult to talk at times, with or without liquor; difficult to achieve the actual act of saying. Sitting still we listen further to the rattle of the wind; not knowing where nor how we should begin. Again the glasses are refilled.

"When she married in Toronto," he says at last, "we figured that maybe John should be with her and with her husband. That maybe he would be having more of a chance there in the city. But we would be putting it off and it weren't until nigh on two years ago that he went. Went with a woman from down the cove going to visit her daughter. Well, what was wrong was that we missed him wonderful awful. More fearful than we ever thought. Even the dog. Just pacing the floor and looking out the window and walking along the rocks of the shore. Like us had no moorings, lost in the fog or on the ice-floes in a snow squall. Nigh sick unto our hearts we was. Even the grand-mother who before that was maybe thinking small to herself that he was trouble in her old age. Ourselves having never had no sons, only daughters."

He pauses, then, rising, goes upstairs and returns with an envelope. From it he takes a picture that shows two young people standing self-consciously before a half-ton pickup with a wooden extension ladder fastened to its side. They appear to be in their middle twenties. The door of the truck has the infor-mation: "Jim Farrell, Toronto: Housepainting, Eavestroughing, Aluminum Siding, Phone 535-3484," lettered on its surface.

"This was in the last letter," he says. "That Farrell I guess was a nice enough fellow, from Heartsick Bay he was.

"Anyway, they could have no more peace with John than we could without him. Like I says, he was here too long before his going and it all took ahold of us the way it will. They sent word that he was coming on the plane to St. John's with a woman they'd met through a Newfoundland club. I was to go to St. John's to meet him. Well, it was all wrong the night before the going. The signs all bad; the grandmother knocked off the lamp-shade and it broke in a hunnerd pieces – the sign of death; and the window blind fell and clattered there on the floor and then lied still. And the dog runned around like he was crazy, moanen and cryen worse than the swiles does out on the ice, and throwen hisself against the walls and jumpen on the table and at the window where the blind fell until we would have to be letten him out. But it be no better for he runned and throwed hisself in the sea and then come back and howled outside the same window and jumped against the wall, splashen the water from his coat all over it. Then he be runnen back to the sea again. All the neighbours heard him and said I should bide at home and not go to St. John's at all. We be all wonderful scared and not know what to do and the next mornen, first thing I drops me knife.

"But still I feels I has to go. It be foggy all the day and every-one be thinken the plane won't come or be able to land. And I says, small to myself, now here in the fog be the bad luck and the death but then there the plane be, almost like a ghost ship comen out the fog with all its lights shinen. I think maybe he won't be on it but soon he comen through the fog, first with the woman and then see'n me and starten to run, closer and closer till I can feel him in me arms and the tears on both our cheeks. Powerful strange how things will take one. That night they be killed."

From the envelope that contained the picture he draws forth a tattered clipping:

Jennifer Farrell of Roncesvalles Avenue was instantly killed early this morning and her husband James died later in emergency at St. Joseph's Hospital. The accident occurred about 2 A.M. when the pickup truck in which they were travelling went out of control on Queen St. W. and struck a utility pole. It is thought that bad visibility caused by a heavy fog may have contributed to the accident. The Farrells were originally from Newfoundland.

Again he moves to refill the glasses. "We be all alone," he says. "All our other daughters married and far away in Montreal, Toronto, or the States. Hard for them to come back here, even to visit; they comes only every three years or so for perhaps a week. So we be hav'n only him."

And now my head begins to reel even as I move to the filling of my own glass. Not waiting this time for the courtesy of his offer. Making myself perhaps too much at home with this man's glass and this man's rum and this man's house and all the feelings of his love. Even as I did before. Still locked again for words.

Outside we stand and urinate, turning our backs to the seeming gale so as not to splash our wind-snapped trousers. We are almost driven forward to rock upon our toes and settle on our heels, so blow the gusts. Yet in spite of all, the stars shine clearly down. It will indeed be a good day for the fishing and this wind eventually will calm. The salt hangs heavy in the air and the water booms against the rugged rocks. I take a stone and throw it against the wind into the sea.

Going up the stairs we clutch the wooden bannister unsteadily and say good night.

The room has changed very little. The window rattles in the wind and the unfinished beams sway and creak. The room is full of sound. Like a foolish Lockwood I approach the window although I hear no voice. There is no Catherine who cries to be let in. Standing unsteadily on one foot when required I manage to undress, draping my trousers across the wooden chair. The bed is clean. It makes no sound. It is plain and wooden, its mattress stuffed with hay or kelp. I feel it with my hand and pull back the heavy patchwork quilts. Still I do not go into it. Instead I go back to the door which has no knob but only an ingenious latch formed from a twisted nail. Turning it, I go out into the hallway. All is dark and the house seems even more inclined to creak where there is no window. Feeling along the wall with my outstretched hand I find the door quite easily. It is closed with the same kind of latch and not difficult to open. But no one waits on the other side. I stand and bend my ear to hear the even sound of my one son's sleeping. He does not beckon any more than the nonexistent voice in the outside wind. I hesitate to touch the latch for fear that I may waken him and disturb his dreams. And if I did, what would I say? Yet I would like to see him in his sleep this once and see the room with the quiet bed once more and the wooden chair beside it from off an old wrecked trawler. There is no boiled egg or shaker of salt or glass of water waiting on the chair within this closed room's darkness.

Once, though, there was a belief held in the outports, that if a girl would see her own true lover she should boil an egg and scoop out half the shell and fill it with salt. Then she should take it to bed with her and eat it, leaving a glass of water by her bedside. In the night her future husband or a vision of him would appear and offer her the glass. But she must only do it once.

It is the type of belief that bright young graduate students were collecting eleven years ago for the theses and archives of North America and also, they hoped, for their own fame. Even as they sought the near-Elizabethan songs and ballads that had sailed from County Kerry and from Devon and Cornwall. All about the wild, wide sea and the flashing silver dagger and the lost and faithless lover. Echoes to and from the lovely, lonely hills and glens of West Virginia and the standing stones of Tennessee.

Across the hall the old people are asleep. The old man's snoring rattles, as do the windows; except that now and then there are catching gasps within his breath. In three or four short hours he will be awake and will go down to light his fire. I turn and walk back softly to my room.

Within the bed the warm sweetness of the rum is heavy and intense. The darkness presses down upon me, but still it brings no sleep. There are no voices and no shadows that are real. There are only walls of memory touched restlessly by flickers of imagination.

Oh, I would like to see my way more clearly. I, who have never understood the mystery of fog. I would perhaps like to capture it in a jar like the beautiful childhood butterflies that always die in spite of the airholes punched with nails in the covers of their captivity – leaving behind the vapours of their lives and deaths; or perhaps as the unknowing child who collects the grey moist condoms from the lovers' lanes, only to have them taken from him and to be told to wash his hands. Oh, I have collected many things I did not understand.

And perhaps now I should go and say, oh son of my *summa cum laude* loins, come away from the lonely gulls and the silver trout and I will take you to the land of the Tastee Freeze where you may sleep till ten of nine. And I will show you the elevator to the apartment on the sixteenth floor and introduce you to the buzzer system and the yards of the wrought-iron fences where the Doberman pinscher runs silently at night. Or may I offer you the money that is the fruit of my collecting and my most successful life? Or shall I wait to meet you in some known or unknown bitterness like Yeats's Cuchulain by the wind-whipped sea or like Sohrab and Rustum by the future flowing river?

Again I collect dreams. For I do not know enough of the fog on Toronto's Queen St. West and the grinding crash of the pickup, and of lost and misplaced love.

I am up early in the morning as the man kindles the fire from the driftwood splinters. The outside light is breaking and the wind is calm. John tumbles down the stairs. Scarcely stopping to splash his face and pull on his jacket, he is gone, accompanied by the dog. The old man smokes his pipe and waits for the water to boil. When it does, he pours some into the teapot, then passes the kettle to me. I take it to the washstand and fill the small tin basin in readiness for my shaving. My face looks back from the mirrored cabinet. The woman softly descends the stairs.

"I think I will go back today," I say while looking into the mirror at my face and at those in the room behind me. I try to emphasize the "I." "I just thought I would like to make this trip — again. I think I can leave the car in St. John's and fly back directly." The woman begins to move about the table, setting out the round white plates. The man quietly tamps his pipe.

The door opens and John and the dog return. They have been down along the shore to see what has happened throughout the night. "Well, John," says the old man, "what did you find?"

He opens his hand to reveal a smooth round stone. It is of the deepest green, inlaid with veins of darkest ebony. It has been worn and polished by the unrelenting restlessness of the sea, and buffed and burnished by the gravelled sand. All of its inadequacies have been removed, and it glows with the lustre of near perfection.

"It is very beautiful," I say.

"Yes," he says, "I like to collect them." Suddenly he looks up to my eyes and thrusts the stone toward me. "Here," he says, "would you like to have it?"

Even as I reach out my hand I turn my head to the others in the room. They are both looking out through the window to the sea.

"Why, thank you," I say. "Thank you very much. Yes, I would. Thank you. Thanks." I take it from his outstretched hand and place it in my pocket.

We eat our breakfast in near silence. After it is finished the boy and dog go out once more. I prepare to leave.

"Well, I must go," I say, hesitating at the door. "It will take me a while to get to St. John's." I offer my hand to the man. He takes it in his strong fingers and shakes it firmly.

"Thank you," says the woman. "I don't know if you know what I mean but thank you."

"I think I do," I say. I stand and fiddle with the keys. "I would somehow like to help or keep in touch but . . ."

"But there is no phone," he says, "and both of us can hardly write. Perhaps that's why we never told you. John is getting to be a pretty good hand at it, though."

"Good-bye," we say again, "good-bye, good-bye."

The sun is shining clearly now and the small boats are putt-putting about the harbour. I enter my unlocked car and start its engine. The gravel turns beneath the wheels. I pass the house and wave to the man and woman standing in the yard.

On a distant cliff the children are shouting. Their voices carol down through the sun-washed air and the dogs are curving and dancing about them in excited circles. They are carrying something that looks like a crippled gull. Perhaps they will make it well. I toot the horn. "Good-bye," they shout and wave, "good-bye, good-bye."

The airport terminal is strangely familiar. A symbol of imper-manence, it is itself glisteningly permanent. Its formica surfaces have been designed to stay. At the counter a middle-aged man in mock exasperation is explaining to the girl that it is Newark he wishes to go to, *not* New York.

There are not many of us and soon we are ticketed and lifting through and above the sun-shot fog. The meals are served in tinfoil and in plastic. We eat above the clouds, looking at the tips of wings.

The man beside me is a heavy-equipment salesman who has been trying to make a sale to the developers of Labrador's resources. He has been away a week and is returning to his wife and children.

Later in the day we land in the middle of the continent. Because of the changing time zones, the distance we have come seems eerily unreal. The heat shimmers in little waves upon the runway. This is the equipment salesman's final destination, whereas for me it is but the place where I must change flights to continue even farther into the heartland. Still we go down the wheeled-up stairs together, donning our sunglasses and stepping across the heated concrete and through the terminal's electronic doors. The salesman's wife stands waiting along with two small children who are the first to see him. They race toward him with their arms outstretched. "Daddy, Daddy," they cry, "what did you bring me? What did you bring me?"

THE ROAD TO RANKIN'S POINT

(1 9 7 6)

I am speaking now of a July in the early 1970s and it is in the morning just after the sun has risen following a night of heavy rains. My car moves through the quiet village which is yet asleep except for those few houses which have sent fishermen to their nets and trawls some hours before. From such houses the smoke whisks and curls lazily before slanting off at the insistence of the almost imperceptible southeast wind. Upon my right the Gulf of St. Lawrence is flat and blue, dotted here and there with the white fishing boats intent on their quiet work. It has been a bad year for lobsters because of the late ice and then the early storms which destroyed so much of the precious gear. During the last week of the lobster season many of the fishermen did not even visit their traps, preferring to remain drunk and discouraged on the beach or within the dampened privacy of their little shanties.

Now since the lobster season's conclusion on July first, it can be at least thankfully forgotten along with the vague feelings of hope tinged with guilt that accompanied its final days. The boats riding on the Gulf today are after a variety of "ground fish," with some few after salmon. They are getting six cents a pound for hake and twelve for cod and no one has seen a haddock for a long, long time. In the cities of Ontario fresh cod sells for $1.65 a pound and the "dried cod" upon which most of us were raised and which we so heartily despised has become almost a delicacy which sells for $2.15 a pound. "Imagine that," says my grandmother, "who would have ever thought?" Across Cabot Strait in Newfoundland the prices are three to four cents lower and there is talk that the fishermen may strike. All this runs through my mind now, although it does not really occupy it. Like the vaguely heard melody of some turned-down radio station heard softly in the background.

At the outskirts of the village the narrow paved road turns to the left, away from the sea, and begins its journey inland and outward. If followed relentlessly it will take you almost anywhere in North America; perhaps to Central and to South America as well. It will remain narrow and unpretentious and "slow" in the caution that it demands of its drivers for approximately fifty miles. Then it will join the maple-leafed Trans-Canada Highway and together they will boom across the Canso Causeway and off Cape Breton Island and out into the world. As the water of the tributary joins the major river, its traffic and its travellers will blend and mingle within the rushing stream. They will become the camper trailers with their owners' names emblazoned on their sides, and the lumbering high-domed motor homes and the overcrowded station wagons with the dogs forever panting through the rear windows. They will become the high-powered "luxury" products of Detroit, loaded with extras and zooming at eighty miles per hour from service station to service station, as if by speed alone they might somehow outrace the galloping depreciation which even now threatens to overtake and engulf them. They will become the scuttling Volkswagens in the "slow" lanes on the long hills and the grinding trucks with their encased and T-shirted drivers carrying the continent's goods and the weaving, swerving motorcyclists with their helmets reflecting the slanting sun.

By night these travellers will all be miles away; comparing mileages, filling their radiators and looking at their maps. They will be sitting around campfires and sweating in the motels. Some will be in the havens of their homes while others will follow the probing paths of their bug-spattered headlights deep into the darkened night. Some few will end in twisted, spectacular wreckages, later moaning incoherently in the unknown hospitals or lying beneath the quiet sheets of death while authorities search through glove compartments and check out licence numbers prior to notifying the next of kin. It is a big, fast, brutal road that leads into the world on this July day and there is no longer any St. Christopher to be the patron saint of travellers.

But for me, in this my twenty-sixth year, it is not into the larger world that I go today. And the road that I follow feeds into no other that will take the traveller to the great adventures of the wild unknown. Instead, at the village's end it veers sharply to the right, leaves the pavement behind and almost immediately begins to climb along the rocky cliffs that hang high above the sea. It winds its tortuous, clinging way for some eight miles before it ends quite abruptly and permanently in my grandmother's yard. There the sea cliff slants down almost vertically and it is as if the road runs into it as it would into a wall. At the wall's base and at the road's end nestles my grandmother's tiny farm; her buildings and her home. Above this last small cultivated outpost and jutting beyond it out to sea is the rocky promontory of Rankin's Point. As one cannot drive beyond it, neither can one see beyond it farther up the coast. It is an end in every way and it is to the beginning of this conclusion that my car now begins its long ascent.

For the first two miles there are still houses strung out along both sides of the road but soon such signs of formal habitation fall behind; and as the road becomes steeper, rockier and more narrow the wildness of the summer's beauty falls and splashes down upon it even to the extent that it is close to lost. The over-reaching branches of the silver birch, the maple and the poplar slap across the hood and windshield, impeding vision and almost the passage of the road itself. The alders lean and hang from the left bank, their sticky buds smearing the car door's sides and leaving stains that will annoy car washers for a long, long time. The wild flowers burst and hang in all their short-lived, giddy, aromatic profusion. When the tough but delicate red-and-white roses are nudged by the car they cascade and strew their fragile, perfumed petals across its hood even as their thorns scratch the finished lacquer of its sides. *Everything has its price*, they seem to say. The sweet red-and-white clover swarms with bees. The yellow buttercups flutter and the white and gold-green daisies dip and sway. The prickly Scottish thistles are in their lavender bloom and the wild buckwheat and rioting raspberry bushes form netted tapestries of the darkest green. As the road dips and twists around many of its hairpinned turns the icy little streams cascade across it; washing it out in a minor way, the water flowing across the gullied roadbed instead of beneath it through the broken, plugged and unused wooden sluices. At such spots near the fresh water's edge the bluebells cling to the velvet-mossed stones and the blue-and-purple irises march downward to the wetness. The gentle, large-eyed rabbits hop trustingly near the road which is so untravelled that it holds for them neither fear nor any threat of death. The road is now but a minor intrusion that the wildness will reclaim.

Before the final two-mile climb there is one last almost right-angled turn and again the spilling, cascading brook and the washed-over roadbed and the plugged and useless sluice. The road rising from the spot is solid rock, and on wet days it is impossible for a car to make the climb. The tires will spin and the rear of the car will slew to the right and hang above the four-hundred-foot drop that falls to the crashing surf which booms and pounds the smooth and rounded boulders far below. Three years ago a lovers' quarrel resulted in a car being stolen from the village below and then pushed over the towering cliff. For weeks the police and the insurance companies and various high-priced towing companies attempted to reach it but with no success. All of the cables and the extended booms and the huge tow trucks that were reared back on their hind and doubled wheels, and the men motioning with their gloved hands or hanging on ropes at the sea cliff's wall did nothing to raise the twisted bits of metal that were scattered far below. Finally some men in a small fishing dory were able to get close enough to the cliff's base to wade ashore in water up to their waists and retrieve what remained of the engine. Now if one hangs over the perilous edge the remaining bits of automobile can still be seen strewn along the wet cliff's base. Here the twisted chassis and there the detached body and yards away the steering wheel and the trunk lid and a crumpled, twisted door. The cormorants and the gulls walk carefully amidst the twisted wreckage as if hoping that each day may bring them something that they had previously missed. They peck with curiosity at the gleaming silver knobs and the selector buttons of the once-expensive radio.

The sharp, right-angled turn and its ascending steepness has always been called by us "The Little Turn of Sadness" because it is here that my grandfather died so many years ago on a February night when he somehow fell as he walked or staggered toward his home which was a steep two miles away. He had already covered the six miles from the village when he lost his footing on the ice-covered rock, falling backwards and shattering the rum bottle he carried within his safe back pocket. Now as I feel my own blood, diseased and dying, I think of his, the brightest scarlet, staining the moon-white snow while the joyous rabbits leaped and pirouetted beneath the pale, clear moon. It was a bright and quiet night without a breath of wind, as my grandmother has often told us. All night she kept looking out across the death-white fields for the form of her returning husband. Her eyes became so strained that as the dawn approached the individual spruce trees at the clearing's edge began to take his shape and size and seemed to move toward the house. First one and then another appearing to move and take on human form. Once she was so certain that she went to the door and opened it, only to stare again across the whitened, empty stillness of the silent winter snow.

In the morning she sent her oldest son, who was ten at the time, to walk along the frozen cliffs; and when he returned, white and breathless, the news he brought was already expected. Shortly after he left, she has often said, she began to hear the death ring or the sound of the death bell in her right ear. It came from off the frozen Gulf of St. Lawrence, borne on the stillness and, no, it was not to be confused with the crying of the white and drifting seals. And then, almost in response to the bell, she had heard the howls of the three black-and-white border collies that had accompanied her son. Their howls drifted back along the coastline, first the oldest dog and then the second and then the third. She had been able to distinguish each dog's cry and to comprehend the message that their anguished voices bore. At that time and in those sounds she realized that life for her and for her children would never be the same. She was twenty-six and expecting her seventh child.

Later she and her older children hitched the best of their brown-dappled horses to the wood sleigh and went forth to meet their husband and father for the final time. The children cried and the tears froze to their reddened cheeks. The horse began to snort and tremble long before he reached the rigid, log-like figure, and then to rear and plunge. Finally he lunged to the side, breaking the shafts of the precious sleigh and adding another stick of destruction to the steadily mounting pile. They had had to abandon the sleigh then and return with the horse and then come back again with the children's coasting sleigh and lengths of rope with which to bind the grisly burden it was to bear.

The dogs lay restlessly about the stiffened corpse, black against the silent snow. Sometimes they whined softly and licked the frozen opened eyes or the grotesquely parted purple lips with the protruding tongue or nuzzled an out-flung half-curved arm. Then they would flop back again into the snow, covering their noses with their paws while following everything with their deep brown eyes. Sensing too that their lives had changed, and not knowing what to do.

Somehow they managed the final two miles, though their own feet slipped on the icy rocks and they fell forward several times when the strained rope parted. Because the sleigh was so small there was only room for the upper part of the body, and the legs and heels hung over the end and dragged along the jagged, stony road. Twice the body almost slipped off completely and when they reached the house the heels of the rubber boots were worn through to the frozen flesh. The heel of the bottle which had killed him still contained, almost miraculously, a half inch of the dark sweet rum, while the neck with its firmly fastened cork was also still intact. Between the perfect top and the perfect bottom all was shattered and splintered and driven deeply into the frozen hip and thigh.

Now this scene of winter death seems strangely out of place amidst the drunken intensity of the summer's splendour. Like an improbable sequence of old black-and-white pictures taken once in the long ago. Taken of people it is impossible to ever know or to fully understand.

The sun is rising above the mountains and touching the freshly washed earth. The raindrops glisten and sparkle, and the fog and mists that hang above the dirt roads of high places rise and vanish toward the sky. The bobolinks and red-winged blackbirds bounce and sing from the tips of their springing willows. Orange butterflies glide and float on the drafts of air and the chattering squirrels and chipmunks sprint along the fallen logs like busy proprietors doing morning inspection. The earth is alive, refreshed and new.

It does not take long for the rocks above "The Little Turn of Sadness" to dry, and my car in its lowest gear grinds slowly and reluctantly up the steep incline, nearly swinging out and over the hanging ledge, then settling more steadily to the stony and almost familiar roadbed.

For the next two miles the road continues to climb and wind along the cliff's high ledge. In some places erosion has caused the roadside to crumble and fall into the sea. It would be impossible for two vehicles to meet and pass upon such narrowness, but there is little likelihood of such an occurrence.

Now and then upon the left I see the remains of the old stone fences and also tiny patches of still-cleared land indicating where houses had once stood. The grey granite stones of their foundations are still visible, covered now with green and velvet moss. Now and then a stone flue stands with phallic reality amidst the rubble of the house that has fallen down around it. Only the strength of stone has survived the ravages of time and seasons.

A mile from my grandmother's house her sheep begin to appear, grazing or lying along the roadside and sometimes right

in the middle of the road. They are the white-faced Cheviots
that she has had for as long as I can remember and there is
almost a timelessness about them. Open-faced and independent, they do not flock together as do the more conventional
Oxfords and Suffolks. As the car approaches, the young lambs
bound and scramble out of its way, bleating over their shoulders
to the patient, watchful ewes. The thick-shouldered rams, with
their heavy, swinging scrota almost dragging on the ground,
move only at the last minute and then begrudgingly. Their
flickering eyes seem to say they would as soon lower their heads
and charge as relinquish this stony trail which they obviously
consider to be theirs.

For decades my grandmother has been concerned about the
purity and well-being of these sheep. She has worried about
strange rams interbreeding and diluting her "stock." And she has
worried about young dogs wild with spring and bloodlust
running them over the cliffs to sea-washed deaths. Now there is
no need to worry. All the other flocks and dogs from the fallen
houses have gone, and it is only her sheep whose bleating cries
reverberate across these high cleansed hills.

At the road's end I stop to slide back the poles of the old gate
before the final entrance to her yard. As I bend, the blood bursts
from my nostrils, splashing scarletly upon my shoes, and there is
a dizzying lightness bordering on black within my head. I
straighten and place my hands on the gateposts for steadiness and
lift my face to the sun to reverse the blood's thick flow. I can feel
it coursing sweetly through the back of my mouth and down the
darkened passages of my throat. To avoid further bending, I slide
the bottom pole back by hooking my right foot underneath it

and then stand and wait for the bleeding to cease. I dab at my nostrils and lips with the pieces of Kleenex that I now carry in place of standard handkerchiefs.

The car, with its clutch disengaged, rolls easily down the small incline into the yard. There is no need to even start the motor. I close the gate, watched with interest by various farm animals who are not in the least alarmed. Almost all of my grandmother's animals are descended from livestock that has been here for a long, long time and over the years they have taken on distinctive colourings and characteristics that are all their own. They seem now the same animals that I have always known and heard described, and seen in the faded photographs of the albums of my mind. The three brown-dappled horses, rolling in the slickness of their summer fat, have an almost maroon tinge to their coats when the sun strikes them at certain angles. They have identical white stars in their foreheads and a solitary white spot the size of a large coin on their barrelled chests. They have always been called either Star or Tena. They have always held their heads high when drawing even the heaviest of loads and have been perfectly in step with each other, their hoofbeats falling in unison through the regulated choreography of their fiercely inbred generations. They have been sure-footed in the snow and long-winded on the hills. They have crossed the drift ice in the blinding blizzards and galloped the cartloads of seaweed ashore across the briny rocks. For years they have refused to eat any hay except that grown upon this hilly farm; as if smelling and tasting within it their own urine, manure and sweat. As if they are part of some great ecological plan, converting themselves into hay and the hay in turn into their wine-dappled sun-strong selves.

Now standing about this yard, whisking their too-long tails and tossing their forelocks out of their eyes, they are idle and at ease. They have felt neither bridle nor harness nor shoes for years and the youngest, who is close to ten, has never felt them at all. He is so old now, in the years of a horse, that it is unlikely that he ever will.

They have become almost pets, waiting for my grandmother to open her door and offer them bits of apple or pieces of stale, dried bread. Yet in their deep, dark eyes and in the muscles that bunch and ripple within their shoulders their power can still be seen. They are like the eyes and muscles of certain animals at the zoo; eyes and muscles that say, *Yes, we are here and we are alive and we eat our food, but we were not bred for this kind of life nor did we come from it nor is this all we are. Look closely at us and you will see.*

The brindled cows with their in-curved horns are busily grazing about the grassy knolls. Because my grandmother no longer tends them as she used to, nor uses their cream-rich milk for her butter and cheese, they too seem wasted and unused. They are followed by overgrown calves who nurse and butt at their swollen and distended udders. Some of their udders are caked and hardened, and mastitis has set in. It would be close to impossible to redeem them now and they will never more fill to overflowing the warm and brimming pails. A black hen with gold flecks around her neck is clucking to her chickens. The chickens are too young for this time of year and will not likely survive the fall.

Entering the porch that leads to my grandmother's house it is necessary to step down. With the passage of the years the house has sunk into the earth. The stone foundation of more than a century has worked itself deep into the soil and now all doors are forced to open inward. The porch is filled with tools and clothes and items from the past. A manual cream separator is on the left, a hand scythe hangs on the wall to the right, and beside it a wire stretcher and a meat grinder. Bits of harness and rope and cans of fence staples, nails, hammers, gunny sacks and fishing rods hang from the spikes driven deep into the wooden beams. Shapeless rain jackets, hats, gloves, and worn-out shoes and boots hang and lie cluttered in a corner.

In the kitchen my grandmother sits at her table drinking her morning tea. She has not seen nor heard my arrival and she is staring out the window that looks upon the sea. There the gulls are curving and turning in the sparkling sun. The three black-and-white border collies raise their eyes when I enter but they do not move. They lie about the floor like tossed and familiar rugs. One is under the table, one against the wood box at the stove, and the third beside my grandmother's chair. Unlike my grandmother, they have been aware of my approach for some time. They have recognized the sound of the motor groaning along the cliff's edge and heard the gate poles slide and the opening of the door and the footstep on the sill. They have heard it all and felt no cause for movement or alarm. I enter now to make my presence fully known and to take my place in time.

Turning from the window with her teacup in her hand, my grandmother is startled to see me and also embarrassed that I have come upon her so silently and unannounced. She is becoming frightened, although she will not admit it, of the loss of her senses, and she fears the silence of the deaf and the darkness of the blind. None of this has happened to her as yet but there are clutching moments seen in her face, as now, that say such thoughts are there.

"Oh, you are here, Calum," she says. "I've been expecting you."

I know that she has as I have been expecting to come, lying in the bed at my parents' house in the village below since three A.M., listening to the rain upon the roof and thinking of how slippery the rocks of the road might be. Thinking of walking the eight-mile distance in the almost unfathomable rural darkness when the rain clouds blot out the moon and stars and there is only the sound of water: the thunking of the large-dropped rain into the earth and into the splashing, invisible brooks and on the right the lapping and moaning of the sea. Knowing that I will never walk that skin-drenched journey again, any more than will my never-seen grandfather, dead now for seventy years, the biblical life span of three score years and ten.

"I came as soon as I could," I say. "As soon as I thought the cliff would be dry enough for the car to climb."

"Oh yes," she says. "Would you like some tea? The kettle has just finished boiling."

"Yes, all right, I will get it myself," I say as I move about her familiar kitchen, digging into the old square tea can which drifted ashore from one of the long-ago wrecked vessels carrying the precious cargo from Ceylon. I gather the tea into my fist and drop it into the teapot and add the water from the steaming kettle.

"They will not be here for a while," she says, "not likely until the afternoon."

She seats herself more comfortably at the end of the table.

"Get yourself some biscuits from out of the tin. I made them early this morning. Give some to the dogs."

Obediently I go to another tin and take out four biscuits. They are still warm to the touch. I butter one for myself and toss one to each of the lying, watchful dogs. They catch them while they are still in the air, then flick out their long, pink tongues for any crumbs that may have fallen on the floor. The floor remains as spotless as before, as if the action had never happened. Like footsteps in the water, I think. No trace remains behind.

I sit opposite my grandmother at the other end of the table and look with her out across the azure sea. The sun is higher now and the mists have all burned off. It is the kind of day that at one time would have allowed us to see Prince Edward Island. *On a clear day you can see Prince Edward Island*, we would say. Not "forever," just Prince Edward Island. Now it does not seem to matter.

Today is the first day of the rest of your life, comes to my mind. The slogan from the many "modern" posters, desk mottoes, greeting cards, bookmarks, record jackets, bumper stickers and graffiti walls. I raise the teacup to my lips, half-hopeful it might burn me more fiercely into life.

"Why do you drink your tea like that?" asks my grandmother. "You will burn yourself. One would think you had never drunk tea before."

"It is all right," I say. "I was only trying something."

We sit for a long time, quietly sipping our tea and looking through the window. We do not say what is on our minds nor make inquiries of each other. We are resting and appearing normal, almost as athletes quietly conserving our energy for the game that lies some hours down our road. The bees buzz from the lilacs at the base of the house and bounce drunkenly against the window. The barn swallows with their delicately forked tails flash their orange breasts and dart and swoop after invisible insects. The dogs lie silently, moving only their eyes, conserving their strength as well. We are drowsy and waiting in the summer's heat.

I have come to see my grandmother on this day almost as the double agent of the spy movies. I have come somehow hoping that I might find a way of understanding and of coming to terms with death; yet deep down I know that I will find only the intensity of life and that I am, after all, but twenty-six, and in the eyes of others, in the youngness of my years.

My grandmother gets up and goes for her violin, which hangs on a peg inside her bedroom door. It is a very old violin and came from the Scotland of her ancestors, from the crumbled foundations that now dot and haunt Lochaber's shores. She plays two Gaelic airs – *Gun Bhris Mo Chridh' On Dh 'Fhalbh Thu* (My Heart Is Broken Since Thy Departure) and *Cha Till Mi Tuille* (Never More Shall I Return, or, MacCrimmon's Lament). Her hands have suffered stiffness and the lonely laments waver and hesitate, as do the trembling fingers upon the four taut strings. She is very moved by the ancient music and there are tears within her eyes.

On the night of this day and on this afternoon as well, two of her grandchildren and one great-grandchild will gyrate and play the music of their time, the music of the early 1970s. They are at other destinations on that other road that leads into the larger world. One is in Las Vegas and two on Toronto's Yonge Street strip. They swivel and stomp beneath kaleidoscopic lights, stepping nimbly over the cords that bind their instruments to the high-powered amplifiers. Their long hair floats and swirls about their shoulders and their hard-driving booted heels are as insistent as their rhythms. Here in the quietness of Rankin's Point, at another road's end, the body out of which they came and to which they owe their lives has trouble controlling the last quavering notes of Never More Shall I Return.

"That is the lament of the MacCrimmons," she says when she has finished. "Your grandfather was part MacCrimmon. They were the greatest musicians in the Scottish Highlands. There is a cairn erected to their memory on the Isle of Skye. Your uncles saw it during the war."

"Yes, I know," I say. "You've told me."

"The MacCrimmons were said to be given two gifts," she says, "the gift of music and the gift of foreseeing their own deaths. Those gifts are supposed to follow in all their bloodlines. They are not gifts of the ordinary world."

High on the rafters of the barn that stands outside, my grandfather had written in the blackest of ink the following statement: "We are the children of our own despair, of Skye and Rum and Barra and Tiree." No one knows why he wrote it or when, and even the "how" gives cause for puzzlement. In that time before ballpoint pens or even fountain pens, did he climb such heights holding an ink bottle in one hand and a straight nibbed pen in the other? And what is the significance of ancestral islands long left and never seen? Blown over now by Atlantic winds and touched by scudding foam. What does it mean to all of us that he died as he did? And had he not, how would our grandmother's life have been different and the lives of her children and even mine as I have known it, and still feel it as I sit here on this day?

I can know my grandfather only through recreated images of his life and death. Images of the frozen snow and the hot blood turned to crust upon it; blood, hot and sweet with rum and instantly converted like the sweet and boiling maple sap upon the winter's snow.

I would like to realize and understand now my grandmother's perception of death in all its vast diversity. For even the fixedness of death and the accidents that are its agents have changed throughout the years of her many-sequenced life. Three of her brothers, as young men, perished in the accidental ways that grew out of their lives – lives that were as intensely physical as the deaths that marked their end. One as a young man in the summer sun when the brown-dappled horses bolted and he fell into the teeth of a mowing machine. A second in a storm at sea when the vessel sank while plying its way across the straits to Newfoundland. A third frozen upon the lunar ice fields of early March when the sealing ship became separated from its men in a sudden obliterating blizzard.

How lonely now and distant these lives and deaths of my grandmother's early life. And how different from the lives and deaths of the three sons she has outlived. Men who left the crying gulls and hanging cliffs of Rankin's Point to take the road into the larger world to fashion careers and lives that would never have been theirs on this tiny sea-washed farm. Careers that were as modern and as affluent as the deaths that marked their termination. Real estate brokers and vice-presidents of grocery chains and buyers for haberdashery firms seldom die in the daily routines of the working lives that they have chosen. The pencil and the telephone replace the broken, dangling reins and the marlinespike and the sealing club; and the adjusted thermostats and the methodic Muzak produce a regulated urban order far removed from the uncertainty of the elements and the unpredictability of suddenly frightened animals.

None of these men died at their work or directly from it, yet die they did in deaths that seem even more bizarre and Grecianly ironic than those of the previous generation. One of them choked on a piece of steak in an expensive Montreal restaurant. A second died at Pompano Beach from too much of the sun he had gone to find. The third died while jogging through the streets of Mississauga at five A.M. Yet perhaps death by affluence is but the same in the end as that achieved through physical labour and perhaps it is only because I now have no choice of either that first one and then the other seems desperately more frightening.

Outside the window the blackbirds and cowbirds hop with familiarity around the brindled cows. They call out their raucous comments to one another and sometimes perch boldly upon the cattle's spines. A single, white-tailed hawk glides silently back and forth, sometimes above the land and then beyond the cliff's edge out toward the sea. His shadow slides beneath him across the summer grass but is not reflected within the deep, blue water. It is as if the mirror were perhaps too profound. He does not go far out to sea but circles and climbs and returns across the land; silent and graceful, holding his wings with rigid and controlled beauty, he bears with eloquence the message of his gifted life.

Within the house all is silent except for the ticking of the white Westclox on its shelf above the table. The dogs drowse with half-closed eyes. Lost within our own thoughts, we stay, as in a picture, quiet and immobile for a long, long time.

"Well, I suppose I must get ready. They will soon be here," says my grandmother, rising from her seat at the end of the table and seeming to break the spell.

Within her bedroom which opens off the kitchen, I can see or sense the combing of her long, white hair. She leans to one side and combs it away from her body, her left hand running along its electric smoothness ahead and behind of the comb she wields with her right.

Later she emerges, fastening a brooch of entwined Scottish thistles to the collar of her recently ironed dress. I recognize both the brooch and the dress as gifts that I have purchased for her at earlier times. For an instant I see myself once more in the press of pre-Christmas shoppers in Toronto, jostling and elbowing, moving on and off the crowded elevators and the humming, slanting escalators that stretch between the floors.

I know that in her trunks and scattered jewel boxes there are layers of dresses and mounds of brooches as good as these; yet she has chosen what she has quite consciously. Few of the others, I realize, will recognize what she wears, and there is of course no reason that they should. I am struck once more by the falseness of the brooch, for Scottish thistles do not twine.

Perhaps at the time of its purchase I was being more symbolic than I had ever thought.

Returning to her bedroom she emerges once more with a pair of scissors and draws her chair up close to mine. Without saying anything I begin to trim her fingernails. They are long and yellowed and each is bordered by a thin layer of grime.

Trimming the yellowed, unclean fingernails of my grandmother I realize that I am admitted now to the silent, secret communication that the strong have always known in their relationship with the weak. It is the strength and knowledge that my grandmother has previously so fiercely exercised over her own children and in many cases her children's children as well. The strength and knowledge leading into and from the awful privacy of all our secret inadequacies, which is the standard that the previous generation waves always over the one that follows. The awareness and memory of dirty diapers and bed wettings and the first attempts at speech and movement; of the birth and death of Santa Claus and of the myriad childish hopes and fears of the lost time; of the lonely screaming nightmares of childhood terror; of nocturnal emissions and of real and imagined secret sins. The strength and knowledge of actual physical support and the giving and sustaining of such physical life and perhaps even love. I have never thought of my grandmother so much in terms of love as in terms of strength. Perhaps, I think now, because the latter has always been so much more visible.

Down in the village at this time I imagine my own father, now nearing seventy, preparing for his journey here to meet us. Nervously brushing his snow-white hair and slapping his face with talcum powder, still half-afraid of his mother's inspection, bound too by those complex cords of strength and knowledge. He cannot, of course, remember ever seeing the father that was his own.

Suddenly my grandmother seizes my right hand and presses it fiercely between both of hers. The scissors that I have held clatter to the floor and I can feel the intensity of her life yearning and pressing outward through the pressure of her palms. "Oh, Calum," she says, "what are you going to do with the rest of your life?"

I do not know whether I am more shocked by the unexpectedness of the question or by what seems to be its enormity, given the circumstances. The doctor has said that I should try to live "the rest of my life" in as normal a fashion as possible. I have, he has said, "perhaps some months," in which I may continue to live and to appear as normal. I am reminded of the summer chickens outside my grandmother's door, doomed by their time of life not to survive the fall.

"Oh stay with me, Calum," she says, "and I will tell them so when they come. Find yourself a nice girl and get married. You are twenty-six and it is time to be thinking of such things. You have always liked it here, and the land and the animals are as good as ever. You can make a good life here for all of us. I have left you everything in my will."

Outside the window I see the piles of roughened field stones picked by the strong, worn fingers of my grandmother's hands in earlier times. I see the falling rail fences and the outbuildings in need of paint and shingles. And the barn that contains my grandfather's only message. This is the "everything" left to me,

I am told, by my grandmother's will. Yet no one has ever given me "everything" before, and it is true that I have always liked it here amidst the loneliness and the privacy and the crying gulls. And I have thought of it many times during my "absent" years spent teaching the over-urbanized high school students of Burlington and Don Mills in the classrooms that always seemed so overheated. I have returned now, I think, almost as the diseased and polluted salmon, to swim for a brief time in the clear waters of my earlier stream. The returning salmon knows of no "cure" for the termination of his life.

I feel the blackened dizziness as it swirls within my head and clutch the chair's seat for support.

"What is the matter with you?" asks my grandmother. "You look like you are going to faint. Do you want a drink of water?"

"No," I say. "It will soon pass. It will soon be over."

The dogs, as if in concert, lift their heads and cock their ears and rise from their recumbent positions to move toward the door. They have heard the cars grinding along the cliff's edge some miles away. Neither my grandmother nor I can hear anything but we know that we are seeing the coming of sound to finer ears than ours. It is almost as if we can see the sound itself through an exchanging of the senses. Sometimes by looking at the face of the person on the telephone, you can see the nature of the news that is received although your ears hear only the silence that is no sound at all.

"They are coming," says my grandmother, giving a final pat to her hair.

The distant procession consists of members of her family, and they are bound on an expedition which might best be entitled "What to do about Grandma?" It is an expedition which has set out with various degrees of optimism for the past fifteen years or so, and it has always been launched in the summer when the maximum forces are available. In the summer, numbers of my grandmother's children and grandchildren and great-grandchildren and even great-great-grandchildren return from their scattered destinations on the roads of the larger world. Joining forces with the relatives who are residents of the region, they map and plan strategies which they hope will suit their purpose. Each year in the face of pleas and tears and petitions and almost threats, my grandmother has remained firm in her refusal to be moved from this her home. I see her quietly gathering her inner resources now, preparing her front of strength almost as if she is checking out her equipment. Images of old Cecil B. DeMille spectaculars come to mind, those pictures in which the attackers are repulsed from their desired heights by having boulders rolled down upon them or balls of flaming fire; sometimes they feel their scaling ladders tipped backwards so that they fall with screams and outstretched limbs. And yet our sympathy seems never to lie with them, but instead with those who are besieged.

This year's strategy involves the nursing home in the village below and it is planned as an alternative to last year's failure which was called "living with us" and which was put forth by different people who varied greatly in their enthusiasm and reluctance. The advantages of the nursing home are "privacy" and "being with people near her own age" and "not having to worry about her meals" and receiving what is vaguely described as "care." There are various other "advantages" of the same type. On and on.

My grandmother has visited the nursing home at different times to see certain people who are her friends, and she has hated it as much as do the friends she goes to see. Clutching her fingers in parchment hands they whisper to her in Gaelic which most of the staff can no longer understand. They tell her of real and imagined atrocities: that when the visitors leave the staff steal the Kleenex and the chocolates, that poison is being put in the food, that they are strapped to armchairs and wheelchairs for a long time, sitting in their own excrement and urine until their heads flop over onto their shoulders. What does it mean that old women in nursing homes suffer from real and imagined atrocities? And are the imagined ones less terrifying because they are not true?

Perhaps all of us, if we think of it, can see ourselves at some future time unable to use the bedpan in some place called Sunny Brae or Sunny Brook or Sunny Acres or Sunshine Villa; listening while the nurses' aides chew gum and talk about their dates (also real and imagined), "Oh he didn't." "Did he?" "You've got to be kidding!" Having our bodies hosed down by people who know too much about bodies and what they do or fail to do and how they finally end. This now I know is bearing down on me. It is ironically too distant and too close.

Once more I am concerned with my falseness and my cowardice. For I have been sent here on this day even as I have come of my own volition. I have been sent to make the initial request of my grandmother. "Perhaps she will go if Calum asks her," they have said. "If anyone can convince her, it will be Calum." But Calum has done nothing but sit here all this morning. He has done nothing because he does not believe in this year's strategy any more than he did in that of the previous year. And in a secret place within his heart he hopes that it will fail.

Now as the cars begin to appear before the pole gate, I see myself as the failed advance rider sent out to scout the territory for the war party that is to follow. Or as an upside-down St. John the Baptist sent to prepare a false way for unlikely prophets. Or as the anguished and befuddled Judas already too close to his halter. At least I will not have to kiss her on the cheek.

After the cars have rolled into the yard, the people spill from them in all their vast variety. I stand at the door as an uncertain welcoming committee of one while my grandmother sits inside as she always does on such occasions. They are almost as a group of brightly coloured summer birds, these members of my family, chatting and laughing in plaid pants (with and without cuffs) and floral tops and sport shirts. Slacks, flares, denims, sandals and various "looks" that come from the variety of the worlds they inhabit and the ages that they are going through. Vaguely I think that they do not look much like people who are supposed to have the "gift" of foreseeing their own deaths.

They move into the house, smiling at me and patting me on the shoulder, some of them looking hopefully into my eyes for any message that might be found. Within the house, which has not enough chairs, they arrange themselves as best they can, the children sitting on the floor with their arms around their knees. Soon they will run outside to play or to be frightened by the animals that are so alien to many of them, but for the present they must sit quietly because it is "polite."

Soon they begin to take the pictures. "Here is one of three generations," they say. "And now one of you and Mary and the baby. Four generations." Dutifully my grandmother holds her latest great-grandchild on her lap while her son and his daughter stand on either side of her. The people appear frozen as they look into the camera's lens.

Once as boys in the summer following the last year of high school, my first cousin and I worked with my uncle on a ship taking barrels of salt fish to the islands of the West Indies and bringing back puncheons of dark and illegal rum. Upon our return we would anchor off the village in the still summer nights while the small local fishing boats plied diligently back and forth without lights and with muffled engines, landing the puncheons on the sandy beaches for the men who waited for them in the darkened pickup trucks.

Once, in Jamaica, my cousin and I were stopped on a street by a boy our own age who showed us a card and asked us to follow him. He took us to a brothel which was so unlike anything we had ever seen that we were actually afraid. When we finally convinced him we did not want "fun" he ushered us into the "picture room" which was only slightly less spectacular. Beautiful girls of all colours and races were being photographed in erotic poses with frightened young men who were about our own age. They undressed the young men and twined their hair about their genitals and brushed their penises with their lips. An energetic little dark-skinned man raced from one posing couple to the next, wheeling a bulky camera before him, shouting directions and asking the first names of the young men. Periodically he would disappear behind a curtain and emerge with the pictures. Across the front of each picture the same hand had written almost identical messages: "To John, my one and only love, Zelda." "To Tim, my one and only love, Tanya." "To George, my one and only love, Goldie."

"Coast Guard, mon!" said our acquaintance. Later we learned that the frightened and virginal-looking young men were members of a group of naval cadets from a Florida-based ship. They would keep the pictures in their wallets and show them secretly to their future friends, saying something like, "That's my girlfriend back home," and wait for the appreciative wows.

I think now that the photographs being taken here today share that same artificiality. In the family groupings in which people are relentlessly encouraged to smile, one cannot always see the desperate hopes and fears that flutter behind the eyes, or fully reach the darkest truth.

Glancing through the window I see my grandmother's maroon-coloured horses and darkly brindled cattle moving about the automobiles that seem to fill the yard. Some of the automobiles bear the names of animals: Mustang, Pinto, Maverick. Soon children will have to be dispatched so that the real animals will not scratch or mar their metallized near-namesakes.

As the afternoon moves on, the conversation rises and falls. People take flasks of rum from their pockets and pour drinks. My father and my uncles and aunts take the violin from its peg and play the complicated jigs and reels gracefully and without effort. All of them grasp the bow in the same spot and in the same manner and bend their wrists in an identical way. It is a style older than any of our memories and produces what we call "our sound." People remove harmonicas from handbags and pockets and the younger ones bring in guitars. Others rattle the kitchen spoons between their fingers and upon their thighs. My grandmother dances with each of her sons and then with the other men. She swings lightly and easily within my arms. There is no one in the nursing home who has lived as long as she.

The afternoon grows heightened and more animated while the question hovers like a whining, buzzing insect at the backs of all our minds. No one dares ask it and yet we are afraid to leave. From time to time people look hopefully toward me, raising their eyebrows, looking for a sign. My grandmother continues to dance and swing with easy grace. She is getting through her day. *If I can only hang on for another little while,* her eyes seem to say, *I can win this. I will not be defeated.* I think of her at twenty-six, pregnant and surrounded by weeping children, pulling home the frozen corpse of her husband on a children's sleigh. Perhaps saying the same thing. I cannot fathom how many times she must have said it in the seventy years between.

Too well I know all of the reasons put forth against her staying here. That it is lonely and isolated. That the house is old and heated only by stoves and illuminated but dimly by kerosene lamps. That there is no telephone. That in the winter, members of her family must bring up her few groceries on snowmobiles when they can get through, and that they are uncertain of what they then might find. That the animals are awkward and expensive and that she might fall and stumble while moving about them within their winter barns.

But I know also, as do most of us here, those other aspects of her life. Her dislike of institutions and her scorn of the "ease" associated with them. After her husband's death it was suggested by "authorities" from Halifax that she could never survive here and that it would "be better for everyone" if she were to move or put some of her children up for adoption or even in an orphanage. It would be "easier," they said. All of us here in this overcrowded room in the early 1970s with our rum and with our music are in some ways the result of her contradiction of such suggestions. Seventy years later. "I would never have my children taken from me to be scattered about like the down of a dead thistle," she has often said. "I would not be that dead. It does not matter that some things are difficult. No one has ever said that life is to be easy. Only that it is to be lived." I have come today, partially at least, hoping to find such strength for the living of my life and the meeting of my death.

The music stops and the sun moves westward. Younger children begin to whisper in their parents' ears that they are hungry and that they would like to leave. The tension seems to mount and crackle. We are waiting for the lightning that will provide us with release; looking at the balancing stone and waiting for its fall.

Suddenly and unexpectedly my grandmother says, "I hope none of you are worrying about me. Calum has said that he is going to stay here with me and now everything will be just fine."

There is a period of unbelieving silence followed by a great gush of relief. As if the plug of a bathtub or the valve of a tire has suddenly set free the contents that had been so controlled and well contained. People look at one another and at me in stunned amazement. The solution seems so perfect that it is almost impossible to comprehend. Much too good really to be true. My parents look at me in wonder that is mingled with relief. They have been uncertain concerning my unexpected return here from Ontario with what seems like no thought of ever going back. "Perhaps he will teach in the high school here," I have heard them say to one another. "Perhaps he is tired and needs a rest." I have not told them or anyone else that I have returned because I know I am to die and do not know where else to do it.

Now it seems that their questions have been temporarily answered and they are glad to know that I have had some plan during the days of this past time. They nod their heads and smile across the room, though still in wonder. My grandmother smiles as if she has just played her great trump card and looks about her in temporary triumph. I have not the courage to destroy the lie she so wishes to be true.

Almost immediately there is a great movement toward departure. It is as if they are afraid that their unexpected and magical gift might suddenly vanish should they stay too long within its presence. "Good-bye for now," they say. "See you later." "So long." "Take care."

The car doors slam, the motors start and the tires turn. The poles of the gate are slid back and then replaced by my father who is the last to leave. He waves to my grandmother and to me as we remain standing in the doorway. He is the middle link of our three generations. Then he too gets into his car beside my mother and drives away. We are left all alone.

Going back into the kitchen my grandmother busies herself in setting out the supper dishes. She takes the plates from the shelves and the knives and forks from the sliding drawers. The dogs who have been outside for most of the afternoon now return to flop upon the floor and resume their roles of quiet watchfulness. The sun is moving toward the sea.

"It is no good, Grandma," I say finally. "It is not going to work."

"What?" she says, keeping her back to me and reaching for the cups and saucers.

"What you told them. That I will stay here. It is not going to work." For a moment I teeter in hesitation but it seems that now I must go on. "It is not going to work," I say, "because I am going to die."

She turns and looks at me sharply and there is a flicker of fear upon her face which she banishes quickly. "Yes, I know," she laughs. "We all are. Sometime."

"It is no longer sometime," I say. "It is very soon. Only months. I am not going to see another spring. I will be of no use to you here nor any to myself. The doctors have said so."

"Don't be silly," she says. "You are only twenty-six. Your life is just beginning."

She looks at me with almost an indulgent tolerance for the silliness of my ideas and for my distortion of reality. Like the fond mother who is told by her imaginative child that he has seen a giraffe and an elephant upstairs in his bedroom. *I feel great affection for you*, the look says, *even though you do not know what you are talking about.*

For an instant I wish that it were so. To be as silly as she thinks I am and to be back in the time when bruises could be washed away by kisses and for her to be right and me thankfully wrong.

"No," I say. "It is true. Really true."

"What do you mean?" she asks, and now the true note of fear begins to sound in her voice. I wonder if it matches my own.

We sit at opposite ends of the kitchen table and look across at each other, across what seems the vast difference of our separated years. We make some attempts at conversation but they are not very successful.

Suddenly my grandmother leans across the table and grasps my hand in hers. "Oh Calum, Calum," she says. "What are we going to do? What are we going to do? What is to become of us?"

The gesture is almost a replica of the one from the earlier afternoon. In looking at her hands I notice that I have never finished trimming her fingernails. I do not know what to say. She holds my hand so fiercely, as if I might pull her from the dark waters of a dream. I try to respond to the pressure with my own hands, for I too had somehow hoped I might be saved. Suddenly both of us burst into tears. We are weeping for each other and for ourselves. We two who had hoped to find strength in each other meet now instead in only this display of weeping weakness. The dogs cock their ears and whine softly. Moving from one of us to the other they rest their trusting heads upon our laps and look into our eyes.

Sometimes in the darkness of our fear it is difficult to distinguish the dream from the truth. Sometimes we wake from the dream beyond the midnight hour and it is so much better than the world to which we wake that we would will ourselves back into its soothing comfort. Sometimes the reverse is true and we would pinch ourselves or scrape our knuckles against the bed frame's steel. Sometimes the nightmare knows no lines.

Lying rigid now in this bed of my parents' house all the images and emotions of the past day meet and swirl in the outer and inner darkness. The hopes and fears of my past and present jostle and intertwine. Sometimes when seeing the end of our present, our past looms ever larger, because it is all we have or think we know. I feel myself falling back into the past now, hoping to have more and more past as I have less and less future. My twenty-six years are not enough and I would want to go farther and farther back through previous generations so that I might have more of what now seems so little. I would go back through the superstitions and the herbal remedies and the fatalistic war cries and the haunting violins and the cancer cures of cobwebs. Back through the knowledge of being and its end as understood through second sight and spectral visions and the intuitive dog and the sea bird's cry. I would go back to the priest with the magic hands. Back to the faith healer if only I had more faith. Back to anything rather than to die at the objective hands of mute, cold science.

I see that old but young MacCrimmon quietly composing the music of his own death before leaving permanently the darkened shores of his misty Skye. I hear the music now and it is almost like a bell, even as I see him falling silently through the dark. How strange, I think, that anyone should even consider a violin as sounding like a bell.

I get up from my bed and put on my clothes and walk silently and carefully through the sleeping house. Outside it is very quiet. There is no industry in this region and late at night the silence is profound. The music seems to come from the ocean, off the quiet Gulf, and, no, it is not to be confused with anything else. It is not a bird or a radio or a shunting train or a passing car. It is not coming from anyone's party. It is only itself, strangely familiar in its unfamiliar way.

And then almost in response to the bell I hear the howls of the three black-and-white border collies. They come borne on the night's stillness, drifting along the lonely coastline that leads from Rankin's Point. First the oldest dog and then the second and then the third. I can distinguish each dog's cry and I can comprehend the message that their anguished voices bear. I will not be able to save my grandmother now, I know, any more than I was able to save her in the earlier afternoon.

My car follows its probing headlights up and down and around the hairpinned darkness of the road to Rankin's Point. Some of the turns are so extreme that it is easy to overdrive the headlights. Sometimes the lights shine straight ahead into the darkness of the green foliage even as the road cuts unexpectedly to the right or to the left and becomes at least temporarily invisible. I follow it easily as if guided through a dream.

At "The Little Turn of Sadness" my headlights pick up the eyes of the waiting dogs. They are lying in different positions in the middle of the road and their eyes glow out of the darkness like the highlighted points of a waiting triangle. Red and gleaming they serve as markers and as warnings; somewhat, I think, like the signal buoys of the harbour or the lights along an airstrip's edge.

When I leave the car they are glad to see me. *He will know what to do,* they seem to say. They are dogs who for centuries have been bred for the guiding and guarding of life. They are not the guardians of junkyards or used-car lots or closed-down supermarkets. Not the guardians of steel and stone but of lives as fragile and as uncertain as their own. Running silently to protect the sheep from the crumbling cliff or crouched beside the lamb with the broken leg, they have always worked closely with their human masters and have waited for them when faced with problems beyond their strength. Now they are glad that I have come and move toward me.

My grandmother lies in the middle of the road at the spot where the little brook washes over the roadbed before the steepness of the final climb. I kneel beside her and take her hands into mine. They are still warm to the touch and the fingernails are still untrimmed. No need for that now. There are no marks visible upon her body and her eyes are open and stare upwards into the darkness of the sky. The twining Scottish thistles are still pinned to the collar of her dress. This is the ending that we have.

I rise and climb the steep road until I am standing at the cliff's edge which faces out to sea. I turn my head to the left and try to look up the coast to the home and buildings of Rankin's Point, but I cannot see in the darkness. For the first time in the centuries since the Scottish emigrations there is no human life at the end of this dark road. I turn again to the open sea and concentrate very hard on seeing something but it is no use. My grandmother cannot see Prince Edward Island now nor ever will again. I look down into the darkness beneath my feet but there too there is only a darkened void although I can hear the water lapping gently on the boulders far below.

The music that my grandmother played in the long-ago morning of this day moves slowly through my mind. I cannot tell if it comes from without or from within and then it does not seem to matter. The darkness rises within me in dizzying swirls and seems to yearn for that other darkness that lies without. I reach for the steadying gate post or the chair's firm seat but there is nothing for the hand to touch. And then as with the music, the internal and the external darkness reach to become as one. Flowing toward one another they become enjoined and indistinct and as single as perfection. Without a seam, without a sound, they meet and unite all.

The Closing Down of Summer

(1 9 7 6)

It is August now, towards the end, and the weather can no longer be trusted. All summer it has been very hot. So hot that the gardens have died and the hay has not grown and the surface wells have dried to dampened mud. The brooks that flow to the sea have dried to trickles and the trout that inhabit them and the inland lakes are soft and sluggish and gasping for life. Sometimes they are seen floating dead in the over-warm water, their bodies covered with fat grey parasites. They are very unlike the leaping, spirited trout of spring, battling and alive in the rushing, clear, cold water; so electrically filled with movement that it seems no parasite could ever lodge within their flesh.

The heat has been bad for fish and wells and the growth of green, but for those who choose to lie on the beaches of the summer sun the weather has been ideal. This is a record year for tourists in Nova Scotia, we are constantly being told. More motorists have crossed the border at Amherst than ever before. More cars have landed at the ferry docks in Yarmouth. Motels and campsites have been filled to capacity. The highways are heavy with touring buses and camper trailers and cars with the inevitable lobster traps fastened to their roofs. Tourism is booming as never before.

Here on this beach, on Cape Breton's west coast, there are no tourists. Only ourselves. We have been here for most of the summer. Surprised at the endurance and consistency of the heat. Waiting for it to break and perhaps to change the spell. At the end of July we said to ourselves and to each other, "The August gale will come and shatter all of this." The August gale is the traditional storm that comes each August, the forerunner of the hurricanes that will sweep up from the Caribbean and beat and lash this coast in the months of autumn. The August gale with its shrieking winds and crashing muddied waves has generally signalled the unofficial end of summer and it may come in August's very early days. But this year, as yet, it has not come and there are only a few days left. Still we know that the weather cannot last much longer and in another week the tourists will be gone and the schools will reopen and the pace of life will change. We will have to gather ourselves together then in some way and make the decisions that we have been postponing in the back of our minds. We are perhaps the best crew of shaft and development miners in the world and we were due in South Africa on the seventh of July.

But as yet we have not gone and the telegrams from Renco Development in Toronto have lain unanswered and the telephone calls have been unreturned. We are waiting for the change in the weather that will make it impossible for us to lie longer on the beach and then we will walk, for the final time, the steep and winding zigzagged trail that climbs the rocky face of Cameron's Point. When we reach the top of the cliff we will all be breathing heavily and then we will follow the little path that winds northward along the cliff's edge to the small field where our cars are parked, their hoods facing out to sea and their front tires scant feet from the cliffside's edge. The climb will take us some twenty minutes but we are all still in good shape after a summer of idleness.

The golden little beach upon which we lie curves in a crescent for approximately three-quarters of a mile and then terminates at either end in looming cliffs. The north cliff is called Cameron's Point after the family that once owned the land, but the south cliff has no name. Both cliffs protect the beach, slowing the winds from both north and south and preserving its tranquillity.

At the south cliff a little brook ends its journey and plummets almost vertically some fifty feet into the sea. Sometimes after our swims or after lying too long in the sand, we stand underneath its fall as we would a shower, feeling the fresh water fall upon our heads and necks and shoulders and run down our bodies' lengths to our feet which stand within the sea.

All of us have stood and turned our naked bodies unknown, unaccountable times beneath the spraying shower nozzles of the world's mining developments. Bodies that when free of mud and grime and the singed-hair smell of blasting powder are white almost to the colour of milk or ivory. Perhaps of leprosy. Too white to be quite healthy; for when we work we are often twelve hours in the shaft's bottom or in the development drifts, and we do not often feel the sun. All summer we have watched our bodies change their colour and seen our hair grow bleached and ever lighter. Only the scars that all of us bear fail to respond to the healing power of the sun's heat. They seem to stand out even more vividly now, long running pink welts that course down our inner forearms or jagged saw-toothed ridges on the taut calves of our legs.

Many of us carry one shoulder permanently lower than the other where we have been hit by rockfalls or the lop of the giant clam that swings down upon us in the narrow closeness of the shaft's bottom. And we have arms that we cannot raise above our heads, and touches of arthritis in our backs and in our shoulders, magnified by the water that chills and falls upon us in our work. Few of us have all our fingers and some have lost either eyes or ears from falling tools or discharged blasting caps or flying stone or splintering timbers. Yet it is damage to our feet that we fear most of all. For loss of toes or damage to the intricate bones of heel or ankle means that we cannot support our bodies for the gruelling twelve-hour stand-up shifts. And injury to one foot means that the other must bear double its weight, which it can do for only a short time before poor circulation sets in to numb the leg and make it, too, inoperative. All of us are big men, over six feet tall and near two hundred pounds, and our feet have at the best of times a great deal of pressure bearing down upon them.

We are always intensely aware of our bodies and the pains that course and twinge through them. Even late at night when we would sleep they jolt us unexpectedly as if from an electric current, bringing tears to our eyes and causing our fists to clench in the whiteness of knuckles and the biting of nails into palms. At such times we desperately shift our positions, or numb ourselves from the tumblers of alcohol we keep close by our sides.

Lying now upon the beach we see the external scars on ourselves and on each other and are stirred to the memories of how they occurred. When we are clothed the price we pay for what we do is not so visible as it is now.

Beside us on the beach lie the white Javex containers filled with alcohol. It is the purest of moonshine made by our relatives back in the hills and is impossible to buy. It comes to us only as a gift or in exchange for long-past favours: bringing home of bodies, small loans of forgotten dollars, kindnesses to now-dead grandmothers. It is as clear as water, and a teaspoonful of it when touched by a match will burn with the low blue flame of a votive candle until it is completely consumed, leaving the teaspoon hot and totally dry. When we are finished here we will pour what remains into forty-ounce vodka bottles and take it with us on the long drive to Toronto. For when we decide to go we will be driving hard and fast and all of our cars are big: Cadillacs with banged-in fenders and Lincolns and Oldsmobiles. We are often stopped for speeding on the stretch outside Mt. Thom, or going through the Wentworth Valley, or on the narrow road to Fredericton, or on the fast straight road that leads from Rivière-du-Loup to Lévis, sometimes even on the 401. When we say that we must leave for Africa within hours we are seldom fined or in odd instances are allowed to pay our speeding fines upon the spot. We do not wish to get into the entanglement of moonshine brought across provincial lines and the tedium that accompanies it. The fine for open commercial liquor is under fifteen dollars in most places and the transparent vodka bottles both show and keep their simple secret.

But we are not yet ready to leave, and in the sun we pour the clear white fluid into styrofoam cups and drink it in long burning swallows, sometimes following such swallows with mouthfuls of Teem or Sprite or Seven-Up. No one bothers us here because we are so inaccessible. We can see any figure that would approach us from more than a mile away, silhouetted on the lonely cliff and the rocky and treacherous little footpath that is the only route to where we are. None of the RCMP who police this region are in any way local and it is unlikely that they even know this beach exists. And in the legal sense there is no public road that leads to the cliff where our cars now stand. Only vague paths and sheep trails through the burnt-out grass and around the clumps of alders and blueberry bushes and protruding stones and rotted stumps. The resilient young spruce trees scrape against the mufflers and oilpans of our cars and scratch against the doors. Hundreds of miles hence, when we stop by the roadsides in Quebec and Ontario, we will find small sprigs of this same spruce still wedged within the grillework of our cars or stuck beneath the headlight bulbs. We will remove them and take them with us to Africa as mementos or talismans or symbols of identity. Much as our Highland ancestors, for centuries, fashioned crude badges of heather or of whortleberries to accompany them on the battlefields of the world. Perhaps so that in the closeness of their work with death they might find nearness to their homes and an intensified realization of themselves. We are lying now in the ember of summer's heat and in the stillness of its time.

Out on the flatness of the sea we can see the fishermen going about their work. They do not make much money any more and few of them take it seriously. They say that the grounds have been over-fished by the huge factory fleets from Russia, Spain and Portugal. And it is true that on the still warm nights we can see the lights of such floating factories shining brightly off the coast. They appear as strange, moveable, brilliant cities and when they are far out their blazing lights seem to mingle with those of the stars. The fishermen before us are older men or young boys. Grandfathers with their grandsons acting out their ancient rituals. At noon or at one or two, before they start for home, they will run their little boats into our quiet cove until their bows are almost touching the sand. They will toss us the gleaming blue-black mackerel and the silver herring and the brown-and-white striped cod and talk to us for a while, telling us anything that they think we should know. In return we toss them the whitened Javex bottles so that they may drink the pure clear contents. Sometimes the older men miss the toss and the white cylindrical bottles fall into the sea where they bob and toss like marker buoys or a child's duck in the bathtub until they are gaffed by someone in the boat or washed back in to shore. Later we cook the fish over small, crackling driftwood fires. This, we know too, cannot go on much longer.

In the quiet graveyards that lie inland the dead are buried. Behind the small white wooden churches and beneath the monuments of polished black granite they take their silent rest. Before we leave we will visit them to pray and take our last farewell. We will perhaps be afraid then, reading the dates of our brothers and uncles and cousins; recalling their youth and laughter and the place and manner of each death.

Death in the shafts and in the drifts is always violent and very often the body is so crushed or so blown apart that it can not be reassembled properly for exposure in the coffin. Most of us have accompanied the grisly remains of such bodies trussed up in plastic bags on trains and planes and automobiles, and delivered them up to the local undertaker. During the two or three days of the final wake and through the lonely all-night vigils kept in living rooms and old-fashioned parlours only memories and youthful photographs recall the physical reality that lies so dismembered and disturbed within each grey, sealed coffin. The most flattering photograph is placed upon the coffin's lid in an attempt to remind us of what was. I am thinking of this now, of the many youthful deaths I have been part of, and of the long homeward journeys in other seasons of other years. The digging of graves in the bitterness of February's cold, the shovelling of drifts of snow from the barren earth, and then the banging of the pick into the frozen ground, the striking of sparks from steel on stone and the scraping of shovels on earth and rock.

Some twenty years ago, when first I went to the uranium shafts of Ontario's Elliot Lake and short-lived Bancroft, we would have trouble getting our dead the final few miles to their high white houses. Often, in winter, we would have to use horses and sleighs to get them up the final hills, standing in chest-high snow, taking out window casings so that we might pass the coffin in and then out again for the last time. Or sometimes in the early spring we would again have to resort to horses when the leaving of the frost and the melting of the winter snow turned the brooks into red and roiling rivers and caused the dirt roads that led into the hills to become greasy and impassable. Sometimes in such seasons the underground springs beneath such roads erupt into tiny geysers, shooting their water upward and changing the roadbeds around them into quivering bogs that bury vehicles up to their hubs and axles.

And in November the rain is chill and cold at the graveside's edge. It falls upon our necks and splatters the red mud upon our gleaming shoes and on the pantlegs of our expensive suits. The bagpiper plays "Flowers of the Forest," as the violinist earlier played his haunting laments from the high choir loft. The music causes the hair to bristle on the backs of our necks and brings out the wildness of our grief and dredges the depths of our dense dark sorrow. At the graveside people sometimes shout farewells in Gaelic or throw themselves into the mud or upon the coffin as it is being lowered on its straps into the gaping earth.

Fifteen years ago when the timbers gave way in Springdale, Newfoundland, my younger brother died, crushed and broken amidst the constant tinkle of the dripping water, and lying upon a bed of tumbled stone. We could not get him up from the bottom in time, as his eyes bulged from his head and the fluids of his body seeped quietly onto the glistening rock. Yet even as we tried we realized our task was hopeless and that he would not last, even on the surface. Would not last long enough for any kind of medical salvation. And even as the strength of his once-powerful grip began to loosen on my hand and his breath to rattle in his throat, we could see the earthly road that stretched before us as the witnesses and survivors of his death: the report to the local authorities, the statements to the company, to the police, to the coroner and then the difficult phone calls made on badly connected party lines or, failing those, the more efficient and more impersonal yellow telegrams. The darkness of the midnight phone call seems somehow to fade with the passing of time, or to change and be recreated like the ballads and folktales of the distant lonely past. Changing with each new telling as the tellers of the tales change, as they become different, older, more bitter or more serene. It is possible to hear descriptions of phone calls that you yourself have made some ten or fifteen years ago and to recognize very little about them except the undeniable kernel of truth that was at the centre of the messages they contained. But the yellow telegram is more blunt and more permanent in the starkness of its message and it is never, ever thrown away. It is kept in vases and in Bibles and in dresser drawers beneath white shirts and it is stumbled upon sometimes unexpectedly, years later, sometimes by other hands, in little sandalwood boxes containing locks of the baby's hair or tucked inside the small shoes in which he learned to walk. A simple obituary of a formal kind.

When my brother died in Springdale, Newfoundland, it was the twenty-first of October and when we brought his body home we were already deep into fall. On the high hardwood hills the mountain ash and the aspen and the scarlet maple were ablaze with colour beneath the weakened rays of the autumn sun. On alternate days the rain fell; sometimes becoming sleet or small hard hailstones. Sometimes the sun would shine in the morning, giving way to the vagaries of precipitation in the afternoon. And sometimes the cloud cover would float over the land even as the sun shone, blocking the sun out temporarily and casting shadows as if a giant bird were passing overhead. Standing beneath such a gliding cloud and feeling its occasional rain we could see the sun shining clearly at a distance of only a mile away. Seeing warmth so reachably near while feeling only the cold of the icy rain. But at the digging of his grave there was no sun at all. Only the rain falling relentlessly down upon us. It turned the crumbling clay to the slickest of mud, as slippery and glistening as that of the potter's wheel but many times more difficult to control. When we had dug some four feet down, the earthen walls began to slide and crumble and to give way around us and to fall upon our rubber boots and to press against the soaking pantlegs that clung so clammily to our blue-veined legs. The deeper we dug, the more intensely the rain fell, the drops dripping from our eyebrows and from our noses and the icy trickles running down the backs of our necks and down our spines and legs and into our squishing and sucking boots. When we had almost reached the required depth one of the walls that had been continuously crumbling and falling suddenly collapsed and with a great whoosh rolled down upon us. We were digging in our traditional family plot and when the wall gave way it sent the box that contained my father's coffin sliding down upon us. He had been dead for five years then, blown apart in Kirkland Lake, and at the time of his burial his coffin had been sealed. We were wildly and irrationally frightened by the slide and braced our backs against the splintered and disintegrating box, fearful lest it should tip and fall upon us and spill and throw whatever rotting relics remained of that past portion of our lives. Of little flesh but maybe green decaying bones or strands of silver matted hair.

We had held it there, braced by our backs in the pouring rain, until timbers were brought to shore up the new grave's side and to keep the past dead resting quietly. I had been very frightened then, holding the old dead in the quaking mud so that we might make room for the new in that same narrow cell of sliding earth and cracking wood. The next day at his funeral the rain contin- ued to fall and in the grave that received him the unsteady timbers and the ground they held so temporarily back seemed but an extension of those that had caused his life to cease.

Lying now in the precarious heat of this still and burning summer I would wish that such thoughts and scenes of death might rise like the mists from the new day's ocean and leave me dry and somehow emptied on this scorching fine-grained sand.

In Africa it will be hot, too, in spite of the coming rainy season, and on the veldt the heat will shimmer and the strange, fine-limbed animals will move across it in patterns older than memory. The nomads will follow their flocks of bleating goats in their constant search for grass and moisture, and the women will carry earthen jars of water on their heads or baskets of clothes to slap against the rocks where the water is found.

In my own white house my wife does her declining wash among an increasingly bewildering battery of appliances. Her kitchen and her laundry room and her entire house gleam with porcelain and enamel and an ordered cleanliness that I can no longer comprehend. Little about me or about my work is clean or orderly and I am always mildly amazed to find the earnings of the violence and dirt in which I make my living converted into such meticulous brightness. The lightness of white and yellow curtains rustling crisply in the breeze. For us, most of our working lives are spent in rough, crude bunkhouses thrown up at the shafthead's site. Our bunks are made of two-by-fours sometimes roughly hammered together by ourselves, and we sleep two men to a room or sometimes four or sometimes in the development's early stages in the vast "ram pastures" of twenty or thirty or perhaps even forty men crowded together in one vast, rectangular, unpartitioned room. Such rooms are like hospital wards without the privacy of the dividing curtains and they are filled, constantly, day and night, with the sounds of men snoring and coughing or spitting into cans by their bedsides, the incoherent moans and mumbles of uneasy sleepers and the thuds of half-conscious men making groaning love to their passive pillows. In Africa we will sleep, mostly naked, under incongruous structures of mosquito netting, hearing the occasional rain on the roofs of corrugated iron. In the near twenty-four-hour winter darkness of the Yukon, we have slept in sleeping bags, weighted down with blankets and surrounded by various heaters, still to wake to our breath as vapour in the coldness of the flashlight's gleam.

It is difficult to explain to my wife such things, and we have grown more and more apart with the passage of the years. Meeting infrequently now almost as shy strangers, communicating mostly over vast distances through ineffectual say-nothing letters or cheques that substitute money for what once was conceived as love. Sometimes the cheques do not even come from me, for in the developing African nations the political situation is often uncertain and North American money is sometimes suddenly and almost whimsically "frozen" or "nationalized," making it impossible to withdraw or remove. In times and places of such uneasiness, shaft crews such as ours often receive little or no actual money, only slips of paper to show our earnings, which are deposited in the metropolitan banks of New York or Toronto or London and from which our families are issued monthly cheques.

I would regain what was once real or imagined with my wife. The long nights of passionate lovemaking that seemed so short, the creating and birth of our seven children. Yet I was never home for the birth of any of my children, only for their fathering. I was not home when two of them died so shortly after birth, and I have not been home to participate or to share in many of the youthful accomplishments of the other five. I have attended few parents' nights or eighth-grade graduations or father-and-son hockey banquets, and broken tricycle wheels and dolls with crippled limbs have been mended by other hands than mine.

Now my wife seems to have gone permanently into a world of avocado appliances and household cleanliness and vicarious experiences provided by the interminable soap operas that fill her television afternoons. She has perhaps gone as deeply into that life as I have into the life of the shafts, seeming to tunnel ever downward and outward through unknown depths and distances and to become lost and separated and unavailable for communication. Yet we are not surprised or critical of each other for she, too, is from a mining family and grew up largely on funds sent home by an absentee father. Perhaps we are but becoming our previous generation.

And yet there are times, even now, when I can almost physically feel the summer of our marriage and of our honeymoon and of her singing the words of the current popular songs into my then-attentive ears. I had been working as part of a crew in Uranium City all winter and had been so long without proper radio reception that I knew nothing of the music of that time's hit parade. There was always a feeling of mild panic then, on hearing whole dance floors of people singing aloud songs that had come and flourished since my departure and which I had never heard. As if I had been on a journey to the land of the dead.

It would be of little use now to whisper popular lyrics into my ears for I have become partially deaf from the years of the jackleg drill's relentless pounding into walls of constant stone. I cannot hear much of what my wife and children say to me, and communicate with the men about me through nods and gestures and the reading of familiar lips. Musically, most of us have long abandoned the modern hit parades and have gone, instead, back to the Gaelic songs remembered from our early youth. It is these songs that we hum now on the hotness of this beach and which we will take with us on our journey when we go.

We have perhaps gone back to the Gaelic songs because they are so constant and unchanging and speak to us as the privately familiar. As a youth and as a young man I did not even realize that I could understand or speak Gaelic and entertained a rather casual disdain for those who did. It was not until the isolation of the shafts started that it began to bubble up somehow within me, causing a feeling of unexpected surprise at finding it there at all. As if it had sunk in unconsciously through some strange osmotic process while I had been unwittingly growing up. Growing up without fully realizing the language of the conversations that swirled around me. Now in the shafts and on the beach we speak it almost constantly, though it is no longer spoken in our homes. There is a "Celtic Revival" in the area now, fostered largely by government grants, and the younger children are taught individual Gaelic words in the classrooms for a few brief periods during each month. It is a revival that is very different from our own and it seems, like so much else, to have little relevance for us and to have largely passed us by. Once, it is true, we went up to sing our Gaelic songs at the various Celtic concerts which have become so much a part of the summer culture and we were billed by the bright young schoolteachers who run such things as MacKinnon's Miners' Chorus; but that too seemed as lonely and irrelevant as it was meaningless. It was as if we were parodies of ourselves, standing in rows, wearing our miners' gear, or being asked to shave and wear suits, being plied with rum while waiting for our turn on the program, only then to mouth our songs to batteries of tape recorders and to people who did not understand them. It was as if it were everything that song should not be, contrived and artificial and non-spontaneous and lacking in communication.

I have heard and seen the Zulus dance until they shook the earth. I have seen large splendid men leap and twist and bend their bodies to the hard-baked flatness of the reddened soil. And I have followed their gestures and listened to their shouts and looked into their eyes in the hope that I might understand the meaning of their art. Hoping to find there a message that is recognizable only to primitive men. Yet, though I think I have caught glimpses of their joy, despair or disdain, it seems that in the end they must dance mainly for themselves. Their dancing speaks a language whose true meaning will elude me forever; I will never grasp the full impact of the subtleties and nuances that are spoken by the small head gesture or the flashing fleck of muscle.

I would like to understand more deeply what they have to say in the vague hope that it might be in some way akin to what is expressed in our own singing. That there might be some message that we share. But I can never enter deeply enough into their experience, can never penetrate behind the private mysteries of their eyes. Perhaps, I think sometimes, I am expecting too much. Yet on those occasions when we did sing at the concerts, I would have liked to reach beyond the tape recorders and the faces of the uninvolved to something that might prove to be more substantial and enduring. Yet in the end it seemed we too were only singing to ourselves. Singing songs in an archaic language as we too became more archaic, and recognizing the nods of acknowledgement and shouted responses as coming only from our own friends and relatives. In many cases the same individuals from whom we had first learned our songs. Songs that are for the most part local and private and capable of losing almost all of their substance in translation. Yet in the introduction to the literature text that my eldest daughter brings home from university it states that "the private experience, if articulated with skill, may communicate an appeal that is universal beyond the limitations of time or landscape." I have read that over several times and thought about its meaning in relation to myself.

When I was a boy my father told me that I would never understand the nature of sex until I had participated in it in some worthwhile way, and that there was little point in trying to grasp its meaning through erotic reading or looking at graphic pictures or listening to the real or imagined experiences of older men. As if the written or the spoken word or the mildly pornographic picture were capable of reaching only a small portion of the distance it might hope to journey on the road to understanding. In the early days of such wistful and exploratory reading the sexual act seemed most frequently to be described as "like flying." A boggling comparison at the time to virginal young men who had never been airborne. In the future numbness of our flight to Africa we will find little that is sexual if it is to be like our other flights to such distant destinations.

We will not have much to say about our flight to those we leave behind, and little about our destinations when we land. Sending only the almost obligatory postcards that talk about the weather continents and oceans away. Saying that "things are going as expected," "going well." Postcards that have as their most exciting feature the exotic postage stamps sought after by the younger children for games of show and tell.

I have long since abandoned any hope of describing the sexual act or having it described to me. Perhaps it is enough to know that it is not at all like flying, though I do not know what it is really like. I have never been told, nor can I, in my turn, tell. But I would like somehow to show and tell the nature of my work and perhaps some of my entombed feelings to those that I would love, if they would care to listen.

I would like to tell my wife and children something of the way my years pass by on the route to my inevitable death. I would like to explain somehow what it is like to be a gladiator who fights always the impassiveness of water as it drips on darkened stone. And what it is like to work one's life in the tightness of confined space. I would like somehow to say how I felt when I lost my father in Kirkland Lake or my younger brother in Springdale, Newfoundland. I would like to say how frightened I am sometimes of what I do. And of how I lie awake at night aware of my own decline and of the diminishing of the men around me. For all of us know we will not last much longer and that it is unlikely we will be replaced in the shaft's bottom by members of our own flesh and bone. For such replacement, like our Gaelic, seems to be of the past and now largely over.

Our sons will go to the universities to study dentistry or law and to become fatly affluent before they are thirty. Men who will stand over six feet tall and who will move their fat, pudgy fingers over the limited possibilities to be found in other people's mouths. Or men who sit behind desks shuffling papers relating to divorce or theft or assault or the taking of life. To grow prosperous from pain and sorrow and the desolation of human failure. They will be far removed from the physical life and will seek it out only through jogging or golf or games of handball with friendly colleagues. They will join expensive private clubs for the pleasures of perspiration and they will not die in falling stone or chilling water or thousands of miles from those they love. They will not die in any such manner, partially at least because we have told them not to and have encouraged them to seek out other ways of life which lead, we hope, to gentler deaths. And yet because it seems they will follow our advice instead of our lives, we will experience, in any future that is ours, only an increased sense of anguished isolation and an ironic feeling of confused bereavement. Perhaps it is always so for parents who give the young advice and find that it is followed. And who find that those who follow such advice must inevitably journey far from those who give it, to distant lonely worlds which are forever unknowable to those who wait behind. Yet perhaps those who go find in the regions to which they travel but another kind of inarticulate loneliness. Perhaps the dentist feels mute anguish as he circles his chair, and the lawyer who lives in a world of words finds little relationship between professional talk and what he would hope to be true expression. Perhaps he too in his quiet heart sings something akin to Gaelic songs, sings in an old archaic language private words that reach to no one. And perhaps both lawyer and dentist journey down into an Africa as deep and dark and distant as ours. I can but vaguely imagine what I will never know.

I have always wished that my children could see me at my work. That they might journey down with me in the dripping cage to the shaft's bottom or walk the eerie tunnels of the drifts that end in walls of staring stone. And that they might see how articulate we are in the accomplishment of what we do. That they might appreciate the perfection of our drilling and the calculation of our angles and the measuring of our powder, and that they might understand that what we know through eye and ear and touch is of a finer quality than any information garnered by the most sophisticated of mining engineers with all their elaborate equipment.

I would like to show them how professional we are and how, in spite of the chill and the water and the dark and the danger, there is perhaps a certain eloquent beauty to be found in what we do. Not the beauty of stillness to be found in gleaming crystal or in the polished hardwood floors to which my wife devotes such care but rather the beauty of motion on the edge of violence, which by its very nature can never long endure. It is perhaps akin to the violent motion of the huge professional athletes on the given days or nights of their many games. Men as huge and physical as are we; polished and eloquent in the propelling of their bodies toward their desired goals and in their relationships and dependencies on one another, but often numb and silent before the microphones of sedentary interviewers. Few of us get to show our children what we do on national television; we offer only the numbness and silence by itself. Unable either to show or tell.

I have always wished to be better than the merely mediocre and I have always wanted to use the power of my body in the fulfilling of such a wish. Perhaps that is why I left the university after only one year. A year which was spent mainly as an athlete and as a casual reader of English literature. I could not release myself enough physically and seemed always to be constricted and confined. In sleeping rooms that were too low, by toilet stalls that were too narrow, in lecture halls that were too hot, even by the desks in those lecture halls, which I found always so difficult to get into and out of. Confined, too, by bells and buzzers and curfews and deadlines, which for me had little meaning. I wanted to burst out, to use my strength in some demanding task that would allow me somehow to feel that I was breaking free.

And I could not find enough release in the muddy wars on the football field or in the thudding contact of the enclosed and boarded rink. I suppose I was drawn too by the apparent glamour of the men who followed the shafts. Impressed by their returning here in summer with their fast cars and expensive clothes; also by the fact that I was from a mining family that has given itself for generations to the darkened earth.

I was aware even then of the ultimate irony of my choice. Aware of how contradictory it seemed that someone who was bothered by confinement should choose to spend his working days in the most confined of spaces. Yet the difference seems to be that when we work we are never still. Never merely entombed like the prisoner in the passive darkness of his solitary confinement. For we are always expanding the perimeters of our seeming incarceration. We are always moving downward or inward or forward or, in the driving of our raises, even upward. We are big men engaged in perhaps the most violent of occupations and we have chosen as our adversary walls and faces of massive stone. It is as if the stone of the spherical earth has challenged us to move its weight and find its treasure and we have accepted the challenge and responded with drill and steel and powder and strength and all our ingenuity. In the chill and damp we have given ourselves to the breaking down of walls and barriers. We have sentenced ourselves to enclosures so that we might taste the giddy joy of breaking through. Always hopeful of breaking through, though we know we never will break free.

Drilling and hammering our way to the world's resources, we have left them when found and moved on. Left them for others to expand or to exploit and to make room for the often stable communities that come in our wake: the sewer lines and the fire hydrants and the neat rows of company houses; the over-organized athletic leagues and the ever-hopeful schools; the junior Chambers of Commerce. We have moved about the world, liberating resources, largely untouched by political uncertainties and upheavals, seldom harmed by the midnight plots, the surprising coups and the fast assassinations. We were in Haiti with Duvalier in 1960 and in Chile before Allende and in the Congo before it became associated with Zaire. In Bolivia and Guatemala and in Mexico and in a Jamaica that the tourists never see. Each segment of the world aspires to the treasure, real or imagined, that lies encased in its vaults of stone, and those who would find such booty are readily admitted and handsomely paid, be they employed by dictator or budding democracy or capitalists expanding their holdings and their wealth. Renco Development on Bay Street will wait for us. They will endure our summer on the beach and our lack of response to their seemingly urgent messages. They will endure our Toronto drunkenness and pay our bail and advance us personal loans. And when we go they will pay us thousands of dollars for our work, optimistically hoping that they may make millions in their turn. They will wait for us because they know from years of many contracts that we are the best bet to deliver for them in the end.

There are two other crews in Canada as strong, perhaps even stronger than we are. They are in Rouyn-Noranda; and as our crew is known as MacKinnon, theirs are known by the names of Lafrenière and Picard. We have worked beside them at various times, competed with them and brawled with them in the hall-like beer parlours of Malarctic and Temiskaming, and occasionally we have saved one another's lives. They will not go to Africa for Renco Development because they are imprisoned in the depths of their language. And because they speak no English they will not move out of Quebec or out of northern or northeastern Ontario. Once there was also the O'Leary crew, who were Irish Newfoundlanders. But many of them were lost in a cave-in in India, and of those who remained most have gone to work with their relatives on high-steel construction in New York. We see them sometimes, now, in the bars of Brooklyn or sometimes in the summers at the ferry terminal in North Sydney before they cross to Port-aux-Basques. Iron work, they say, also pays highly for the risk to life; and the long fall from the towering, swaying skyscrapers can occur for any man but once. It seems, for them, that they have exchanged the possibility of being fallen upon for that of falling itself. And that after years of dodging and fearing falling objects from above, they have become such potential objects themselves. Their loss diminishes us, too, because we know how good they were at what they did, and know, too, that the mangled remnants of their dead were flown from India in sealed containers to lie on such summer days as these beneath the nodding wild flowers that grow on outport graves.

I must not think too much of death and loss, I tell myself repeatedly. For if I am to survive I must be as careful and calculating with my thoughts as I am with my tools when working so far beneath the earth's surface: I must always be careful of sloppiness and self-indulgence lest they cost me dearly in the end.

Out on the ocean now it is beginning to roughen and the southwest wind is blowing the smallish waves into larger versions of themselves. They are beginning to break upon the beach with curling whitecaps at their crests, and the water that they consist of seems no longer blue but rather a dull and sombre grey. There are no longer boats visible on the once-flat sea, neither near at hand nor on the horizon's distant line. The sun no longer shines with the fierceness of the earlier day and the sky has begun to cloud over. Evening is approaching. The sand is whipped by the wind and blows into our faces and stings our bodies as might a thousand pinpricks or the tiny tips of many scorching needles. We flinch and shake ourselves and reach for our protective shirts. We leave our prone positions and come restlessly to our feet, coughing and spitting and moving uneasily like nervous animals anticipating a storm. In the sand we trace erratic designs and patterns with impatient toes. We look at one another, arching our eyebrows like bushy question marks. Perhaps this is what we have been waiting for? Perhaps this is the end and the beginning?

And now I can feel the eyes of the men upon me. They are waiting for me to give interpretations of the signals, waiting for my sign. I hesitate for a moment, running my eyes along the beach, watching water touching sand. And then I nod my head. There is almost a collective sigh that is more sensed than really heard. Almost like distant wind in far-off trees. Then suddenly they begin to move. Rapidly they gather their clothes and other belongings, shaking out the sand, folding and packing. Moving swiftly and with certainty they are closing down their summer even as it is closing down on them. MacKinnon's miners are finished now and moving out. We are leaving the beach of the summer sun and perhaps some of us will not see it any more. For some of us may not return alive from the Africa for which we leave.

We begin to walk. First along the beach toward the north cliff of Cameron's Point, and then up the steep and winding zigzagged trail that climbs its face. When I am halfway up I stop and look back at the men strung out in single file behind me. We are mountain climbers in our way, though bound together by no physical ropes of any kind. They stop and look back, too; back and down to the beach we have so recently vacated. The waves are higher now and are breaking and cresting and rolling farther in. They have obliterated the outlines of our bodies in the sand and our footprints of brief moments before already have been washed away. There remains no evidence that we have ever been. It is as if we have never lain, nor ever walked nor ever thought what thoughts we had. We leave no art or mark behind. The sea has washed its sand slate clean.

And then the rain begins to fall. Not heavily but almost hes-itantly. It is as if it has been hot and dry for so long that the act of raining has almost been forgotten and has now to be slowly and almost painfully relearned

We reach the summit of the cliff and walk along the little path that leads us to our cars. The cars are dusty and their metal is still hot from the earlier sun. We lean across their hoods to lift the windshield wipers from the glass. The rubber of the wiper blades has almost melted into the windshields because of heat and long disuse, and when we lift them, slender slivers of rubber remain behind. These blades will have to be replaced.

The isolated raindrops fall alike on windshield and on roof, on hood and trunk. They trace individual rivulets through the layers of grime and then trickle down to the parched and waiting earth.

And now it is two days later. The rain has continued to fall and in it we have gone about preparing and completing our rituals of farewell. We have visited the banks and checked out all the dates on our insurance policies. And we have gathered our working clothes, which when worn continents hence will make us loom even larger than we are in actual life. As if we are Greek actors or mastodons of an earlier time. Soon to be replaced or else perhaps to be extinct.

We have stood bareheaded by the graves and knelt in the mud by the black granite stones. And we have visited privately and in tiny self-conscious groups the small white churches which we may not see again. As we have become older it seems we have become strangely more religious in ways that border on super-stition. We will take with us worn family rosaries and faded charms, and loop ancestral medals and crosses of delicate worn fragility around our scar-lashed necks and about the thickness of our wrists, seemingly unaware of whatever irony they might project. This, too, seems but a further longing for the past, far removed from the "rational" approaches to religion that we sometimes encounter in our children.

We have said farewells to our children, too, and to our wives, and I have offered kisses and looked into their eyes and wept outwardly and inwardly for all I have not said or done and for my own clumsy failure at communication. I have not been able, as the young say, "to tell it like it is," and perhaps now I never shall.

By four o'clock we are ready to go. Our cars are gathered with their motors running and we will drive them hard and fast and be in Toronto tomorrow afternoon. We will not stop all night except for a few brief moments at the gleaming service stations and we will keep one sober and alert driver at the wheel of each of our speeding cars. Many of the rest of us will numb ourselves with moonshine for our own complex and diverse reasons: perhaps to loosen our thoughts and tongues or perhaps to deaden and hold them down; perhaps to be as the patient who takes an anaesthetic to avoid operational pain. We will hurtle in a dark night convoy across the landscapes and the borders of four waiting provinces.

As we move out, I feel myself a figure in some mediaeval ballad who has completed his formal farewells and goes now to meet his fatalistic future. I do not particularly wish to feel this way and again would shake myself free from thoughts of death and self-indulgence.

As we gather speed the land of the seacoast flashes by. I am in the front seat of the lead car, on the passenger side next to the window. In the side mirror I can see the other cars stretched out behind us. We go by the scarred and abandoned coal workings of our previous generations and drive swiftly westward into the declining day. The men in the back seat begin to pass around their moonshine and attempt to adjust their long legs within the constricted space. After a while they begin to sing in Gaelic, singing almost unconsciously the old words that are so worn and so familiar. They seem to handle them almost as they would familiar tools. I know that in the other cars they are doing the same even as I begin silently to mouth the words myself.

There is no word in Gaelic for good-bye, only for farewell.

More than a quarter of a century ago in my single year at university, I stumbled across an anonymous lyric from the fifteenth century. Last night while packing my clothes I encountered it again, this time in the literature text of my eldest daughter. The book was very different from the one that I had so casually used, as different perhaps as is my daughter from me. Yet the lyric was exactly the same. It had not changed at all. It comes to me now in this speeding car as the Gaelic choruses rise around me. I do not particularly welcome it or want it, and indeed I had almost forgotten it. Yet it enters now, regardless of my wants or wishes, much as one might see out of the corner of the eye an old acquaintance one has no wish to see at all. It comes again, unbidden and unexpected and imperfectly remembered. It seems borne up by the mounting, surging Gaelic voices like the flecked white foam on the surge of the towering, breaking wave. Different yet similar, and similar yet different, and in its time unable to deny:

I wend to death, knight stith in stour;
Through fight in field I won the flower;
No fights me taught the death to quell –
I wend to death, sooth I you tell.

I wend to death, a king iwis;
What helpes honour or worlde's bliss?
Death is to man the final way –
I wende to be clad in clay.

To Every Thing There Is A Season

(1 9 7 7)

 I am speaking here of a time when I was eleven and lived with my family on our small farm on the west coast of Cape Breton. My family had been there for a long, long time and so it seemed had I. And much of that time seems like the proverbial yesterday. Yet when I speak on this Christmas 1977, I am not sure how much I speak with the voice of that time or how much in the voice of what I have since become. And I am not sure how many liberties I may be taking with the boy I think I was. For Christmas is a time of both past and present and often the two are imperfectly blended. As we step into its nowness we often look behind.

We have been waiting now, it seems, forever. Actually, it has been most intense since Hallowe'en when the first snow fell upon us as we moved like muffled mummers upon darkened country roads. The large flakes were soft and new then and almost generous, and the earth to which they fell was still warm and as yet unfrozen. They fell in silence into the puddles and into the sea where they disappeared at the moment of contact. They disappeared, too, upon touching the heated redness of our necks and hands or the faces of those who did not wear masks. We carried our pillowcases from house to house, knocking on doors to become silhouettes in the light thrown out from kitchens (white pillowcases held out by whitened forms). The snow fell between us and the doors and was transformed in shimmering golden beams. When we turned to leave, it fell upon our footprints, and as the night wore on obliterated them and all the records of our movements. In the morning everything was soft and still and November had come upon us.

My brother Kenneth, who is two and a half, is unsure of his last Christmas. It is Hallowe'en that looms largest in his memory as an exceptional time of being up late in magic darkness and falling snow. "Who are you going to dress up as at Christmas?" he asks. "I think I'll be a snowman." All of us laugh at that and tell him Santa Claus will find him if he is good and that he need not dress up at all. We go about our appointed tasks waiting for it to happen.

I am troubled myself about the nature of Santa Claus and I am trying to hang on to him in any way that I can. It is true that at my age I no longer *really* believe in him, yet I have hoped in all his possibilities as fiercely as I can; much in the same way, I think, that the drowning man waves desperately to the lights of the passing ship on the high sea's darkness. For without him, as without the man's ship, it seems our fragile lives would be so much more desperate.

My mother has been fairly tolerant of my attempted perpetuation. Perhaps because she has encountered it before. Once I overheard her speaking about my sister Anne to one of her neighbours. "I thought Anne would *believe* forever," she said. "I practically had to tell her." I have somehow always wished I had not heard her say that as I seek sanctuary and reinforcement even in an ignorance I know I dare not trust.

Kenneth, however, believes with an unadulterated fervour, and so do Bruce and Barry, who are six-year-old twins. Beyond me there is Anne who is thirteen and Mary who is fifteen, both of whom seem to be leaving childhood at an alarming rate. My mother has told us that she was already married when she was seventeen, which is only two years older than Mary is now. That, too, seems strange to contemplate and perhaps childhood is shorter for some than it is for others. I think of this sometimes in the evenings when we have finished our chores and the supper dishes have been cleared away and we are supposed to be doing our homework. I glance sideways at my mother, who is always knitting or mending, and at my father, who mostly sits by the stove coughing quietly with his handkerchief at his mouth. He has "not been well" for over two years and has difficulty breathing whenever he moves at more than the slowest pace. He is most sympathetic of all concerning my extended hopes, and says we should hang on to the good things in our lives as long as we are able. As I look at him out of the corner of my eye, it does not seem that he has many of them left. He is old, we think, at forty-two.

Yet Christmas, in spite of all the doubts of our different ages, is a fine and splendid time, and now as we pass the midpoint of

December our expectations are heightened by the increasing coldness that has settled down upon us. The ocean is flat and calm and along the coast, in the scooped-out coves, has turned to an icy slush. The brook that flows past our house is almost totally frozen and there is only a small channel of rushing water that flows openly at its very centre. When we let the cattle out to drink, we chop holes with the axe at the brook's edge so that they can drink without venturing onto the ice.

The sheep move in and out of their lean-to shelter, restlessly stamping their feet or huddling together in tightly packed groups. A conspiracy of wool against the cold. The hens perch high on their roosts with their feathers fluffed out about them, hardly feeling it worthwhile to descend to the floor for their few scant kernels of grain. The pig, who has little time before his butchering, squeals his displeasure to the cold and with his snout tosses his wooden trough high in the icy air. The splendid young horse paws the planking of his stall and gnaws the wooden cribwork of his manger.

We have put a protective barricade of spruce boughs about our kitchen door and banked our house with additional boughs and billows of eel grass. Still, the pail of water we leave standing in the porch is solid in the morning and has to be broken with the hammer. The clothes my mother hangs on the line are frozen almost instantly and sway and creak from their suspending clothespins like sections of dismantled robots: the stiff-legged rasping trousers and the shirts and sweaters with unyielding arms outstretched. In the morning we race from our frigid upstairs bedrooms to finish dressing around the kitchen stove.

We would extend our coldness half a continent away to the Great Lakes of Ontario so that it might hasten the Christmas coming of my oldest brother, Neil. He is nineteen and employed on the "lake boats," the long flat carriers of grain and iron ore whose season ends any day after December 10, depending on the ice conditions. We wish it to be cold, cold on the Great Lakes of Ontario, so that he may come home to us as soon as possible. Already his cartons have arrived. They come from different places: Cobourg, Toronto, St. Catharines, Welland, Windsor, Sarnia, Sault Ste. Marie. Places that we, with the exception of my father, have never been. We locate them excitedly on the map, tracing their outlines with eager fingers. The cartons bear the lettering of Canada Steamship Lines, and are bound with rope knotted intricately in the fashion of sailors. My mother says they contain his "clothes" and we are not allowed to open them.

For us it is impossible to know the time or manner of his coming. If the lakes freeze early, he may come by train because it is cheaper. If the lakes stay open until December 20, he will have to fly because his time will be more precious than his money. He will hitchhike the last sixty or hundred miles from either station or airport. On our part, we can do nothing but listen with straining ears to radio reports of distant ice formations. His coming seems to depend on so many factors which are out there far beyond us and over which we lack control.

The days go by in fevered slowness until finally on the morning of December 23 the strange car rolls into our yard. My mother touches her hand to her lips and whispers "Thank God." My father gets up unsteadily from his chair to look through the window. Their longed-for son and our golden older brother is

213

here at last. He is here with his reddish hair and beard and we can hear his hearty laugh. He will be happy and strong and confident for us all.

There are three other young men with him who look much the same as he. They, too, are from the boats and are trying to get home to Newfoundland. They must still drive a hundred miles to reach the ferry at North Sydney. The car seems very old. They purchased it in Thorold for two hundred dollars because they were too late to make any reservations, and they have driven steadily since they began. In northern New Brunswick their windshield wipers failed, but instead of stopping they tied lengths of cord to the wipers' arms and passed them through the front window vents. Since that time, in whatever precipitation, one of them has pulled the cords back and forth to make the wipers function. This information falls tiredly but excitedly from their lips and we greedily gather it in. My father pours them drinks of rum and my mother takes out her mincemeat and the fruitcakes she has been carefully hoarding. We lean on the furniture or look from the safety of sheltered doorways. We would like to hug our brother but are too shy with strangers present. In the kitchen's warmth, the young men begin to nod and doze, their heads dropping suddenly to their chests. They nudge each other with their feet in an attempt to keep awake. They will not stay and rest because they have come so far and tomorrow is Christmas Eve and stretches of mountains and water still lie between them and those they love. After they leave we pounce upon our brother physically and verbally. He laughs and shouts and lifts us over his head and swings us in his muscular arms. Yet in spite of his happiness he seems surprised at the appearance of his father, whom he has not seen since March. My father merely smiles at him, while my mother bites her lip.

Now that he is here there is a great flurry of activity. We have left everything we could until the time he might be with us. Eagerly I show him the fir tree on the hill which I have been watching for months and marvel at how easily he fells it and carries it down the hill. We fall over one another in the excitement of decoration.

He promises that on Christmas Eve he will take us to church in the sleigh behind the splendid horse that until his coming we are all afraid to handle. And on the afternoon of Christmas Eve he shoes the horse, lifting each hoof and rasping it fine and hammering the cherry-red horseshoes into shape upon the anvil. Later he drops them hissingly into the steaming tub of water. My father sits beside him on an overturned pail and tells him what to do. Sometimes we argue with our father, but our brother does everything he says.

That night, bundled in hay and voluminous coats, and with heated stones at our feet, we start upon our journey. Our parents and Kenneth remain at home, but all the rest of us go. Before we leave we feed the cattle and sheep and even the pig all that they can possibly eat, so that they will be contented on Christmas Eve. Our parents wave to us from the doorway. We go four miles across the mountain road. It is a primitive logging trail and there will be no cars or other vehicles upon it. At first the horse is wild with excitement and lack of exercise and my brother has to stand at the front of the sleigh and lean backwards on the reins. Later he settles down to a trot and still later to a walk as the mountain rises before him. We sing all the Christmas songs we know and watch for the rabbits and foxes scudding across the open patches of snow and listen to the drumming of partridge wings. We are never cold.

When we descend to the country church we tie the horse in a grove of trees where he will be sheltered and not frightened by the many cars. We put a blanket over him and give him oats. At the church door the neighbours shake hands with my brother. "Hello, Neil," they say. "How is your father?"

"Oh," he says, just "Oh."

The church is very beautiful at night with its festooned branches and glowing candles and the booming, joyous sounds that come from the choir loft. We go through the service as if we are mesmerized.

On the way home, although the stones have cooled, we remain happy and warm. We listen to the creak of the leather harness and the hiss of runners on the snow and begin to think of the potentiality of presents. When we are about a mile from home the horse senses his destination and breaks into a trot and then into a confident lope. My brother lets him go and we move across the winter landscape like figures freed from a Christmas card. The snow from the horse's hooves falls about our heads like the whiteness of the stars.

After we have stabled the horse we talk with our parents and eat the meal our mother has prepared. And then I am sleepy and it is time for the younger children to be in bed. But tonight my father says to me, "We would like you to stay up with us a while," and so I stay quietly with the older members of my family.

When all is silent upstairs Neil brings in the cartons that contain his "clothes" and begins to open them. He unties the intricate knots quickly, their whorls falling away before his agile fingers. The boxes are filled with gifts neatly wrapped and bearing tags. The ones for my younger brothers say "from Santa Claus" but mine are not among them any more, as I know with certainty they will never be again. Yet I am not so much surprised as touched by a pang of loss at being here on the adult side of the world. It is as if I have suddenly moved into another room and heard a door click lastingly behind me. I am jabbed by my own small wound.

But then I look at those before me. I look at my parents drawn together before the Christmas tree. My mother has her hand upon my father's shoulder and he is holding his ever-present handkerchief. I look at my sisters, who have crossed this threshold ahead of me and now each day journey farther from the lives they knew as girls. I look at my magic older brother who has come to us this Christmas from half a continent away, bringing everything he has and is. All of them are captured in the tableau of their care.

"Every man moves on," says my father quietly, and I think he speaks of Santa Claus, "but there is no need to grieve. He leaves good things behind."

SECOND SPRING

(1 9 8 0)

It was the summer after the seventh grade that saw me truly smitten with the calf club wish. It was not, of course, a really dazzlingly new idea because, living on a farm, I had always been surrounded by numerous animals. Not a day went by without my touching them and the insistence of their presence affected the living of my life and the lives of the other members of my family in very real and tangible ways. Their closeness and the manner of their closeness varied with the time of seasons.

In the winter, when they were less plentiful, they crowded together in the shared and dense confinement of their stables; stamping their hooves on the manure-strong planking and tossing their impatient heads and uttering the sounds of their different species. If you ventured into the silent barn at night the wave of their communal warmth rolled out to meet you at the creaking, opened door and the sound of the different rhythms of their breathing rose and fell in the softened darkness. If the flashlight was flicked on, or the carried lantern raised, the luminous eyes of those who were awakened glowed from their stalls and across their mangers, and then various sounds seemed to respond to the presence of the light; the creak of the wooden stanchion posts rubbed by the necks of restless cattle, the murmured grunts of half-asleep pigs, the nickering snorts of horses, the zing of suddenly tightened rope or leather, the jangle of moving halter chains.

By March conditions were even more overcrowded as the females grew awkward and ponderous with the weight of their unborn young. When they lay down in their expanded heaviness the ripples of movement from deep within their wombs were visible against the drum-tight skin of their extended sides. The promise of the future lay warm and heavy within their deep, dark bodies.

Inside the winter house the dogs and cats lay like scattered rugs beneath the kitchen couches and under dining tables or stretched at length behind the wood-filled stoves. At night my dog Laddie lay across my feet; a warm and living comforter whose heartbeat could be felt through the fabric of the bedclothes. His wet, cold nose was covered by his paws.

By the end of March the birth cycle would begin and would extend sometimes deep into June. First the sheep, then some cattle and later the pigs and finally the wobbly foals with their long, ungainly legs. There would be chickens and kittens and puppies with at-first-unopened eyes. The number of animals would double or almost triple within the allotted weeks and there would be a flurry of activity surrounding the new arrivals

and the rapidity of their growth. New pens would be con-
structed and, amidst squeals of protest, there would be separa-
tions, weanings and brandings and the pulling of teeth and the
flashing of knives used for the cutting of testicles, the docking
of tails and the notching of ears. They would spill out then,
according to their kind, to the larger yards and fields or the
mountain-high pastures washed by the blue-white sea.

By July first, which always seemed unbelievably soon, the
haying season which would ensure their winter's survival would
begin. During the summer months, while the animals grew
sleek and fat and haughty, we, their human owners, would grow
thin and burned and irritable; rising often before sunrise and
working sometimes until after dark. Only the work horses
seemed to share in our drudgery and weight loss; the burns from
their collars and the chafings caused by their rubbing traces corresponding to the blisters and calluses upon our hands.
Sometimes at night we would rub ourselves with diluted horse
liniment to alleviate the sprains and bruises which we accumu-
lated during the day.

Throughout this season, as I said, the animals of summer
grew strong and free. Only the milk cows were brought to the
barn twice daily for their milking, and even they seemed to take
on an air of independence that bordered on arrogance. The
others grazed openly and heedlessly through the long days of
their summer vacation. From the tops of our hay wagons we
could see them, especially on the hottest days, lying on the sandy
beaches which separated their pastures from the sea, or danger-
ously close to the rocky edge of the sea cliff's fall. It was always
cooler near the sea and there was always a slight breeze and they

were not bothered there by the flies that tormented inland animals. Throughout the working days of summer we spent little time ourselves beside or within the turquoise sea.

As the summer progressed and as the season's young became more independent, the mature animals would yearn again to be sexually active. They would demonstrate their needs in various ways, again depending on their species and their sex, and they would continue to do so until they were fulfilled. We, as the humans who depended on them as they did on us, would frequently and of necessity interfere with their needs and desires. We would tether the lusty and often ill-tempered rams to iron stakes driven deep into the earth or isolate them in all-male pens where they frequently took out their frustrations by battering their thick-boned skulls against each other. We would keep them from the ewes until late in the fall, knowing that early matings resulted in the birth of winter lambs who stood little chance of surviving the bitter coldness of the season of their birth. We would keep the young heifers from the heavy bulls, knowing that they were often injured and sometimes permanently maimed in their first sexual encounters, and knowing also that even if they did survive the breeding, great difficulty awaited them in such youthful pregnancies, and that often they would die attempting to give birth. Another year would make a great difference to them as well as to us. In the same manner we would discourage nesting and maternal hens from bringing forth autumnal chickens who would not be matured enough to meet the demands of cold, rain-lashed November and the harsher months to follow. Like highly protective parents we would hover over such lives, hoping that our attempts at control would result in what was "best" for all. This is for your own good, we would think, as well as for ours, although we would never articulate it in such a manner.

In the fall we would reduce the population that had so flourished through the long, hot summer days. As it had doubled or tripled in the spring, it was reduced by similar numbers in the fall, and reduced in a variety of ways. Livestock buyers came, sometimes walking to the pastures to view their intended victims, offering prices, quoting possibilities, leaving and return-ing. All of the male lambs would go, and most of the females except a select few singled out to continue the reproductive cycle. When they left, they would be strong and rambunctious, unlike their earlier wobbly-legged selves. They would crowd against one another and jostle as they were ushered up the ramps of the waiting trucks and sometimes they would attempt to leap over the slatted sides of their new confinement. We would hear their indignant bleatings as the trucks took them permanently from the single environment of their one and only summer. Sounds of angered indignation tinged with the very real sound of fear. Later the cheques we had exchanged them for would come and we, in our turn, would enter a phase of rejuvenation and hopeful, though temporary, self-confidence.

Sometimes, depending on different factors, it would be more profitable to butcher animals and sell them locally than to trust to the simpler yet more bureaucratic expedient of the truck or train which would take them to more distant killing stations. There was always butchering in the late fall to supply meat for ourselves and our urban relatives, but in some years there would be more than in others. It would always be a melancholy time then, especially if there was a lot of it. The night before we would lay out the ceremonial clothes of death, splattered with bloodstains and bearing the distinctive odour which could never be fully washed away. We would sit on chairs in the kitchen, sharpening the various knives and testing the keenness of the blades with the balls of our callused thumbs. We would pay attention to the weather and nearly always kill according to the phases of the moon. From the barn we could hear the protesting moans of the unknowing and condemned animals. Unlike condemned prisoners, they would receive neither food nor water before their executions. This was to reduce the bulk of their weight and their body fluids for the day that was to follow; so that their weight, which would so soon become dead, would be less ponderous and easier to handle.

On the day of the actual butchering we would rise early so that we would get a good start. In the late fall the days would be short, and since we would normally work by natural light, adjustments would have to be made. The animal would be taken to that part of the barn called the threshing floor and stationed beneath the chain pulleys which would soon be used to elevate its carcass. If it were a huge animal, it would be shot. Sometimes we would draw lines on its trusting head with a crayon, from behind each ear and across its forehead. Generally the point of intersection would be the marksman's target – almost a literal bull's-eye. If the animal were less huge, it would be merely hit between the eyes by a sledgehammer or the blunt side of an axe wielded by the strongest man. Even as its front legs buckled and its eyes glazed, the knife used for the severing of the jugular would be passed handle-first to the waiting hands which had tossed aside the sledgehammer or axe – much as the nurse might pass the scalpel. If done well, it would take but ten or twelve seconds to change life into death. The pigs were always the hardest to kill because their skulls slanted backwards and were more difficult to strike than the flattened foreheads of others. As the blood gushed from the slashed throats, we would gather it in pans so that it might later be used for blood puddings – *maragan*, they were called in Gaelic. One person would hold the pan beneath the neck of the fallen animal while another would raise and steady the convulsing and partly severed head so that the blood would be pumped into the pan and not wasted on the barn-planked floor. Later we would take the hind legs and cut the flesh between the hocks and the main tendons and insert a horizontal stick. To this stick we would fasten the now-descended chain pulleys and we would raise the animal by its widespread legs even as we skinned and disembowelled it. Sometimes the flesh would continue to twitch for a long time after the actual death and even after the hide had been removed. The contents of the body would generally spill into a huge washtub and we would sort them out in their steaming warmth with bloodied slippery hands. We would save at least the heart and the liver and the stomach and the strips of marbled fat; sometimes other portions as well. And if there was time, our father would point out and explain the functions of the myste-rious and until-now invisible internal organs. "This is the bladder, and this is the spleen and this is the large intestine. This is the windpipe. These are the lungs. This is the passage that the seed follows from the testicles to the end of the penis." We would listen and watch intently, like those involved in a formal autopsy or like intense medical students about their still cadaver.

Often there would be surprises. Sometimes shingle nails or fence staples or bits of twisted wire would be found embedded in the stomach, and one time the neck of a beer bottle was found completely surrounded by a strange almost translucent knob of gristle. It seemed to glow like a huge, obscene pearl. We remembered then how more than a year ago the cow had stood for days unable to eat or give milk, and for a while barely able to walk. We had no way of knowing then how the sharp-edged amber glass she had carelessly swallowed in her grazing cut into her stomach's lining, and we did not know when the gristle began to surround it and isolate it, thus allowing her to move and function once again. Another time we found an unborn calf within the womb of a young cow we had considered sterile. We had tried various matings and solutions, but she had always failed to conceive. In her fourth year of life her sterility became a luxury we could not afford. "We cannot take her through another winter like that," was the verdict. "She will have to be fattened and killed." When found within the womb of the slaughtered mother, the embryonic calf continued to move for a brief and borrowed time. Its delicate limbs had begun to form and were folded compactly back upon themselves, while its eyes seemed large and luminous. Its ears were exquisite and fragile and flatly pressed, like the memory of ferns found deep within the darkened earth. No one knew who had fathered the calf, although the time could be roughly estimated. What we had wanted we had found achieved, when it was ironically too late to save the life of either.

Such scenes of selling and butchering would repeat themselves until a rough balance between livestock and available hay was achieved. In dry seasons when the hay crop was less lush there would have to be a corresponding reduction in animal numbers. In years that were more bountiful we could afford to winter individuals who would not have survived the more rigorous selectivity of leaner years. The selection of those who would remain and those who would "go" was always a tight and careful process. Like shrewd and thoughtful managers of athletic teams preparing their lists of protected players, we would go over the strengths and weaknesses of each individual. Age was always a factor, as was general strength; fertility, as I mentioned, another, and sometimes even what might be called "personality." Animals who were particularly ill-tempered or high-strung or who had developed bad habits, like leaping fences or raiding summer vegetable gardens, received thoughtful scrutiny as the deadline approached. And as always, if the troublesome individuals had outstanding positive traits, they would be given additional leeway and allowed to make it for another year. Sheep who produced "weighty" lambs or a high proportion of twins were forgiven balancing weaknesses, and the cows who were the leading milk producers were generally grudgingly indulged, regardless of how unpleasant they actually might be. They were often the "stars" on not overly strong teams and were catered to accordingly.

I say all of this now so that you might understand the environment in which the calf club wish was born, and also so that you might see the situation in which it existed for a while – wobbly and uncertain but grounded in a kind of realism similar to the animals and the people who were its basic source.

The idea itself, however, came from a new person in our midst. In the late winter and early spring of the seventh grade a new and dynamic agricultural representative began to visit our two-room school. He was young and athletic and brimming with vigour. He was one year away from the completion of his degree and had interrupted his formal studies for a year of "in-the-field" practical experience; and we were to be part of his field. He was almost contagious. We had always had visits from agricultural representatives but they were for the most part men who were older and gave the impression of wishing they were somewhere else. One used to wear a suede jacket and a pair of grey trousers covered with cigarette ashes and other interesting stains. He would sit at the desk in the front of the room and ask if there were any questions. There would seldom be any, so he would ask one: "Well, then what will we talk about?" Then he would look out the window rather longingly, as would we, hoping for, if not a discussion topic, a sort of mutual deliverance. Another used to show slides of "common North American weeds." He seemed to come later in the year, in May or June, and always in the afternoon. Each slide bore the name of the weed which was illustrated, and he would read the label aloud to us in a ritual which we came to call the weed parade. "Common Ragwort," he would say, or "Scottish Thistle" or "Wild Onion" or "Broad-leaved Dock." He would always glance surreptitiously at his watch and drink from a thermos bottle of coffee laced with whisky. In the drowsy hot afternoons, as weed followed weed and their names became more slurred and the vapours from the whiskied coffee rose around us, we would find it almost impossible to stay awake. But our new man changed all that.

First he said that in addition to our present vegetable garden clubs we should start a calf club. He had been doing research, he said, and all we needed was a minimum of ten heifer calves produced by a pure-bred sire. These would be born the following spring, so it was not too early to begin thinking of their conception. The mothers could be "any cow of high quality." Such quality would hopefully be transferred to her daughter. We would need a paper signed by the keeper of the pure-bred sire, indicating the breeding date and the hopeful conception of the desired calf. We were to check our cattle at home and speak with our parents. We were interested in dairy cattle, so we should not select a beef-type mother. Neither should we "cross" breeds if we could help it. We should not breed a cow with heavy Holstein characteristics to an Ayrshire bull, for example, because the breed characteristics would become confused. His research had shown that the predominant strain in the area was Ayrshire and there were two Ayrshire bulls approximately ten miles apart and subsidized by the Department of Agriculture. These bulls, he said, were not being "utilized to their full potential." We copied it all down in our scribblers to refer to at a later time.

On our way home I considered all the cattle that we owned, thinking of their backgrounds and their breeding and when they were due to give birth that spring. I was already a year ahead of myself in searching for my candidate for mother of the year. I settled mentally on a large and consistently gentle cow whom we called Morag. She was basically white with cherry-red markings and long and sweeping elegant Ayrshire horns. She possessed almost all of the "high-quality" requirements which had been mentioned and she would deliver her current "ordinary" calf quite early in the spring. She had always conceived quickly and easily following the births of her other calves, and I could not believe my good fortune.

When I entered our house my father was fixing harness in the kitchen. He was not in a good mood, I realized, but I was so enthusiastic that I told him all about the new agricultural representative and our potential calf club, falling over my words in my excitement.

"Oh," he said with something like vague annoyance, "I've heard all that before. Those agricultural representatives are all the same. They just talk and talk and talk and never do anything. They come in their fancy cars in the middle of the haying season and expect you to drop everything and talk to them. Almost everything they say is common sense anyway: 'Plant early and you will harvest early.' 'Rotate your crops.' 'Use lime.' 'Heavy rainfall results in a high yield.' 'Turkeys are needed for the Thanksgiving market.' Who doesn't know that? What they say is all baloney."

"Well," I said, thinking I had best keep on, "it would just be one cow. I was thinking of Morag after her calf is born. There is a pure-bred Agricultural Society bull at MacDougall's five miles away. We could breed her there in the summer."

"Not me," he said. "I'm not dragging any more cows on the end of a rope to one of those bulls. I kept one of those Agricultural Society bulls here myself about fifteen years ago. More trouble than he was worth. Took up too much space in the barn. Had to haul feed and water to him all the time because he was too dangerous to let out. Then if he didn't get exercise he wouldn't breed properly. And people always came with cows at the damnedest times. Seven o'clock on Sunday morning. Any time there was a wedding or a funeral. Any time you were leaving the house you'd be sure to meet someone with a cow and have to go back in and change your clothes and go handle the bull for them. Bull got so he wouldn't let anyone else around him but me, so I could never leave the house. People would come with their cows and if I weren't home they'd complain. Not that they didn't have a right to, I suppose."

He began to gather up his harness from the floor in preparation for the evening chores. I felt that perhaps I should point out that all of our best cattle were still descendants of that long-departed bull but it somehow did not seem a good day for that kind of logic. After he had gone to the barn, my mother said: "He is not having a good day but you realize he did not say 'No.' Ask him something definite and volunteer to do the work yourself. He is getting tired. You know that if he gives you his word, he will always keep it."

It was true. Whatever uneven moods my father was prone to, he possessed a memory that did not permit him to forget anything and he was always true to his word. In retrospect, it does not seem that we were certain of many things, dwelling in the realm of fluctuating weather and fickle seasons and aggressive insects and indifferent soil; but of those traits we were sure, and we clung to them as the uneasy swimmer to his certain log.

In the barn it was growing dark. My father moved about the animals with a tired familiarity, leaning against them, pushing them with his shoulder as he moved towards their mangers, talking to them in a sort of abbreviated private language, pulling manure with his fork from beneath them, tightening their halter chains, distributing their feed so that it was within their reach.

"Okay," he said before I had time to speak. "I didn't say you couldn't, just that I wouldn't. If you raise the fee, you can have the cow."

It was, it seemed, fair enough.

The fee was probably part of the reason we had stopped using the Agricultural Society bull in the first place. Another was that it took valuable time in a period before the widespread use of trucks and artificial insemination. "He," the bull, had gone too far away, and it was no longer considered worth it. It was expensive, as I mentioned, and there was also a feeling that paying money for the simple breeding act was a bit too much – as if it were somehow unnatural, a kind of perversion or animal prostitution in which we did not care to be involved; as if there were an uneasy idea that no one should have to "pay for it." There was also the shrewd and pragmatic observation that after a few years of such selective breeding most cattle already contained "good," if not exactly royal, blood and further exalted matings were perhaps a waste of time. It was probably a reaction to such spreading ideas that the agricultural representative had come among us in the first place to plant the seeds of the calf club wish.

In any case, I had achieved the first step. Before the birth of Morag's present calf, I had already willed her pregnant once again. I entered my name with the agricultural representative and told my fellow schoolmates that I would "go." The snow had not yet melted, nor had the wild ducks flown north, nor had the first spring lambs and early kittens yet been born, but I was already well into not only this spring but the next as well.

After the birth of Morag's "ordinary" calf, there followed the long period of waiting. If she were to deliver the magic calf by early next spring, she would have to conceive in the middle of summer. It took nine months from conception to birth – "just like people," as we used to say. "Cattle are the only animals that take the same length of time."

As the spring passed and the early summer approached, the hectic pace of our lives increased. School drew to a close and during the last few weeks we attended it irregularly. We were needed at home, and whatever we had learned during the year was already in our past. Feverish preparations for the approaching haying season began: the repairing of machinery, the sending away for parts, improvements to the barn and also a myriad of other activities involving gardening, canning and the making of cheese. The short intense summer was upon us and we had no time to lose.

Meanwhile the animals grew sleek and fat and were distant from us most of the time as we prepared to gather in their winter sustenance. In the early weeks of July we began our haying in earnest; cutting the most mature fields and leaving them to dry, then raking and finally pitching onto the wagons, then driving into the barn and pitching off, and returning again and then again. Always threatened by broken harness and non-functioning machinery and always fearful of the sudden spectre of rain.

On the evening of the fourteenth of July I noticed the signs in Morag when I was bringing the milk cows home from their pasture by the sea. She was coming into her breeding cycle and it caused a restlessness and tension not only within herself but among the other cattle as well. It was late in the evening when I first noticed it and there was nothing I could do that day. That night the radio told us of the approaching rain squalls which were to hit on the following day.

"Goddamn it," said my father, "and us with all that hay out."

We had just recently cut a new field, so much of it was still undried. In the morning we were up at five, moving feverishly about our tasks, racing against the weather. At the morning milking Morag's situation was truly obvious, although my father did not notice. He was not around the cattle much but busy harnessing the horses and shouting directions to animals and people alike. The clouds were already bunching, although they still seemed far enough away, hanging over the ocean and visible from a distance.

"Hurry up," he said, coming into the barn where I was milking the cows. "It's going to rain. We haven't got all day."

"I think we should keep Morag in the barn today," I stammered quickly, fearful lest he should get away before I broached the subject.

"What for?" he asked and I could see that he was so harried and preoccupied that he had given my words but little thought.

"She's in heat," I said. "She began last night."

For a moment his eyes seemed to cloud over with non-comprehension, but then they cleared and became filled almost with panic, as he understood the significance of my words. It was as if he were trapped by his memory and his word. Trapped by them at this, his busiest time.

"But there is no time today," he sputtered. "We have other things to do than just worry about this one goddamn cow."

"Okay," I said. "We will just keep her in and see what the day brings. I didn't say I wanted to go with her now."

"Okay," he said, as if he were relieved of an earlier capricious promise. "Take the others down to the shore. We have to get going."

What the day brought was a forenoon of furious activity. First we raked the driest hay and then followed with the groaning wagons. The sun shone erratically, but the air was so humid that little actual drying took place. At times the clouds blotted out the sun, and once we could actually see the rain falling out to sea, although it had not yet started to fall upon the land. All morning as we raced about, raising new blisters upon the calluses already formed on our hands, Morag moaned and bawled her passion from the barn. When we came in with the loaded wagons, we could hear her threshing about in the frustration of her captivity and her desire.

I would have liked to bring her a pail of water to ease her thirst, although I knew that was not what she really wanted – but there was no time even for that. On one or two occasions I thought I heard an answering call from what seemed like a great distance but I could not really be sure. She was safe in the barn anyway, I thought. Safe for me, if not satisfied for herself. Our work intensified, as did the weather which surrounded us.

When the storm finally broke, it announced itself first in two thunderous cracks and a jagged scar of lightning across the sky, and then the rain seemed to hurl itself down as if pressurized forth from the hanging, laden clouds. Everything and everyone became immediately drenched and to save even the half-loaded wagon of imperfectly dried hay we had to shout to the horses and swing the reins over their already steaming backs. They broke into a gallop then, jolting the wagon behind them until they careened into the still, dignified safety of the waiting barn. Within five minutes it was obvious that the day's haying was over and that at a future time we would have to begin again with what was now being so thoroughly soaked. But by then the hay would not be the same, but only of the second grade.

The rain poured down all afternoon; rivulets streamed down the windows and the sides of the buildings and cascaded down the laneways, pushing erratic, insistent trenches through the softened earth. Nothing but the water seemed to move. The ocean was still and we were still ourselves after all our desperate activity. Even Morag's passion seemed to lull as if she were cooled and covered by the soothing of the rain. It was late that evening before I could venture down to the shore to bring the milk cows home, and by the next morning Morag was ravenously hungry but otherwise in no way outwardly exceptional. The hope for the mid-April calf was gone and would not come again.

For two days it was overcast and there were sporadic showers, and the cut and sodden hay began gradually to turn black. On the third day it cleared in the afternoon and by the fourth day the sun shone again and we began to pick up where we had left off prior to the storm. We did not pick up at the same place, for part of our crop was gone or greatly deteriorated. I set my sights on the approximate three-week future and rationalized that a mid-May calf would, after all, not really be so bad.

I was ready in August because I had mentally noted the earlier date. We were still at our haying, although many of the fields had now been cleared. We were all thinner and more irritable and beset by various nagging injuries which bore witness to the activities of our past days and weeks. A thumbnail torn off by a running rope, a back spasm caused by lifting too heavy a pitch, a swollen jaw caused by the unexpected disturbance of a wasp's nest within the deepened grass, a purplish plate-sized bruise on the thigh caused by the kick of a horse irritated by flies.

When I recognized the August signs in Morag, it was in the morning and the day promised to be clear and hot. We were on the home stretch of our summer's haying and things were not as desperate as they had been in the earlier month. I mentioned the situation to my father and he said that I should keep Morag in the barn that day. That evening, after we had done a reasonable day's work, he said, I could be free to go on my five-mile journey. All day as we worked I was intent on my future mission. I was actually a bit afraid as the time drew closer, contemplating the twists and turns of the road I must go, and realizing even then how erratic it might be. From the barn Morag moaned and bawled, her voice sounding like the theme music for the day's production. The answer seemed to come from far away.

In the evening, after the other milk cows were stabled, I placed a halter on Morag's head, looped an additional length of rope around her sweeping horns and prepared to set off.

"Don't wrap the rope too tightly around your hand," said my father, "because if she bolts she might pull your shoulder out of its socket." He was on his way to finish the last hay load of the evening.

"Okay," I said, doubling the rope within my hand.

The five-mile journey was on a narrow dirt road which followed the erratic indentations of the sea. It was apparently the original path followed by the first settlers in the 1770s when they walked along the shore on their way to their new lands. Now it was almost a private road, rarely used by any automotive traffic because it was so narrow and so dangerous, but used by people on missions such as mine, by people on foot, or those on horseback; sometimes by lovers, sometimes by drunkards or a variety of others who did not appreciate detection. At times it clung to the cliffs and in certain places the edges of it had crumbled and fallen down into the sea some two hundred feet below.

As we began the journey, Morag moved rapidly and I was forced to run to keep by her side. I could feel the strength of her head and shoulders almost surging back along the rope like a current and thought uneasily that if she were to lunge I would not be able to control her. Contrary to what I had been told, I wrapped the rope around my hand, figuring that if she had to drag me, she at least would not escape. We covered the first mile rapidly and both of us were breathing heavily. She will soon tire, I thought, and then she will be easier to handle.

After the first mile the road began to climb steeply and the small rocks rolled beneath our feet, but still she did not seem to slacken much.

In one way this is good, I thought. At least we are getting there in a hurry.

I had had an earlier vision of her standing stubbornly in the middle of the road while I tried in vain to urge her on. This was obviously not going to be the case – at least not for the first two miles. After the climb the road passed through a sort of upland plateau for perhaps three hundred yards and then became a series of hairpin turns. Suddenly and unexpectedly it dipped and rose and twisted in such a manner as to make it impossible to see what was ahead. It was in the middle of the second turn that we saw him, or perhaps heard him first. There was a low rumble in his throat, which he continually repeated as he approached us, coming down the hill.

The hill at this spot rose from the cliff edge of the sea which was on our right and ascended steeply before levelling off into another plateau. On that plateau I could now see a herd of cattle in the distance and he was coming from them and rapidly bearing down on us. He weighed perhaps a ton, with immense shoulders and an enormous chest. He was mostly white but his head and neck were a brindled grey which shaded at times almost into blue. He carried his head low as he moved and moaned towards us with strands of bead-like saliva falling from his lower jaw. His horns were thick and yellowed, and spiralled downward and outward like those of a mountain sheep. No formal heritage was visible in the way he looked or the way he moved, and there was nothing like him in any book entitled *Standard Breeds of Cattle*.

He was approaching quickly now, coming down the hill towards us, the grade of the hill seeming to give him added momentum. He was walking very rapidly and determinedly with that low moaning rumble in his throat, but he was not running. He was not running at all like those bulls run in the jokes about bulls after cows. None of us, I knew, were in any joke. At the base of the hill beside the road there was a rail fence, which formed a separation, but I could see that the rails and the posts were rotten and that they represented perhaps more the idea of a fence than the fact of one. I thought that with his size and speed and the downward grade of the hill he would perhaps jump over it, but instead he merely walked through it as if it did not exist at all. The whole section of the fence parted to his progress like the furrow before the breaking plough or the water before the ongoing ship. The edges of the rotted, broken rails seemed to cling to his flanks as he passed through their destruction but they had no effect upon his movement. He continued to bear down upon us rapidly but also unhurriedly, as if he were very certain of everything and very much in control.

In romantic retrospect, I see myself sometimes as one of those "guides" in the Gothic novels, attempting to guard my tremulous female figure from the lascivious, slobbering male who, in the fulfilling of his desires, will cause irrevocable pain. Or by another extension the "concerned father" who will do almost anything to keep his vulnerable daughter from the one he knows to be not right for her. Defence against the figure "with but one thing on his mind."

But in the reality of that evening's dusty road, she swung her head toward him with swift and arching strength. Her sweeping horns seemed almost to whistle through the air and she lifted me, with the rope wrapped tightly around my hand, completely off my feet. As if I were some slight and ridiculous irritant she could no longer tolerate. She swung my body almost into his looming head and I could see, as under a microscope, the dark and deepened liquid of his eyes, the gnarled, yellow rings at the base of his horns, his grey-blue jowls and the strings of beaded saliva trailing from his jaw. I could smell the sweet, heavy hotness of his grass-filled breath as their muzzles touched, and for an instant I thought I might lose my own life if either horned head should swing in the wrong direction. Then with a moan he swung behind her and reared up massively, his heavy shoulders silhouetted and rising into the evening sun which was settling now to the waiting sea. It seemed in that moment as if Morag were approaching her answer even as I was to be denied mine.

"Is that what you want?" came a voice near at hand.

"No," I said or perhaps sobbed, "no" almost before noticing where the voice came from.

"Christ," he said, sliding from the back of the horse almost in one motion.

He too had come upon us suddenly and unexpectedly around the hairpin turn. He was apparently coming from the village, judging from the two rum bottles which protruded from his faded blue overalls, and it seemed he had not been hurrying because the huge, black horse which immediately began to crop the roadside grass showed no signs of perspiration. He was an old man then, deep into his seventies, and was my grandfather's cousin and therefore also mine. He was a tremendously big man and had lived the kind of reckless life that big men sometimes lead in such communities – perhaps because there was often no one to stop them from doing almost anything they wanted. He was to die at a future time, late at night and in mysterious darkness, falling or pushed from the rickety balcony outside a bootlegger's second-storey door. His neck was broken when he was discovered and his money gone and someone had cut the reins of his black horse and its companion as they stood hitched to the steel-wheeled wagon and waiting as on so many other nights. They had galloped home then, wildly through the night, the sparks flashing from the steel of their shoes as they swung the wagon behind them, lifting it off its wheels in the tightest turns and suspending it for seconds over the cliff's edge and above the darkened sea. The people who lived along the road had been awakened by the sound of the rushing horses and had recognized them from the sure-footed terror of their hoofbeats in the same manner that their descendants now recognize the individual motor sounds of different cars. They had heard the sounds before and did not know that on this occasion the black horses were careening through the night, driverless and without a human guide.

When the horses arrived home they were covered with froth, the muscles of their shoulders and flanks trembled and twitched and their eyes were glassy and wild. The people of the house came out then and with lanterns and flashlights began to retrace the journey of the wagon, seeking to find him in the roadside ditch or over the cliff's edge on the boulders touched by the sea, or even perhaps lying sprawled in the middle of the road. But they did not find him all that night and in the morning someone brought the official, final news. They noticed then that the reins had been cut, and wondered why they had not noticed it before.

But that is ahead of my story. For at that meeting on the narrow road and in the presence of the bull, we did not know what future was in store for any of us. Our present seemed too real.

In memory, now, he moved with tremendous speed, although he did not seem to hurry and the illusion was probably due to the length of his legs and the amount of ground he covered in a single step. Without breaking stride, he bent down and his right hand scooped up a large rock which lay by the roadside. It seemed almost the size of a bowling ball yet he carried it easily and lightly in his gigantic hand. As he approached the rearing, lunging bull, he extended his left hand up and forward until it grasped one of the mountain sheep horns and then in one fluid arc of motion and follow-through, he brought the rocky boulder down between the bull's concentrated, widespread eyes. The thud of the rock on skull was like the sound on the butchering days and the bull toppled sideways and to his knees. His eyes, drained of their passion, rolled glassily upwards in their sockets, and two thin streams of saliva, now green from regurgitated grass, trickled from his nostrils and back into his sagging mouth. His penis, still dripping fluid, collapsed limply within its sheath. His day's breeding or attempted breeding was over.

"Did he get it in?" he said, wiping his hand on his overalls and then reaching for one of the rum bottles.

"I don't know," I said. "I couldn't see."

"If he got it in," he said, "you never can be sure. What are you doing here anyway, apart from trying to get yourself killed?"

Briefly and disjointedly I stammered out the nature of my mission.

"Well," he said, "you may as well keep going. I'll go with you partway if you want. Here, you jump on the horse."

Easily and with the same arm he had used for the rock, he lifted me up to the back of the horse and then passed me the reins. He took Morag's rope in his hand and almost automatically she began to move in step with him while I followed behind on the horse. I looked back once at the bull and he was still kneeling and partially lying by the roadside where he had been struck down. His head seemed to loll to one side.

After we had negotiated the remainder of the hairpin turns and had travelled perhaps a mile, he stopped and passed Morag's rope towards me. I dismounted from the horse, exchanging the reins for the proffered rope.

"You should be all right now," he said. "Perhaps you should go back by the other road."

Taking a deep pull from one of his rum bottles, he mounted the black horse and turned him in the direction of his original homeward journey.

Morag and I continued on our way more quietly and more slowly than when we had set out. When we entered the laneway to the MacDougall yard, the sun was almost setting and I could see that they were hurrying to get their last load of hay into the barn before darkness. Mr. MacDougall was on top of the hay wagon, organizing the pitches tossed up by the others, and he was not awfully glad to see us.

"Jesus H. Christ, another goddamn cow," he said, driving his fork deep into the hay before him. I was reminded of my father's earlier remarks.

Nevertheless, he climbed down from the wagon and his place was taken by one of his sons. On the way to the barn, I told him what had happened.

"Did he get it in?" he asked.

"I don't know," I said, "I couldn't see."

"He probably didn't," he said, "if it happened as fast as you say. Perhaps he didn't reach her. Sometimes it takes them a while to get set. Anyway, we'll just have to see."

I stood in the dusky yard, clutching Morag's rope and waiting for the cherry-red and white bull with all the proper characteristics to come moaning forth, guided by a long wooden staff snapped into the ring of his nose. The breeding was almost leisurely and seemed thorough.

"Well, this one is sure as hell in," said MacDougall appreciatively. "No doubt about that. It should be all right."

After the bull was returned to his barn, I paid MacDougall the fee and he went into his house and then returned with a scribbler from which he tore a page. On it he wrote the date, and Morag's ownership, and the fact that the breeding had occurred. He squinted his eyes in the dusky gloom and his hands were heavy and thick and unaccustomed to holding the stubby, yellow pencil. The funky odour of the bull's perspiration and semen still hung about his hands and about the man himself.

On the return we took a more travelled route and I was afraid as the darkness descended that we might be hit by a passing car or truck, but there was little traffic and we walked steadily and briskly. Although the route was longer, the return journey seemed much shorter than the outgoing one, the way return journeys often do. It was totally dark when we entered our own yard and my father was in the barn, where he seemed to be waiting.

"How did you get along?" he asked.

Again, I stated my story.

"Do you think he got it in?" he asked.

"I don't know," I said.

I was so exhausted I could hardly stand. My father took Morag's rope from me and led her into the barn. I went into the house and to bed without eating any supper. The mark from Morag's rope still burned and circled redly about my hand and wrist.

During the weeks that followed I played and replayed the events of the day within the privacy of my mind. I half hoped she had not conceived so that we could perhaps start over again; but I knew that if she had not, valuable time would already be lost and a September mating would at best produce a summer calf instead of a spring one; and that would perhaps be too late for the calf club's organization. When the September dates came, I watched Morag anxiously but there were no signs. She grazed contentedly and lay in the sun by the sea and walked home placidly to be milked. She seemed at ease with everything.

We went into September seriously then with a new round of activities: grain crops had to be harvested, and preparations began for the digging of potatoes. School reopened and I was in the eighth grade. There were various fall fairs and exhibitions, and our agricultural representative was everywhere. The first truckload of lambs was hauled away, bleating in the autumn sun, and the vines and tendrils of the vegetable gardens turned to russet and then to darker brown.

In October Morag was still quiet and calm when the serious butchering and selling began, and by Hallowe'en, when the first snow fell, she and the other animals entered the stables for their winter confinement.

All winter I watched her anxiously and nervously, almost as if I were the young expectant father. When she began to grow heavier I moved her to a special stall so she might have more room, and sometimes I would place my hands and arms around her expanded girth, hoping I might feel life. When first I felt it, we were already out of the coldest depth of winter and into the erratic, gale-filled month of March. The calf became even more real then, as I led her through my mind in various elegant postures and positions.

Spring came early that year and although the nights remained cold, during the days the sun shone warmly down upon our backs as we went about repairing fences and replacing sluices and generally rectifying the ravages of winter. By May first the cattle were out during the day busily seeking the first adventurous blades of grass. During the first week the older, more mature, animals still sought the relative warmth of the stable at night while the younger ones seemed quite willing to give up warmth for the advantages of freedom. I was torn between Morag's giving birth outside where there would be less chance of infection but possible dangers from the cold, or keeping her inside where her surroundings would be warmer but more constricted and less sanitary. She was now so heavy that she seemed almost to fall when she lay down and she had great difficulty in getting up.

In the late afternoon of the tenth of May when I went down to the shore for the cows I could not see Morag among them and I knew then that her time had come, apart from any decision that might be mine. I searched for half an hour, knowing that she would not give birth near the sea, which was still dotted with the winter's ice floes and the source of chilling winds, so I began to criss-cross the wooded hollows and the inland sheltered gatherings of spruce. Finally I found her heavy tracks deep in the wet spring earth. They were already nearly filled with water, indicating that she had passed a considerable time before. I followed them across a small stream which trickled from a marsh and then around the edge of the marsh itself and then up a steep incline and finally to the edge of a considerable grove of spruce and fir.

The trees of the grove were closely crowded together. Parting the branches and still following the heavy tracks in the brown needled floor, I came suddenly into a small clearing which was almost like a room. The edges of it were bordered by wild brambles which had not yet begun to bud, and there were also several older heavier trees which had been uprooted and toppled by the winter winds and now lay like heavy barriers along the wooded perimeter. There seemed no way out of it except through the entranceway that we had used. Morag was lying on her side when I entered. She was already greatly dilated and the mucus discharge had begun. She struggled to her feet when I entered and swung her horns towards me and for a moment I was afraid that she might charge even as the unborn calf began to protrude. But then she became calmer, and after pacing several preparatory circles she flopped heavily down upon her side once more.

As in all births, it seemed surprisingly fast once it actually began. After all the months of our waiting, it seemed to take no time at all.

His shoulders were heavy and thick and his chest was large. He was mostly white but his head and neck were a brindled grey that shaded at times almost into blue. No formal heritage was visible in the way he looked and there was nothing like him in any book entitled *Standard Breeds of Cattle*. Morag rose and turned to lick the mucus from his nostrils and nudged him with her nose. Almost immediately he tried to struggle to his feet, clothed in the shimmering curtains of placenta which hung transparently from about his newborn frame.

He tottered and fell and tottered and fell but then seemed to gain control of his wobbly legs even as his mother's nose pushed him firmly but gently towards his first nursing. They seemed very glad to see each other, and if disappointment was mine it obviously was not shared by them.

The calf club wish ended there in the tiny groved room on the tenth of May, when the eighth grade was not yet completed.

I do not think I had to work as hard that summer. Perhaps it was just that the weather was better. Or that I was older. Or that my parents were doing more than I realized. Perhaps all of them together. Anyway, there seemed to be more free time, and that was the summer I flung myself into baseball with a passionate enthusiasm.

We played some evenings and on Sunday afternoons and we travelled considerable distances. I found that I could hit the ball naturally and easily but it was the fielding that I loved most of all. I played third base and the shortstop and I divided up our territory and responsibilities.

I would wait then for the bouncers and the line drives and the ground balls with delicious intensity. I would hope that each ball would be hit to me, and I do not recall any of them getting by. I would lunge and leap and bend and fall and pivot and turn and then hope that the next one might once again be mine. In my small area of the earth it seemed that everything was under my control.

WINTER DOG

(1 9 8 1)

 I am writing this in December. In the period close
to Christmas, and three days after the first snowfall
in this region of southwestern Ontario. The snow
came quietly in the night or in the early morning. When we
went to bed near midnight, there was none at all. Then early in
the morning we heard the children singing Christmas songs
from their rooms across the hall. It was very dark and I rolled
over to check the time. It was 4:30 a.m. One of them must have
awakened and looked out the window to find the snow and then
eagerly awakened the others. They are half crazed by the
promise of Christmas, and the discovery of the snow is an unexpected giddy surprise. There was no snow promised for this area,
not even yesterday.

"What are you doing?" I call, although it is obvious.

"Singing Christmas songs," they shout back with equal obvi-
ousness, "because it snowed."

"Try to be quiet," I say, "or you'll wake the baby."

"She's already awake," they say. "She's listening to our singing. She likes it. Can we go out and make a snowman?"

I roll from my bed and go to the window. The neighbouring houses are muffled in snow and silence and there are as yet no lights in any of them. The snow has stopped falling and its whitened quietness reflects the shadows of the night.

"This snow is no good for snowmen," I say. "It is too dry."

"How can snow be dry?" asks a young voice. Then an older one says, "Well, then can we go out and make the first tracks?"

They take my silence for consent and there are great sounds of rustling and giggling as they go downstairs to touch the light switches and rummage and jostle for coats and boots.

"What on earth is happening?" asks my wife from her bed. "What are they doing?"

"They are going outside to make the first tracks in the snow," I say. "It snowed quite heavily last night."

"What time is it?"

"Shortly after 4:30."

"Oh."

We ourselves have been nervous and restless for the past weeks. We have been troubled by illness and uncertainty in those we love far away on Canada's east coast. We have already considered and rejected driving the fifteen hundred miles. Too far, too uncertain, too expensive, fickle weather, the complications of transporting Santa Claus.

Instead, we sleep uncertainly and toss in unbidden dreams. We jump when the phone rings after 10:00 p.m. and are then reassured by the distant voices.

"First of all, there is nothing wrong," they say. "Things are just the same."

Sometimes we make calls ourselves, even to the hospital in Halifax, and are surprised at the voices which answer.

"I just got here this afternoon from Newfoundland. I'm going to try to stay a week. He seems better today. He's sleeping now."

At other times we receive calls from farther west, from Edmonton and Calgary and Vancouver. People hoping to find objectivity in the most subjective of situations. Strung out in uncertainty across the time zones from British Columbia to Newfoundland.

Within our present city, people move and consider possibilities:

If he dies tonight we'll leave right away. Can you come?

We will have to drive as we'll never get air reservations at this time.

I'm not sure if my car is good enough. I'm always afraid of the mountains near Cabano.

If we were stranded in Rivière-du-Loup we would be worse off than being here. It would be too far for anyone to come and get us.

My car will go but I'm not so sure I can drive it all the way. My eyes are not so good any more, especially at night in drifting snow.

Perhaps there'll be no drifting snow.

There's always drifting snow.

We'll take my car if you'll drive it. We'll have to drive straight through.

John phoned and said he'll give us his car if we want it or he'll drive — either his own car or someone else's.

He drinks too heavily, especially for long-distance driving, and at this time of year. He's been drinking ever since this news began.

He drinks because he cares. It's just the way he is.

Not everybody drinks.

Not everybody cares, and if he gives you his word, he'll never drink until he gets there. We all know that.

But so far nothing has happened. Things seem to remain the same.

Through the window and out on the white plane of the snow, the silent, laughing children now appear. They move in their muffled clothes like mummers on the whitest of stages. They dance and gesture noiselessly, flopping their arms in parodies of heavy, happy, earthbound birds. They have been warned by the eldest to be aware of the sleeping neighbours so they cavort only in pantomime, sometimes raising mittened hands to their mouths to suppress their joyous laughter. They dance and prance in the moonlight, tossing snow in one another's direction, tracing out various shapes and initials, forming lines which snake across the previously unmarked whiteness. All of it in silence, unknown to and unseen and unheard by the neighbouring world. They seem unreal even to me, their father, standing at his darkened window. It is almost as if they have danced out of the world of folklore like happy elves who cavort and mimic and caper through the private hours of this whitened dark, only to vanish with the coming of the morning's light and leaving only the signs of their activities behind. I am tempted to check the recently vacated beds to confirm what perhaps I think I know.

Then out of the corner of my eye I see him. The golden collie-like dog. He appears almost as if from the wings of the stage or as a figure newly noticed in the lower corner of a winter painting. He sits quietly and watches the playful scene before him and then, as if responding to a silent invitation, bounds into its midst. The children chase him in frantic circles, falling and rolling as he doubles back and darts and dodges between their legs and through their outstretched arms. He seizes a mitt loosened from its owner's hand, and tosses it happily in the air and then snatches it back into his jaws an instant before it reaches the ground and seconds before the tumbling bodies fall on the emptiness of its expected destination. He races to the edge of the scene and lies facing them, holding the mitt tantalizingly between his paws, and then as they dash towards him, he leaps forward again, tossing and catching it before him and zigzagging through them as the Sunday football player might return the much sought-after ball. After he has gone through and eluded them all, he looks back over his shoulder and again, like an elated athlete, tosses the mitt high in what seems like an imaginary end zone. Then he seizes it once more and lopes in a wide circle around his pursuers, eventually coming closer and closer to them until once more their stretching hands are able to actually touch his shoulders and back and haunches, although he continues always to wriggle free. He is touched but never captured, which is the nature of the game. Then he is gone. As suddenly as he came. I strain my eyes in the direction of the adjoining street, toward the house where I have often seen him, always within a yard enclosed by woven links of chain. I see the flash of his silhouette, outlined perhaps against the snow or the light cast by the street lamps or the moon. It arcs upward and seems to hang for an instant high above the top of the fence and then it descends on the other side. He lands on his shoulder in a fluff of snow and with a half roll regains his feet and vanishes within the shadow of his owner's house.

"What are you looking at?" asks my wife.

"That golden collie-like dog from the other street was just playing with the children in the snow."

"But he's always in that fenced-in yard."

"I guess not always. He jumped the fence just now and went back in. I guess the owners and the rest of us think he's fenced in but he knows he's not. He probably comes out every night and leads an exciting life. I hope they don't see his tracks or they'll probably begin to chain him."

"What are the children doing?"

"They look tired now from chasing the dog. They'll probably soon be back in. I think I'll go downstairs and wait for them and make myself a cup of coffee."

"Okay."

I look once more toward the fenced-in yard but the dog is nowhere to be seen.

I first saw such a dog when I was twelve and he came as a pup of about two months in a crate to the railroad station which was about eight miles from where we lived. Someone must have phoned or dropped in to say: "Your dog's at the station."

He had come to Cape Breton in response to a letter and a cheque which my father had sent to Morrisburg, Ontario. We had seen the ads for "cattle collie dogs" in *The Family Herald*, which was the farm newspaper of the time, and we were in need of a good young working dog.

His crate was clean and neat and there was still a supply of dog biscuits with him and a can in the corner to hold water. The baggage handlers had looked after him well on the trip east, and he appeared in good spirits. He had a white collar and chest and four rather large white paws and a small white blaze on his forehead. The rest of him was a fluffy, golden brown, although his eyebrows and the tips of his ears as well as the end of his tail were darker, tingeing almost to black. When he grew to his full size the blackish shadings became really black, and although he had the long, heavy coat of a collie, it was in certain areas more grey than gold. He was also taller than the average collie and with a deeper chest. He seemed to be at least part German Shepherd.

It was winter when he came and we kept him in the house, where he slept behind the stove in a box lined with an old coat. Our other dogs slept mostly in the stables or outside in the lees of woodpiles or under porches or curled up on the banking of the house. We seemed to care more for him because he was smaller and it was winter and he was somehow like a visitor; and also because more was expected of him and also perhaps because we had paid money for him and thought about his coming for some time – like a "planned" child. Sceptical neighbours and relatives who thought the idea of paying money for a dog was rather exotic or frivolous would ask: "Is that your Ontario dog?" or "Do you think your Ontario dog will be any good?"

He turned out to be no good at all, and no one knew why. Perhaps it was because of the suspected German Shepherd blood. But he could not "get the hang of it." Although we worked him and trained him as we had other dogs, he seemed always to bring panic instead of order and to make things worse instead of better. He became a "head dog," which meant that instead of working behind the cattle he lunged at their heads,

255

impeding them from any forward motion and causing them to turn in endless, meaningless bewildered circles. On the few occasions when he did go behind them, he was "rough," which meant that instead of being a floating, nipping, suggestive presence, he actually bit them and caused them to gallop, which was another sin. Sometimes in the summer the milk cows suffering from his misunderstood pursuit would jam pell mell into the stable, tossing their wide horns in fear, and with their great sides heaving and perspiring while down their legs and tails the wasted milk ran in rivulets mingling with the blood caused by his slashing wounds. He was, it was said, "worse than nothing."

Gradually everyone despaired, although he continued to grow grey and golden and was, as everyone agreed, a "beautiful-looking dog."

He was also tremendously strong, and in the winter months I would hitch him to a sleigh, which he pulled easily and willingly on almost any kind of surface. When he was harnessed I used to put a collar around his neck and attach a light line to it so that I might have some minimum control over him, but it was hardly ever needed. He would pull home the Christmas tree or the bag of flour or the deer which was shot far back in the woods; and when we visited our winter snares he would pull home the gunny sacks which contained the partridges and rabbits which we gathered. He would also pull us, especially on the flat wind-swept stretches of land beside the sea. There the snow was never really deep and the water that oozed from a series of freshwater springs and ponds contributed to a glaze of ice and crisply crusted snow which the sleigh runners seemed to sing over without ever breaking through. He would begin with an easy lope and then increase his swiftness until both he and the sleigh seemed to touch the surface at only irregular intervals. He would stretch out then with his ears flattened against his head and his shoulders bunching and contracting in the rhythm of his speed. Behind him on the sleigh we would cling tenaciously to the wooden slats as the particles of ice and snow dislodged by his nails hurtled towards our faces. We would avert our heads and close our eyes and the wind stung so sharply that the difference between freezing and burning could not be known. He would do that until late in the afternoon when it was time to return home and begin our chores.

On the sunny winter Sunday that I am thinking of, I planned to visit my snares. There seemed no other children around that afternoon, and the adults were expecting relatives. I harnessed the dog to the sleigh, opened the door of the house and shouted that I was going to look at my snares. We began to climb the hill behind the house on our way to the woods when we looked back and out toward the sea. The "big ice," which was what we called the major pack of drift ice, was in solidly against the shore and stretched out beyond the range of vision. It had not been "in" yesterday, although for the past weeks we had seen it moving offshore, sometimes close and sometimes distant, depending on the winds and tides. The coming of the big ice marked the official beginning of the coldest part of winter. It was mostly drift ice from the Arctic and Labrador, although some of it was freshwater ice from the estuary of the St. Lawrence. It drifted down with the dropping temperatures, bringing its own mysterious coldness and stretching for hundreds of miles in craters and pans, sometimes in grotesque shapes and sometimes in dazzling architectural forms. It was blue and white and sometimes grey and at other times a dazzling emerald green.

The dog and I changed our direction toward the sea, to find what the ice might yield. Our land had always been beside the sea and we had always gone toward it to find newness and the extraordinary; and over the years we, as others along the coast, had found quite a lot, although never the pirate chests of gold that were supposed to abound, or the reasons for the mysterious lights that our elders still spoke of and persisted in seeing. But kegs of rum had washed up, and sometimes bloated horses and various fishing paraphernalia and valuable timber and furniture from foundered ships. The door of my room was apparently the galley door from a ship called the *Judith Franklin* which was wrecked during the early winter in which my great-grandfather was building his house. My grandfather told of how they had heard the cries and seen the lights as the ship neared the rocks, and of how they had run down in the dark and tossed lines to the people while tying themselves to trees on the shore. All were saved, including women clinging to small children. The next day the builders of the new house went down to the shore and salvaged what they could from the wreckage of the vanquished ship. A sort of symbolic marriage of the new and the old: doors and shelving, stairways, hatches, wooden chests and trunks and various glass figurines and lanterns which were miraculously never broken.

People came too. The dead as well as the living. Bodies of men swept overboard and reported lost at sea, and the bodies of men still crouched within the shelter of their boats' broken bows. And sometimes in late winter young sealers who had quit their vessels would walk across the ice and come to our doors. They were usually very young – some still in their teens – and had signed on for jobs they could not or no longer wished to handle. They were often disoriented and did not know where they were, only that they had seen land and had decided to walk toward it. They were often frostbitten and with little money and uncertain as to how they might get to Halifax. The dog and I walked toward the ice upon the sea.

Sometimes it was hard to "get on" the ice, which meant that at the point where the pack met the shore there might be open water or irregularities caused by the indentations of the coastline or the workings of the tides and currents, but for us on that day there was no difficulty at all. We were "on" easily and effortlessly and enthusiastic about our new adventure. For the first mile there was nothing but the vastness of the white expanse. We came to a clear stretch where the ice was as smooth and unruffled as that of an indoor arena and I knelt on the sleigh while the dog loped easily along. Gradually the ice changed to an uneven terrain of pressure ridges and hummocks, making it impossible to ride farther; and then suddenly, upon rounding a hummock, I saw the perfect seal. At first I thought it was alive, as did the dog, who stopped so suddenly in his tracks that the sleigh almost collided with his legs. The hackles on the back of his neck rose and he growled in the dangerous way he was beginning to develop. But the seal was dead, yet facing us in a frozen perfection that was difficult to believe. There was a light powder of snow over its darker coat and a delicate rime of frost still formed the outline of its whiskers. Its eyes were wide open and it stared straight ahead towards the land. Even now in memory it seems more real than reality – as if it were trans-formed by frozen art into something more arresting than life itself. The way the sudden seal in the museum exhibit freezes your eyes with the touch of truth. Immediately I wanted to take it home.

It was frozen solidly in a base of ice, so I began to look for something that might serve as a pry. I let the dog out of his harness and hung the sleigh and harness on top of the hummock to mark the place and began my search. Some distance away I found a pole about twelve feet long. It is always surprising to find such things on the ice field but they are, often amazingly, there, almost in the same way that you might find a pole floating in the summer ocean. Unpredictable but possible. I took the pole back and began my work. The dog went off on explorations of his own.

Although it was firmly frozen, the task did not seem impos-sible and by inserting the end of the pole under first one side and then the other and working from the front to the back, it was possible to cause a gradual loosening. I remember thinking how very warm it was because I was working hard and perspiring heavily. When the dog came back he was uneasy, and I realized it was starting to snow a bit but I was almost done. He sniffed without interest at the seal and began to whine a bit, which was something he did not often do. Finally, after another quarter of an hour, I was able to roll my trophy onto the sleigh and with the dog in harness we set off. We had gone perhaps two hundred yards when the seal slid free. I took the dog and the sleigh back and once again managed to roll the seal on. This time I took the

line from the dog's collar and tied the seal to the sleigh, reasoning that the dog would go home anyway and there would be no
need to guide him. My fingers were numb as I tried to fasten the
awkward knots, and the dog began to whine and rear. When I
gave the command he bolted forward, and I clung at the back of
the sleigh to the seal. The snow was heavier now and blowing in
my face but we were moving rapidly, and when we came to the
stretch of arena-like ice we skimmed across it almost like an
iceboat, the profile of the frozen seal at the front of the sleigh
like those figures at the prows of Viking ships. At the very end
of the smooth stretch, we went through. From my position at
the end of the sleigh I felt him drop almost before I saw him,
and rolled backwards seconds before the sleigh and seal followed
him into the blackness of the water. He went under once,
carried by his own momentum, but surfaced almost immediately
with his head up and his paws scrambling at the icy, jagged edge
of the hole; but when the weight and momentum of the sleigh
and its burden struck, he went down again, this time out of sight.

I realized we had struck a "seam" and that the stretch of
smooth ice had been deceivingly and temporarily joined to the
rougher ice near the shore and now was in the process of breaking away. I saw the widening line before me and jumped to the
other side just as his head miraculously came up once more. I lay
on my stomach and grabbed his collar in both my hands and
then in a moment of panic did not know what to do. I could feel
myself sliding towards him and the darkness of the water and
was aware of the weight that pulled me forward and down. I was
also aware of his razor-sharp claws flailing violently before my
face and knew that I might lose my eyes. And I was aware that

his own eyes were bulging from their sockets and that he might think I was trying to choke him and might lunge and slash my face with his teeth in desperation. I knew all of this but somehow did nothing about it; it seemed almost simpler to hang on and be drawn into the darkness of the gently slopping water, seeming to slop gently in spite of all the agitation. Then suddenly he was free, scrambling over my shoulder and dragging the sleigh behind him. The seal surfaced again, buoyed up perhaps by the physics of its frozen body or the nature of its fur. Still looking more genuine than it could have in life, its snout and head broke the open water and it seemed to look at us curiously for an instant before it vanished permanently beneath the ice. The loose and badly tied knots had apparently not held when the sleigh was in a near vertical position and we were saved by the ineptitude of my own numbed fingers. We had been spared for a future time.

He lay gasping and choking for a moment, coughing up the icy salt water, and then almost immediately his coat began to freeze. I realized then how cold I was myself and that even in the moments I had been lying on the ice, my clothes had begun to adhere to it. My earlier heated perspiration was now a cold rime upon my body and I imagined it outlining me there, beneath my clothes, in a sketch of frosty white. I got on the sleigh once more and crouched low as he began to race towards home. His coat was freezing fast, and as he ran the individual ice-coated hairs began to clack together like rhythmical castanets attuned to the motion of his body. It was snowing quite heavily in our faces now and it seemed to be approaching dusk, although I doubted if it were so on the land which I could now no longer see. I realized all the obvious things I should have considered earlier. That if the snow was blowing in our faces, the wind was off the land, and if it was off the land, it was blowing the ice pack back out to sea. That was probably one reason why the seam had opened. And also that the ice had only been "in" one night and had not had a chance to "set." I realized other things as well. That it was the time of the late afternoon when the tide was falling. That no one knew where we were. That I had said we were going to look at snares, which was not where we had gone at all. And I remembered now that I had received no answer even to that misinformation, so perhaps I had not even been heard. And also if there was drifting snow like this on land, our tracks would by now have been obliterated.

We came to a rough section of ice: huge slabs on their sides and others piled one on top of the other as if they were in some strange form of storage. It was no longer possible to ride the sleigh but as I stood up I lifted it and hung on to it as a means of holding on to the dog. The line usually attached to his collar had sunk with the vanished seal. My knees were stiff when I stood up; and deprived of the windbreak effect which the dog had provided, I felt the snow driving full into my face, particularly my eyes. It did not merely impede my vision, the way distant snow flurries might, but actually entered my eyes, causing them to water and freeze nearly shut. I was aware of the weight of ice on my eyelashes and could see them as they gradually lowered and became heavier. I did not remember ice like this when I got on, although I did not find that terribly surprising. I pressed the soles of my numb feet firmly down upon it to try to feel if it was moving out, but it was impossible to tell because there was no

fixed point of reference. Almost the sensation one gets on con-
veyor belts at airports or on escalators; although you are standing still you recognize motion, but should you shut your eyes
and be deprived of sight, even that recognition may become
ambiguously uncertain.

The dog began to whine and to walk around me in circles,
binding my legs with the traces of the harness as I continued
to grasp the sleigh. Finally I decided to let him go as there
seemed no way to hold him and there was nothing else to do.
I unhitched the traces and doubled them up as best I could and
tucked them under the backpad of his harness so they would
not drag behind him and become snagged on any obstacles. I
did not take off my mitts to do so as I was afraid I would not
be able to get them back on. He vanished into the snow almost
immediately.

The sleigh had been a gift from an uncle, so I hung on to it
and carried it with both hands before me like an ineffectual
shield against the wind and snow. I lowered my head as much
as I could and turned it sideways so the wind would beat
against my head instead of directly into my face. Sometimes
I would turn and walk backward for a few steps. Although I
knew it was not the wisest thing to do, it seemed at times the
only way to breathe. And then I began to feel the water slosh-
ing about my feet.

Sometimes when the tides or currents ran heavily and the ice
began to separate, the water that was beneath it would well up
and wash over it, almost as if it were reflooding it. Sometimes
you could see the hard ice clearly beneath the water but at other
times a sort of floating slush was formed mingling with snow

and "slob" ice which was not yet solid. It was thick and dense and soupy and it was impossible to see what lay beneath it. Experienced men on the ice sometimes carried a slender pole so they could test the consistency of the footing which might or might not lie before them, but I was obviously not one of them, although I had a momentary twinge for the pole I had used to dislodge the seal. Still, there was nothing to do but go forward.

When I went through, the first sensation was almost of relief and relaxation, for the water initially made me feel much warmer than I had been on the surface. It was the most dangerous of false sensations, for I knew my clothes were becoming heavier by the second. I clung to the sleigh somewhat as a raft and lunged forward with it in a kind of up-and-down motion, hoping that it might strike some sort of solidity before my arms became so weighted and sodden that I could no longer lift them. I cried out then for the first time into the driving snow.

He came almost immediately, although I could see he was afraid and the slobbing slush was up to his knees. Still, he seemed to be on some kind of solid footing, for he was not swimming. I splashed towards him and when almost there, desperately threw the sleigh before me and lunged for the edge of what seemed like his footing, but it only gave way as if my hands were closing on icy insubstantial porridge. He moved forward then, although I still could not tell if what supported him would be of any use to me. Finally I grasped the breast strap of his harness. He began to back up then, and as I said, he was tremendously strong. The harness began to slide forward on his shoulders but he continued to pull as I continued to grasp and then I could feel my elbows on what seemed like solid ice and I was able to hook them on the edge and draw myself, dripping and soaking, like another seal out of the black water and onto the whiteness of the slushy ice. Almost at once my clothes began to freeze. My elbows and knees began to creak when I bent them as if I were a robot from the realm of science fiction and then I could see myself clothed in transparent ice as if I had been coated with shellac or finished with clear varnish.

As the fall into the winter sea had at first seemed ironically warm, so now my garments of ice seemed a protection against the biting wind, but I knew it was a deceptive sensation and that I did not have much time before me. The dog faced into the wind and I followed him. This time he stayed in sight, and at times even turned back to wait for me. He was cautious but certain and gradually the slush disappeared, and although we were still in water, the ice was hard and clear beneath it. The frozen heaviness of my clothes began to weigh on me and I could feel myself, ironically, perspiring within my suit of icy armour. I was very tired, which I knew was another dangerous sensation. And then I saw the land. It was very close and a sudden surprise. Almost like coming upon a stalled and unex-pected automobile in a highway's winter storm. It was only yards away, and although there was no longer any ice actually touch-ing the shore, there were several pans of it floating in the region between. The dog jumped from one to the other and I followed him, still clutching the sleigh, and missing only the last pan which floated close to the rocky shore. The water came only to my waist and I was able to touch the bottom and splash noisily on land. We had been spared again for a future time and I was never to know whether he had reached the shore himself and come back or whether he had heard my call against the wind.

We began to run toward home, and the land lightened and there were touches of evening sun. The wind still blew but no snow was falling. Yet when I looked back, the ice and the ocean were invisible in the swirling squalls. It was like looking at another far and distant country on the screen of a snowy television.

I became obsessed, now that I could afford the luxury, with not being found disobedient or considered a fool. The visitors' vehicles were still in the yard, so I imagined most of the family to be in the parlour or living room, and I circled the house and entered through the kitchen, taking the dog with me. I was able to get upstairs unnoticed and get my clothes changed, and when I came down I mingled with everybody and tried to appear as normal as I could. My own family was caught up with the visitors and only general comments came my way. The dog, who could not change his clothes, lay under the table with his head on his paws and he was also largely unnoticed. Later as the ice melted from his coat, a puddle formed around him, which I casually mopped up. Still later someone said, "I wonder where that dog has been, his coat is soaking wet." I was never to tell anyone of the afternoon's experience, or that he had saved my life.

Two winters later I was sitting at a neighbour's kitchen table when I looked out the window and saw the dog as he was shot. He had followed my father and also me and had been sitting rather regally on a little hill beside the house and I suppose had presented an ideal target. But he had moved at just the right or wrong time and instead of killing him, the high-powered bullet smashed into his shoulder. He jumped into the air and turned his snapping teeth upon the wound, trying to bite the cause of the pain he could not see. And then he turned towards home, unsteady but still strong on three remaining legs. No doubt he felt, as we all do, that if he could get home he might be saved, but he did not make it, as we knew he could not, because of the amount of blood on the snow and the wavering pattern of his three-legged tracks. Yet he was, as I said, tremendously strong and he managed almost three-quarters of a mile. The house he sought must have been within his vision when he died, for we could see it quite clearly when we came to his body by the roadside. His eyes were open and his tongue was clenched between his teeth and the little blood he had left dropped red and black on the winter snow. He was not to be saved for a future time any more.

I learned later that my father had asked the neighbour to shoot him and that we had led him into a kind of ambush. Perhaps my father did so because the neighbour was younger and had a better gun or was a better shot. Perhaps because my father did not want to be involved. It was obvious he had not planned on things turning out so messy.

The dog had become increasingly powerful and protective, to the extent that people were afraid to come into the yard. And he had also bitten two of the neighbour's children and caused them to be frightened of passing our house on their journeys to and from school. And perhaps there was also the feeling in the community that he was getting more than his share of the breeding: that he travelled farther than other dogs on his nightly forays and that he fought off and injured the other smaller dogs who might compete with him for female favours. Perhaps there was fear that his dominance and undesirable characteristics did not bode well for future generations.

This has been the writing down of a memory triggered by the sight of a golden dog at play in the silent snow with my own excited children. After they came in and had their hot chocolate, the wind began to blow; and by the time I left for work, there was no evidence of their early-morning revels or any dog tracks leading to the chain-link fence. The "enclosed" dog looked impassively at me as I brushed the snow from the buried wind-shield. What does he know? he seemed to say.

The snow continues to drift and to persist as another uncer-tainty added to those we already have. Should we be forced to drive tonight, it will be a long, tough journey into the wind and the driving snow which is pounding across Ontario and Quebec and New Brunswick and against the granite coast of Nova Scotia. Should we be drawn by death, we might well meet our own. Still, it is only because I am alive that I can even consider such possibilities. Had I not been saved by the golden dog, I would not have these tight concerns, or children playing in the snow or, of course, these memories. It is because of him that I have been able to come this far in time.

It is too bad that I could not have saved him as well, and my feelings did him little good as I looked upon his bloodied body there beside the road. It was too late and out of my control and even if I had known the possibilities of the future it would not have been easy.

He was with us only for a while and brought his own changes, and yet he still persists. He persists in my memory and in my life and he persists physically as well. He is there in this winter storm. There in the golden-grey dogs with their black-tipped ears and tails, sleeping in the stables or in the lees of woodpiles or under porches or curled beside the houses which face toward the sea.

THE TUNING OF PERFECTION

(1 9 8 4)

He thought of himself, in the middle of that April, as a man who had made it through another winter. He was seventy-eight years old and it seems best to give his exact age now, rather than trying to rely on such descriptions as "old" or "vigorous" or "younger than his years." He was seventy-eight and a tall, slim man with dark hair and brown eyes and his own teeth. He was frequently described as "neat" because he always appeared clean-shaven and the clothes he wore were clean and in order. He wore suspenders instead of a belt because he felt they kept his trousers "in line" instead of allowing them to sag sloppily down his waist, revealing too much of his shirt. And when he went out in public, he always wore shoes. In cold or muddy weather, he wore overshoes or rubbers or what he called the "overboots" – the rubber kind with the zippers in the front, to protect his shoes. He never wore the more common rubber boots in public – although, of course, he owned them and kept them neatly on a piece of clean card-board in a corner of his porch.

He lived alone near the top of the mountain in a house which he himself had built when he was a much younger man. There had once been another house in the same clearing, and the hollow of its cellar was still visible as well as a few of the moss-covered stones that had formed its early foundation. This "ex-house" had been built by his great-grandfather shortly after he had come from the Isle of Skye and it was still referred to as "the first house" or sometimes as "the old house," although it was no longer there. No one was really sure why his great-grandfather had built the house so high up on the mountain, especially when one considered that he had been granted a great deal of land and there were more accessible spots upon it where one might build a house. Some thought that since he was a lumberman he had wanted to start on top of the mountain and log his way down. Others thought that because of the violence he had left in Scotland he wanted to be inaccessible in the new world and wanted to be able to see any potential enemies before they could see him. Others thought that he had merely wanted to be alone, while another group maintained that he had built it for the view. All of the reasons became confused and intermingled with the passing of the generations and the distancing of the man from Skye. Perhaps the theory of the view proved the most enduring because although the man from Skye and the house he built were no longer visible, the view still was. And it was truly spec-tacular. One could see for miles along the floor of the valley and over the tops of the smaller mountains and when one looked to the west there was the sea. There it was possible to see the various fishing boats of summer and the sealing ships of winter and the lines of Prince Edward Island and the flat shapes of the Magdalen Islands and, more to the east, the purple mass of Newfoundland.

The paved road or the "main road" which ran along the valley floor was five miles by automobile from his house, although it was not really that far if one walked and took various short cuts: paths and footbridges over the various tumbling brooks and creeks that spilled down the mountain's side. Once there had been a great deal of traffic on such paths, people on foot and people with horses, but over the years as more and more people obtained automobiles, the paths fell into disuse and became overgrown, and the bridges that were washed away by the spring freshets were no longer replaced very regularly or very well.

The section of winding road that led to his house and ended in his yard had been a bone of contention for many years, as had some of the other sections as well. Most of the people on the upper reaches of the mountain were his relatives, and they were all on sections of the land granted to the man from Skye. Some of the road was "public" and therefore eligible to be maintained by the Department of Highways. Other sections of it, including his, were "private," so they were not maintained at all by government but only by the people living along them. As he lived a mile above the "second last" or the "second" house – depending upon which way you were counting – he did not receive visits from the grader or the gravel truck, or the snow plough in winter. It was generally assumed that the Department of Highways was secretly glad that it did not have to send its men or equipment up the twisting switchbacks and around the hairpin turns that skirted the treacherous gullies containing the wrecks of rolled and abandoned cars. The Department of Highways was not that fussy about the slightly lower reaches of the road, either, and there were always various petitions being circulated, demanding "better service for the tax dollar." Still, whenever the issue of making a "private" section of the road "public" was raised, there were always counter-petitions that circulated and used phrases like "keeping the land of our fathers *ours.*" Three miles down the mountain, though (or two miles up), there was a nice wide "turn-around" for the school bus, and up to and including that spot the road was maintained as well as any other of its kind.

He did not mind living alone up on the mountain, saying that he got great television reception, which was of course true – although it was a relatively new justification. There was no television when he built the house in the two years prior to 1927 and when he was filled with the fever of his approaching marriage. Even then, people wondered why he was "going up the mountain" while many of the others were coming down, but he paid them little mind, working at it in determined perfection in the company of his twin brother and getting the others only when it was absolutely necessary: for the raising of the roof beams and the fitting of the gables.

He and his wife had been the same age and were almost consumed by one another while they were still quite young. Neither had ever had another boyfriend or girlfriend but he had told her they would not marry until he had completed the house. He wanted the house so that they could be "alone together" as soon as they were married, rather than moving in with in-laws or relatives for a while, as was frequently the custom of the time. So he had worked at it determinedly and desperately, anticipating the time when he could end "his life" and begin "their lives."

He and his twin brother had built it in "the old way," which meant making their own plans and cutting all the logs themselves and "snigging" them out with their horses and setting up their own saw mill and planing mill. And deciding also to use wooden pegs in the roof timbers instead of nails; so that the house would move in the mountain's winds – like a ship – move but not capsize, move yet still return.

In the summer before the marriage, his wife-to-be had worked as hard as he, carrying lumber and swinging a hammer; and when her father suggested she was doing too much masculine work, she had replied, "I am doing what I want to do. I am doing it for *us*."

During the building of their house, they often sang together and the language of their singing was Gaelic. Sometimes one of them would sing the verses and the other the chorus and, at other times, they would sing the verses and choruses together and all the way through. Some of the songs contained at least fifteen or twenty verses and it would take a long time to complete them. On clear still days all of the people living down along the mountain's side and even below in the valley could hear the banging of their hammers and the youthful power of their voices.

They were married on a Saturday in late September and their first daughter was born exactly nine months later, which was an item of brief and passing interest. And their second daughter was born barely eleven months after their first. During the winter months of that time he worked in a lumber camp some fifteen miles away, cutting pulp for $1.75 a cord and getting $40.00 a month for his team of horses as well. Rising at five-thirty and working until after seven in the evening and sleeping on a bunk with a mattress made from boughs.

Sometimes he would come home on the weekends, and on the clear, winter nights she would hear the distinctive sound of his horses' bells as they left the valley floor to begin their ascent up the mountain's side. Although the climb was steep, the horses would walk faster because they knew they were coming home, even breaking into a trot on the more level areas and causing their bells to accelerate accordingly. Sometimes he would get out of the wood sleigh and run beside the horses or ahead of them in order to keep warm and also to convince himself that he was getting home faster.

When she heard the bells she would take the lamp and move it from one window to the other and then take it back again and continue to repeat the procedure. The effect was almost that of a regularly flashing light, like that of a lighthouse or someone flicking a light switch off and on at regulated intervals. He would see the light now at one window and then in the other, sent down like the regulated flashing signals his mares gave off when in heat; and although he was exhausted, he would be filled with desire and urge himself upwards at an even greater rate.

After he had stabled his horses and fed them, he would go into their house and they would meet one another in the middle of the kitchen floor, holding and going into one another sometimes while the snow and frost still hung so heavily on his clothes that they creaked when he moved or steamed near the presence of the stove. The lamp would be stilled on the kitchen table and they would be alone. Only the monogamous eagles who nested in the hemlock tree even farther up the mountain seemed above them.

They were married for five years in an intensity which it seemed could never last, going more and more into each other and excluding most others for the company of themselves.

When she went into premature labour in February of 1931, he was not at home because it was still six weeks before the expected birth and they had decided that he would stay in the camp a little longer in order to earn the extra money they needed for their fourth child.

There had been heavy snows in the area and high winds and then it had turned bitterly cold, all in the span of a day and a half. It had been impossible to get down from the mountain and get word to him in the camp, although his twin brother managed to walk in on the second day, bringing him the news that everyone on the mountain already knew: that he had lost his wife and what might have been his first-born son. The snow was higher than his twin brother's head when they saw him coming into the camp. He was soaked with perspiration from fighting the drifts, and pale and shaking, and he began to throw up in the yard of the camp almost before he could deliver his message.

He had left immediately, leaving his brother behind to rest, while following his incoming tracks back out. He could not believe it, could not believe that she had somehow gone without him, could not believe that in their closeness he was still the last to know and that in spite of hoping "to live alone together" she had somehow died surrounded by others, but without him and really alone in the ultimate sense. He could not believe that in the closeness of their beginning there had been separation in their end. He had tried to hope that there might be some mistake; but the image of his brother, pale and shaken and vomiting in the packed-down snow of the lumber camp's yard, dispelled any such possibility.

He was numb throughout all of the funeral preparations and the funeral itself. His wife's sisters looked after his three small daughters who, while they sometimes called for their mother, seemed almost to welcome the lavish attention visited upon them. On the afternoon following the funeral the pneumonia which his twin brother had developed after his walk into the camp worsened, and he had gone to sit beside his bed, holding his hand, at least able to be *present* this time, yet aware of the disapproving looks of Cora, his brother's wife, who was a woman he had never liked. Looks which said: If he had not gone for *you*, this would never have happened. Sitting there while his brother's chest deepened in spite of the poultices and the liniments and even the administrations of the doctor who finally made it up the mountain road and pronounced the pneumonia "surprisingly advanced."

After the death of his brother the numbness continued. He felt as those who lose all of their family in the midnight fire or on the sinking ship. Suddenly and without survivors. He felt guilt for his wife and for his brother's fatherless children and for his daughters who would now never know their mother. And he felt terribly alone.

His daughters stayed with him for a while as he tried to do what their mother had done. But gradually his wife's sisters began to suggest that the girls would be better off with them. At first he opposed the idea because both he and his wife had never been overly fond of her sisters, considering them somehow more vulgar than they were themselves. But gradually it became apparent that if he were ever to return to the woods and earn a living, someone would have to look after three children under the age of four. He was torn for the remainder of the winter months and into the spring, sometimes appreciating what he felt was the intended kindness of his in-laws and at other times angry at certain overheard remarks: "It is not right for three little girls to be alone up on that mountain with that man, a *young* man." As if he were more interesting as a potential child molester than simply as a father. Gradually his daughters began to spend evenings and weekends with their aunts, and then weeks, and then, in the manner of small children, they no longer cried when he left, or clung to his legs, or sat in the window to await his approach. And then they began to call him "Archibald," as did the other members of the households in which they lived. So that in the end he seemed neither husband nor brother nor even father but only "Archibald." He was twenty-seven years old.

He had always been called Archibald or sometimes in Gaelic "Gilleasbuig." Perhaps because of what was perceived as a kind of formality that hung about him, no one ever called him "Arch" or the more familiar and common "Archie." He did not look or act "like an Archie," as they said. And with the passing of the years, letters came that were addressed simply to "Archibald" and that bore a variety of addresses covering a radius of some forty miles. Many of the letters in the later years came from the folklorists who had "discovered" him in the 1960s and for whom he had made various tapes and recordings. And he had come to be regarded as "the last of the authentic old-time Gaelic singers." He was faithfully recorded in the archives at Sydney and Halifax and Ottawa and his picture had appeared in various scholarly and less scholarly journals; sometimes with the arms of the folklorists around him, sometimes holding one of his horses and sometimes standing beside his shining pickup truck which bore a bumper sticker which read "Suas Leis A' Ghaidlig." Sometimes the articles bore titles such as "Cape Breton Singer: The Last of His Kind" or "Holding Fast on Top of the Mountain" or "Mnemonic Devices in the Gaelic Line" – the latter generally being accompanied by a plethora of footnotes.

He did not really mind the folklorists, enunciating the words over and over again for them, explaining that "bh" was pronounced as "v" (like the "ph" in phone is pronounced "f," he would say), expanding on the more archaic meanings and footnoting himself the words and phrases of local origin. Doing it all with care and seriousness in much the same way that he filed and set his saws or structured his woodpile.

Now in this April of the 1980s he thought of himself, as I said earlier, as a man of seventy-eight years who had made it through another winter. He had come to terms with most things, although never really with the death of his wife; but that too had become easier during the last decades, although he was still bothered by the sexual references which came because of his monastic existence.

Scarcely a year after "the week of deaths," he had been visited by Cora, his twin brother's wife. She had come with her breath reeking of rum and placed the bottle on the middle of his kitchen table.

"I've been thinking," she said. "It's time me and you got together."

"Mmmm," he said, trying to make the most non-committal sound he could think of.

"Here," she said, going to his cupboard and taking down two of his sparkling glasses and splashing rum into them. "Here," she said, sliding a glass towards him across the table and seating herself opposite him. "Here, have a shot of this. It will put lead in your pencil," and then after a pause, "although from what I've *heard* there's no need of that."

He was taken aback, somehow imagining her and his twin brother lying side by side at night discussing his physicality.

Heard *what?* he wondered. *Where?*

"Yeah," she said. "There's not much need of you being up here on this mountain by yourself and me being by myself farther down. If you don't use it, it'll rust off."

He was close to panic, finding her so lonely and so drunkenly available and so much unlike the memory of his own wife. He wondered if she remembered how much they disliked each other, or thought they did. And he wondered if he were somehow thought of as being interchangeable with his dead brother. As if, because they were twins, their bodies must somehow be the same, regardless of their minds.

"I bet it's rusty right now," she said and she leaned the upper part of her body across the table so that he could smell the rum heavy on her breath even as he felt her fingers on his leg.

"Mmmm," he said, getting up rapidly and walking towards the window. He was rattled by her overt sexuality, the way a shy middle-aged married man might be when taken on a visit to a brothel far from his home – not because what is discussed is so foreign to him, but rather because of the manner and the approach.

Outside the window the eagles were flying up the mountain, carrying the twigs, some of them almost branches, for the building of their home.

"Mmmm," he said, looking out the window and down the winding road to the valley floor below.

"Well," she said, getting up and downing her drink. "I guess there's no fun here. I just wanted to say hello."

"Yes," he said. "Well, thank you."

She lurched towards the door and he wondered if he should open it for her or if that would be too rash.

But she opened it herself.

"Well," she said as she went out into the yard, "you know where I'm at."

"Yes," he said, gaining confidence from her departing back, "I know where you are."

Now on this morning in April half a century later, he looked out his window at the eagles flying by. They were going down into the valley to hunt, leaving their nest with their four precious eggs for the briefest time. Then he recognized the sound of a truck's motor. He recognized it before it entered the yard, in the way his wife had once recognized the individual sound of his horses' bells. The truck was muddy and splattered, not merely from this spring trip up the mountain but from a sort of residual dirt perhaps from the previous fall. It belonged to his married granddaughter, who had been christened Sarah but preferred to be known as Sal. She wheeled her truck into the yard, getting out of it inches from his door and almost before it had stopped. She wore her hair in a ponytail, although she seemed too old for that, and her tight-fitting jeans were slipped inside her husband's rubber boots. He was always slightly surprised at her ability to chew gum and smoke cigarettes at the same time and was reminded of that now as she came through his door, her lipstick leaving a red ring around her cigarette as she removed it from her mouth and flicked it out into the yard. She wore a tight-fitting T-shirt with the words "I'm Busted" across her chest.

"Hi, Archibald," she said, sitting in the chair nearest the window.

"Hi," he said.

"What's new?"

"Oh, nothing much," he replied, and then after a pause, "Would you like some tea?"

"Okay," she said. "No milk. I'm watching my figure."

"Mmmm," he said.

He looked at her from the distance of his years, trying to find within her some flashes of his wife or even of himself. She was attractive in her way, with her dark eyes and ready mouth, although shorter than either he or his wife.

"Had two phone calls," she said.

"Oh," he said, always feeling a bit guilty that he had no telephone and that messages had to be left with others farther down the mountain.

"One is from a guy who wants to buy your mare. You're still interested in selling?"

"Yes, I guess so."

"The other is about Gaelic singing. They want us to sing in Halifax this summer. This is the year of 'Scots Around the World.' All kinds of people will be there, even some of the Royal Family. We'll be there for a week. They haven't decided on the pay yet but it'll be okay and they'll pay our accommodation and our transportation."

"Oh," he said, becoming interested and cautious at the same time. "What do you mean by us?"

"*Us*. You know, the family. They want twenty of us. There'll be a few days of rehearsal there and then some concerts and we'll be on television. I can hardly wait. I have to do lots of shopping in Halifax and it will be a chance to sleep in without Tom bothering me. We won't even have to be at the theatre or studio or whatever until noon." She lit another cigarette.

"What do they want us to sing?" he asked.

"Oh, who cares?" she said. "It's the trip that's important. Some of the old songs. They're coming to audition us or something in two or three weeks. We'll sing *Fear A' Bhata* or something," she said, and butting her cigarette on her saucer and laying her gum beside it on the table, she began to sing in a clear, powerful voice:

Fhir a' bhata, na ho ro eile,
Fhir a' bhata, na ho ro eile,

284

Fhir a' bhata, na ho ro eile,
Mho shoraidh slan leat 's gach ait' an teid thu

Is tric mi 'sealltainn o 'n chnoc a 's airde
Dh'fheuch am faic mi fear a' bhata,
An tig thu 'n diugh, no 'n tig thu 'maireach;
'S mur tig thu idir, gur truagh a tha mi.

Only when she sang did she remind him somewhat of his wife, and again he felt the hope that she might reach that standard of excellence.

"You're singing it too fast," he said cautiously when she had finished. "But it is good. You're singing it like a milling song. It's supposed to be a lament for a loved one that's lost."

He sang it himself slowly, stressing the distinction of each syllable.

She seemed interested for a while, listening intently before replacing her gum and lighting another cigarette, then tossing the still-lighted match into the stove.

"Do you know what the words mean?" he said when he had finished.

"No," she said. "Neither will anybody else. I just make the noises. I've been hearing the things since I was two. I know how they go. I'm not dumb, you know."

"Who else are they asking?" he said, partially out of interest and partially to change the subject and avoid confrontation.

"I don't know. They said they'd get back to us later. All they wanted to know now was if we were interested. The man about the mare will be up later. I got to go now."

She was out of the door almost immediately, turning her truck in a spray of gravel that flicked against his house, the small stones pinging against his windowpane. A muddied bumper sticker read: "If you're horny, honk your horn."

He was reminded, as he often was, of Cora, who had been dead now for some fifteen years and who had married another man within a year of her visit to him with her open proposal. And he was touched that his granddaughter should seem so much like his brother's wife instead of like his own.

The man who came to buy the mare was totally unlike any other horse buyer he had ever seen. He came in a suit and in an elaborate car and spoke in an accent that was difficult to identify. He was accompanied by Carver, who was apparently his guide, a violent young man in his thirties from the other side of the mountain. Carver's not-unhandsome face was marred by a series of raised grey scars and his upper lip had been thickened as a result of a fight in which someone had swung a logging chain into his mouth, an action which had also cost him his most obvious teeth. He wore his wallet on a chain hooked to his belt and scuffed his heavy lumberman's boots on the cardboard in Archibald's porch before entering the kitchen. He was by the window and rolled a cigarette while the horse buyer talked to Archibald.

"How old is the mare?"

"Five," said Archibald.

"Has she ever had a colt?"

"Why, yes," said Archibald, puzzled by the question. Usually buyers asked if the horse would work single or double or something about its disposition or its legs or chest. Or if it would work in snow or eat enough to sustain a heavy work schedule.

"Do you think she could have another colt?" he asked.

"Why, I suppose," he said, almost annoyed, "if she had a stallion."

"No problem," said the man.

"But," said Archibald, driven by his old honesty, "she has never worked. I have not been in the woods that much lately and I always used the old mare, her mother, before she died. I planned to train her but never got around to it. She's more like a pet. She probably will work, though. They've always worked. It's in the stock. I've had them all my life." He stopped, almost embarrassed at having to apologize for his horses and for himself.

"Okay," said the man. "No problem. She has had a colt, though?"

"Look," said Carver from his seat near the window, snuffing out his cigarette between his callused thumb and forefinger, "he already told you that. I told you this man don't lie."

"Okay," said the man, taking out his chequebook.

"Don't you want to see her first?" asked Archibald.

"No, it's okay," the man said. "I believe you."

"He wants nine hundred dollars," said Carver. "She's a young mare."

"Okay," said the man, to Archibald's amazement. He had been hopeful of perhaps seven hundred dollars or even less since she had never worked.

"You'll take her down in your truck later?" the man said to Carver.

"Right on!" said Carver and they left, the man driving with a peculiar caution as if he had never been off pavement before and was afraid that the woods might swallow him.

After they left, Archibald went out to his barn to talk to the mare. He led her out to the brook to drink, then to the door of the house where she waited while he went in and rummaged for some bread to offer her as a farewell treat. She was young and strong and splendid and he was somehow disappointed that the buyer had not at least seen her so that he could appreciate her excellent qualities.

Shortly after noon Carver drove his truck into the yard. "Do you want a beer?" he said to Archibald, motioning towards the open case on the seat beside him.

"No, I don't think so," Archibald said. "We may as well get this over with."

"Okay," said Carver. "Do you want to lead her on?"

"No, it's okay," said Archibald. "She'll go with anybody."

"Yeah," said Carver. "Perhaps that's a good way to be."

They went into the barn. In spite of what he had said, Archibald found himself going up beside the mare and untying the rope and leading her out into the afternoon sun which reflected on her dappled shining coat. Carver backed his truck up to a small incline beside the barn and lowered the tailgate. Then Archibald handed him the rope and watched as she followed him willingly into the truck.

"This is the last of all them nice horses you had up here, eh?" said Carver after he had tied the rope and swung down from the truck.

"Yes," said Archibald, "the last."

"I guess you hauled a lot of wood with them horses. I heard guys talking, older guys who worked with you in the camps."

"Oh, yes," said Archibald.

"I heard guys say you and your brother could cut seven cords of pulp a day with a crosscut saw, haul it and stack it."

"Oh, yes," he said. "Some days we could. Days seemed longer then," he added with a smile.

"Christ, we're lucky to get seven with a power saw unless we're in a real good stand," said Carver, pulling up his trousers and starting to roll a cigarette. "Your timber here on your own land is as good as ever, they say."

"Yes," he said. "It's pretty good."

"'That Archibald,' they say, 'no one knows where he gets all them logs, hauls them out with them horses and doesn't seem to disturb anything. Year after year. Treats the mountain as if it were a garden.'"

"Mmmm," he said.

"Not like now, eh? We just cut 'em all down. Go in with heavy equipment, tree farmers and loaders and do it all in a day, to hell with tomorrow."

"Yes," said Archibald. "I've noticed."

"You don't want to sell?" asked Carver.

"No," he said. "Not yet."

"I just thought . . . since you were letting your mare go. No work for the mare, no work for you."

"Oh, she'll probably work somewhere," he said. "I'm not so sure about myself."

"Nah, she won't work," said Carver. "They want her for birth control pills."

"For what?" said Archibald.

"This guy says, I don't know if it's true, that there's this farm outside of Montreal that's connected to a lab or something.

Anyway, they've got all these mares there and they keep them bred all the time and they use their water for birth control pills."

It seemed so preposterous that Archibald was not sure how to react. He scrutinized Carver's scarred yet open face, looking for a hint, some kind of touch, but he could find nothing.

"Yeah," said Carver. "They keep the mares pregnant all the time so the women won't be."

"What do they do with the colts?" said Archibald, thinking that he might try a question for a change.

"I dunno," said Carver. "He didn't say. I guess they just throw them away. Got to go now," he said, swinging into the cab of his truck, "and take her down the mountain. I think he's almost got a boxcar of these mares, or a transport truck. In two days she'll be outside Montreal and they'll get her a stallion and that'll be it."

The truck roared into action and moved from the incline near the barn. Archibald had been closer to it than he thought and was forced to step out of the way. As it passed, Carver rolled down the window and shouted, "Hey, Archibald, do you sing any more?"

"Not so much," he said.

"Got to talk to you about that sometime," he said above the engine's roar and then he and the truck and the splendid mare left the yard to begin their switchbacked journey down the mountain.

For a long time Archibald did not know what to do. He felt somehow betrayed by forces he could not control. The image of his mare beneath the weight of successive and different stallions came to his mind but the most haunting image was that of the dead colts which Carver had described as being "thrown away." He imagined them as the many dead unwanted animals he had seen thrown out on the manure piles behind the barns, their skulls smashed in by blows from axes. He doubted that there was anything like that outside of Montreal and he doubted – or wanted to doubt – somehow more than he could what Carver had said. But he had no way to verify the facts or disprove them, and the images persisted. He thought, as he always did at times of loss, of his wife. And then of the pale, still body of his quiet and unbreathing son, with the intricate blue veins winding like the map lines of roads and rivers upon his fragile, delicate skull. Both wife and son gone from him, taken in the winter's snow. And he felt somehow that he might cry.

He looked up to the sound of the whooshing eagles' wings. They were flying up the mountain, almost wavering in their flight. Like weary commuters trying to make it home. He had watched them through the long winter as they were forced to fly farther and farther in search of food and open water. He had noticed the dullness of their feathers and the dimming lustre in their intense green eyes. Now, and he was not sure if perhaps it was his eyesight or his angle of vision, the female's wing tips seemed almost to graze the bare branches of the trees as if she might falter and fall. And then the male who had gone on ahead turned and came back, gliding on the wind with his wings outstretched, trying to conserve what little energy he had left. He passed so close to Archibald that he could see, or imagined that he could see, the desperate fear in his fierce, defiant eyes. He was so intent on his mission that he paid little attention to Archibald, circling beside his mate until their wing tips almost touched. She seemed to gain strength from his presence and almost to lunge with her wings, like a desperate swimmer on her final lap, and they continued together up the mountain. In the dampness of the late spring Archibald feared, as perhaps did they, for the future of their potential young.

He had seen the eagles in other seasons and circumstances. He had seen the male seize a branch in his powerful talons and soar towards the sky in the sheer exuberance of his power and strength; had seen him snap the branch in two (in the way a strong man might snap a kindling across his knee), letting the two sections fall towards the earth before plummeting after one or the other and snatching it from the air; wheeling and somersaulting and flipping the branch in front of him and swooping under it again and again until, tired of the game, he let it fall to earth.

And he had seen them in the aerial courtship of their mating; had seen them feinting and swerving high above the mountain, outlined against the sky. Had seen them come together, and with talons locked, fall cartwheeling over and over for what seemed like hundreds of feet down toward the land. Separating and braking, like lucky parachutists, at the last minute and gliding individually and parallel to the earth before starting their ascent once more.

The folklorists were always impressed by the bald eagles.

"How long have they been here?" the first group asked.

"Forever, I guess," had been his answer.

And after doing research they had returned and said, "Yes, Cape Breton is the largest nesting area on the eastern seaboard north of Florida. And the largest east of the Rockies. It's funny, hardly anybody knows they're here."

"Oh, some people do," Archibald said with a smile.

"It's only because they don't use pesticides or herbicides in the forest industry," the folklorists said. "If they start, the eagles will be gone. There are hardly any nests any more in New Brunswick or in Maine."

"Mmmm," he said.

In the days that followed they tried to prepare for the "singing" in Halifax. They had several practices, most of them at Sal's because she had talked to the producer and had become the contact person, and also because she seemed to want to go the most. They managed to gather a number of people of varying talent, some more reluctant than others. One or two of the practices were held at Archibald's. The number in the group varied. It expanded sometimes to as many as thirty, including various in-laws and friends of in-laws and people who simply had little else to do on a given evening. Throughout it all, Archibald tried to maintain control and to do it in "his way," which meant enunciating the words clearly and singing the exact number of verses in the proper order. Sometimes the attention of the younger people wandered and the evenings deteriorated quite early and rapidly, with people drifting off into little knots to gossip or tell jokes or to drink what was in Archibald's opinion too much. As the pressures of the spring season increased and many of the men left logging to fish or work upon their land, there were fewer and fewer male voices at the practice sessions. Sometimes the men joked about this and the future make-up of the group.

"Do you think you'll be able to handle all these women by yourself in Halifax, Archibald?" someone might ask, although not really asking the question of him.

"Sure, he will," another voice would respond. "He's well rested. He hasn't used it in fifty years – not that we know of, anyway."

Then at one practice Sal announced with some agitation that she had been talking to the producer in Halifax. He had told her, she said, that two other groups from the area had contacted him and he would be auditioning them as well. He would be coming in about ten days.

Everyone was dumbfounded.

"What other groups?" asked Archibald.

"One," said Sal, pausing for dramatic effect, "is headed by *Carver*."

"Carver!" they said in unison and disbelief. And then in the midst of loud guffaws, "Carver can't sing. He can hardly speak any Gaelic. Where will he get a group?"

"Don't ask me," said Sal, "unless it's those guys he hangs around with."

"Who else?" said Archibald.

"MacKenzies!" she said.

No one laughed at the mention of MacKenzies. They had been one of the oldest and best of the singing families. They lived some twenty miles away in a small and isolated valley, but Archibald had noticed, over the past fifteen years or so, more and more of their houses becoming shuttered and boarded, and a few of the older ones starting to lean and even to fall to the pressures of the wind.

"They don't have enough people any more," someone said.

"No," added another voice. "All of their best singers have gone to Toronto."

"There are two very good young men there," said Archibald, remembering a concert of a few years back when he had seen the two standing straight and tall a few feet back from the microphone, had seen them singing clearly and effortlessly with never a waver or a mispronunciation or a missed note.

"They've gone to Calgary," said a third voice. "They've been there now for over a year."

"I was talking to some people from over that way after the call from Halifax," said Sal. "They said that the MacKenzies' grandmother was going to ask them to come back. They said she was going to try to get all her singers to come home."

Archibald was touched in spite of himself, touched that Mrs. MacKenzie would try so hard. He looked around the room and realized that there were very few people in it who knew that Mrs. MacKenzie was his cousin and by extension theirs. Although he did not know her well and had only nodded to her and exchanged a few words with her over a lifetime, he felt very close to her now. He was not even sure of the degree of the relationship (although he would work it out later), remembering only the story of the young woman from an earlier generation of his family who had married the young man from the valley of the MacKenzies who was of the "wrong religion." There had been great bitterness at the time and the families had refused to speak to one another until all those who knew what the "right religion" was had died. The young woman who left had never visited her parents or they her. It seemed sad to Archibald, feeling almost more kinship to the scarcely known Mrs. MacKenzie than to those members of his own flesh and blood who seemed now so agitated and squabbly.

"She will never get them home," said the last voice. "They've all got jobs and responsibilities. They can't drop everything and come here or to Halifax for a week to sing four or five songs."

The voice proved right, although in the following ten days before the producer's visit Archibald thought often of Mrs. MacKenzie making her phone calls and of her messengers fanned out across Toronto, visiting the suburbs and the taverns, asking the question to which they already knew the answer but feeling obliged to ask it, nonetheless. In the end four MacKenzies came home, two young men who had been hurt at work and were on compensation and a middle-aged daughter and her husband who managed to take a week of their vacation earlier than usual. The *really* good young men were unable to come.

When the producer came he brought with him two male assistants with clipboards. The producer was an agitated man in his early thirties. He had dark curly hair and wore thick glasses and a maroon T-shirt with "If you've got it, flaunt it" emblazoned across the front. When he spoke, he nervously twisted his right ear lobe.

Archibald's group was the last of the three he visited. "He's saved the best for the last," laughed Sal, not very convincingly.

He came in the evening and explained the situation briefly. If chosen, they would be in Halifax for six days. They would practise and acquaint themselves with the surroundings for the first two days and on the next four there would be a concert each evening. There would be various acts from throughout the province. They would be on television and radio, and some of the Royal Family would be in attendance.

Then he said, "Look, I really don't understand your language so we're here mainly to look for effect. We'd like you to be ready with three songs. And then maybe we'll have to cut it back to two. We'll see how it goes."

They began to sing, sitting around the table as if they were "waulking the cloth" as their ancestors had done before them. Archibald sat at the head of the table, singing loudly and clearly, while the other voices rose to meet him. The producer and his assistants took notes.

"Okay, that's enough," he said after about an hour and a half.

"We'll take the third one," he said to one of his assistants.

"What's it called?" he asked Archibald.

"*Mo Chridhe Trom*," said Archibald. "It means my heart is heavy."

"Okay," said the producer. "Let's do it again."

They began. By the twelfth verse the music took hold of Archibald in a way that he had almost forgotten it could. His voice soared above the others with such clear and precise power that they faltered and were stilled.

'S ann air cul nam beanntan ard,
Tha aite comhnuidh mo ghraidh,
Fear dha 'm bheil an chridhe blath,
Do 'n tug mi 'n gradh a leon mi.

'S ann air cul a' bhalla chloich,
'S math an aithnichinn lorg do chos,
Och 'us och, mar tha mi 'n nochd
Gur bochd nach d'fhuair mi coir ort.

Tha mo chridhe dhut cho buan,
Ris a' chreag tha 'n grunnd a' chuain,
No comh-ionnan ris an stuaidh
A bhuaileas orr' an comhnuidh.

He finished the song alone. There was a silence that was almost embarrassing.

"Okay," said the producer after a pause. "Try another one, number six. The one that doesn't sound like all the others. What's it called?"

"*Oran Gillean Alasdair Mhoir*," said Archibald, trying to compose himself. "Song to the Sons of Big Alexander. Sometimes it's known simply as The Drowning of the Men."

"Okay," said the producer. "Let's go." But when they were halfway through, he said, "Cut, okay, that's enough."

"It's not finished," said Archibald. "It's a narrative."

"That's enough," said the producer.

"You can't cut them like that," said Archibald, "if you do, they don't make any sense."

"Look, they don't make any sense to me, anyway," said the producer. "I told you I don't understand the language. We're just trying to gauge audience impact."

Archibald felt himself getting angrier than perhaps he should, and he was aware of the looks and gestures from his family. "Be careful," they said, "don't offend him or we won't get the trip."

"Mmmm," he said, rising from his chair and going to the window. The dusk had turned to dark and the stars seemed to touch the mountain. Although in a room filled with people, he felt very much alone, his mind running silently over the verses of *Mo Chridhe Trom* which had so moved him moments before.

Over lofty mountains lies
The dwelling place of my love,
One whose heart was always warm,
And whom I loved too dearly.

And behind the wall of stone
I would recognize your steps,
But how sad am I tonight
Because we're not together.

Still my love you will last
Like the rock beneath the sea,
Just as long as will the waves
That strike against it always.

"Okay, let's call it a night," said the producer. "Thank you all very much. We'll be in touch."

The next morning at nine the producer drove into Archibald's yard. His assistants were with him, packed and ready for Halifax. The assistants remained in the car while the producer came into Archibald's kitchen. He coughed uncomfortably and looked about him as if to make sure that they were alone. He reminded Archibald of a nervous father preparing to discuss "the facts of life."

"How were the other groups?" asked Archibald in what he hoped was a noncommittal voice.

"The young man Carver and his group," said the producer, "have tremendous *energy*. They have a lot of male voices."

"Mmmm," said Archibald. "What did they sing?"

"I don't remember the names of the songs, although I wrote them down. They're packed away. It doesn't matter all that much, anyway. They don't know as many songs as you people do, though," he concluded.

"No," said Archibald, trying to restrain his sarcasm, "I don't suppose they do."

"Still, that doesn't matter so much either as we only need two or three."

"Mmmm."

"The problem with that group is the way they look."

"The way they *look*?" said Archibald. "Shouldn't it be the way they sing?"

"Not really," said the producer. "See, these performances have a high degree of *visibility*. You're going to be on stage for four nights and the various television networks are all going to be there. This is, in total, a *big show*. It's not a regional show. It will be national and international. It will probably be beamed back to Scotland and Australia and who knows where else. We want people who *look right* and who'll give a good impression of the area and the province."

Archibald said nothing.

"You see," said the producer, "we've got to have someone we can zoom in on for close-ups, someone who looks the part. We don't want close-ups of people who have had their faces all carved up in brawls. That's why you're so good. You're a great-looking man for your age, if you'll pardon me. You're tall and straight and have your own teeth, which helps both your singing and appearance. You have a *presence*. The rest of your group have nice voices, especially the women, but without you, if you'll pardon me, they're kind of ordinary. And then," he added almost as an afterthought, "there is your reputation. You're known to the folklorists and people like that. You have *credibility*. Very important."

Archibald was aware of Sal's truck coming into the yard and knew that she had seen the producer's car on its way up the mountain.

"Hi," she said, "what's new?"

"I think you're all set but it's up to your grandfather," the producer said.

"What about the MacKenzies?" asked Archibald.

"Garbage. No good at all. An old woman playing a tape recorder while seven or eight people tried to sing along with it. Wasted our time. We wanted people that were alive, not some scratchy tape."

"Mmmm," said Archibald.

"Anyway, you're on. But we'd like a few changes."

"Changes?"

"Yeah, first of all we'll have to cut them. That was what I was trying to get around to last night. You're only going to be on stage for three or four minutes each night and we'd like to get two songs in. They're too long. The other problem is they're too mournful. Jesus, even the titles, 'My Heart is Heavy,' 'The Drowning of the Men.' Think about it."

"But," said Archibald, trying to sound reasonable, "that's the way those songs are. You've got to hear them in the original way."

"I've got to go now," said Sal. "Got to see about babysitters and that. See you."

She left in her customary spray of gravel.

"Look," said the producer, "I've got to put on a big show. Maybe you could get some songs from the other group."

"The other group?"

"Yeah," he said, "Carver's. Anyway, think about it. I'll call you in a week and we can finalize it and work out any other details." And then he was gone.

In the days that followed Archibald *did* think about it. He thought about it more than he had ever thought he would. He thought of the impossibility of trimming the songs and of changing them and he wondered why he seemed the only one in his group who harboured such concerns. Most of the others did not seem very interested when he mentioned it to them, although they did seem interested in shopping lists and gathering the phone numbers of long-absent relatives and friends in Halifax.

One evening Carver met Sal on her way to Bingo and told her quite bluntly that he and his group were going.

"No, you're not," she said, "we are."

"Wait and see," said Carver. "Look, we need this trip. We need to get a boat engine and we want to buy a truck. You guys are done. Done like a dinner. It matters too much to that Archibald and you're all dependent on him. *Us*, we're *adjustable*."

"As if we couldn't be adjustable!" said Sal with a laugh as she told of the encounter at their last practice before the anticipated phone call. The practice did not go well as far as Archibald was concerned, although no one else seemed to notice.

The next day when Archibald encountered Carver at the general store down in the valley, he could not resist asking: "What did you sing for that producer fellow?"

"*Brochan Lom*," said Carver with a shrug.

"*Brochan Lom*," said Archibald incredulously. "Why, that isn't even a song. It's just a bunch of nonsense syllables strung together."

"So what!" said Carver. "He didn't know. No one knows."

"But it's before the Royal Family," said Archibald, surprising even himself at finding such royalist remnants still within him.

"Look," said Carver, wiping his mouth with the back of his hand, "what did the Royal Family ever do for *me*?"

"Of course people know," said Archibald, pressing on with weary determination. "People in audiences know. Other singers know. Folklorists know."

"Yeah, maybe so," said Carver with a shrug, "but me, I don't know no folklorists."

He looked at Archibald intently for a few seconds and then gathered up his tobacco and left the store.

Archibald was troubled all of that afternoon. He was vaguely aware of his relatives organizing sitters and borrowing suitcases and talking incessantly but saying little. He thought of his conversation with Carver, on the one hand, and strangely enough, he thought of Mrs. MacKenzie on the other. He thought of her with great compassion, she who was probably the best of them all and who had tried the hardest to impress the man from Halifax. The image of her in the twilight of the valley of the MacKenzies playing the tape-recorded voices of her departed family to a man who did not know the language kept running through his mind. He imagined her now, sitting quietly with her knitting needles in her lap, listening to the ghostly voices which were there without their people.

And then that night Archibald had a dream. He had often had dreams of his wife in the long, long years since her death and had probably brought them on in the early years by visiting her grave in the evenings and sometimes sitting there and talking to her of their hopes and aspirations. And sometimes in the nights following such "conversations" she would come to him and they would talk and touch and sometimes sing. But on this night she only sang. She sang with a clarity and a beauty that caused the hairs to rise on the back of his neck even as the tears welled to his eyes. Every note was perfect, as perfect and clear as the waiting water droplet hanging on the fragile leaf or the high suspended eagle outlined against the sky at the apex of its arc. She sang to him until four in the morning, when the first rays of light began to touch the mountain top. And then she was gone.

Archibald awoke relaxed and refreshed in a way that he had seldom felt since sleeping with his wife so many years before. His mind was made up and he was done thinking about it.

Around nine o'clock Sal's truck came into the yard. "That producer fellow is on the phone," she said. "I told him I'd take the message but he wants to talk to you."

"Okay," said Archibald.

In Sal's kitchen the receiver swung from its black spiral cord.

"Yes, this is Archibald," he said, grasping it firmly. "No, I don't think I can get them down to three minutes or speed them up at all. No, I don't think so. Yes, I have thought about it. Yes, I have been in contact with others who sing in my family. No, I don't know about Carver. You'll have to speak to him. Good-bye."

He was aware of the disappointment and grumpiness that spread throughout the house, oozing like a rapid ink across a blotter. In the next room he heard a youthful voice say: "All he had to do was shorten the verses in a few stupid, old songs. You'd think he would have done it for *us*, the old coot."

"I'm sorry," he said to Sal, "but I just couldn't do it."

"Do you want a drive home in the truck?" she asked.

"No," he said, "never mind, I can walk."

He began to walk up the mountain with an energy and purpose that reminded him of himself as a younger man. He felt that he was "right" in the way he had felt so many years before when he had courted his future bride and when they had decided to build their house near the mountain's top, even though others were coming down. And he felt as he had felt during the short and burning intensity of their brief life together. He began almost to run.

In the days that followed, Archibald was at peace. One day Sal dropped in and said that Carver was growing a moustache and a beard.

"They told him the moustache would cover his lip and with the beard his scars would be invisible on TV," she sniffed. "Make-up will do wonders."

Then one rainy night after he was finished watching the international and national and regional news, Archibald looked out his window. Down on the valley floor he could see the headlights of the cars following the wet pavement of the main highway. People bound for larger destinations who did not know that he existed. And then he noticed one set of lights in particular. They were coming hard and fast along the valley floor and although still miles away, they seemed to be coming with a purpose all their own. They "looked" different from the other headlights, and in one of those moments of knowledge mixed with intuition Archibald said aloud to himself. "That car is coming here. It is coming for *me*."

He was rattled at first. He was aware that his decision had caused ill feelings among some members of his family, as well as various in-laws and others strung out in a far-flung and complicated web of connections he could barely comprehend. He knew also that because of the rain many of the men had not been in the woods that much lately and were perhaps spending their time in the taverns talking too much about him and what he had done. He watched as the car swung off the pavement and began its ascent, weaving and sloughing up the mountain in the rain.

Although he was not a violent man, he did not harbour any illusions about where or how he lived. "That Archibald," they said, "is nobody's fool." He thought of this now as he measured the steps to the stove where the giant poker hung. He had had it made by a blacksmith in one of the lumber camps shortly after his marriage. It was of heavy steel, and years of poking it into the hot coals of his stove had sharpened its end to a clean and burnished point. When he swung it in his hand its weight seemed like an ancient sword. He lifted his wooden table easily and placed it at an angle which he hoped was not too obvious in the centre of the kitchen, with its length facing the door.

"If they come in the door," he said, "I will be behind the table and in five strides I can reach the poker." He practised the five strides just to make sure. Then he put his left hand between his legs to adjust himself and straightened his suspenders so that they were perfectly in line. And then he went to the side of the window to watch the coming car.

Because of the recent rains, sections of the road had washed away and at certain places freshets and small brooks cut across it. Sometimes the rains washed down sand and topsoil as well, and the trick was never to accelerate on such washed-over sections for fear of being buried in the flowing water and mud. Rather, one gunned the motor on the relatively stable sections of the climb (where there was "bottom") and trusted to momentum to get across the streams.

Archibald watched the progress of the car. Sometimes he lost its headlights because of his perspective and the trees, but only momentarily. As it climbed, swerving back and forth, the wet branches slapping and silhouetted against its headlights, Archibald began to read the dark wet roadway in his own mind. And he began to read the driver's reflexes as he swung out from the gullies and then in close to the mountain's wall. He began almost to admire the driver. Whoever that is, he thought, is very drunk but also very good.

The car hooked and turned into his yard without any apparent change in speed, its headlights flashing on his house and through his window. Archibald moved behind his table and

307

stood, tall and balanced and ready. Before the sound of the slamming car door faded, his kitchen door seemed to blow in and Carver stood there unsteadily, blinking in the light with the rain blowing at his back and dripping off his beginning beard.

"Yeah," he said over his shoulder, "he's here, bring it in."

Archibald waited, his eyes intent upon Carver but also sliding sideways to his poker.

They came into his porch and there were five of them, carrying boxes.

"Put them on the floor here," said Carver, indicating a space just across the threshold. "And try not to dirty his floor."

Archibald knew then he would be all right and moved out from behind his table.

"Open the boxes," said Carver to one of the men. The boxes were filled with forty-ounce bottles of liquor. It was as if someone were preparing for a wedding.

"These are for you," said Carver. "We bought them at a bootlegger's two hours ago. We been away all day. We been to Glace Bay and to New Waterford and we were in a fight in the parking lot at the tavern in Bras D'Or, and a couple of us got banged up pretty bad. Anyway, not much to say."

Archibald looked at them framed in the doorway leading to his porch. There was no mystery about the kind of day they had had, even if Carver had not told him. Even now, one of them, a tall young man, was rocking backwards on his heels, almost literally falling asleep on his feet as he stood in the doorway. There was a fresh cut on Carver's temple which could not be covered by either his moustache or his beard. Archibald looked at all the liquor and was moved by the total inappropriateness of the gift; bringing all of this to him, the most abstemious man on the mountain. Somehow it moved him even more. And he was aware of its cost in many ways.

He also envied them their closeness and their fierceness and what the producer fellow had called their tremendous energy. And he imagined it was men like them who had given, in their recklessness, all they could think of in that confused and stormy past. Going with their claymores and the misunderstood language of their war cries to "perform" for the Royal Families of the past. But he was not sure of that either. He smiled at them and gave a small nod of acknowledgement. He did not quite know what to say.

"Look," said Carver, with that certainty that marked everything he did. "Look, Archibald," he said. "We know. We know. We *really* know."

AS BIRDS BRING FORTH THE SUN

(1 9 8 5)

Once there was a family with a Highland name who lived beside the sea. And the man had a dog of which he was very fond. She was large and grey, a sort of staghound from another time. And if she jumped up to lick his face, which she loved to do, her paws would jolt against his shoulders with such force that she would come close to knocking him down and he would be forced to take two or three backward steps before he could regain his balance. And he himself was not a small man, being slightly over six feet and perhaps one hundred and eighty pounds.

She had been left, when a pup, at the family's gate in a small handmade box and no one knew where she had come from or that she would eventually grow to such a size. Once, while still a small pup, she had been run over by the steel wheel of a horse-drawn cart which was hauling kelp from the shore to be used as fertilizer. It was in October and the rain had been falling for some weeks and the ground was soft. When the wheel of the cart passed over her, it sunk her body into the wet earth as well as crushing some of her ribs; and apparently the silhouette of her small crushed body was visible in the earth after the man lifted her to his chest while she yelped and screamed. He ran his fingers along her broken bones, ignoring the blood and urine which fell upon his shirt, trying to soothe her bulging eyes and her scrabbling front paws and her desperately licking tongue.

The more practical members of his family, who had seen run-over dogs before, suggested that her neck be broken by his strong hands or that he grasp her by the hind legs and swing her head against a rock, thus putting an end to her misery. But he would not do it.

Instead, he fashioned a small box and lined it with woollen remnants from a sheep's fleece and one of his old and frayed shirts. He placed her within the box and placed the box behind the stove and then he warmed some milk in a small saucepan and sweetened it with sugar. And he held open her small and trembling jaws with his left hand while spooning in the sweetened milk with his right, ignoring the needle-like sharpness of her small teeth. She lay in the box most of the remaining fall and into the early winter, watching everything with her large brown eyes.

Although some members of the family complained about her presence and the odour from the box and the waste of time she involved, they gradually adjusted to her; and as the weeks passed by, it became evident that her ribs were knitting together in some form or other and that she was recovering with the resilience of the young. It also became evident that she would grow to a tremendous size, as she outgrew one box and then another and the grey hair began to feather from her huge front paws. In the spring she was outside almost all of the time and followed the man everywhere; and when she came inside during the following months, she had grown so large that she would no longer fit into her accustomed place behind the stove and was forced to lie beside it. She was never given a name but was referred to in Gaelic as *cù mòr glas*, the big grey dog.

By the time she came into her first heat, she had grown to a tremendous height, and although her signs and her odour attracted many panting and highly aroused suitors, none was big enough to mount her, and the frenzy of their disappointment and the longing of her unfulfilment were more than the man could stand. He went, so the story goes, to a place where he knew there was a big dog. A dog not as big as she was, but still a big dog, and he brought him home with him. And at the proper time he took the *cù mòr glas* and the big dog down to the sea where he knew there was a hollow in the rock which appeared only at low tide. He took some sacking to provide footing for the male dog and he placed the *cù mòr glas* in the hollow of the rock and knelt beside her and steadied her with his left arm under her throat and helped position the male dog above her and guided his blood-engorged penis. He was a man used to working with the breeding of animals, with the guiding of rams and bulls and stallions and often with the funky smell of animal semen heavy on his large and gentle hands.

The winter that followed was a cold one and ice formed on the sea and frequent squalls and blizzards obliterated the offshore islands and caused the people to stay near their fires much of the time, mending clothes and nets and harness and waiting for the change in season. The *cù mòr glas* grew heavier and even larger until there was hardly room for her around the stove or under the table. And then one morning, when it seemed that spring was about to break, she was gone.

The man and even his family, who had become more involved than they cared to admit, waited for her but she did not come. And as the frenzy of spring wore on, they busied themselves with readying their land and their fishing gear and all of the things that so desperately required their attention. And then they were into summer and fall and winter and another spring which saw the birth of the man and his wife's twelfth child. And then it was summer again.

That summer the man and two of his teenaged sons were pulling their herring nets about two miles offshore when the wind began to blow off the land and the water began to roughen. They became afraid that they could not make it safely back to shore, so they pulled in behind one of the offshore islands, knowing that they would be sheltered there and planning to outwait the storm. As the prow of their boat approached the gravelly shore, they heard a sound above them, and looking up they saw the *cù mòr glas* silhouetted on the brow of the hill which was the small island's highest point.

"*M'eudal cù mòr glas*," shouted the man in his happiness – *m'eudal* meaning something like dear or darling; and as he shouted, he jumped over the side of his boat into the waist-deep water, struggling for footing on the rolling gravel as he waded eagerly and awkwardly toward her and the shore. At the same time, the *cù mòr glas* came hurtling down toward him in a shower of small rocks dislodged by her feet; and just as he was emerging from the water, she met him as she used to, rearing up on her hind legs and placing her huge front paws on his shoulders while extending her eager tongue.

The weight and speed of her momentum met him as he tried to hold his balance on the sloping angle with the water rolling gravel beneath his feet, and he staggered backwards and lost his footing and fell beneath her force. And in that instant again, as the story goes, there appeared over the brow of the hill six more huge grey dogs hurtling down towards the gravelled strand. They had never seen him before; and seeing him stretched prone beneath their mother, they misunderstood, like so many armies, the intention of their leader.

They fell upon him in a fury, slashing his face and tearing aside his lower jaw and ripping out his throat, crazed with blood-lust or duty or perhaps starvation. The *cù mòr glas* turned on them in her own savagery, slashing and snarling and, it seemed, crazed by their mistake; driving them bloodied and yelping before her, back over the brow of the hill where they vanished from sight but could still be heard screaming in the distance. It all took perhaps little more than a minute.

The man's two sons, who were still in the boat and had witnessed it all, ran sobbing through the salt water to where their mauled and mangled father lay; but there was little they could do other than hold his warm and bloodied hands for a few brief moments. Although his eyes "lived" for a small fraction of time, he could not speak to them because his face and throat had been torn away, and of course there was nothing they could do except to hold and be held tightly until that too slipped away and his eyes glazed over and they could no longer feel his hands holding theirs. The storm increased and they could not get home and so they were forced to spend the night huddled beside their father's body. They were afraid to try to carry the body to the rocking boat because he was so heavy and they were afraid that they might lose even what little of him remained and they were afraid also, huddled on the rocks, that the dogs might return. But they did not return at all and there was no sound from them, no sound at all, only the moaning of the wind and the washing of the water on the rocks.

In the morning they debated whether they should try to take his body with them or whether they should leave it and return in the company of older and wiser men. But they were afraid to leave it unattended and felt that the time needed to cover it with protective rocks would be better spent in trying to get across to their home shore. For a while they debated as to whether one should go in the boat and the other remain on the island, but each was afraid to be alone and so in the end they managed to drag and carry and almost float him toward the bobbing boat. They laid him face-down and covered him with what clothes there were and set off across the still-rolling sea. Those who waited on the shore missed the large presence of the man within the boat and some of them waded into the water and others rowed out in skiffs, attempting to hear the tearful messages called out across the rolling waves.

The *cù mòr glas* and her six young dogs were never seen again, or perhaps I should say they were never seen again in the same way. After some weeks, a group of men circled the island tentatively in their boats but they saw no sign. They went again and then again but found nothing. A year later, and grown much braver, they beached their boats and walked the island carefully, looking into the small sea caves and the hollows at the base of the wind-ripped trees, thinking perhaps that if they did not find the dogs, they might at least find their whitened bones; but again they discovered nothing.

The *cù mòr glas*, though, was supposed to be sighted here and there for a number of years. Seen on a hill in one region or silhouetted on a ridge in another or loping across the valleys or glens in the early morning or the shadowy evening. Always in the area of the half perceived. For a while she became rather like the Loch Ness monster or the Sasquatch on a smaller scale. Seen but not recorded. Seen when there were no cameras. Seen but never taken.

The mystery of where she went became entangled with the mystery of whence she came. There was increased speculation about the handmade box in which she had been found and much theorizing as to the individual or individuals who might have left it. People went to look for the box but could not find it. It was felt she might have been part of a *buidseachd* or evil spell cast on the man by some mysterious enemy. But no one could go much farther than that. All of his caring for her was recounted over and over again and nobody missed any of the ironies.

What seemed literally known was that she had crossed the winter ice to have her pups and had been unable to get back. No one could remember ever seeing her swim; and in the early months at least, she could not have taken her young pups with her.

The large and gentle man with the smell of animal semen often heavy on his hands was my great-great-great-grandfather, and it may be argued that he died because he was too good at breeding animals or that he cared too much about their fulfilment and well-being. He was no longer there for his own child of the spring who, in turn, became my great-great-grandfather, and he was perhaps too much there in the memory of his older sons who saw him fall beneath the ambiguous force of the *cù mòr glas*. The youngest boy in the boat was haunted and tormented by the awfulness of what he had seen. He would wake at night screaming that he had seen the *cù mòr glas a' bhàis*, the big grey dog of death, and his screams filled the house and the ears and minds of the listeners, bringing home again and again the consequences of their loss. One morning, after a night in which he saw the *cù mòr glas a' bhàis* so vividly that his sheets were drenched with sweat, he walked to the high cliff which faced the island and there he cut his throat with a fish knife and fell into the sea.

The other brother lived to be forty, but, again so the story goes, he found himself in a Glasgow pub one night, perhaps looking for answers, deep and sodden with the whisky which had become his anaesthetic. In the half darkness he saw a large, grey-haired man sitting by himself against the wall and mumbled something to him. Some say he saw the *cù mòr glas a' bhàis* or uttered the name. And perhaps the man heard the phrase through ears equally affected by drink and felt he was being called a dog or a son of a bitch or something of that nature. They rose to meet one another and struggled outside into the cobblestoned passageway behind the pub where, most improbably, there were supposed to be six other large, grey-haired men who beat him to death on the cobblestones, smashing his bloodied head into the stone again and again before vanishing and leaving him to die with his face turned to the sky. The *cù mòr glas a' bhàis* had come again, said his family, as they tried to piece the tale together.

This is how the *cù mòr glas a' bhàis* came into our lives, and it is obvious that all of this happened a long, long time ago. Yet with succeeding generations it seemed the spectre had somehow come to stay and that it had become *ours* – not in the manner of an unwanted skeleton in the closet from a family's ancient past but more in the manner of something close to a genetic possibility. In the deaths of each generation, the grey dog was seen by some – by women who were to die in childbirth; by soldiers who went forth to the many wars but did not return; by those who went forth to feuds or dangerous love affairs; by those who answered mysterious midnight messages; by those who swerved on the highway to avoid the real or imagined grey dog and ended in masses of crumpled steel. And by one professional athlete who, in addition to his ritualized athletic superstitions, carried another fear or belief as well. Many of the man's descendants moved like careful haemophiliacs, fearing that they carried unwanted possibilities deep within them. And others, while they laughed, were like members of families in which there is a recurrence over the generations of repeated cancer or the diabetes that comes to those beyond middle age. The feeling of those who may say little to others but who may say often and quietly to themselves, "It has not happened to me," while adding always the cautionary "*yet.*"

I am thinking all of this now as the October rain falls on the city of Toronto and the pleasant, white-clad nurses pad confidently in and out of my father's room. He lies quietly amidst the whiteness, his head and shoulders elevated so that he is in that hospital position of being neither quite prone nor yet sitting. His hair is white upon his pillow and he breathes softly and sometimes unevenly, although it is difficult ever to be sure.

My five grey-haired brothers and I take turns beside his bedside, holding his heavy hands in ours and feeling their response, hoping ambiguously that he will speak to us, although we know that it may tire him. And trying to read his life and ours into his eyes when they are open. He has been with us for a long time, well into our middle age. Unlike those boys in that boat of so long ago, we did not see him taken from us in our youth. And unlike their youngest brother who, in turn, became our great-great-grandfather, we did not grow into a world in which there was no father's touch. We have been lucky to have this large and gentle man so deep into our lives.

No one in this hospital has mentioned the *cù mòr glas a' bhàis*. Yet as my mother said ten years ago, before slipping into her own death as quietly as a grownup child who leaves or enters her parents' house in the early hours, "It is hard to *not* know what you do know."

Even those who are most sceptical, like my oldest brother who has driven here from Montreal, betray themselves by their nervous actions. "I avoided the Greyhound bus stations in both Montreal and Toronto," he smiled upon his arrival, and then added, "Just in case."

He did not realize how ill our father was and has smiled little since then. I watch him turning the diamond ring upon his finger, knowing that he hopes he will not hear the Gaelic phrase he knows too well. Not having the luxury, as he once said, of some who live in Montreal and are able to pretend they do not understand the "other" language. You cannot *not* know what you do know.

Sitting here, taking turns holding the hands of the man who gave us life, we are afraid for him and for ourselves. We are afraid of what he may see and we are afraid to hear the phrase born of the vision. We are aware that it may become confused with what the doctors call "the will to live" and we are aware that some beliefs are what others would dismiss as "garbage." We are aware that there are men who believe the earth is flat and that the birds bring forth the sun.

Bound here in our own peculiar mortality, we do not wish to see or see others see that which signifies life's demise. We do not want to hear the voice of our father, as did those other sons, calling down his own particular death upon him.

We would shut our eyes and plug our ears, even as we know such actions to be of no avail. Open still and fearful to the grey hair rising on our necks if and when we hear the scrabble of the paws and the scratching at the door.

VISION

(1 9 8 6)

I don't remember when I first heard the story but I remember the first time that I heard it and remembered it. By that I mean the first time it made an impression on me and more or less became *mine*; sort of went into me the way such things do, went into me in such a way that I knew it would not leave again but would remain there forever. Something like when you cut your hand with a knife by accident, and even as you're trying to staunch the blood flowing out of the wound, you know the wound will never really heal totally and your hand will never look quite the same again. You can imagine the scar tissue that will form and be a different colour and texture from the rest of your skin. You know this even as you are trying to stop the blood and trying to squeeze the separated edges of skin together once more. Like trying to squeeze together the separated banks of a small and newly discovered river so that the stream will be subterranean once again. It is something like that, although you know in one case the future scar will be forever on the outside, while the memory will remain forever deep within.

Anyway, on this day we were about a mile and a half offshore but heading home on the last day of the lobster season. We could see the trucks of the New Brunswick buyers waiting for us on the wharf and because it was a sunny day, light reflected and glinted off the chrome trim and bumpers of the waiting trucks and off their gleaming rooftops as well. It was the last day of June and the time was early afternoon and I was seventeen.

My father was in good spirits because the season was over and we had done reasonably well and we were bringing in most of our gear intact. And there seemed no further need to rush.

The sea was almost calm, although there was a light breeze at our backs and we throttled down our engine because there really was no reason to hurry into the wharf for the last and final time. I was in the stern of the boat steadying the piled lobster traps that we had recently raised from the bottom of the sea. Some of them still gleamed with droplets of salt water and streamers of seaweed dangled from their laths. In the crates beside my feet the mottled blue-green lobsters moved and rustled quietly, snapping their tails as they slid over one another with that peculiar dry/wet sound of shell and claws over shell and claws. Their hammer claws had been pegged and fastened shut with rubber bands so they would not mutilate each other and so decrease their value.

"Put some of those in a sack for ourselves," said my father, turning his head back over his right shoulder as he spoke. He was standing ahead of me, facing the land and urinating over the side. His water fell into the sea and vanished into the rolling swell of the boat's slow passage.

"Put them in the back there," he said, "behind the bait bucket, and throw our oilers over them. They will want everything we've got, and what they won't see won't hurt them. Put in some markets too, not just canners."

I took a sack and began to pick some lobsters out of the crate, grasping them at the end of their body shells or by the ends of their tails and being careful not to get my fingers snapped. For even with their hammer claws banded shut there was still a certain danger.

"How many do you want?" I asked.

"Oh," he said, turning with a smile and running his hand along the front of his trousers to make sure his fly was closed, "as many as you want. Use your own good judgement."

We did not often take home lobsters for ourselves because they were so expensive and we needed the money they would bring. And the buyers wanted them with a desperation almost bordering on frenzy. Perhaps even now as I bent over the crate they were watching from the wharf with binoculars to see if any were being concealed. My father stood casually in front of me, once more facing the land and shielding my movements with his body. The boat followed its set course, its keel cutting the blue-green water and turning it temporarily into white.

There was a time long ago when the lobsters were not thought to be so valuable. Probably because the markets of the larger world had not yet been discovered or were so far away. People then ate all they wanted of them and even used them for fertilizer on their fields. And those who did eat them did not consider them to be a delicacy. There is a quoted story from the time which states that in the schools you could always identify the children of the poor because they were the ones with lobster in their sandwiches. The well-do-do were able to afford bologna.

With the establishment of the New England market, things changed. Lobster factories were set up along the coast for the canning of the lobsters at a time before good land transportation and refrigeration became common. In May and June and into July the girls in white caps and smocks packed the lobster meat into burnished cans before they were steam sealed. And the men in the smack boats brought the catches to the rickety piers which were built on piles and jutted out into the sea.

My father's mother was one of the girls, and her job was taking the black vein out of the meat of the lobster's tail before the tail was coiled around the inside of the can. At home they ate the black vein along with the rest of the meat, but the supervisors at the factory said it was unsightly. My father's father was one of the young men standing ready in the smack boat, wearing his cap at a jaunty angle and uttering witty sayings and singing little songs in Gaelic to the girls who stood above him on the wharf. All of this was, of course, a long time ago and I am just trying to recreate the scene.

On the day of the remembered story, though, the sea was almost serene as I placed the lobsters in the sack and prepared to hide them behind the bait bucket and under our oilers in the stern of the boat. Before we secreted the sack, we leaned over the side and scooped up water in the bailing bucket and soaked the sack to insure the health and life of the lobsters kept within. The wet sack moved and cracked with the shape and sound of the lobsters and it reminded me vaguely of sacks of kittens which were being taken to be drowned. You could see the movement but not the individuals.

My father straightened from his last dip over the side and passed the dripping bucket carefully to me. He steadied himself with his left hand on the gunwale and then seated himself on the thwart and faced toward the north. I gave the lobsters another soaking and moved to place them behind the bait bucket. There was still some bait remaining but we would not have need of it any more so I threw it over the side. The pieces of blue-grey mackerel turned and revolved before I lost sight of them within the water. The day before yesterday we had taken these same mackerel out of the same sea. We used nets for the spring mackerel because they were blind and could not see to take a baited hook; but in the fall, when they returned, the scales had fallen from their eyes and they would lunge at almost anything thrown before them. Even bits of other mackerel ground up and mixed with salt. Mackerel are a windward fish and always swim against the wind. If the wind is off the land, they swim toward the shore and perhaps the waiting nets; but if the wind blows in the opposite direction, they face out to sea and go so far out some years that we miss them altogether.

I put the empty bait bucket in front of the sack of lobsters and placed an empty crate upside down and at an angle over them so that their movements would not be noticeable. And I casually threw our oilers over them as well.

Ahead of us on the land and to the north of the wharf with its waiting trucks was the mile-long sandy beach cut by the river that acted as an erratic boundary between the fishing grounds of

ourselves and our neighbours, the MacAllesters. We had traditionally fished to the right of the river and they to the left, and
apparently for many years it was constant in its estuary. But in
recent years the river mouth, because of the force of storms and
tides and the build-up of sand, had become undependable as a
visual guide. The shifting was especially affected by the ravages
of the winter storms, and some springs the river might empty
almost a mile to the north or the south of its previous point of
entry. This had caused a tension between ourselves and the
MacAllesters because, although we traditionally went to the
same grounds, the boundary was no longer fixed and we had
fallen into accusations and counter-accusations; sometimes
using the actual river when it suited our purpose, and when it
did not, using an earlier and imaginary river which we could no
longer see.

The MacAllesters' boat was going in ahead of us now and I
waved to Kenneth MacAllester, who had become a rather luke-
warm friend because of the tension between our families. He
was the same age as I, and he waved back, although the other
two men in the boat did not.

At an earlier time when Kenneth MacAllester and I were
friends and in about grade six he told me a story while we were
walking home from school in the spring. He told me that his
grandmother was descended from a man in Scotland who possessed *Da Shealladh*, two sights or the second sight, and that by
looking through a hole in a magical white stone he could see
distant contemporary events as well as those of the future.
Nearly all of his visions came true. His name was either Munro
or MacKenzie and his first name was Kenneth and the eye he

placed to the stone for his visions was *cam* or blind in the sense of ordinary sight. He was a favourite of the powerful man for whom he worked, but he and the man's wife were jealous and disliked each other. Once when the powerful man was in Paris there was a big party on his estate. In one version "the prophet" commented rather unwisely on the paternity of some of the children present. In another version the man's wife asked him mockingly if he could "see" her husband in Paris but he refused. However, she insisted. Putting the stone to his eye he told her that her husband was enjoying himself rather too much with ladies in Paris and had little thought of her. Enraged and embarrassed, she ordered him to be burned in a barrel of tar into which spikes had been driven from the outside. In one version the execution took place right away, but in another it did not take place until some days later. In the second version the man was returning home when he heard the news and saw the black smoke rising. He spurred his horse at utmost speed toward the point where he saw the billowing smoke and called out in an attempt to stop the burning and save his friend, but his horse died beneath him, and though he ran the rest of the way, he arrived too late for any salvation.

Before the prophet died he hurled his white stone as far as he could out into the lake and told the lady that the family would come to an end years hence. And he told her that it would end when there was a deaf-and-dumb father who would outlive his four sons and then all their lands would pass into the hands of strangers. Generations later the deaf-and-dumb father was apparently a fine, good man who was helpless in the face of the prophecy he knew too much about and which he saw unfolding around him with the death of each of his four loved sons. Unable again to offer any salvation.

I thought it was a tremendous story at the time, and Kenneth picked up a white stone from the roadside and held it to his eye to see if "prophecy" would work for him.

"I guess I really wouldn't want it to work," he said with a laugh. "I wouldn't want to be blind," and he threw the stone away. At that time he planned on joining the Air Force and flying toward the sun and being able to see over the tops of mountains and across the sea.

When we got to his house we were still talking about the story and his mother cautioned us not to laugh at such things. She went and found a poem by Sir Walter Scott, which she read aloud to us. We did not pay much attention to it, but I remember the lines which referred to the father and his four doomed sons:

Thy sons rose around thee in light and in love
All a father could hope, all a friend could approve;
What 'vails it the tale of thy sorrows to tell?
In the springtime of youth and of promise they fell!

Now, as I said, the MacAllesters' boat was going in ahead of us, loaded down with its final catch and with its stern and washboard piled high with traps. We had no great wish to talk to the MacAllesters at the wharf and there were other boats ahead of us as well. They would unload their catches first and pile their traps upon the wharf and it would be some time before we would find a place to dock. My father cut our engine. There was no need to rush.

"Do you see Canna over there?" he asked, pointing to the north where he was facing. "Do you see the point of Canna?"

"Yes," I said, "I see it. There it is."

There was nothing very unusual about seeing the point of Canna. It was always visible except on the foggiest days or when there was rain or perhaps snow. It was twenty miles away by boat, and on the duller days it reached out low and blue like the foot of a giant's boot extended into the sea. On sunny days like this one it sparkled in a distant green. The clearings of the old farms were visible and above them the line of the encroaching trees, the spruce and fir of a darker green. Here and there the white houses stood out and even the grey and weather-beaten barns. It was called after the Hebridean island of Canna, "the green island" where most of its original settlers were born. It was the birthplace of my grandmother, who was one of the girls in the white smocks at the Canna lobster factory in that long-ago time.

"It was about this time of year," said my father, "that your Uncle Angus and I went by ourselves to visit our grandmother at the point of Canna. We were eleven at the time and had been asking our parents for weeks to let us go. They seemed reluctant to give us any answer and all they would say was 'We will see' or 'Wait and see.' We wanted to go on the smack boat when it was making its final run of the season. We wanted to go with the men on the smack who were buying lobsters and they would set us ashore at the wharf at Canna point and we would walk the mile to our grandmother's house. We had never gone there by ourselves before. We could hardly remember being there because if you went by land you had to travel by horse and buggy and it was a long way. First you had to go inland to the main road and drive about twenty miles and then come back down toward the shore. It was about twice as far by land as it was by sea and our parents went about once a year. Usually by themselves, as there was not enough room for others in the buggy. If we did not get to go on the smack, we were afraid that we would not get to go at all. 'Wait and see' was all they said."

It seemed strange to me, as my father spoke, to think of Canna as far away. By that time it took perhaps three-quarters of an hour by car, even though the final section of the road was often muddy and dangerous enough in the wet months of spring and fall and often blocked by snow in the winter. Still, it was not hard to get there if you really wanted to, and so the old letters from Canna which I discovered in the upstairs attic seemed quite strange and from another distant time. It seemed hard to believe that people only twenty miles away would write letters to one another and visit only once a year. But at that time the distance was hard to negotiate, and there were no telephones.

My father and his brother Angus were twins and they had been named after their grandfathers so their names were Angus and Alex. It was common for parents to name their first children after their own parents and it seemed that almost all of the men were called Angus or Alex. In the early years of the century the Syrian and Lebanese pedlars who walked the muddy country roads beneath their heavy backpacks sometimes called themselves Angus or Alex so that they would sound more familiar to their potential customers. The pedlars, like the Gaelic-speaking people in the houses which they visited, had very little English, so anything that aided communication was helpful. Sometimes they unfolded their bolts of cloth and displayed their shining needles before admirers who were unable to afford them, and sometimes, sensing the situation, they would leave the goods behind. Later, if money became available, the people would say, "Put aside what we owe Angus and Alex in the sugar bowl so that we can pay them when they come."

Sometimes the pedlars would carry letters from one community to the other, to and from the families of the different Anguses and Alexes strung out along the coast. Distinguishing the different families, although their names were much the same, and delivering letters which they could not read.

My father and his brother continued to pester their parents who continued to say "Wait and see," and then one day they went to visit their father's mother who lived in a house quite close to theirs. After they had finished the lunch she had given them, she offered to "read" their teacups and to tell them of the future events revealed in the tea leaves at the bottoms of their cups: "You are going on a journey," she said, peering into the cups as she turned them in her hands. "You are going to cross water. And to take food with you. You will meet a mysterious woman who has dark hair. She will be quite close to you. And . . ." she said, turning the cups in her hands to see the formation of the leaves better, "and . . . oh . . . oh . . . oh."

"What?" they asked. "What?"

"Oh, that's enough for today," she said. "You had better be getting home or they will be worrying about you."

They ran home and burst into their parents' kitchen. "We are going on a trip to Canna," they said. "Grandma told us. She saw it in the tea leaves. She read it in our cups. We are going to take a lunch. We are going across the water. She said we were going."

The morning they left they were dressed in their best clothes and waiting at the wharf long before the smack was due, clutching their lunches in their hands. It was sunny when the boat left the wharf but as they proceeded along the coast it became cloudy and then it began to rain. The trip seemed long in the rain and the men told them to go into the boat's cabin where they would be dry and where they could eat their lunch. The first part of the trip seemed to be spoiled by rain.

It was raining heavily when the boat approached the wharf at Canna point. It was almost impossible to see the figures on the wharf or to distinguish them as they moved about in their heavy oil slickers. The lobster buyers were in a hurry, as were the wet men impatiently waiting for them in the rain.

"Do you know where you're going?" said the men in the smack to their young passengers.

"Yes," they said, although they were not quite sure because the rain obscured the landmarks that they thought they would remember.

"Here," said the men in the smack, handing them two men's oil slickers from the boat's cabin. "Wear these to help keep you dry. You can give them back to us sometime."

They climbed up the iron ladder toward the wharf's cap and the busy men reached their hands down to help and pull them up.

The men were busy and because of the rain no one on the wharf asked them where they were going, and they were too shy and too proud to ask. So they turned the cuffs of the oil slickers back over their wrists and began to walk up the muddy road from the wharf. They were still trying to keep their best clothes clean and pick their spots carefully, placing their good shoes where there were fairly dry spots and avoiding the puddles and little rivulets which rolled the small stones along in their course. The oil slickers were so long that the bottoms of them dragged on the muddy road and sometimes they lifted them up in the way that older ladies might lift the hems of their skirts when stepping over a puddle or some other obstacle in the roadway. When they lifted them, the muddy bottoms rubbed against their good trousers so they let them fall again. Then their shoes were almost invisible and they could hear and feel the tails of the coats dragging behind them as they walked. They were wet and miserable inside the long coats, as well as indistinguishable to anyone who might see the small forms in the long coats walking along the road.

After they had walked for half a mile they were overtaken by an old man in a buggy who stopped and offered them a ride. He, too, was covered in an oil coat, and his cap was pulled down almost to his nose. When he stopped to pick them up, the steam rose from his horse as they clambered into the wagon beside him. He spoke to them in Gaelic and asked them their names and where they were from and where they were going.

"To see our grandmother," they said.

"Your grandmother?" he asked.

"Yes," they said. "Our grandmother."

"Oh," he said. "Your grandmother, are you sure?"

"Of course," they said, becoming a bit annoyed. For although they were more uncertain than they cared to admit, they did not want to appear so.

"Oh," he said, "all right then. Would you like some peppermints?" And he reached deeply into a pocket beneath his oil coat and brought out a brown paper bag full of peppermints. Even as he passed the bag to them, the raindrops pelted upon it and it became soggy and began to darken in deterioration.

"Oh," he said, "you may as well keep all of them. I got a whole lot more of them for the store. They just came in on the boat." He pointed to some metal containers in the back of the buggy.

"Are you going to spend the night with your grandmother?" he asked.

"Yes," they said.

"Oh," he answered, pulling on the reins and turning the horse into the laneway of a yard.

He drove them to the door of the house and helped them down from the buggy while his horse stomped its impatient hooves in the mud and tossed its head in the rain.

"Would you like me to go in with you?" he asked.

"No," they said, impatient for him to be gone and out of sight.

"All right," he said and spoke to his uneasy horse which began to trot down the laneway, the buggy wheels throwing hissing jets of mud and water behind them.

They hesitated for a while outside the doorway of the house, waiting for the man to go out of sight and feeling ridiculous for standing in the rain. But halfway down the lane he stopped and looked back. And then he stood up in the buggy and shouted to them and made a "go-forward" gesture with his hand toward the house. They opened the door then and went in because they felt embarrassed and did not want to admit that he had brought them to the wrong house.

When they went in, they found themselves in the middle of a combined porch and entranceway which was cluttered with an odd collection of household and farming utensils. Baking pans and jars and sealers and chamber pots and old milk pails and rakes and hoes and hayforks and bits of wire and lengths of chain. There was very little light, and in the gloom something started up from their feet and bounced against their legs and then into a collection of jars and pails, causing a crashing cacophony of sound. It was a half-grown lamb, and it bleated as it bounded toward the main door, dropping bits of manure behind it. In the same instant and in response to the sound, the main door opened and the lamb leaped through it and into the house.

Framed in the doorway was a tall old woman clad in layers of clothing, even though it was summer, and wearing wire-framed glasses. On either side of her were two black dogs. They were like collies, although they had no white markings. They growled softly but deep within their throats and the fur on the back of their necks rose and they raised their upper lips to reveal their gleaming teeth. They were poised on the tips of their paws and their eyes seemed to burn in the gloom. She lowered a hand to each of their heads but did not say anything. Everyone seemed to stare straight ahead. The boys would have run away but they were afraid that if they moved, the dogs would be upon them, so they stayed where they were as still as could be. The only sound was the tense growling of the dogs. "*Cò a th'ann?*" she said in Gaelic. "Who's there?"

The boys did not know what to say because all the possible answers seemed so complicated. They moved their feet uneasily, which caused the dogs to each take two steps forward as if they were part of some rehearsed choreography. "*Cò a th'ann?*" she said, repeating the question. "Who's there?"

"We're from Kintail," they said finally. "Our names are Alex and Angus. We're trying to find our grandmother's house. We came on the smack boat."

"Oh," she said. "How old are you?"

"Eleven," they said. "Both of us. We're twins."

"Oh," she said. "Both of you. I have relatives in Kintail. Come in."

They were still afraid, and the dogs remained poised, snarling softly, with their delicate, dangerous lips flickering above the whiteness of their teeth.

"All right," they said. "We'll come in, but just for a minute. We can't stay long."

Only then did she speak to the dogs. "Go and lie under the table and be quiet," she said. Immediately they relaxed and vanished behind her into the house.

"Did you know these dogs were twins?" she asked.

"No," they said. "We didn't."

"Well," she said. "They are."

Inside the house they sat on the first chairs that they could find and moved them as close to the door as possible. The room that they were in was a primitive kitchen and much of its floor was cluttered with objects not unlike the porch, except that the objects were smaller – knives and forks and spoons and the remains of broken cups and saucers. There was a half-completed partition between the kitchen and what might have been a living room or dining room. The upright studs of the partition were firmly in place and someone had nailed wainscotting on either side of them but it extended only halfway to the ceiling. It was difficult to tell if the partition had been left incomplete or if it was gradually being lowered. The space between the walls of the partition was filled with cats. They pulled themselves up by their paws and looked curiously at the visitors and then jumped back down into the space. From the space between the uncompleted walls the visitors could hear the mewing of newborn kittens. Other cats were everywhere. They were on the table, licking what dishes there were, and on the backs of the chairs and in and out of a cavern beneath an old couch. Sometimes they leaped over the half-completed partition and vanished into the next room. Sometimes they snarled at one another and feinted with their paws. In one corner a large tiger-striped tomcat was energetically breeding a small grey female flattened out beneath him. Other tentative males circled the breeding pair, growling deeply within their throats. The tiger cat would interrupt his movements from time to time to snarl at them and keep them at bay. The female's nose was pressed against the floor and her ears flattened down against her head. Sometimes he held the fur at the back of her neck within his teeth.

The two black dogs lay under the table and seemed oblivious to the cats. The lamb stood watchfully behind the stove. Everything in the house was extremely dirty – spilled milk and cat hair and unwashed and broken dishes. The old woman wore men's rubber boots upon her feet and her clothing seemed to consist of layers of petticoats and skirts and dresses and sweaters upon sweaters. All of it was very dirty and covered with stains of spilled tea and food remnants and spattered grease. Her hands seemed brown, and her fingernails were long, and there was a half inch of black grime under each of them. She raised her hands to touch her glasses and they noticed that the outside lenses were smeared and filthy as well. It was then that they realized that she was blind and that the glasses served no useful purpose. They became even more uncertain and frightened than they were before.

"Which one of you is Alex?" she asked, and he raised his hand as if answering a question at school before realizing that she could not see him.

"I am," he answered then, and she turned her face in his direction.

"I have a long association with that name," she said, and they were surprised at her use of a word like "association."

Because of the rain the day seemed to darken early and they could see the fading light through the grimy windows. They wondered for a moment why she did not light a lamp until they realized that there was none and that to her it made no difference.

"I will make you a lunch," she said. "Don't move."

She went to the partial partition and ripped the top board off with her strong brown hands and then she leaned it against the partition and stomped on it with her rubber-booted foot. It splintered and she repeated the action, feeling about the floor for the lengths of splintered wood. She gathered them up and went to the stove and, after removing the lids, began to feed them into the fire. She moved the kettle over the crackling flame.

She began to feel about the cupboards for food, brushing away the insistent cats which crowded about her hands. She found two biscuits in a tin and placed them on plates which she put into the cupboard so the cats would not devour them. She put her hand into a tea tin and took a handful of tea which she placed in the teapot and then she poured the hot water in as well. She found some milk in a dirty pitcher and, feeling for the cups, she splashed some of it into each.

Then she took the teapot and began to pour the tea. She turned her back to them but as she poured they could see her quickly dip her long brown finger with the half inch of grimy fingernail quickly into each cup. They realized she was doing it because she had no other way of knowing when the cups were full but their stomachs revolved and they feared they might throw up.

She brought them a cup of tea each and retrieved the biscuits from the cupboard and passed the plates to them. They sat holding the offerings on their laps while she faced them. Although they realized she could not see them, they still felt that she was watching them. They looked at the tea and the biscuits with the cat hair and did not know what to do. After a while they began to make slurping sounds with their lips.

"Well, we will have to be on our way," they said. Carefully they bent forward and placed the still-full teacups under their chairs and the biscuits in their pockets.

"Do you know where you are going?" she asked.

"Yes," they said with determination.

"Can you see your way in the dark?"

"Yes," they said again with equal determination.

"We will meet again?" she said, raising her voice to form a question.

"Yes," they said.

"Some are more loyal than others," she said. "Remember that."

They hurried down the laneway, surprised to find that it was not so dark outside as it seemed within the blind woman's house. When they got to the main road, they followed it in the direction that led away from the wharf and it seemed that in a short time they could make out the buildings of their original destination.

It was still raining as they entered the laneway to the buildings, and by this time it was indeed quite dark. The laneway ended at the door of the barn and the house was some yards farther. The barn door was open and they stepped inside for a moment to compose themselves. It was very quiet within the barn, for all of the animals were away in their summer pastures. They hesitated for a moment in the first stall and then they were aware of a rhythm of sound coming from the next area, the threshing floor. They opened the small connecting door and stepped inside and waited for their eyes to adjust to the gloom. And then in the farthest corner they noticed a lantern turned to its lowest and hanging on a nail. And beyond it they could make out the shape of a man. He was tall and wore rubber boots and bib overalls and had a tweed cap pulled down upon his head. He was facing the south wall of the barn but was sideways to them and presented a profile. He was rhythmically rocking from his heels to the balls of his feet and thrusting his hips back and forth and moaning and talking to himself in Gaelic. But it did not seem that he was talking to himself but to someone of the opposite sex who was not there. The front of his overalls was open and he had a hold of himself in his right hand which he moved to the rhythm of his rocking body.

They did not know what to do. They did not recognize the man, and they were terrified that he might turn and see them, and they were afraid that if they tried to make a retreat they might cause a sound which would betray their presence. At home they slept upstairs while their parents slept below in a private room ("to keep an eye on the fire," their parents said); and although they were becoming curious about sex, they did not know a great deal about it. They had seen the mating of animals, such as the cats earlier, but they had never seen a fully aroused grown man before, although they recognized some of the words he was moaning to himself and his imaginary partner. Suddenly, with a groan, he slumped forward as the grey jets of seed spurted onto the south wall of the barn and down to the dry and dusty hay before his feet. He placed his left arm against the wall and rested his forehead against it. They stepped back quietly through the little door and then out of the barn and then they walked rapidly but on their tiptoes through the rain toward the house.

When they entered the porch and the screen door slammed behind them, they heard a voice from within the kitchen. It was harsh and angry and seemed to be cursing, and then the door flew open and they were face to face with their grandmother. At first she did not recognize them in their long coats, and her face remained suspicious and angry, but then her expression changed and she came forward to hug them.

"Angus and Alex," she said. "What a surprise!" Looking over their shoulders, she said, "Are you alone? Did you come by yourselves?" And then, "Why didn't you tell us you were coming? We would have gone to meet you."

It had never entered their minds that their arrival would be such a surprise. They had been thinking of the trip with such intensity that in spite of the day's happenings they still somehow assumed that everyone knew they were coming.

"Well, come in, come in," she said, "and take those wet clothes off. How did you say you came again? And are you just arriving now?"

They told her they had come on the smack and of their walk and the ride with the man who had the peppermints and of their visit to the blind woman, but they omitted the part about the man in the barn. She listened intently as she moved about the kitchen, hanging up their coats and setting the teapot on the stove. She asked for a description of the man with the peppermints and they told her he said he owned a store, and then she asked them how the blind woman was. They told her of the tea she had served them which they had left and she said, "Poor soul!"

And then the screen door banged again and a heavy foot was heard in the porch, and in through the kitchen door walked the man they had seen in the barn.

"Your grandchildren are here to see you," she said with an icy edge to her voice. "They came on the smack from Kintail."

He stood blinking and swaying in the light, trying to focus his eyes upon them. They realized then that he was quite drunk and having difficulty comprehending. His eyes were red-rimmed and bloodshot and a white stubble speckled with black indicated that he had not shaved for a number of days. He swayed back and forth, looking at them carefully and trying to see who they really were. They could not help looking at the front of his overalls to see if there were flecks of semen, but he had been out in the rain and all of his clothing was splattered with moisture.

"Oh," he said, as if a veil had been lifted from his eyes. "Oh," he said. "I love you. I love you." And he came forward and hugged each of them and kissed them on the cheek. They could smell the sourness of his breath and feel the rasping scratch of his stubble on their faces.

"Well," he said, turning on his heel, "I am going upstairs to rest for awhile. I have been out in the barn and have been busier than you might think. But I will be back down later." And then he kicked off his boots, steadying himself with one hand on a kitchen chair, and swayed upstairs.

The visitors were shocked that they had not recognized their grandfather. When he came to visit them perhaps once a year, he was always splendid and handsome in his blue serge suit, with a gold watch chain linked across the expansiveness of his vest, and with his pockets filled with peppermints. And when they visited in the company of their parents, he had always been gracious and clear-headed and well attired.

When they could no longer hear his footsteps, their grandmother again began to talk to them, asking them questions, inquiring of their parents and of their school work as she busied herself about the stove and began to set the table.

Later he came back downstairs and they all sat around the table. He had changed his clothes, and his face was covered with bleeding nicks because he had tried to shave. The meal was uncomfortable as he knocked over his water glass and dropped his food on his lap. The visitors were as exhausted as he was, and only their grandmother seemed in control. He went back upstairs as soon as the meal was finished, saying, "Tomorrow will be a better day," and their grandmother suggested that they go to bed soon after.

"We are all tired," she said. "He will be all right tomorrow. He tried to shave in honour of your coming. I will talk to him myself. We are glad that you have come."

They slept together under a mountain of quilts and in a room next to their grandparents'. Before they went to sleep they could hear them talking in Gaelic, and the next thing they remembered was waking in the morning. Their grandparents were standing near their bed and the sun was shining through the window. Each of their grandparents held a tray containing porridge and sugar and milk and tea and butter. They were both rather formally dressed and like the grandparents they thought they knew. The drunk moaning man in the barn was like a dream they wished they had not had.

When they got up to put on their clothes they discovered bits of the blind woman's biscuits still in their pockets, and when they went outside they threw them behind the barn.

They stayed a week at Canna and all during that time the sun shone and the days were golden. They went visiting with their grandfather in his buggy – visiting women in houses and sometimes standing in barns with men. One day they visited the store and had trouble identifying the man behind the counter with the one who had offered them the ride and the peppermints. He seemed equally surprised when he recognized them and said to their grandfather, "I'm sorry if I made a mistake."

During their week in Canna they noticed small differences in the way of doing things. The people of Canna tied their horses with ropes around their necks instead of with halters. They laid out their gardens in beds instead of in rows and they grew a particular type of strawberry whose fruit grew far from the original root. When they drew water from their wells they threw away the first dipperful and the water itself had a slightly different taste. They set their tables for breakfast before retiring for the night. They bowed or curtsied to the new moon, and in the Church of St. Columba the women sat on one side of the aisle and the men on the other.

The Church of St. Columba, said their grandfather, was called after the original chapel on the island of Canna. St. Columba of Colum Cille was a brilliant, dedicated missionary in Ireland and he possessed *Da Shealladh*, the second sight, and used a stone to "see" his visions. He was also a lover of beauty and very strong-willed. Once, continued their grandfather, he copied a religious manuscript without permission but believed the copy was rightfully his. The High King of Ireland who was asked to judge the dispute ruled against Colum Cille, saying, "To every cow its calf and to every book its copy." Later the High King of Ireland also executed a young man who had sought sanctuary under the protection of Colum Cille. Enraged at what he perceived as injustice and bad judgement, Colum Cille told the High King he would lead his relations and clansmen against him in battle. On the eve of the battle, as they prayed and fasted, the archangel Michael appeared to Colum Cille in a vision. The angel told him that God would answer his prayers and allow him to win the battle but that He was not pleased with him for praying for such a worldly request and that he should exile himself from Ireland and never see the country any more, or its people, or partake of its food and drink except on his outward journey. The forces of Colum Cille won the battle and inflicted losses of three thousand men, and perhaps he could have been the King of Ireland, but he obeyed the vision. Some said he left also to do penance for the three thousand lives he had cost. In a small boat and with a few followers who were his relatives, he crossed the sea to the small islands of Scotland and spent the last thirty-four years of his life establishing monasteries and chapels and travelling among the people. Working as a missionary, making predictions, seeing visions and changing forever that region of the world. Leaving Ireland, he said:

> *There is a grey eye*
> *Looking back on Ireland,*
> *That will never see again*
> *Her men or her women.*
>
> *Early and late my lamentation,*
> *Alas, the journey I am making;*
> *This will be my secret bye-name*
> *"Back turned on Ireland."*

"Did he ever go back?" they asked.

"Once," said their grandfather, "the poets of Ireland were in danger of being banned and he crossed the sea from Scotland to speak on their behalf. But when he came, he came blindfolded so that he could not see the country or its people."

"Did you know him?" they asked. "Did you ever see him?"

"That was a very long time ago," he laughed. "Over thirteen hundred years ago. But, yes, sometimes I feel I know him and I think I see him as well. This church, as I said, is called after the chapel he established on Canna. That chapel is fallen a long time ago, too, and all of the people gone, and the well beside the chapel filled up with rocks and the Celtic crosses of their grave-yards smashed down and used for the building of roads. But sometimes I imagine I still see them," he said, looking toward the ocean and across it as if he could see the "green island" and its people. "I see them going about their rituals: riding their horses on Michaelmas and carrying the bodies of their dead round toward the sun. And courting and getting married. Almost all of the people on Canna got married before they were twenty. They considered it unlucky to be either a single man or woman so there were very few single people among them. Perhaps they also found it difficult to wait," he added with a smile, "and that is why their population rose so rapidly. Anyway, all gone."

"You mean dead?" they asked.

"Well, some of them, yes," he said, "but I mean gone from there, scattered all over the world. But some of us are here. That is why this place is called Canna and we carry certain things within us. Sometimes there are things within us which we do not know or fully understand and sometimes it is hard to stamp out what you can't see. It is good that you are here for this while."

Toward the end of the week they learned that there was a government boat checking lighthouses along the coast. It would stop at the point of Canna and later, on its southern journey, also at Kintail. It was an excellent chance for them to get home, and it was decided that they should take it. The night before they left, their grandparents served them a splendid dinner with a white tablecloth and candles.

As they prepared to leave on the following morning, the rain began to fall. Their grandmother gave them some packages to deliver to their mother, and also a letter, and packed a lunch with lobster sandwiches for them. She hugged and kissed them as they were leaving and said, "Thank you for coming. It was good to have you here and it made us feel better about ourselves." She looked at her husband and he nodded.

They climbed into their grandfather's buggy as the rain fell upon them, and carefully placed their packages beneath the seat. On the road down to the wharf they passed the lane to the blind woman's house. She was near the roadway with the two black dogs. She was wearing her men's rubber boots and a large kerchief and a heavy rubber raincoat. When she heard the buggy approaching, she called out, "*Cò a th'ann? Cò a th'ann?* Who's there? Who's there?"

But their grandfather said nothing.

"Who's there?" she called. "Who's there? Who's there?"

The rain fell upon her streaked and empty glasses and down her face and along her coat and her strong protruding hands with their grimy fingernails.

"Don't say anything," said their grandfather under his breath. "I don't want her to know you're here."

As the horse approached, she continued to call, but none of them said anything. Above the regular hoofbeats of the horse her voice seemed to rise through the falling rain, causing a tension within all of them as they tried to pretend they could not hear her.

"*Cò a th'ann?*" she called. "Who's there? Who's there?"

They lowered their heads as if she could see them. But when they were exactly opposite her, their grandfather could not stand it any longer and suddenly reined in the horse.

"*Cò a th'ann?*" she called. "Who's there?"

"'*Se mi-fhìn*," he answered quietly. "It's myself!"

She began to curse him in Gaelic and he became embarrassed.

"Do you understand what she's saying?" he said to them.

They were uncertain. "Some of it," they said.

"Here," he said, "hold the horse," and he passed the reins to them. He took the buggy whip out of its socket as he descended from the buggy, and they were uncertain about that, too, until they realized he was taking it protect himself from the dogs who came snarling towards him, but kept their distance because of the whip. He began to talk to the blind woman in Gaelic and they both walked away from the buggy along the laneway to her house until they were out of earshot. The dogs lay down on the wet roadway and watched and listened carefully.

The visitors could not hear the conversation, only the rising and falling of the two voices through the descending rain. When their grandfather returned, he seemed upset and took the reins from them and spoke to the horse immediately.

"God help me," he said softly and almost to himself, "but I could not pass her by."

There was water running down his face and they thought for a moment he might be crying; but just as when they had looked for the semen on his overalls a week earlier, they could not tell because of the rain.

The blind woman stood in the laneway facing them as they moved off along the road. It was one of those situations which almost automatically calls for waving but even as they began to raise their hands they remembered her blindness and realized it was no use. She stood as if watching them for a long time and then, perhaps when she could no longer hear the sound of the horse and buggy, she turned and walked with the two dogs back toward her house.

"Do you know her well?" they asked.

"Oh," said their grandfather, as if being called back from another time and place, "yes, I do know her quite well and since a long, long time."

Their grandfather waited with them on the wharf for the coming of the government boat, but it was late. When it finally arrived, the men said they would not be long checking the light-house and told them to go into the boat to wait. They said their good-byes then, and their grandfather turned his wet and impatient horse towards home.

Although the wait was not supposed to be long, it was longer than expected and it was afternoon before the boat left the protection of the wharf and ventured out into the ocean. The rain was still falling and a wind had come up and the sea was choppy. The wind was off the land, so they stood with their backs toward Canna and to the wind and the rain. When they were far enough out to sea to have perspective, one of the men said, "It looks like there is a fire back there." And when they looked back they could see the billowing smoke, somehow seeming ironic in the rain. It rose in the distance and was carried by the wind but it was difficult to see its source not only because of the smoke but also because of the driving rain. And because the perspective from the water was different from what it was on the land. The government men did not know any of the local people and they were behind schedule and already well out to sea, so there was no thought of turning back. They were mildly concerned, too, about the rising wind, and wanted to make as much headway as possible before conditions worsened.

It was that period of the day when the afternoon blends into evening before the boat reached the Kintail wharf. During the last miles the ocean had roughened and within the rocking boat the passengers had become green and seasick and vomited their lobster sandwiches over the side. Canna seemed very far away and the golden week seemed temporarily lost within the reality of the swaying boat and the pelting rain. When the boat docked, they ran to their house as quickly as they could. Their mother gave them soup and dry clothes and they went to bed earlier than usual.

They slept late the next day, and when they awoke and went downstairs it was still raining and blowing. And then the Syrian pedlars, Angus and Alex, knocked on the door. They put their heavy wet leather packs upon the kitchen floor and told the boys' mother that there had been a death in Canna. The Canna people were sending word but they had heard the news earlier in the day from another pedlar arriving from that direction and he had asked them to carry the message. The pedlars and the boys' parents talked for a while and the boys were told to "go outside and play" even though it was raining. They went out to the barn.

Almost immediately the boys' parents began to get ready for the journey. The ocean was by this time too rough for a boat, and they had already hauled their boat up at the end of the lobster season. They readied their horse and buggy, and later in the afternoon they were gone. They were away for five days, and when they returned they were drawn and tired.

Through bits and pieces of conversation, the boys learned that it was the blind woman's house that had burned and she within it.

Later, and they were not sure just when, they gathered other details and bits of information. She had been at the stove, it was thought, and her clothes had caught fire. The animals had burned with her. Most of their bones were found before the door to which they had gone to seek escape but she had been unable to open it for them or, it seemed, for herself.

Over the weeks the details blended in with their own experience. They imagined her strong hands pulling down the wainscotting of her own house and placing it in the fire, consuming her own house somehow from within as it was later to consume her. And they could see the fire going up the front of her layers of dirty clothing. Consuming the dirt which she herself had been unable to see. Rising up the front of her clothing, rising up above her shoulders toward her hair, the imaginary orange flames flickering and framing her face and being reflected in the staring lenses of her glasses.

And they imagined the animals, too. The savage faithful dogs which were twins snarling at the doorway with their fur in flames, and the lusty cats engaged in their growling copulation in the corner, somehow keeping on, driven by their own heat while the other heat surrounded them, and the bleating lamb with its wool on fire. And in the space between the walls the mewing unseen kittens, dying with their eyes still closed.

And sometimes they imagined her, too, in her porch or in her house or standing by the roadside in the rain. *Cò a th'ann?* they heard her call in their imagination and in their dreams. *Cò a th'ann? Cò a th'ann?* Who's there? Who's there? And one night they dreamed they heard themselves answer. *'Se mi-fhìn* they heard themselves say as with one voice. It is myself.

My father and his brother never again spent a week on the green hills of Canna. Perhaps their lives went by too fast or circumstances changed or there were reasons that they did not fully understand themselves.

And one Sunday six years later when they were in church the clergyman gave a rousing sermon on why young men should enlist in World War I. They were very enthusiastic about the idea and told their parents that they were going to Halifax to enlist although they were too young. Their parents were very upset and went to the clergyman in an attempt to convince him it was a mistake. The clergyman was their friend and came to their house and told them it was a general sermon for the day. "I didn't mean *you*," he added, but his first success was better than his second.

They left the next day for Halifax, getting a ride to the nearest railroad station. They had never been on a train before and when they arrived, the city of Halifax was large and awesome. At the induction centre their age was easily overlooked but the medical examination was more serious. Although they were young and strong, the routine tests seemed strange and provoked a tension within them. They were unable to urinate in a bottle on request and were asked to wait a while and then try again. But sitting on two chairs wishing for urine did little good. They drank more and more water and waited and tried but it did not work. On their final attempt, they were discussing their problem in Gaelic while standing in a tiny cubicle with their legs spread apart and their trousers opened. Unexpectedly a voice from the next cubicle responded to them in Gaelic.

The voice belonged to a young man from Canna who had come to enlist as well but who did not have their problem. "Can we 'borrow' some of that?" they asked, looking at his full bottle of urine.

"Sure," he said, "no need to give it back," and he splashed some of his urine into each of their waiting bottles. All of them "passed" the test; and later in the alleyway behind the induction centre, standing in the steam of their own urine, they began to talk to the young man from Canna. His grandfather owned the store in Canna, he said, and was opposed to his coming to enlist.

"Do you know Alex?" they asked and mentioned their grandfather's formal name.

He seemed puzzled for a moment and then brightened. "Oh," he said, "*Mac an Amharuis*, sure, everyone knows him. He's my grandfather's friend."

And then, perhaps because they were far from home and more lonely and frightened than they cared to admit, they began to talk in Gaelic. They began with the subject of *Mac an*

Amharuis, and the young man told them everything he knew. Surprised perhaps at his own knowledge and at having such attentive listeners. *Mac an Amharuis* translates as "Son of Uncertainty," which meant that he was illegitimate or uncertain as to who his father was. He was supposed to be tremendously talented and clever as a young man but also restless and reluctant to join the other young men of Canna in their fishing boats. Instead he saved his money and purchased a splendid stallion and travelled the country offering the stallion's services. He rode on the stallion's back with only a loose rope around its neck for guidance.

He was also thought to be handsome and to possess a "strong nature" or "too much nature," which meant that he was highly sexed. "Some say," said the young man, "that he sowed almost as much seed as the stallion and who knows who might be descended from him. If we only knew, eh?" he added with a laugh.

Then he became involved with a woman from Canna. She was thought to be "odd" by some because she was given to rages and uncertainty and sometimes she would scream and shout at him in public. At times he would bring back books and sometimes moonshine from wherever he went with the stallion. And sometimes they would read quietly together and talk and at other times they would curse and shout and become physically violent.

And then he became possessed of *Da Shealladh*, the second sight. It seemed he did not want it and some said it came about because of too much reading of the books or perhaps it was inherited from his unknown father. Once he "saw" a storm on the evening of a day which was so calm that no one would believe him. When it came in the evening the boats could not get back and all the men were drowned. And once when he was away with the stallion, he "saw" his mother's house burn down, and when he returned he found that it had happened on the very night he saw it, and his mother was burned to death.

It became a weight upon him and he could not stop the visions or do anything to interfere with the events. One day after he and the woman had had too much to drink they went to visit a well-known clergyman. He told the clergyman he wanted the visions to stop but it did not seem within his power. He and the woman were sitting on two chairs beside each other. The clergyman went for the Bible and prayed over it and then he came and flicked the pages of the Bible before their eyes. He told them the visions would stop but that they would have to give up one another because they were causing a scandal in the community. The woman became enraged and leaped at the clergyman and tried to scratch out his eyes with her long nails. She accused *Mac an Amharuis* of deceiving her and said that he was willing to exchange their stormy relationship for his lack of vision. She spat in his face and cursed him and stormed out the door. *Mac an Amharuis* rose to follow her but the clergyman put his arms around him and wrestled him to the floor. He was far gone in drink and within the clergyman's power.

They stopped appearing with one another and *Mac an Amharuis* stopped travelling with the stallion and bought himself a boat. He began to visit the woman's younger sister, who was patient and kind. The woman moved out of her parents' house and into an older house nearer the shore. Some thought she moved because she could not stand *Mac an Amharuis* visiting her sister, and others thought that it was planned to allow him to visit her at night without anyone seeing.

Within two months *Mac an Amharuis* and the woman's sister were married. At the wedding the woman cursed the clergyman until he warned her to be careful and told her to leave the building. She cursed her sister, too, and said, "You will never be able to give him what I can." And as she was going out the door, she said to *Mac an Amharuis* either "I will never forgive you" or "I will never forget you." Her voice was charged with emotion but her back was turned to them and the people were uncertain whether it was a curse or a cry.

The woman did not come near anyone for a long time and people saw her only from a distance, moving about the house and the dilapidated barn, caring for the few animals which her father had given her, and muffled in clothes as autumn turned to winter. At night people watched for a light in her window. Sometimes they saw it and sometimes they did not.

And then one day her father came to the house of his daughter and *Mac an Amharuis* and said that he had not seen a light for three nights and he was worried. The three of them went to the house but it was cold. There was no heat when they put their hands on the stove and the glass of the windowpanes was covered with frost. There was nobody in any of the rooms.

They went out into the barn and found her lying in a heap. Most of the top part of her body was still covered by layers of clothes, although the lower part was not. She was unconscious or in something like a frozen coma and her eyes were inflamed, with beads of pus at their corners. She had given birth to twin girls and one of them was dead but the other somehow still alive, lying on her breast amidst her layers of clothing. Her father and *Mac an Amharuis* and her sister carried the living into the house and started a fire in the stove, and sent for the nearest medical attention, which was some miles away. Later they also carried in the body of the dead baby and placed it in a lobster crate, which was all that they could find. When the doctor came, he said he could not be certain of the baby's exact time of birth but he felt that it would live. He said that the mother had lost a great deal of blood and he thought she might have lacerated her eyes during the birth with her long fingernails and that infection had set in, caused perhaps by the unsanitary conditions within the barn. He was not sure if she would live and, if she did, he feared her sight would never be restored.

Mac an Amharuis and his wife cared for the baby throughout the days that the woman was unconscious, and the baby thrived. The woman herself began to rally and the first time she heard the baby cry she reached out instinctively for it but could not find it in the dark. Gradually, as she recognized by sound the people around her, she began to curse them and accused them of having sex when she could not see them. As she grew stronger, she became more resentful of their presence and finally asked them to leave. She began to rise from her bed and walk with her hands before her, sometimes during the day and some-times during the night because it made no difference to her. And once they saw her with a knife in her hand. They left her then, as she had requested them to do and perhaps because they were afraid. And because there seemed no other choice, they took the baby with them.

They continued to bring her food and to leave it at the door of her porch. Sometimes she cursed at them but at other times she was quieter. One day while they were talking she extended her hand with the long fingernails to the face of *Mac an Amharuis*. She ran the balls of her fingers and the palm of her hand from his hair down over his eyes and nose and his lips and his chin and down along the buttons of his shirt and below his belt to between his legs; and then her hand closed for an instant and she grasped what she had held before but would never see again.

Mac an Amharuis and his wife had no children of their own. It was thought that it caused a great sadness within her and perhaps a tension because, as people said, "It's sure as hell not *his* fault." Their childlessness was thought also to prey on him and to lead to periodic drinking binges, although he never mentioned it to anyone. For the most part, they were helpful and supportive of each other and no one knew what they talked about when they were alone and together in their bed at night.

This, I guess, is my retelling of the story told by the young man of Canna to my father and his brother at a time when they were all young and on the verge of war. All of the information that spilled out of him came because it was there to be released and he was revealing more than he realized to his attentive listeners. The story was told in Gaelic, and as the people say, "It is not the same in English," although the images are true.

When the war was over, the generous young man from Canna was dead; and my father's brother had lost his leg.

My father returned to Kintail and the life that he had left, the boat and the nets and the lobster traps. All of them in the cycle of the seasons. He married before World War II; and when he was asked to go again, he went with the other Highlanders from Cape Breton, leaving his wife pregnant, perhaps without realizing it.

On the beach at Normandy they were emptied into ten feet of water as the rockets and shells exploded around them. And in the mud they fell face-down, leaving the imprints of their faces temporarily in the soil, before clawing their way some few feet forward. At the command they rose, as would a wave trying to break farther forward on the shore. And then all of it seemed to happen at once. Before my father's eyes there rose a wall of orange flame and a billowing wave of black smoke. It rose before him even as he felt the power of the strong hand upon his left shoulder. The grip was so powerful that he felt the imprint of the fingers almost as a bruise; and even as he turned his searing eyes, he fell back into his own language. "*Cò a th'ann?*" he said. "*Cò a th'ann?* Who's there?" And in the instant before his blindness, he recognized the long brown fingers on his shoulder with their pointed fingernails caked in dirt. "*'Se mi-fhìn,*" she said quietly. "It is myself."

All of the soldiers in front of my father were killed and in the spot where he stood there was a crater, but this was told to him because he was unable ever to see it for himself.

Later he was told that on the day of his blinding, his grandfather, the man known to some as *Mac an Amharuis*, died. *Mac an Amharuis* was a man of over a hundred years at the time of his death and his eyes had become covered with the cataracts of age. He did not recognize, either by sight or sound, any of the people around him, and much of his talk was of youth and sex and of the splendid young stallion with the loose rope around its neck. And much of it was of the green island of Canna which he had never literally seen and of the people riding their horses at Michaelmas and carrying the bodies of their dead round toward the sun. And of the strong-willed St. Columba determined to be ascetic with his "back turned on Ireland" and the region of his early love. And of walls of flame and billowing smoke.

When I began this story I was recounting the story which my father told to me as he faced the green hills of Canna on the last day of the lobster season a long time ago. But when I look on it now I realize that all of it did not come from him, exactly as I have told it, on that day. The part about seeing his grandfather in the barn and much of the story of the young man from Canna came instead from his twin brother who participated in most of the events. Perhaps because of the loss of his leg, my father's brother became one of those veterans from World War I who spent a lot of their time in the Legion Hall. When he spoke to me he had none of the embarrassment which my father sometimes showed when discussing certain subjects. Perhaps my father, by omitting certain parts of his story, was merely repeating the custom of his parents who did not reveal to him at once everything there was to be shown.

But perhaps the story also went into me because of other events which happened on that day. After my father had finished, we started our engine and went into the wharf. By the time we arrived, the MacAllesters had gone and many of the other men as well. We hoisted the lobsters to the wharf's cap and I looked at the weight that the scales showed.

Whether the buyers noticed the concealed lobsters behind the crate we were never to know, but they said nothing. We unloaded our traps on the wharf and then climbed up the iron ladder and talked casually to the buyers and received our money. We planned to come back later for the lobsters behind the crate.

There were still other fishermen about and most of them shared my father's good mood because they were glad that the season had ended and pleased to have the money which was their final payment. Someone offered us a ride in a truck to the Legion and we went.

The Legion Hall was filled with men, most of them fishermen, and the noise was loud and the conversation boister- ous. Toward the back of the hall I noticed Kenneth MacAllester with a number of his relatives. Both of us were underage but it did not matter a great deal. If you looked as if you were old enough, no one asked any questions. My father's brother and a number of our own relatives were at a table in the middle. They waved to us and I moved toward them. Behind me, my father followed, touching my belt from time to time for guidance. Most of the men pulled in their feet as we approached so that my father would not stumble. The crutch my uncle used in place of his missing leg was propped up across a chair and he removed it as we approached and leaned it against the table so that he could offer the chair to my father. We sat down and my uncle gave me some money to go to the bar for beer. Coming back, I passed another table of MacAllesters. They were relatives of our neighbours and although I recognized them I did not know them very well. One of them said something as I passed but I did not hear what he said and it seemed best not to stop. The afternoon grew more boisterous and bottles and glasses began to shatter on the cement floor. And then there was a shower of droplets over our head.

"What's that?" said my father.

Two of the MacAllesters from the table I had passed were throwing quarts of beer to their relatives at the back of the hall. They were standing up like quarterbacks and spiralling the open quarts off the palms of their hands and I saw Kenneth reach up and catch one as if he were a wide receiver. The quarts, for the most part, stayed upright; but as they revolved and spun, their foaming contents sprinkled or drenched those seated beneath them.

"Those bastards," said my uncle.

The two of them came over to the table. They were about thirty, and strong and heavily muscled.

"Who are you talking to?" one of them said.

"Never mind," said my uncle. "Go and sit down."

"I asked you a question," he said. And then turning to me he added, "I asked you a question before, too. What's the matter, can't some of you hear? I just thought that some of you couldn't see."

There was a silence then that began to spread to the neighbouring tables and the conversations slowed and the men took their hands off their bottles and their glasses.

"I asked you your age," he said, still looking at me. "Are you the oldest or the youngest?"

"He's the only one," said the other man. "Since the war, his father is so blind he can't find his way into his wife's cunt to make any more."

I remember my uncle reaching for the bottom of his crutch, and he swung it like a baseball bat from his sitting position. And I remember the way he planted his one leg onto the floor even as he swung. And I remember the crutch exploding into the nose and mouth of the man and his blood splashing down upon us and then the overturning of tables and chairs and the crashing of broken glass. And I remember also two of the MacAllesters who were our neighbours reaching our table with amazing speed. Each of them went to a side of my father's chair, and they lifted it up with him still sitting upon it. And they carried him as carefully as if he were eggs or perhaps an object of religious veneration, and the men who were smashing their fists into one another's mouths moved out of their way when they saw them coming. They deposited him with great gentleness against the far wall where they felt no harm could come to him, bending their knees in unison as they lowered his chair to the floor. And then each of them placed a hand upon his shoulder as one might comfort a frightened child. And then one of them picked up a chair and smashed it over the head of my cousin, who had his brother by the throat.

Someone grabbed me and spun me around but I could see by his eyes that he was intent on someone across the hall and that I was merely in his way. And then I saw Kenneth coming toward me, as I half expected him to. It was like the bench-clearing brawls at the hockey games when the goalies seek each other out because they have the most in common.

I saw him coming with his eyes intent upon me and because I knew him well I believed that he would leap from a spot about three strides ahead of him and that the force of his momentum would carry us backward and I would be on the bottom with my head on the cement floor. It all took perhaps a fraction of a second, his leap and my bending and moving forward and side-ways, either to go toward him or to get out of the way, and my shoulder grazing his hip as he was airborne with his hands stretched out before him and his body parallel to the floor. He came crashing down on top of the table, knocking it over and forward and beneath him to the cement.

He lay face-down and still for a moment and I thought he was unconscious, and then I saw the blood spreading from beneath his face and reddening the shards of different-coloured glass.

"Are you all right?" I said, placing my hand upon his shoulder.

"It's okay," he said. "It's just my eye."

He sat up then with his hands over his face and the blood streaming down between his fingers. I was aware of a pair of rubber boots beside us, and then a man's voice. "Stop," he shouted to the brawling hall. "For Christ's sake, stop, someone's been hurt."

In retrospect, and even then, it seemed like a strange thing to say because when one looked at the bloodied men it seemed that almost everyone had been hurt in some way, although not to the same degree. But given the circumstances, he said exactly the right thing, and everyone stopped and unclenched his fist and released his grip on his opponent's throat.

In the rush to the doctor and to the hospital, everyone's orig-inal plans went awry. No one thought of the lobsters we had hidden and saved for our end-of-the-season feast; and when we discovered them days later, it was with something like surprise. They were dead and had to be thrown back into the sea, perhaps to serve as food for the spring mackerel with the scales upon their eyes.

That night two cars of MacAllesters came to our house. They told us that Kenneth's eye was lost; and Mr. MacAllester, who was about my father's age, began to cry. The two young men who were throwing the beer held their caps in their hands, and their knuckles were still raw and bleeding. Both of them apologized to my father. "We didn't see it getting that out of hand," one of them said. My uncle came in from another room and said that he shouldn't have swung the crutch.

Mr. MacAllester said that if my father would agree, all of us should stop using the fickle river as the boundary between our fishing grounds and take our sightings instead from the two rocky promontories on either side of the beach. One family would fish off the beach one year and the other the next. My father agreed. "I can't see the boundary anyway," he said with a smile. It all seemed so simple in hindsight.

This has been the telling of a story about a story but like most stories it has spun off into others and relied on others and perhaps no story every really stands alone. This began as the story of two children who long ago went to visit their grandparents but who, because of circumstances, did not recognize them when they saw them. As their grandparents did not see them. And this is a story related by a man who is a descendant of those people. The son of a father who never saw his son but knew him only through sound or by the running of his fingers across the features of his face.

As I write this, my own small daughter comes in from kindergarten. She is at the age where each day she asks a riddle and I am not supposed to know the answer. Today's question is, "What has eyes but cannot see?" Under the circumstances, the question seems overwhelmingly profound. "I don't know," I say and I feel I really mean it.

"A potato," she shouts and flings herself into my arms, elated and impressed by her own cleverness and by my lack of understanding.

She is the great-great-granddaughter of the blind woman who died in flames and of the man called *Mac an Amharuis*; and both of us, in spite of our age and comprehension, are indeed the children of uncertainty.

Most of the major characters in this story are, as the man called *Mac an Amharuis* once said of others, "all gone" in the literal sense. There remains only Kenneth MacAllester, who works as a janitor for a soap company in Toronto. Unable ever to join the Air Force and fly toward the sun and see over the tops of mountains and across the ocean because of what happened to his eye on that afternoon so long ago. Now he has an artificial eye and, as he says, "Only a few people know the difference."

When we were boys we would try to catch the slippery spring mackerel in our hands and look into the blindness of their eyes, hoping to see our own reflections. And when the wet ropes of the lobster traps came out of the sea, we would pick out a single strand and then try to identify it some few feet farther on.

It was difficult to do because of the twisting and turning of the different strands within the rope. Difficult ever to be certain in our judgements or to fully see or understand. Difficult then to see and understand the twisted strands within the rope. And forever difficult to see and understand the tangled twisted strands of love.

ISLAND

(1 9 8 8)

All day the rain fell upon the island and she waited. Sometimes it slanted against her window with a pinging sound, which meant it was close to hail, and then it was visible as tiny pellets for a moment on the pane before the pellets vanished and rolled quietly down the glass, each drop leaving its own delicate trickle. At other times it fell straight down, hardly touching the window at all, but still there beyond the glass, like a delicate, beaded curtain at the entrance to another room.

She poked the fire within the stove, turning the half-burned lengths of wood so that they would burn more evenly. Some of the wood lengths were old fence posts or timbers that had been hauled from the shore before being cut into sizes that would fit the stove. Some of them contained ancient nails which were bent and twisted deep into the wood's core. When the fire was very hot, they glowed to a cherry red, reminiscent of a blacksmith's shop or, perhaps, their earliest casting. They would glow in the intense heat while the wood was consumed around them and, in the morning, they would be shaken down with the ashes, black and twisted but still there in the greyness of the ashpan. On days when the fire burned with less intensity because the wood was damp or the draughts poor, they remained a rusted brown while the damp wood sputtered and hissed reluctantly before releasing them from the coffins in which they were confined. Today was such a day.

She went to the window and looked out once more. Beneath the table the three black-and-white dogs followed her with their eyes but made no other movement. They had been outside several times during the day and the wetness of their coats gave off the odour of damp woollen garments which have been hung to dry. When they came in, they shook themselves vigorously beside the stove, causing a further sputtering and hissing, as the water droplets fell against the heated steel.

Through the window and the beaded sheets of rain she could see the grey shape of *tir mòr*, the mainland, more than two miles away. Because of her failing sight and the nature of the weather she was not sure if she could really see it. But she had seen it in all weathers and over so many decades that the image of it was clearly in her mind, and whether she actually saw it or remembered it, now, seemed to make no difference.

The mainland was itself but another large island although most people did not think of it in that way. It was, as many said, larger than the province of Prince Edward Island and even some European countries and it had paved roads and cars and now even shopping centres and a fairly large population.

On rainy or foggy evenings such as this, it was always hard to see and to understand the mainland, but when the sun shone it was clearly visible with its white houses and red or grey barns, and with the green lawns and fields surrounding the houses while the rolling mountains of dark green spruce rose behind them. At night the individual houses, and the communities they formed, seemed to be magnified because of the lights. In the daytime if you looked at a certain spot you might see only one house and perhaps a barn, but at night there might be several lights shining from the different windows of the house, and perhaps a light at the barn and other lights shining from hydro poles in the yard, or in the driveway or along the road. And there were the moving lights caused by the headlights of the travelling cars. It all seemed more glamorous at night, perhaps because of what you could not see, and conversely a bit more disappointing in the day.

She had been born on the island at a time so long ago that there was now nobody living who could remember it. The event no longer lived in anybody's mind, nor was it recorded with accuracy anywhere on paper. She had been born a month prematurely, at the beginning of the spring break-up when crossing from the island to the mainland was impossible.

At other times her mother had tried to reach the mainland before her children were born. Sometimes she would cross almost a month before the expected delivery because the weather and the water in all seasons, except summer, could never be depended upon. She had planned to do so this time as well but the ice that covered the channel during the winter months began to decay earlier than usual. It would not bear the weight of a horse and sleigh or even a person on foot and there were visible channels of open water running like eager rivers across what seemed like the grey-white landscape of the rotting ice. It was too late for foot travel and too early for a boat because there was not, as yet, enough open water. And then, too, she was born a month earlier than expected. All of this she was, of course, told much later. She was also told that when the winter began her parents did not realize that her mother was pregnant. Her father was sixty at the time and her mother close to fifty and they were already grandparents. They had not had any children for five years and had thought their child-bearing years were past and the usual signs were no longer there or at least not recognized until later in the season. So her birth, as her father said, was "unexpected" in more ways than one.

She was the first person ever born on the island as far as anybody knew.

Later she was brought across to the mainland to be christened. And still later when the clergyman was sending his baptismal records to the provincial capital he included hers along with those of the children who had been born on the mainland. And perhaps to simplify matters he recorded her birthplace as being the same as that of the other children and of her brothers and sisters, or if he did not intend to simplify perhaps he had merely forgotten. He also had the birth date wrong and it was thought that perhaps he had forgotten to ask the parents or had forgotten what they had told him and by the time he was ready to send in his records they had already gone back to the island and he could not contact them. So he seemed to have counted back a number of days before the christening and selected his own date. Her middle name was wrong, too. Her parents had called her Agnes but he had somehow copied it down as Angus. Again perhaps he had forgotten or was preoccupied, and he was a very old man at the time, as evidenced by his shaky, spidery handwriting. And, it was pointed out, his own middle name was Angus. She did not know any of this until years later when she sent for her official birth certificate in anticipation of her own marriage. Everyone was surprised that a single document could contain so many errors and by that time the old clergyman had died.

Although hers was thought to be the only birth to have occurred on the island there had been a number of deaths. One of them was that of her own grandfather, who had died one November from "a pain in the side" after pulling up his boat for the winter – thinking there would be no further need for a boat until the spring. He was only forty when it happened, the death occurring two weeks after his birthday. His widow and children did not know what to do as there was no adequate radio communication and they were not strong enough to get the boat he had so recently hauled up back into the water. They waited for two days hoping the sullen grey waves would subside, and stretching his body out on the kitchen table and covering it with white sheets – afraid to put too much fire in the kitchen stove lest it might hasten the body's decay.

On the third day they launched a small skiff and tried to row across to the mainland. They did not know if they would be strong enough to make it, so they gathered large numbers of dried cattails and reeds from one of the island's marshes and placed them in a metal washtub and doused them with the oil

used for the lamp at the lighthouse. They placed the tub in the
prow of the skiff and when they rowed out beyond the shape of
the island they set the contents of the tub on fire, hoping that it
might act as a signal and a sign. On the mainland someone saw
the rising funnel of grey-black smoke and the shooting flames at
its base and then the skiff moving erratically – rowed by the desperate hands of the woman and her children. Most of the mainland boats had already been pulled up for the winter, but one
was launched and the men went out to what looked like a
burning boat and tossed a line to it and towed it in to the wharf
after first taking off the woman and her children and comforting them and listening to their story. Later the men went out to
the island and brought the man's body over to the mainland so
that, although he died on the island, he was not buried there.
And still later that evening someone went over to light the lamp
in the lighthouse so that it might send out its flashing warning
to possible travellers on the night-time sea. Even in the face of
her husband's death, the woman, as well as her family, harboured
fears that they might lose the job if the Government realized the
lightkeeper was dead. They had already purchased their supplies
for the winter and there was no other place to go so late in the
season, so they decided to say nothing until the spring and
returned to the island after the funeral accompanied by the
woman's brother.

The original family had gone to the island because of death,
or rather to aid in death's reduction. The lighthouse was established in the previous century because of the danger the island
represented to ships travelling in darkness or in uncertain
weather. It was thought that the light would warn sea travellers

of the danger of the island or, conversely, that it might represent hope to those already at the sea's mercy and who yearned so much to reach its rocky shore. Before the establishment of the light there had been a number of wrecks which might or might not have been avoided had there been a light. What was known with certainty was that survivors had landed on the island only to die from exposure and starvation because no one knew that they were there. Their skeletons had been found accidentally by fishermen in the spring – huddled under trees or outcrops of rock in the positions of their deaths. Some still had the remains of their arms around one another. Some still with tattered, flapping clothes covering their bones although the flesh between the clothing and the bones was no longer there.

When the family first went they were told that their job was to keep the light and offer salvation to any of those who might come ashore. The Government erected buildings for them which were better than those of their relatives on the mainland, and helped them with the purchase of livestock and original supplies. To some it seemed they had a good job – a Government job. In answer to the question of the isolation, they told themselves they would get used to it. They told themselves they were already used to it, coming as they did from a people in the far north of Scotland who had for genera- tions been used to the sea and the wind and sleet and rocky out- crops at the edge of their part of Europe. Used to the long nights when no one spoke and to the isolation of islands. Used to seeing their men going to work for the Hudson's Bay Company and the North West Company and not expecting them back for years. Used to seeing their men going to the vast ocean-like tracts of prairie in places like Montana and Wyoming to work as sheepherders. To spend months that sometimes stretched into years, talking only to dogs or to themselves or to imaginary people who blended into ghosts. Startled by the response to their own voices when they appeared, strange and unexpectedly, at the camp or at the store or at the rural trading post. In demand as sheepherders, because it was believed, and because they had been told, that they did not mind the isolation. "Of course I spoke to ghosts," a man was supposed to have said once upon his returning. "Wouldn't you if there was no one else to speak to?"

In the early days on the island, there was no adequate radio communication, and if they were in trouble and unable to get across they would light fires on the shore in the hope that such signs would be visible on the mainland. In the hope that they, who had gone to the island as part of the business of salvation, might themselves be saved. And when the Great War was declared, it was said, they did not know of it for weeks, coming ashore to be told the news by their relatives, coming ashore to a world which would be forever changed.

Gradually, with the passage of the years, the family's name as well as their identity became entwined with that of the island. So that although the island had an official name on the marine and nautical charts it became known generally as MacPhedran's Island while they themselves became known less as MacPhedrans than as people "of the island." Being identified as "John the Island," "James the Island," "Mary of the Island," "Theresa of the Island." As if in giving their name to the island they had received its own lonely designation in return.

All of this was already history by the time she was born and she had no choice in any of it. Not choosing, for herself, to be born on the island (although the records said she was not) and not choosing the rather surprised individuals who became her parents after they had already become the grandparents of others. For by the time she was born the intertwined history of her family and the island was already far advanced. And when she was later told the story of the man who died from the pain in his side, it seemed very far away to her although it was not so for her father, who had been one of the children in the skiff, rowing with small desperate freezing hands at the bidding of his mother. By the time of her early memories, the Government had already built a wharf at the island which was superior to any on the mainland. The wharf was built "to service" the lighthouse, but it also attracted mainland fishermen who were drawn to its superior facilities. Especially during the lobster season months of May and June, men came to live in the shacks and shanties they erected along the shore. Leaving their shanties at four in the morning and returning in the early afternoon to sell their catches to the buyers who came in their big boats from far away. And returning to their mainland homes on Saturday and coming back again on Sunday, late in the afternoon or in the early evening, their weekly supplies of bread and provisions in burlap bags lying at the bottom of their boats. Sometimes lying in the bottoms of the boats there were also yearling calves, with trussed feet and eyes bulging with fear, who were brought to the island for summer pasturage and would be taken off half-wild in the cold, grey months of fall. Later in the summer the energetic,

377

stifled rams would be brought in the same way, to spend monastic, frustrated months in all-male company before returning to
the mainland and the fall fury of the breeding season.

He came to the island the summer she was seventeen. Came
before the rams or the young cattle or the buyers' boats. Came at
the end of April when there were still white cakes of ice floating
in the ocean and when the family's dogs still ran down to the
wharf to bark at the approaching boats and to snarl at the men
who got out of them. In the time before such boats and men
became familiar sights and sounds and odours. Yet even as the
boat came into the wharf the dogs seemed to make less fuss than
was usual and whatever he said quietened them and caused them
to be still. She saw all this from the window of the kitchen. She
was drying the dishes for her mother at the time and she
wrapped the damp dish towel around her hand as if it were a
bandage and then she as quickly unwrapped it again. As he bent
to loop the boat's rope to the wharf, his cap fell off and she saw
the redness of his hair. It seemed to flash and reflect in the April
sun like the sudden and different energy of spring. She and most
of her people were dark-haired and had dark eyes as well.

He had come, she learned, to fish for the season with one of
the regular men from the mainland. He was the nephew of the
man's wife and came from a place located over the mountain.
From a distance of some twenty-five miles, which was a long
distance at the time. He had come early to make preparations for
the season. To work on the shanty and repair the winter's
damages, to repair the man's lobster traps and to make a few new
ones. He told them all of this in the evening when he came up

to the lighthouse to borrow oil for his lamp. He brought them bits and scraps of news from the mainland as well, although they did not have that many people in common. He spoke in both Gaelic and English, although his accent was different from theirs. He seemed about twenty years of age and his eyes were very blue.

They looked at one another often. They were the youngest people in the room.

In the early madness of the lobster season they did not speak to one another although they saw each other almost every day. The men were often up at three in the morning brewing their tea by the flickering lamps, casting their large shadows eerily upon the shanties' walls as they moved about in the semi-darkness. At night they sometimes fell asleep by eight. Sometimes still sitting on their chairs, their heads tilting suddenly forward or backward and their mouths dropping open. She worked with her mother, planting the garden and the potatoes. Sometimes in the evening she would walk down by the shanties, but not very often. Not because her parents openly disapproved but because she felt uncomfortable walking so close to so many men. Sometimes they nodded and smiled as all of them knew her name and who she was and some of them were her distant relatives. But at other times she felt uneasy, hearing only bits of the comments and remarks exchanged among them as they stood in their doorways or sat on their homemade chairs or overturned lobster crates. The remarks seemed mainly for themselves, to demonstrate their wit and masculinity to each other. As if they were young schoolboys instead of being mostly beyond middle age. Sometimes they reminded her of the late summer rams, playful and friendly and generally grazing contentedly in *achadh nan caoraich*, the field of the sheep, although sometimes given to spontaneous rages against those who would trespass into their territory or sometimes unleashing their suppressed fury against one another. Rearing and smashing against one another until their skulls thundered and reverberated like the growling icebergs of spring and their pent-up semen ejaculated in spurting jets, leaving them stunned and weak in the knees.

She and her mother were the only women on the island.

One evening she walked to the back of the island, down to the far shore which did not face the mainland but only the open sea. There was a small cove there which was known as *bagh na long bhriseadh*, bay of the shipwreck, because there were timbers found there in the long-ago time before the lighthouse was established. She sat on *creig a bhoird*, the table rock, which was called so because of its shape, and looked out across the seeming infinity of the sea. And then he was standing beside her. He made no sound in coming and the dog which had accompanied her gave no signal of his approach.

"Oh," she said, on realizing him so unexpectedly close. She stood up quickly.

"Do you come here often?" he said.

"No," she said. "Well yes, sometimes."

The ocean stretched out flat and far before them.

"Were you born here?" he asked.

"Yes," she said. "I guess so."

"Do you stay here all the time? Even in the winter?"

"Yes," she said, "most of the time."

She was defensive, like most of her family, on the subject of the island. Knowing that they were often regarded as slightly eccentric because of how and where they lived. Always anticipating questions about the island's loneliness.

"Some people are lonely no matter where they are," he said as if he were reading her mind.

"Oh," she said. She had never heard anyone say anything quite like that before.

"Would you like to live somewhere else?" he asked.

"I don't know," she said. "Maybe."

"I have to go now," he said. "I'll see you later. I'll come back."

And then he was gone. As suddenly as he had come. Seeming to vanish behind the table rock and the water's edge. She waited for a while, sitting down once more upon the rock to compose herself and then walking up the island's rise toward the lighthouse. Later when she looked down from the kitchen window toward the shanties, she could see him hammering laths onto a broken lobster trap and readying the bait buckets for the morning. His cap was pushed back upon his head and the evening sun caught the golden highlights of his burnished hair. He looked up once and her hand tightened upon the cloth she was holding. Her mother asked her if she would like some tea.

It was into the next week before she again walked down by the shanties. He was sitting on a lobster crate splicing rope. As she went by she thought she heard him say *Áite na cruinneachadh*. She quickened her step as she felt her colour rise, hoping or perhaps imagining that he had said "the meeting place." She went there immediately, down to the bay of shipwrecks and the table rock, and waited. She faced out to the sea and sat in such a way that she could not see him *not* coming if that was the way it was supposed to be. The dog sat at her feet and neither of them moved when he came to stand beside them.

"I told you I'd come back," he said.

"Oh," she said. "Oh yes. You did."

In the weeks that followed they went more frequently to the meeting place. Standing and later sitting on the table rock and looking out across the vastness of the sea. Talking more and sometimes laughing and, in retrospect, she could not remember when he asked her to marry him but only that she had burst into tears when she said "Oh yes" and they joined their hands on the flatness of the table rock which was still warm from the retained heat of the descending sun. "Oh yes," she had said. "Oh yes. Oh yes."

He planned to work in a sawmill, he said, after the lobster season was done; and then in the fall or early winter, after the snows began to fall and the ground became frozen, he would go to work in the winter woods of Maine. He would return to fish with the same man the next spring and then in the summer they would marry. They would go then, he said, "to live somewhere else."

"Oh yes," she said. "Oh yes, we will."

It was in the late fall, on the night following a day of cold and slanting rain, that she was awakened by the dog pulling at the blankets that lay so heavily upon her bed. She sat up, even as she shivered and pulled the blankets about her shoulders, and tried to adjust her eyes to the darkness of the room. The rain slanted against the window with a pinging sound which meant that it was close to hail, and even in the darkness she could see the near-white pellets visible for a moment before they vanished on the pane. The eyes of the dog seemed to glow in the dark and she felt the cold wetness of its nose when she extended her hand beyond the boundary of the bed. She could smell the wetness of its coat, and when she moved her hand across its head and down its neck the water filmed upon her palm. She got up then, throwing on what clothes she could find in the darkness of the room, and followed the clacking nails of the dog as it moved down the hallway and past the closed door behind which her parents snored, sometimes snoring regularly and at other times with fitful catches in their sound. She went down through the kitchen and through the tiny puddles caused by the rain slanting through the opened door. Outside it was wet and windy although nothing like a gale and she followed the dog down the darkened path. In a single white instant she saw the dark shape of the boat bobbing at the wharf and his straight but dripping form by the corner of the shanties.

The creaky door of the summer shanty yielded easily to his familiar shoulder. Inside it was slightly musty although the wind persisted through some of the unsealed cracks. Their eyes adjusted to the gloom and the few sticks of basic furniture that remained. The primitive mattresses had been stored away to protect them from mice and the dampness of the sea. They held one another in their urgency and lay upon the floor fumbling with the encumbrances of their clothes. She felt the wet burden of his garments almost heavy upon her although the length of his body seemed light within them.

"Oh," she said, digging her fingers into the dampness of his neck, "when we are married we can do this all the time."

At the moment of explosion their breaths bonded into a single gasp that bordered on a cry.

She thought of this later as she passed the closed door of her parents' room. Thought of how her breath and his had become one, and contrasted it with the irregular individual snoring which came from beyond her parents' door. She could not imagine them ever being young.

The same wonder was there the next morning as she watched her father in his undershirt preparing the fire and later going to polish the thick glass of the lighthouse lamp. She watched her mother washing the dishes and then reaching for her knitting needles and the always-present ball of yarn.

She went outside and walked down towards the shanties. The door was pulled tight and she had a hard time getting it to move. Inside it all seemed different, probably, she thought, because of the daylight. She looked at the grey boards of the floor thinking she might see the outline of their bodies or even a spot of dampness but there was nothing. She went outside and walked to the wharf, to the spot where the dark boat was moored, but again there was no sign. He had "borrowed" the boat of the man he had fished with and had to have it back before dawn.

The wind was rising as the temperature was dropping. The hail-like rain had given way to stinging snow and the ground was beginning to freeze. She touched her body to see if it had been a dream.

As the winter began she was alive with the prospect of marriage. She sent for her birth certificate without ever revealing why and helped her mother with the knitting. As the winter deepened she looked at the calendar more often.

When the ice began to rot and break in the spring she looked out the window more frequently. It seemed like a later spring than usual although her father said there was nothing unusual about it. One day the channel would be clear of ice but the next day it would again be solid. The wind shifted and blew from inconsistent directions. On the mainland they could see, or imagined they could see, men moving about and readying their gear for the opening of the season. Because of the ice they were still afraid to launch their boats into the water. They all looked very small and far away.

When the first boats finally came, the dogs ran down to the wharf barking and snarling and her father went down also, calling to the dogs and welcoming the men and telling them not to be afraid. She looked out the window but did not see him in the boats or on the wharf nor moving about the familiar shanties. But neither did she see the mainland man he fished with nor his boat.

When her father came in he was filled with news and carried some fresh supplies and a bundle of newspapers and a bag of mail.

In the midst of all the newness it was a long time before he mentioned the mainland fisherman's name and added, almost as an afterthought, "That young man who fished with him last year was killed in the woods this winter. Went to Maine and was killed on a skidway. He's looking for another man right now."

When her father spoke he was already looking at a marine catalogue and had put on his glasses. He raised his eyes above the rims of his spectacles as he lowered the catalogue and looked toward them. "You remember him," he said without emotion, "the young fellow with the red hair."

"Oh poor fellow," said her mother. "God have mercy on his soul."

"Oh," was all she could say. Her hands tightened so whitely on the metal knitting needles that the point of one pierced and penetrated the ball of her thumb.

"Your hand is bleeding," said her mother. "What happened? You'll have to be more careful or you'll get blood on your knitting and everything will be ruined. What happened?" she asked again. "You'll have to be more careful."

"Nothing," she said, rising quickly and going to the door. "Nothing at all. Yes, I'll have to be more careful."

She went outside and looked down towards the shanties where the newly arrived men were busy preparing for the new spring season. The banter of their voices seemed to float on the current of the wind. Sometimes she could hear their actual words but at other times they were lost and unknown. She could not believe the magnitude and suddenness of change. Could not believe the content of the news nor the method of its arrival. Could not believe that news of such outstanding impact could arrive in such a casual manner and mean so little to all of those around her.

She looked down at her bloodied hand. "Why didn't he write?" she asked herself and considered going back in to recheck the contents of the mailbag. But then she thought that both of them were beyond letters and that in the instant of his death it was already too late for that. She did not even know if he could read or write. She had never thought to ask. It had not seemed important at the time. The blood was beginning to darken and dry upon her palm and between her fingers. Suddenly last winter, although it was barely over, seemed like a long, long time ago. She pressed her hand against her stomach and turned her face away from the mainland and the sea.

When it became obvious that she was expecting a child there was great wonder as to how it came to be. She herself was rather surprised that no one had ever seen them together. It was true that she had always walked "over" or "across" the island while he had walked "around," seeming to emerge suddenly and unexpectedly out of the sea by the table rock of their meeting place. Still the island was small and, especially during the fishing season, there was little opportunity for privacy. Perhaps, she thought, they had been more successful, in some ways, than they planned. It was as if he had been invisible to everyone but herself. She was struck by this and tried to relive over and over again their last damp meeting in the dark. Only the single instant of his dark silhouette in the lighthouse beam was recallable to vision. All the rest of it had been touching in the dark. She remembered the lightness of his body in his dark, wet clothes, but it was a memory of feeling rather than of sight. She had never seen him with all his clothes off. Had never slept with him in a bed. She had no photograph to emphasize reality. It was as if in vanishing from her future he had also vanished from her past. It was almost as if he had been a ghost, and as she advanced in her pregnancy she found the idea strangely attractive.

"No," she kept saying to the pressure of their questions. "I don't know. I can't say. No, I can't tell you what he looked like."

She wavered only twice. The first time was a week before her delivery at a time when the approximate date of the conception was more than obvious. They were all on the mainland and the late August heat shimmered in layers above the clear deep water. The shape of the island loomed grey and blue and green across the channel and she who had wished to leave it now wished she might return. They were at her aunt's house and she would remain there until her baby would be born. She and her aunt had never liked each other, and it bothered her now to be dependent upon her. Before her parents left to return to the island they came into her room accompanied by the aunt, who turned to her father and said, "Well, go ahead. Tell her what people are saying."

She was shocked to see the pained embarrassment on his face as he twisted his cloth cap and looked out the window in the direction of the island.

"It is just the way we live," he said. "Some say there was no other man."

She remembered the erratic snoring coming from her parents' room and how she could not imagine that they ever had been young.

"Oh," she said. "I'm sorry."

"Is that all you have to say for yourself?" said her aunt.

She wavered a moment. "Yes," she said. "That's all. That's all I have to say."

After the birth of her daughter with the jet black hair, she received a visit from the clergyman. He was an old man, although not as old as she imagined the one who had confused her own birth records, it seemed to her, so very long ago.

At that time it was in the power of clergymen to refuse to christen children unless they knew the identities of both parents. In cases such as hers the identities could be kept as confidential.

"Well," he said. "Can you tell me who the father is?"

"No," she said. "I can't say."

He looked at her as if he had heard it all before. And as if it were an aspect of his job he did not greatly like. He looked at her daughter and back at her. "We wouldn't want innocent people to burn in hell because of the wilfulness of others," he said.

She was startled and frightened and looked toward the window.

"Tell me," he said quietly. "Is it your father?"

She thought for a flash of her own unexpected birth and of how her father was surprised again although the situation was so very much different.

"No," she said firmly. "It isn't him."

He seemed vastly relieved. "Good," he said. "I didn't think he would ever do anything like that. I will stop the rumours."

He moved toward the door as if one answer were all answers but then he hesitated with his hand upon the knob. "Tell me then," he said, "one more thing. Do I know him? Is he from around here?"

"No," she said, gaining confidence from seeing his hand upon the knob. "He isn't from around here at all."

That fall she stayed on the mainland until quite late into the season. It seemed as if her daughter were constantly sick and each time the journey was planned a new variation of illness appeared to stifle the departure. Out on the island her parents seemed to grow old all at once, or maybe it was just that she saw them in a different light. Of course they had always seemed old to her and she had often thought of having grandparents for parents. But now they seemed for the first time to be almost afraid of the island and the coming of winter. Never since the first year of their marriage had they been there without a child. When her father fell from the ladder leading up to the light-house lamp it was almost as if the fall and the broken arm had been expected.

Ever since her grandfather's death from "a pain in the side," the Government had more or less left them alone. It was as if the officials had been embarrassed by the widow's reluctance to tell them of her husband's death and by her fear that she might lose, in addition to her husband, the only income the family pos-sessed. It was as if the officials had understood that "some MacPhedran" would always be on the island that bore the name and that no further questions ever would be asked. The cheques always arrived and the light always shone.

But when her father fell it brought a deeper seriousness. He could neither climb to the light nor navigate the boat across the channel, nor manage, quite, to look after the house and build-ings and the animals. It seemed best that they should all try to stay on the mainland for the winter.

Her brother came home from Halifax, reluctantly, and manned the light deep into fall. He was a single man who worked on construction crews and who drank quite heavily at times and was given to moods of deep depression. He was uneasy about the island although he understood it and was regarded as "an excellent man in a boat." At the beginning of the winter he said to his father, who stood in the departing boat, "I don't want to stay here. I don't want to stay here at all."

"Oh," said his father, "you'll get used to it," which was what they had always said to one another.

But it seemed he did not get used to it. Deep in the blizzards of February one of the island dogs crossed on the ice to the mainland and came to a familiar door. It was impossible to see or move for three days because of the severe temperatures and the force of the wind-driven snow. Impossible for a man to stand upright in the wind or, as they said, for one "to see the palm of his hand in front of his face." When the storm abated four men started across the vast white landscape of the ice. They could feel parts of their exposed faces freezing and the exhaled moisture of their breath froze upon their eyebrows and they could see their eyelashes drooping heavily with ice. As they neared the island's wharf they could see that it was almost buried under gigantic pans of ice. Some of the pans had been pushed so far up on the shore that they almost tilted against the doors of the summer shanties. There was no smoke from the chimney of the house. The dogs came down snarling and circling at first, but the one who had crossed to the mainland had returned and had a calming effect upon the others. The door of the house was open and the stove was cold. The water in the crockery teapot had frozen, causing the teapot itself to split into two delicate halves. There was nobody in any of the rooms and no answer to their calls. Outside, the barn doors were open and swinging in the wind. The animals were all dead, still tied and frozen in their stalls. The frozen flesh of some of them had been gnawed on by the dogs.

It seemed his coat and cap and winter mitts were missing, but that was all. A loaded rifle and a shotgun were hanging in the porch. The men started a fire in the stove and made themselves something to eat from the store of winter provisions. Later they went outside again. Some walked across the island and some walked around it. They found no tracks other than their own. They looked at the dogs for a signal or a sign. They even spoke to them and asked them questions but they received nothing in return. He had vanished like his tracks beneath the winter snow.

The men remained for the night and the next day crossed back to the mainland. They told what they had found and not found. The sun shone, and although it was a weak February sun it was stronger than it had been a week earlier. It melted the ice upon the window panes and someone pointed out that the days were getting longer and that the winter was more than halfway over.

Under the circumstances they decided to go back but to leave the baby behind.

"There seems almost more reason to go back now," said her father, looking through the melting ice on the windows. His broken arm had healed, although he knew it would never be the same.

She was often to think of why she went back, although at the time there seemed little conscious thought surrounding the decision. While her parents were willing to leave the island to the care of their son they were not willing to abandon it to others. They had found life on the mainland not as attractive as it sometimes seemed when viewed from across the water. They also seemed bothered by the complicated shafts of guilt concerning their lost son and their headstrong daughter, and while these shafts might persist on the island there would be no people to emphasize and expose them. She, herself, as the child of their advanced years, seemed suddenly willing to consider herself old also and to identify with the past now that her future seemed to point in that direction.

She went back with almost a bitter gladness. Glad to leave her carping aunt and her mainland family behind, although worried about leaving her sickly daughter in their care. Still, she knew they were right to say that the winter island was no place for a sick child and she felt also that if she did not go her parents could not manage.

"Who will climb up to the light?" asked her father simply. They viewed her youth as their immediate salvation and thought of her as their child rather than as someone else's mother.

It seemed a long time since the red-haired man had asked her to marry him and to share his life in the magical region of "somewhere else." In her persistent refusal to identify him she had pushed him so far back into the recesses of her mind that he seemed even more ghostly than before. She thought sometimes of his body in the dark and of his silhouette by the sea.

She was struck by the mystery of his age – if he had an age it had suddenly "stopped" and he had become part of a kind of timelessness – unlike the visible deterioration she witnessed in her father.

In the winter cold of February they returned with a certain sense of relief, each harbouring individual reasons. Because of her youth she did most of the work, dressing in her father's heavy, shapeless clothes and following easily the rituals and routines that had become part of her since childhood. More and more her parents remained close to the stove, talking in Gaelic and sometimes playing cards or merely looking at the fire or out the frosted windows.

When March came in with its howling blizzards it seemed that they had been betrayed by the fickle promise of the February sun, and although her father's will was strong his aging body seemed also to contribute to a pattern of betrayal. He was close to eighty and it seemed that each day there was another function which his body refused to perform. It was as if it had suddenly grown tired and was in the process of forgetting.

One day when there was a lull in the storms some of their relatives crossed the ice with a horse and sleigh. They were shocked at the condition and appearance of her father, seeing him changed "suddenly" after an absence of weeks while those who were with him had seen him change but gradually. They insisted that he return with them while the weather was good and the ice still strong. Reluctantly he agreed on the condition that his wife go with him.

After years of isolated permanence he was aware of all the questionable movement.

"Sometimes life is like that," he said to his daughter as he sat bundled in a sleigh at the moment before departure. "It goes on and on at a certain level and then there comes a year when everything changes."

Suddenly a gust of wind passed between them, whipping their faces with fine, sharp granules of snow. And suddenly she knew in that instant that she would never ever see him again. She wanted to tell him, to thank him or perhaps confess now that their time was vanishing between them. The secret of her own loneliness came down upon her and she reached toward his bundled body and his face, which was muffled in scarves except for his eyes, which were filled with water converting to ice.

"It was," she said, "the red-haired man."

"Oh yes," he said but she did not know with what degree of comprehension he said it. And then the sleigh moved off with its runners squeaking on the winter snow.

Although she was prepared for the death of her father, she had not anticipated the loss of her mother, who died ten days after her husband. There was no physical explanation for her death and it seemed not unlike that of certain animals who pine away without their mates or who are unwilling or unable to adjust to new surroundings. As wild birds die in captivity or those who have been caged die from the shock of unexpected freedom or the loss of familiar boundaries.

Because of the spring break-up she was unable to attend either of their funerals, and on the respective days she looked across the high grey waves and the grotesque icebergs that rolled between. From the edge of the island she saw the long funeral processions following the horse-drawn coffins along the muddy roads to the graveyard by the mainland church. She turned her face into the wind and climbed up toward the light.

That spring and summer she continued to tend the light, although she had little to do with the mainland fishermen and never walked down by the shanties. She began to sign the requisition slips for government supplies with the name "A. MacPhedran" because her initial and that of her father were the same. After a while the cheques came in the name of "A. MacPhedran" and she had no trouble cashing any of them. No one came to question the keeper of the light, and the sex of A. MacPhedran seemed ambiguously unimportant. After all, she told herself, wryly, her official birth certificate stated that her given name was Angus.

When the fall came she decided to remain on the island for the winter. Some of her relatives approved because they wanted "some MacPhedran" to remain on the island and they cited her youth and the fact that she was "used to it" as part of their reasoning. They were interested in "maintaining tradition" as long as they were not the ones to maintain that specific part of it. Others disapproved and toward them she was, secretly, most defiant. Her aunt and her aunt's family had grown attached to her daughter, had "gotten used to her" as they said, and regarded the child as their own. When she visited them she experienced a certain fearful hostility on their part, as if they feared that she might snatch the child and flee while they were busy in another room.

Most of her relatives, however, either willingly or unwillingly, agreed to help her with the island, by assisting her with supplies, by doing some of the heavier autumn work, or even by visiting occasionally. She settled into the life with a sort of wilful determination tempered by the fact that she was still waiting for something to happen and to bring about the change.

Two years later on a hot summer afternoon, she was in the lighthouse tower when she saw the boat approaching. She had been restless all day and had walked the length and width of the island twice. She had gone to its edge as if testing the boundaries, somewhat as a restless animal might explore the limitations of its cage. She had walked out into the cold salt water, feeling it move gradually up and through and under the legs of her father's coveralls which had become, for her, a sort of uniform. She walked farther out feeling the water rise as she felt the rocks turning beneath her feet. She looked downward and saw her coveralled limbs distorted in the green water, shot through by the summer sun. They seemed not to be a part of her but to have become disembodied and convoluted and to be almost floating away from her at a horizontal level. When she closed her eyes she could feel them intensely but when she looked at them they did not appear the way they felt. The dogs lay on the shore, just above the water line, and watched her. They were panting in the summer heat and drops of water fell from the extended redness of their tongues.

She returned to the shore, still dripping, and walked among the shanties. The lobster fishermen had departed at the end of the season leaving very little of themselves behind. She walked among the deserted buildings looking at the few discarded objects, sometimes touching and turning them with her toes: a worn woollen sock, a length of spliced and twisted rope, a rusted knife with a broken blade, tobacco packages with bleached and faded lettering, a rubber boot with a hole in it. It was as if she were walking through the masculine remnants of an abandoned and vanished civilization. She went back to the house to put on dry coveralls and to hang the wet ones on the outside clothes-line. As she left to climb to the lighthouse she looked over her shoulder and was startled by the sight of the vertical coveralls. Their dangling legs rasped together with the gentlest of frictions and the moisture had changed their colour up to the waist. Droplets dripped from them onto the summer grass which was visibly distorted by their own moving shadow.

There were four men in the approaching boat and she real-ized that they were mackerel fishing and did not have the island in mind as a specific destination. The boat zigzagged back and forth across the stillness of the blue-green water, stopping fre-quently while the men tossed their weighted lines overboard. They jerked their lines up and down rhythmically hoping to attract the fish by the movement of the lures. Sometimes they dipped their hands into pails or tubs of *gruth*, dried cottage cheese, and flung the white handfuls onto the surface of the water, waiting and hoping for the unseen fish to strike. She turned her head and looked toward the back of the island. From her high vantage point she could see, or thought she could see, pods or schools of mackerel breaking the surface, beyond the meeting place and the table rock, and beyond the bay of the shipwreck. They seemed like moving, floating islands, changing the clear, flat surface into agitated areas that resembled boiling water.

She hurried down from the lighthouse and shouted and ges-tured to the men in the boat. They were still far offshore and, perhaps, saw her before they heard her but were still unable to comprehend her message. They directed the boat toward the island. As they approached she realized that the movement of her arm, which was intended as a pointing gesture to the back of the island, was also a beckoning gesture, as they might understand it.

When they were within earshot she shouted to them, "The mackerel. At the back of the island. Go around."

They stopped the boat and leaned forward trying to catch the meaning of her words. One of the younger men, probably the one with the best hearing, understood her first and relayed the message to the others.

"Behind the island?" shouted the oldest man, cupping his hands to his mouth.

"Yes," she shouted back. "By the bay of the shipwreck."

She almost added "By the meeting place" before realizing that the phrase would be meaningless to them.

"Thank you," shouted the oldest man. He took off his cap and tipped it to her and she could see the whiteness of his hair. "Thank you," he repeated. "We'll go around."

They changed the course of the boat and began to go around the island.

She rushed up to the house and changed out of her coveralls and put on a summer dress which she found in the back of a closet. She walked across the island accompanied by the dogs and went down to the meeting place, where she sat on the table rock and waited. The rock was hot from the heat of the day's sun and burned her thighs and the backs of her legs. She could see the floating islands of frenzied mackerel beyond the mouth of the bay. They were deep into their spawning season and she hoped they would still be there when the men in the boat arrived.

"They seem to be taking an awfully long time," she said to no one in particular. And then she saw the prow of the boat rounding the island's end.

She stood up and pointed to the boiling, bubbling mackerel, but they had already seen them and even as they waved back they were in the process of readying all their available lines. The boat glided silently towards the fish and by the time the first one struck it was almost completely stilled. The mackerel seemed to surround the boat, changing the water to black by their own density. Their snapping mouths fastened on anything thrown their way and when the men jerked up their lines there were sometimes two or three fish on a single hook. Sometimes they broke the surface as if they would jump into the boat and sometimes their bodies were so densely packed that they became "snagged" as the hooks went into their bellies or their eyes or their backs or their tails. The scent of their own blood spreading within the water spurred them to an even greater frenzy and they fell upon their mutilated fellows, snapping the still living flesh from the moving bones. The men moved in their own frenzy as if to keep pace. Hooks snagged in their thumbs and the singing, sizzling lines burned through the calluses on their hands. The fish filled the bottom of the boat and began to rise in a blue-green, flopping, snapping mass to the level of the men's knees. And then, suddenly, they were gone. The hooks brought back nothing but clear drops of water or shreds of mutilated seaweed. There was no indication of them anywhere, either on the surface of the sea or beneath. It was as if they had never been, apart from the heaving weight that caused the boat to ride so low within the water. The men wiped the sweat from their foreheads with swollen hands, sometimes leaving other streaks behind. Some of the streaks contained a mixture of fish blood and their own.

The men looked toward the shore and saw her rise from the table rock and come toward them until she reached the water's edge. They guided the boat across the glass-like sea until its prow grounded heavily on the gravelly shore. They tossed the painter rope to her and she caught it with willing hands.

All afternoon they lay on the table rock. At first they seemed driven by the frenzy of all that had happened and not happened to them. By all the heat and the loneliness and the waiting and all the varied events that had conspired to create their day. The clothes of the men were sprinkled with blackening clots of blood and the golden spawn of the female fish and the milky white semen of the male. She had never seen fully aroused men before, having known only one man at one time, and having experienced in that damp darkness more of feeling than of sight.

She was to remember, for the rest of her life, the oldest man with the white hair. How he took off his cap and then pulled his heavy navy-blue jersey over his shoulders and folded it neatly and placed it on the rock beside her. She was to remember the whiteness of his skin and arms compared with the bronzed redness of his face and neck and that of his bleeding and swollen hands. As if, without clothes, his upper body was still clothed in a costume made of two different materials. The whiteness of his skin and whiteness of his hair were the same colour but totally different as well. After he had folded his jersey he placed his cap neatly upon it. It was as if he were doing it out of long habit and was preparing to lie down with his wife. She almost expected him to brush his teeth.

After the first frenzy they were quieter, lying stretched beneath the sun. Sometimes one of the younger men got up and skipped flat stones across the surface of the sea. The dogs lay above the water line, panting and watching everything. She was later to think how often she had watched them in the fury of their own mating. And how she had seen their surplus young placed in burlap bags, weighted down with rocks and tossed over the boat's side into the sea.

The sun began to decline and the tide began to fall, the water receding from the heavy boat which was in danger of becoming beached. The men got up and adjusted their clothes. Some walked some distance away to urinate. They came back and all four of them put their shoulders to the prow and prepared to push the boat back into the water.

"One, two, three, heave!" they said, moving in concentrated unison on the last syllable. Their bodies were stretched out almost horizontally as they pushed, the toes of their rubber boots scrabbling in the loose beach gravel. The boat began to move, grudgingly at first, and then more rapidly as the water took its weight. The men scrambled over the prow and over the sides, wet up to their waists. They seized their oars to push the boat farther out so there would be room to turn it around and face it toward home.

She watched them leave, standing on the shore. As the boat moved out, she noticed her undergarment crumpled and discarded by the edge of the table rock. The boat moved farther out and farther away and the men waved to her. She felt her arm rising in a similar gesture, almost without her willing it. The man with the white hair tipped his cap. She knew in one of those intuitive flashes that they would never say anything to anyone, or scarcely mention the events of the day among themselves. She also knew that they would never be back. As the boat rounded the island's end, she scrunched up her undergarment and threw it into the sea. She began to walk up toward the lighthouse. She touched her body. It was sticky with blood and fishspawn and human seed. "It will have to happen this time," she thought, "because there was so much of it and it went on so long." Comparing the afternoon to her one previous brief encounter in the dark.

When she reached the lighthouse she heard the cries of the scavenging gulls. She looked in the direction of the sound and saw the boat cutting a V in the placid water on its way to the mainland. The men were bent double, grasping their fishforks and throwing the dead mackerel back into the sea. The gulls swooped and screamed in a whitened noisy cloud.

Two years later she was in a mainland store ordering supplies to take back to the island. Usually she made arrangements with one of her relatives to take the supplies from the store to the water's edge and then ferry them across to the island, but on this day she could not find the particular young man. One of the items was a bag of flour. As she stood paying her bill and looking

403

out the door in some agitation, she saw, out of the corner of her eye, the white-haired man in the navy-blue jersey.

"This is too heavy for you," he said. "Let me help," and he bent down and picked up the hundred-pound flour sack and threw it easily onto his shoulder. When it landed some of the flour puffed out, sprinkling his blue jersey and his cap and his hair with its fine white powder. She remembered the whiteness of his body beneath the blue jersey and the frenzied afternoon beneath the summer sun. As they were going out the door they met her young relative.

"Here, I'll take that," he said, relieving the man of the bag of flour.

"Thank you," she said to the man.

"My pleasure," he said and tipped his cap toward her. The flour dust fell from his cap onto the floor between them.

"He is a real nice fellow," said her young relative as they moved toward the shore. "But of course you don't know him the way we do."

"No," she said. "Of course I don't." She looked across the channel to the stillness of the island. Her expected child had never arrived.

The years of the next decade passed by in a blur of monotonous sameness. She realized that she was becoming more careless of her appearance and that such carelessness was regarded as further evidence of eccentricity. She came ashore less frequently, preferring to try to understand the world through radio. She found her teenage daughter to be foreign and aloof and embarrassed by her presence. Her aunt's family harboured doubts about their decision to rear the girl and, one day, when she was visiting, suggested that she might want to live on the island with her "real mother." The girl laughed and walked into another room.

Gradually during the next years things changed even more, but so quietly that, in retrospect, she could not link the specific events to the specific years. Many of them had to do with changes on the mainland. The Government built a splendid new wharf and the spring fishermen no longer came to inhabit the shanties, which began to fall into disrepair, their doors banging in the wind and the shingles flying from their roofs. Sometimes she looked at the initials carved by the absent men on the shanties' walls, but his, as she knew, would never be among them.

Community pastures were established, with regular attendants, and the bound young cattle and the lusty rams no longer came to the summer pasturage. The sweeping headlights of cars became a regular feature of her night vision, mirroring the beam from her solitary lighthouse. One night after a quarrel with her aunt's family, her daughter left in such a car, and vanished into the mystery of Toronto. She did not know of it until weeks later when she came ashore to purchase supplies.

The wharf at the island began to deteriorate and the visitors came less often. When she sought help from her relatives, she found herself often dealing with members of a newer generation. Many of them were sulky and contributed to the maintaining of island tradition with the utmost reluctance and only because of the badgering of their parents.

Yet the light still shone and the various missives to and from "A. MacPhedran" continued to travel through the mails. The nature of such missives also changed, however gradually. When the first generation of her family went to the island it had been close to the age of sail, when captains were at the mercies of the winds. In her own time she had seen the coming of the larger ships and the increasing sophistication of their technology. There had not been a wreck upon the island in all her time of habitation and no freezing, ice-caked travellers had ever knocked upon her midnight door. The "emergency chest" and its store of supplies remained unopened from one inspection to the next.

One summer she realized with a shock that her child-bearing years were over and that that part of her life was past.

Mainland boat operators began to offer "trips around the island," taking tourists on circumnavigational voyages. Very often because of time limitations they did not land but merely circled or anchored briefly offshore. When the boats approached the dogs barked, bringing her to her door or sometimes to the water's edge. At first she was not aware of the image she presented to the tourists with their binoculars or their cameras. Nor was she aware of how she was described by the operators of the boats. Standing at the edge of the sea in her dishevelled men's clothing and surrounded by her snarling dogs, she later realized, she had passed into folklore. She had, without realizing it, become "the mad woman of the island."

It was on a hot summer's day, some years later, when, in answer to the barking of the dogs, she looked out the window and saw the big boat approaching. The men wore tan-coloured uniforms and the Canadian flag flew from the mast. They tied the boat to the remnants of the wharf and began to climb

toward the house as she called off the dogs. The decision had
been made, they told her quietly, while sitting in the kitchen, to
close the lighthouse officially. The light would still shine but it
would be maintained by "modern technology." It would operate
automatically and be serviced by supply boats which would
come at certain times of the year or, in emergency, they added,
by helicopter. It would, however, be maintained in its present
state for approximately a year and a half. After that, they said, she
would have "to live somewhere else." They got up to leave and
thanked her for her decades of fine service.

After they had gone she walked the length and width of the
island. She repeated all the place names, many of them in
Gaelic, and marvelled that the places would remain but the
names would vanish. "Who would know?" she wondered, that
this spot had once been called *achadh nan caoraich*, or that
another was called *creig a bhoird*. And who, she thought, with a
catch in her heart, would ever know of *Áite na cruinneachadh*
and of what had transpired there. She looked across the landscape, repeating the phrases of the place-names as if they were
those of children about to be abandoned without knowledge
of their names. She felt like whispering their names to them so
they would not forget.

She realized with a type of shock that in spite of generations
of being people "of the island" they had never really owned it
in any legal sense. There was nothing physical of it that was, in
strict reality, formally theirs.

That autumn and winter her rituals seemed without meaning.
There was no need of so many supplies because the future was
shorter and she approached each winter task with the knowledge

that it would be her last. She approached spring with a longing born of confused emotions. She who wanted to leave and wanted to return and wanted to stay felt the approaching ache of those who leave the familiar behind. She felt, perhaps, as those who leave bad places or bad situations or bad marriages behind them. As those who must look over their shoulders one last time and who say quietly to themselves, "Oh, I have given a lot of my life to this, such as it was, and such was I. And no matter where I go, I will never be the same."

That April as the ice broke, for her the final time, she was drying the dishes and looking through the window. Because of her failing eyesight she did not see the boat until it was almost at the remains of the wharf, and the dogs did not make their usual sound. She saw the man bending to loop the boat's rope to the wharf and as he did so his cap fell off and she saw the redness of his hair. It seemed to flash and reflect in the April sun like the sudden and different energy of spring. She wrapped the damp dish towel around her hand as if it were a bandage and then she as quickly unwrapped it again.

He started up the path toward the house and the dogs ran happily beside him. She stood in the doorway uncertainly. As he approached she realized that he was talking to the dogs and his accent was slightly unfamiliar. He seemed about twenty years of age and his eyes were very blue. He had an earring in his ear.

"Hello," he said, extending his hand. "I don't know if you recognize me."

It had been so long and so much had happened that she did not know what to say. Her hand tightened on the cloth she was still holding. She stepped aside to let him enter the house and watched as he sat on a chair.

"Do you stay here all the time?" he asked, looking around the kitchen, "even in the winter?"

"Yes," she said. "Most of the time."

"Were you born here?"

"Yes," she said. "I guess so."

"It must be lonely," he said, "but I guess some people are lonely no matter where they are."

She looked at him as if he were a ghost.

"Would you like to live somewhere else?" he asked.

"I don't know," she said. "Maybe."

He raised his hand and touched the earring as if to make certain it was still there. His glance travelled about the kitchen, seeming to rest lightly on each of the familiar objects. She realized that the kitchen had hardly changed since that other April visit so long ago. She could not think of what to say.

"Would you like some tea?" she asked after a moment of awkward silence.

"No, thank you," he said. "I'm pressed for time right now but perhaps we'll have it later."

She nodded although she was not certain of his meaning. The dogs lay under the table, now and then thumping the floor with their tails. Through the window she could see the white gulls hanging over the ocean which was still dotted with cakes of floating ice.

He looked at her carefully, as if remembering, and he smiled. Neither of them seemed to know just what to say.

"Well," he said getting up suddenly. "I have to go now. I'll see you later. I'll come back."

"Wait," she said rising as quickly, "please don't go," and she almost added the word "again."

"I'll be back," he said, "in the fall. And then I will take you with me. We will go and live somewhere else."

"Yes," she said and then added almost as an afterthought, "Where have you been?"

"In Toronto," he said. "I was born there. They told me on the mainland that you are my grandmother."

She looked at him as if he were a genetic wonder, which indeed he seemed to be.

"Oh," she said.

"I have to go now," he repeated, "but I'll see you later. I'll come back."

"Oh yes," she said. "Oh yes, we will."

And then he was gone. She sat transfixed, not daring to move. Part of her felt that she should rush and call him back and another fearful part told her she should not know what she might see. Finally she went to the window. Halfway across to the mainland there was a single man in a boat but she could make no clear identification. She did not say anything to anyone about the visit. She could think of no way she could tactfully introduce it. After years of secrecy it seemed a dangerous time to bring up the subject of the red-haired man. Perhaps, again, no one else had seen him? She did not wish to add further evidence to her designation as "the mad woman of the island." She scanned the faces of her relatives carefully but could find nothing. Perhaps he had visited them, she thought, and they had

410

told him not to come. Perhaps they considered themselves in the business of not disturbing the disturbed.

Now as the October rain fell she added yet another stick to the fire. She was no longer bothered by the declining stock of wood because she would not need it for the winter. The rains fell, turning more to the consistency of hail and she knew this by the sound as well as by her sight. She looked away from the door as she had so many years ago, the first time at the table rock. Deliberately not looking in the direction of his possible coming so that she could not see him *not* coming if that was the way it was supposed to be. She waited, listening to the regular patterns of the rain, and wondered if she were on the verge of sleep. Suddenly the door blew open and the hail-like rain skittered across the floor. The wet dogs moved from beneath the table and she heard them rather than saw. Perhaps she should mop the wet floor, she thought, but then she remembered that they planned to tear the house down anyway and its cleanliness seemed like a minor virtue. The water rippled across the floor in rolling little wind-driven waves. The dog came in, its nails clacking across the floor even as little spurts of water rose from beneath its padded paws. It came and laid its head upon her lap. She got up, not daring to believe. Outside it was wet and windy and she followed the dog down the darkened path. And then in the revolving cycle of the high lighthouse light she saw in a single white instant the dark shape of the boat bobbing at the wharf and his straight but dripping form by the corner of the shanties.

They moved toward each other.

"Oh," she said, digging her fingernails into the dampness of his neck.

"I told you I'd come back," he said.

"Oh," she said. "Oh yes. You did."

She ran her fingers over his face in the darkness and when the light revolved again she saw the blueness of his eyes and his red hair darkened by the dripping water. He was not wearing any earring.

"How old are you?" she asked, embarrassed by the girlish triviality of the question which had bothered her all these years.

"Twenty-one," he said. "I thought I told you."

He took her hands and walked backward while facing her, down to the darkness of the bobbing boat and the rolling sea.

"Come," he said. "Come with me. It is time we went to live somewhere else."

"Oh yes," she said. "Oh yes we will."

She dug her nails into the palms of his hands as he guided her over the spume-drenched rocks.

"This boat," he said, "has to be back before dawn."

The wind was rising as the temperature was dropping. The hail-like rain had given way to stinging snow and the ground they left behind was beginning to freeze.

A dog barked once. And when the light revolved, its solitary beam found no MacPhedrans on the island or the sea.

CLEARANCES

(1 9 9 9)

*I*n the early morning he was awakened by the dog's pulling at the Condon's woollen blanket, which was the top covering upon his bed. The blanket was now a sort of yellow-beige although at one time, he thought, it must have been white. The blanket was made from the wool of the sheep he and his wife used to keep and it was now over half a century old. When they used to shear the sheep in the spring they would set aside some of the best fleeces and send them to Condon's Woollen Mill in Charlottetown; and after some months, it seemed miraculously, the box of blankets would arrive. In the corner of each blanket would be a label which read, "William Condon and Sons, Charlottetown, Prince Edward Island," and the Condon's Latin motto, which was *Clementia in Potentia.*

Once, when they were much older, their married son, John, and his wife had taken them on a trip to Prince Edward Island.

It was in July and they left Cape Breton on a Friday and came back on Sunday afternoon. This was in the time before the Anne of Green Gables craze and they did not really know what people were supposed to visit on Prince Edward Island, so on Saturday morning they went to look at Condon's Woollen Mill because it was the name that was most familiar to them. And there it sat. He remembered that they had put on their good clothes although they did not know why, and that he had placed his hat upon his knee because of the perspiration that gathered on his hatband and on his brow. They did not get out of their car but merely looked at the woollen mill through the haze of the July heat. Perhaps they had expected to see Mr. Condon or one of his sons busily converting wool into blankets, but they saw nothing. Later his wife was to tell her friends, "We visited Condon's Woollen Mill on Prince Edward Island," as if they had visited a religious shrine or a monument of historical significance and, he thought, she was probably right.

Sometimes in the early passion of their love they would throw the blanket back over his shoulder toward the foot of the bed, or sometimes it would land on the floor by the bed's side. Later, when their ardour had cooled, he would retrieve it and spread it carefully over his wife's shoulders and his own. His wife always slept on the side of the bed closest to the wall, while he slept on the outside in a protective manner. He was always the last person to go to bed and the first to rise. It was the sleeping pattern followed by his own parents and his grandparents as well.

The blanket had been on them when his wife died; died without a sound or a shudder. He had been talking to her for a while in the early morning darkness. He had on his heavy woollen Stanfield's underwear and she her winter nightgown, and the bed was warm from their mutual heat. At first he had thought she was playing a trick on him by refusing to answer or that she was still sleeping, but then in an instant of full wakefulness he recognized the absence of her regular breathing and reached his hand, in the winter darkness, towards her quiet face. It was cool to his touch because of its exposure to the winter air, but when he grasped her hand which lay beneath the blankets it was still warm and seemed to close around his own. He got up, and, trying not to panic, phoned his married children who lived nearby. At first they seemed sceptical in their early morning grogginess, asking him if he was "sure." Perhaps she was only sleeping more soundly than usual? He noticed the whiteness of his knuckles as he grasped the telephone receiver too tightly, trying to get a grip, not only on the receiver, but on the whole frightening situation. Trying to control his voice and remain calm in delivering a message he did not want to deliver and they did not wish to receive. Finally they seemed convinced, but then he noticed the panic rising in their own voices even as he attempted to control it in his own. He found himself trying to recapture the soothing tone of his early fatherhood, speaking to his married, middle-aged children in a manner he might have used thirty or forty years ago in the face of some childhood disaster. With the coming of the VCR and the microwave and the computer and digital recording and so much more, both he and his wife felt that *they* were becoming the children and he sometimes recognized in his children's voices that adult tone of impatience that might have been his at an earlier time. Sometimes he thought the tone bordered on condescension. But now the roles were suddenly reversed once again. "We will have to do the best we can," he heard himself saying. "I will phone the ambulance and the doctor and the clergyman. It is still early in the morning and most of the world is not yet awake. We will contact the authorities before making any long-distance calls. No, there is no reason to come over here right away. I am fine for a while."

He went back to the bed and pulled the Condon's woollen blanket over her face, but before he did so, he laid his cheek against what he thought of as the stilled beating of her heart.

The previous summer she had been given a variety of multi-coloured pills by the doctor, but they had caused dizziness and drowsiness and a variety of skin eruptions, and she had said, "I wanted to feel better, not worse." One summer's day she opened the screen door and flung all of the pills into the yard. The flock of hens, who always responded to the table scraps flying from the door, raced towards the bounty. Later, five of the most aggressive hens were found dead. "If they did that to the hens," she had said, "what would they do to me?" He had agreed, somewhat reluctantly, to join her in a pact of secrecy. "You don't tell children everything," she had said. "You know that."

It was now ten years later and, of course, he did not think all of these thoughts as the dog pulled at the blanket. Still, they would all come to him later, as they had every day since her death.

He still lived in the house his grandfather had built. It was a large wooden house modelled after the others of its time. It had always appeared quite splendid from the outside but the inside, particularly the upstairs, had remained unfinished for years. For him and his wife it had been their project "to finish it" over the decades of their marriage. They had worked at converting the vast upstairs expanse into individual rooms, drywalling one room and wallpapering another whenever money was available. By the time they had finished the upstairs rooms, the children for whom the rooms had been intended had already begun to leave home; their older daughters going first, as had their aunts, to Boston or Toronto. Now there was only himself and his dog, and when he visited the upstairs rooms they seemed like a museum that he had had a hand in creating.

When he was a child, the vast upstairs contained only one room with a door, where his grandfather slept. The rest had been roughly sectioned into a girls' side and a much smaller boys' side, as he was the only boy. The sections were separated by a series of worn blankets strung on wires. His parents had slept downstairs in the room he occupied now.

As his parents' only son he had gone into the fishing boat with his father when he was eleven or twelve. His grandfather would go with them, sitting on an overturned bait bucket, chewing and spitting tobacco and rising frequently to attempt urination over the boat's side. The old man, he realized now, probably suffered from prostate trouble but had never in all his life been to a doctor. His grandfather seemed always to under-stand the weather and the tides and where the fish were, as if operating by private radar. They fished for lobster and haddock and herring and hake. In the summer they set their hereditary salmon net.

They conducted almost all of their lives in Gaelic, as had the previous generations for over one hundred years. But in the years between the two world wars they realized, when selling their cattle or lambs or their catches of fish, that they were

417

disadvantaged by language. He remembered his grandfather growing red in the face beneath his white whiskers as he attempted to deal with the English-speaking buyers. Sending Gaelic words out and receiving English words back; most of the words falling somewhere into the valley of noncomprehension that yawned between them. Across the river the French-speaking Acadians seemed the same, as did the Mi'kmaq to the east. All of them trapped in the beautiful prisons of the languages they loved. "We will have to do better than this," said his grandfather testily. "We will have to learn English. We will have to go forward."

He himself had enlisted in the Second World War to escape what seemed like poverty and, perhaps, as well to seek adventure. Of the latter he found too much and had promised and prayed in the trenches of the dying young that if he were saved he would return home never to leave again. He had prayed in Gaelic, looking across the flames to the German trenches. Prayed in Gaelic because it was more reflexively natural and he felt he could make himself more clearly understood to God in the prayers of his earliest language. It seemed his prayers had been answered and in the subsequent years he was able to repress the most horrific of the memories, choosing to recall only one remarkable week of respite.

In that week, he was on furlough in London and, armed with scraps of paper bearing place names and addresses, he took the train to Glasgow. From Glasgow he took another train and then another. As he switched trains and journeyed farther to the north and to the west, he was aware of the soft sounds of Gaelic around him. At first he was surprised, hearing the language only as what seemed like subliminal whispers, but as the train stopped and started in the small rural stations the Gaelic-speaking population began to intensify and the soft language to dominate. At one station a shepherd got on with his dog. "*Greas ort* (Hurry up)," he said to the dog, and then, "*Dean suidhe* (Sit down)." "*S'e thu fhein a tha tapaidh* (It is yourself that's smart)," he added as the dog sat beside him and looked with interest at the passing moors and mountains.

Sitting there in his Canadian uniform he was aware of his difference and his similarity. Quietly, he took from his pocket the scribbled addresses and bits of information. Haltingly he said to the shepherd "*Ciamar a tha sibh?* (How are you?) *Nach eil e latha breagha a th'ann?* (Isn't it a nice day?)"

Instantly the train coach fell silent and all eyes turned towards him. "*Glé mhath. S'e gu dearbh. Tha e blath agus grianach.* (Very well. Yes, it's sunny and warm)," said the shepherd, and then eyeing his epaulette said in measured English, "You are from Canada? You are from the Clearances?" He uttered both statements in the form of questions and pronounced the word "Clearances" as if it were a place instead of a matter of historical eviction.

"Yes," he replied, "I guess so."

Beyond the train's windows the empty moors stretched to the base of the mist-shrouded mountains. The tumbling white-watered streams cascaded down the mountains' sides and a lonely eagle circled over the stone foundations of a vanished people.

"Long time ago," he said to the shepherd, "since we left for Canada."

"Probably lucky," said the shepherd. "Nothing much here any more."

They were quiet for a time. Each of them alone with his own thoughts.

"Tell me, though," said the shepherd, "is it possible that in Canada you can own and keep your land?"

"Yes," he said, "it is."

"Fancy that," replied the shepherd. He was an older man who reminded him of his father.

During the remainder of the week, he tried to do it all. Aided by the information on the scraps of paper and his new-found friends and friends of friends, he went on boats up the inland lochs and across the straits to the offshore islands which he found inhabited mainly by wind and crying seabirds. He found the crumbled gravestones, some bearing his name, beneath the waist-high bracken. Where once people had lived in their hundreds and their thousands, there now stretched only the unpopulated emptiness of the vast estates with their sheep-covered hills or the islands which had become bird sanctuaries or shooting ranges for the well-to-do. He saw himself as the descendant of victims of history and changing economic times, betrayed, perhaps, by politics and poverty as well.

In the evenings around the hospitable whisky bottle he tried to explain the landscape of Cape Breton.

"How would you plant crops amidst all the trees?" inquired his shy hosts.

"Oh, the trees had to be cleared first," he explained. "I guess beginning with my great-great-grandfather. They cut the trees and cleared the land of stones."

"After the war will you go back to these cleared lands?" they asked.

"Yes," he said, "I will go back if I get the chance."

In the late afternoons and early evenings he looked across the western ocean, beyond the point of Ardnamurchan, and tried to visualize Cape Breton and his family at their tasks.

"After the clearances," said his friend the shepherd, "there were not many people left. Most of them were gone to Canada or America or Australia. Most of our young men now are in the war or in Glasgow, some in the south of England. But I am here," he added rolling a stem of heather between his fingers, "working for an estate and looking after sheep that are not my own. But the dog is mine."

It was late in the afternoon of his final day and he stood with the shepherd and his ever-watchful dog observing the distant grazing sheep.

He had loved the beautiful dog and his fellows, admired their highly developed intelligence and their eagerness to please. "I will show you how to breed them," said the shepherd. "They will be with you until the end."

After the war he returned with the determined gratitude of those who have survived. With his father's help he cleared yet another field which extended to the ocean's edge. They invested in better cattle and sheep. His friend, the shepherd, sent him a detailed breeding chart for the development of border collies. He sent for pups and, as they matured, endeavoured to keep them in pens during the breeding season so that they might maintain their specialness. His wife shared all of his enthusiasms and never complained, even when as newlyweds they moved into his father's house. His widowed father was respectful of their privacy and gave them the bedroom he had once shared with his wife and journeyed to the upstairs bedroom which his own father had inhabited as an older man.

"Things will get better," said his father. "We are going forward. Maybe next year we will get a bigger boat."

Sometimes in the evenings he would look across the ocean, imagining he could see the point of Ardnamurchan and beyond. Sometimes he would try to explain the Highland landscape to his father and his wife, though never mentioning his experiences in the trenches.

On this day when he emerged from his bed, he looked out the window at the rooftops of the houses he had helped build for his two sons in what seemed like another lifetime. He had merely given them the land and had not bothered to draw up deeds to decide if or where his property ended and theirs began. They had all been enthusiastic about the younger men's approaching marriages; all of them interested in "going forward" and doing the best they could. He had not thought of boundaries or borders until his second son's death eight years ago. His strong athletic son breaking his neck in a fall from his rooftop while trying to clean his chimney. It had seemed so bizarre and unexpected as he, like most parents, had not expected to outlive his children. There was no will, nor title to the deceased man's house, as none of them had, originally, thought such documentation to be important. In a fit of delayed guilt he had drawn up a deed so that his daughter-in-law might have title to her house and to a block of surrounding land. As he had not anticipated his son's death, neither had he anticipated that his daughter-in-law would fall in love with someone else and move to Halifax, selling her property to a surly summer couple who erected a seven-foot privacy fence and kept a sullen pitbull who paced restlessly behind it. He had not been in the house he helped to build since the changing of the land.

He looked in the direction of his son John's house and felt like calling him up and asking him to visit but felt that it was too early and that the younger man, perhaps, needed to stay in bed. He felt great sympathy for John, whom he saw now as a harried middle-aged man. He had helped him finance a large boat in order to be competitive, but the fish quotas had changed and now the boat sat idle, unable to be of use and unable to be sold. For the past two seasons, John had been in Leamington, Ontario, fishing with the Portuguese fishermen he had once known off the coast of Newfoundland; fishing Lake Erie for pickerel and bass, perch and smelt; sleeping in a small room on Erie Street with a pull-out couch and a hot plate. The crying gulls followed the boats of Lake Erie too, John said, but they were a different species.

He felt sorrow for John and his family, watching the older children become, he thought, more unruly and their mother more tight-lipped and worn down. He tried to be involved without being intrusive, well aware that a father-in-law was not a husband. John was currently home to celebrate his wife's birthday, having driven 1,500 miles without pausing to sleep.

He spoke to the dog in Gaelic as he proceeded to put on his clothes. "*S'e thu fhein a tha tapaidh* (It is yourself that's smart)," he said. He had always spoken to the dog and his predecessors in Gaelic, thinking it somehow preserved a link with his own and his animal's ancestral past. He knew that people were amused and impressed by his "bilingual dog," as they persisted in calling him. He looked now at the dog's eagerness and felt a twinge of sadness for the unused potential the dog represented. He was, he felt, somewhat like John's unused expensive boat, except that he was vitally and intensely alive. He felt somehow that he had denied the dog his heritage by no longer keeping sheep or livestock of any kind, with the exception of a few scattered hens.

Many of the neighbouring farms no longer maintained fences, and the keeping of livestock had become almost impossible. Sometimes the dog would fall into a herding position behind the annoyed hens or even younger grandchildren, stimulated by what he was born to do. He was aware also of the dog's sexual frustration, aware that he was eager to breed and eager to herd and eager to please, always looking at him with his hopeful brown eyes, constantly seeking direction. Sometimes the dog accompanied him in the passenger seat of his pickup truck, looking out the window at the passing landscape, his excitement quickening if he happened to view livestock on the distant hills.

The dog had been with him when he had backed out of the Co-op parking lot into the fender of an approaching car. While assessing the damage he had overheard someone say, "He is too old to be driving. He's always preoccupied. The dog would be a better driver." He had gone for a driver's test and passed it with flying colours. "I wish I had your reflexes," said the examiner.

He and the dog had just gone outside to the morning sun when the pickup truck drove into the yard. Although he was temporarily surprised, he recognized the young driver as one of a series of "clear-cutters" who yearned for the spruce trees that had gradually reclaimed the field he had once cleared as a younger man. He was torn between sympathy for the young clear-cutters, who were ambitious and attempting to make a living, and annoyance at their rapaciousness. They would option a parcel of land and cut everything in sight, taking the valuable logs and pulp and leaving a desolation of stumpage and slashed limbs and inferior wood behind. They worked rapidly with their heavy power equipment, sometimes leaving behind trenches the height of a man. They would pay owners such as himself a percentage of the cordage.

The young man identified himself through a Gaelic patronymic, adding helpfully, "I'm your cousin."

He was annoyed by the young man's brashness, recalling that he had a particular reputation for leaving disaster behind him and not being overly forthright in his cordage payments.

"I may as well log off your wood," he said. "It will be good for you and good for me. May as well log it off before the damn tourists get everything."

The tourists were a sore point with some people. They had begun to flood into what they saw as prime recreation area, marvelling at the pristine water and the unpolluted air. Many of them were from the New England area and an increasing number from Europe. They slept late and often complained about the whine of the clear-cutters' saws. In the summer the clear-cutters often began their work at four in the morning in order to avoid the extremes of the summer's heat. Some of the tourists had taken pictures of the carnage left behind by the clear-cutters and had them published in environmental magazines.

"I'm just trying to make a living," said the young man. "This isn't my recreational area. This is my home. Yours too." He felt a wave of sympathy for the young man, recognizing familiar echoes within his speech.

"What about it?" continued his visitor. "Soon the tourists and the Government will have everything. Look what happened to the fishing. Look at your salmon nets. Look at the Park to the north. We'll all be living in a wilderness area before we know it."

He was surprised that the young man knew about his salmon nets. For generations they had set the delicate, beautiful nets, and they had been a promise for his sons. They had fished under the threat that the Government would eliminate such customs as theirs because it was thought to be more beneficial if their few salmon entered the mainland rivers for the benefit of the summer anglers. And the rumours had proven, eventually, to be true.

He winced also at the thought of "the Park." Located farther north, it seemed to travel like a slow-moving glacier, claiming more and more land to be used as hiking trails and wilderness areas, while the families in its path worried about eviction notices.

"People like you and me," said the young man, "are no match for the Government and the tourists."

"I'll think about it," he said, trying to be polite in the face of growing frustration.

"Think all you like," said the young man. "Thinking doesn't change facts. Here's my card," he said, offering a white rectangle which he drew from his shirt pocket.

"Never mind the card," he said. "I'll know where to find you."

The truck left in what seemed like a hail of small rocks.

He had wanted to say something like, "When I was your age, I was in the trenches," but it seemed like something an old man might say, and, perhaps, it would not matter very much.

He was still deep in troubled thought and looking at the ground when he became aware of John's approach. He had walked quietly across the field that separated their houses.

"Hello," he said with a start when John appeared suddenly before him. "He wants to buy the wood," he added by way of explaining his recent visitor.

"Yes," said his son, "I recognized the truck."

They were silent for a while, moving the pebbles of the driveway with their shoes, uncomfortable with their private and communal thoughts to the extent that they were almost relieved when the bright new car came rapidly but quietly up the driveway. Both of them recognized the casually dressed real estate salesman, although they did not know the more formally dressed couple in the back seat.

"Hi," said the salesman, stepping out of the car and extending his hand in what seemed like a single motion. "These people are looking for land with ocean frontage," he said. "We have driven forty miles and seen nothing they like as well as yours. They are from Germany," he said, dropping his voice, "but they speak perfect English."

"Oh, it's not for sale," he heard himself say.

"You shouldn't say that until you know what they're willing to pay," said the real estate agent. "They say there is no land like this for sale anywhere in Europe."

He found himself amazed for the second time in the still-early day. He recognized that the real estate agent operated on commission, but was not really certain why that should annoy him.

The German couple emerged from the car. They shook hands very formally. "Nice day," said the man, while his wife smiled pleasantly. "Very nice land," he continued. "Runs down to the ocean?"

"Yes," he said, "runs down to the ocean."

The couple smiled and then walked a few yards away and began to converse in German.

John tapped him on the shoulder and beckoned to him. They, in turn, moved a few yards away, and it took a few seconds before he realized John was talking to him in Gaelic. "You could ask them if they want the wood," he said. "If you were to sell, maybe you could sell the wood first and then the land later."

He was startled by what seemed like a family betrayal. They continued to speak uncomfortably in Gaelic while a short distance away the couple continued to converse in German. The real estate agent stood listlessly between them while the July sun contributed to the perspiration forming on his brow. He looked slightly irritated at being banished to what seemed like a state of unilingual loneliness.

"Ask them if they're interested in the wood," said John, moving toward the real estate agent and speaking in English. He explained his issue in low tones and the real estate agent conveyed the information to the couple, who spoke enthusiastically to one another in German.

The real estate agent came back, seemingly impressed by his role as interpretive negotiator. "They don't care about the wood," he said. "They say it just blocks the view of the ocean. You can do what you want with it. They wouldn't take possession until next spring and you can do anything you want with it until then. They will offer a very good price."

The German gentleman approached and smiled. "Very nice land," he repeated. Then he added, "Not very many people around here."

"No," he heard himself say, "not any more. A lot of them gone to the States. A lot of the younger people gone to Halifax or southern Ontario."

"Oh yes," said the man. "Nice and quiet."

He was aware of the presence of John beside him.

"I'll have to think about it," he said.

"Sure," said the real estate agent and handed him his card, "but the sooner the better."

The Germans smiled and shook his hand. "Very nice land," the man repeated. "Hope to hear from you soon."

They got into the car and waved as they departed.

"Not telling you what to do," said John, "but I've spent almost my whole life here, too. You always said, 'We have to go forward' and 'Things will get better.' Maybe if this worked out I could stay here with my wife and children for a while." He stood uncertainly for a moment, uncomfortable in his father's presence. Finally, he said, "Well, I have to go now. Good-bye. *Sin e ged tha* (That's the way it is)."

"Yes," he said, "good-bye. *Sin e ged tha*."

"It is going to be hot today," he said to himself, "as hot as that day we visited Condon's Woollen Mill." But then he remembered that Condon's Woollen Mill no longer existed.

He and the dog walked down to his little fishing shanty. He opened the door and took down the beautiful salmon nets from the pegs where they were hung. He went to rub the cork buoys between his fingers, but they crumbled at his touch. He came back out and closed the door. He looked at the land once cleared by his great-great-grandfather and at the field once cleared by himself. The spruce trees had been there and had been cleared and now they were back again. They went and came something like the tide, he thought, although he knew his analogy was incorrect. He looked toward the sea; somewhere out there, miles beyond his vision, he imagined the point of Ardnamurchan and the land which lay beyond. He was at the edge of one continent, he thought, facing the invisible edge of another. He saw himself as a man in a historical documentary, probably, he thought, filmed in black and white.

He felt the dog grow tense beside him and emit a low growl. He turned to see his neighbour's pitbull advancing towards them. The large beast wore a collar covered with pointed studs and moved with deliberate measured steps. Its huge jaws were clenched firmly and strings of saliva hung, like beaded curtains, from its bloated, purple lips.

He glanced at his own dog and saw the black and white hair rising determinedly on its neck. "Both of us are overmatched here," he thought, but he heard his voice say softly in Gaelic, "*S'e thu fhein a tha tapaidh* (It is yourself that's smart)."

He looked up at the sun. It had reached its zenith and was about to decline. He looked down at his dog as it trembled beside him. "Neither of us was born for this," he thought, and then, from a great distance, across the ocean and across the years, he heard the voice of his friend the shepherd. He lowered his right hand until his fingertips touched the bristling hair on the dog's neck. A small gesture to give each other courage. And then they both took a step forward at the same time. As the blood roared in his ears, he heard the voice again, "They will be with you until the end."

ACKNOWLEDGEMENTS

The stories in this book originally appeared in the following publications, to which grateful acknowledgement is due:

"The Boat": *The Massachusetts Review*, 1968; *Best American Short Stories*, 1969.

"The Vastness of the Dark": *The Fiddlehead*, Winter 1971.

"The Golden Gift of Grey": *Twigs*, VII, 1971.

"The Return": *The Atlantic Advocate*, November 1971.

"In the Fall": *Tamarack Review*, October 1973.

"The Lost Salt Gift of Blood": *The Southern Review*, Winter 1974; *Best American Short Stories*, 1975.

"The Road to Rankin's Point": *Tamarack Review*, Winter 1976.

"The Closing Down of Summer": *Fiddlehead*, Fall 1976.

"To Every Thing There Is a Season:" *Globe and Mail*, December 24, 1977.

"Second Spring": *Canadian Fiction Magazine*, 1980.

"Winter Dog": *Canadian Fiction Magazine*, 1981.

"The Tuning of Perfection": *The Cape Breton Collection*, Pottersfield Press, Nova Scotia, 1984.

"As Birds Bring Forth the Sun": *event* magazine, 1985.

"Island": *The Ontario Review*, 1988: Thistledown Press Limited Edition, 1989.

"Clearances": "Festival of Fiction," CBC Radio/Canada Council for the Arts, 1999.

I would like to thank Kerstin Mueller of the Eastern Counties
Regional Libraries and Roddie Coady of the Coady and Tompkins
Memorial Library for providing me with much-needed and much-
appreciated writing space.

I would also like to thank A.G. MacLeod, Murdina Stewart, and the
University of Windsor for their different kinds of help and co-
operation. The translations of the longer Gaelic songs are from *Beyond
the Hebrides* (1977), edited by Donald A. Fergusson. Again, my thanks.